Fatherhood
Reclaimed

To Martin and Juliet who lived fatherhood
while I wrote about it

Fatherhood Reclaimed

The Making of the Modern Father

Adrienne Burgess

VERMILION

3 5 7 9 10 8 6 4 2

First published in the United Kingdom in 1997 by Vermilion
an imprint of Ebury Press
Random House · 20 Vauxhall Bridge Road · London SW1V 2SA

Random House Australia (Pty) Limited
20 Alfred Street · Milsons Point · Sydney · New South Wales 2061 · Australia

Random House New Zealand Limited
18 Poland Road · Glenfield · Auckland 10 · New Zealand

Random House South Africa (Pty) Limited
PO Box 2263 · Rosebank 2121 · South Africa

Random House UK Limited Reg. No. 954009

A CIP catalogue record for this book is available from the British Library.

ISBN: 0 09 179015 8 (Hardback)
ISBN: 0 09 179020 4 (Paperback)

Printed and bound in Great Britain by Mackays of Chatham plc.

Papers used by Vermilion are natural, recyclable
products made from wood grown in sustainable forest.

Contents

Acknowledgements

My acknowledgements in the writing of this book go, first and foremost, to Anna Coote (whose idea it was), to Gail Rebuck (who has published it) and to Patricia Hewitt (who supported and guided me, as she always has). No less important are the many fathers who shared their lives with me in interviews and whose voices are heard throughout this book. From all these men I learned a great deal.

Also central to the book's evolution were Sarah Sutton and Fiona MacIntyre at the Ebury Press; Alexander Ruxton, who helped to develop the proposals for public policy; Trefor Lloyd, whose insights are always profound; my mother Dora Burgess, who carried out research and proof-reading; and my assistant Susan Moore, who conducted interviews, undertook research, managed correspondence and references, and acted as a valued sounding-board. Jane Franklin and the staff at the Institute for Public Policy Research gave support on many levels.

Many among the academic fatherhood fraternity were generous with time and information. Chief among these were Charlie Lewis, Michael Lamb, Graeme Russell and Peter Moss, although my conclusions are my own and do not represent their views. Richard Wall of the Cambridge Group set me on track for the historical chapter and offered valuable comments. Geoffrey Godbert identified poems; and Arthur Baker, John Foy, Maurice Mason, Liam O'Gogain and Eugene Hockenjos helped with the resource list. Superb service was provided by the library at the London School of Economics and Political Science, my local library in Pimlico, and by the Bibliotheque Nationale, who entrusted a rare book to me – sent in the post!

My husband Martin Cochrane and daughter Juliet sacrificed much for this book, and to them above all my love and thanks are due. The book is also written in loving memory of my father, Laurence Keith Burgess, who died as I began it.

Preface

During the process of writing this book, all my preconceptions about fathers and fathering have been overturned. I therefore offer this manuscript in a spirit of enquiry.

The book falls into two parts. The first three chapters are concerned with exposing some of the belief-systems which constrain men as fathers, and influence our perceptions of their role and conduct. Chapter 1 examines the images of fatherhood with which we are, and have been, surrounded for centuries, suggesting reasons for their evolution, and exploring some of the ways in which they still hold us in thrall. Chapter 2, by contrast, focuses on fathers' actual behaviour. Illumining men's private lives today, and in times gone by, it exposes deep rifts between image and reality, and outlines the ways in which fathers' and mothers' roles differ, and how they are similar. The third chapter, 'The Natural Father: cad or dad?', goes, perhaps, to the heart of the matter, establishing the extent to which fathers' behaviour is biologically and environmentally determined and indicating what can reasonably be expected of men as fathers, now and in the future.

The second half of the book leaves behind discussion of cultural and biological constraints, to focus on the everyday business of being a father in the post-industrial West. This section explores structural barriers to men's participation in active parenting. Chapter 4 analyses the process of becoming a father, from pre-conception to the early days of parenthood – an area traditionally controlled by women, where men's role is presented ambivalently. Chapter 5 examines the workaday world which, through means both subtle and not-so-subtle, erects barriers between men and their children – a situation which seems to be hardening with every year that passes. Chapter 6 weighs the value of fathers to their families and investigates separation and divorce, establishing which men are likely to lose touch with their children, and why.

It feels, having finished, that this book exposes just the tip of the iceberg, and inevitably some fathers will feel themselves neglected. Not only stepfathers, but widowed fathers, lone fathers, grandfathers, unmarried fathers, older fathers and very young fathers, all have special and interesting tales to tell, which would merit further comment. And although black fathers have been included, it is in nothing like the detail I would have liked. For although some research is now in the pipeline, there is currently no documentation on the behaviour and aspirations of black fathers in Britain. Proposals for public policy have had to be presented in merest outline, with the detail reserved for another document.[1]

Nevertheless, it is my hope that in these six chapters some of the dross is cleared away, to enable us all – whether we are fathers, the mothers of children who have fathers, or the children of fathers – to see fathers and fatherhood more clearly, engage in constructive debate, and offer support to the relationships between men and their children.

Adrienne Burgess
Institute for Public Policy Research
October, 1996

❛ Father's Day is the day to remember the forgotten man ❜
5,000 Jokes for Afterdinner Speakers

Chapter 1
Images of Fatherhood: from god to geek

When Stephen was told that his much-loved father – banker, prisoner-of-war and occasional transvestite – had suddenly died, his own response astonished him. In the split second before grief and disbelief filled the gap, he saw in his mind's eye the thin, anxious face of the man who had emerged from Russia to claim him as his son, the face he had glimpsed, once, ludicrously smeared with lipstick, and a voice spun through his head. 'The King is dead,' said the voice, 'the King is dead – long live the King!' That this long-forgotten line, presumably from some despised examination text, should have lain in wait for this moment was almost more than Stephen could bear. How could such exultation fill his heart? He had loved his father. They had not been engaged in any battle of which he was aware. Yet his response was larger than the event itself – consonant, it seemed, with that of a Prometheus, an Oedipus or a Hamlet. He had experienced in the death of an ordinary man a moment of transcendent liberation.

Great expectations

It was in 1909 that Carl Jung first commented on the 'magical' influence parents have over their children. This he ascribed not to the child's individual helplessness or particular personality, but to the luminosity of parental archetypes activated in the child's psyche. 'Behind the father stands the archetype of the father, and in this pre-existent archetype lies the secret of the father's power, just as the power which forces the bird to migrate is not produced by the bird itself but derives from its ancestors,' wrote Jung. 'The personal father inevitably embodies the archetype, which is what endows this figure with its fascinating power.'[1] Whether or not archetypes are pre-existent (and many would argue not) it is clear that no parent has the luxury of a clean sheet against which to operate. Whatever any father does is measured against images which simultaneously amplify and dwarf the process of human fathering. 'When we relate to the father, we relate also to our expectation of him,' writes political and psychological theorist Andrew Samuels. 'He is strong or weak, castrating or facilitating, depending on how he does or does not fit in with the expectation.'[2]

> 6 My father was a soft, gentle type of man. If my mother was cross he would wipe away the tears – real, role-reversal stuff. So why don't I hold him in high regard? I remember John Mortimer writing about the death of his own father, 'At last a man is free to step out from the shadow into the sunlight'. Never meant anything to me, but it will when my mother dies. 9
>
> *Gerrard, 43, father of two*

Accustomed as we are, in late 20th century Europe, to the marginalising of fatherhood, the most striking fact to be gleaned from the study of fathers and fatherhood is the centrality of the image of the authoritarian father to moral and political debate in the West over many centuries. Until recently it was paternal authority rather than maternal instinct which was deemed to be a natural fact, and fathers, not mothers, of whom great things were expected. In the 18th century the father was so much the dominant parental figure that the words parent and father were used inter-changeably. It must be remembered, however, that paternal imagery and paternal behaviour are not the same thing. Our culture's saturation with patriarchal imagery has tricked us into thinking that this has accurately reflected fathers' daily conduct. It has not. Fathers' behaviour, which will be considered in later chapters, is and always has been immensely varied. Paternal imagery, however, has been selective and limited, and while it has, inevitably, influenced the way some fathers have behaved, its main effect has been to veil other kinds of interaction between men and their children.

Opposing archetypes

The archetypal father as we know him is the King, the Elder, the Father in Heaven, who represents authority and appears as the polar-opposite of the mother. '"Fatherland" implies boundaries, a definite localisation in space,' intoned Jung, as if the word had created its own interpretation, 'whereas the land itself is Mother

Earth, quiescent and fruitful.'[3] Images recognised by Jung to be true archetypes were those which were seen to emerge across time and place in many different cultures. The image of the 'ruler father' does this. He appears as Zeus, Thor, Brahma and a host of others, including 'Darth Vader' (the Dark Father) in the *Star Wars* trilogy.

> 6 You say 'fatherhood' to me or 'being a father', I don't have an overall concept of it. It's the best and the worst. Awful, sometimes when you are trying to cook the tea, and you've got one of them making too much noise and another demanding. Then another time, it's wonderful, like this morning. He was on my lap in the kitchen and we negotiated he would take a big bite of his toast and then I would sing him a nursery rhyme. So he was sitting here eating toast and I was singing 'Little Bo Peep' and 'Baa Baa Black Sheep' ... 9
>
> *Seb, 39, father of three*

Feminist mythologists (among others) have now challenged conventional thinking about archetypes. In *Alone of All Her Sex*, Marina Warner examined the traditional figure of the Virgin Mary, who both Jung and the Catholic Church had claimed was an 'inevitable expression of the Great Mother', and demonstrated that this so-called archetype had been 'socially constructed'. Images of the Virgin Mary had been developed and refined over many centuries by the religious establishment, who had sought to put, and keep, women in their place by persuading them that certain styles of behaviour were right, proper, natural and God-derived.[4] More recently, in *Women who Run with the Wolves*, another feminist mythologist, Clarissa Estes, has taken a different tack. Adopting an approach that could be described as 'I'll-show-you-my-archetype-if-you-show-me-yours', she has unearthed images of 'wild women' from a range of cultures. These images present very different notions of ideal femininity from those found in our society, where Estes contends they have been suppressed.[5]

Among the great achievements of feminist scholarship has been the exposé of ideologies which have defined and promoted women's behaviour. This great unmasking has provided precise perspectives on what was once vaguely referred to as 'conditioning', and has helped many women re-appraise their lives. While a similar exercise in respect of men would be equally liberating, it presents a greater challenge, for in our society, if women have been the 'object', men have been the 'subject'. Their activities have been presented as the benchmark, and the identity of the ruler father offered as their consolation and reward. The simple act of objectifying the male position threatens to cast men down – down among the women, who are not perceived as controlling life's structures and processes but as being at their mercy. 'The subjugated have a decent chance to be onto the god trick and all its dazzling – and therefore blinding – illusions,' observes anthropologist Donna Haraway, 'but how to look from below – that is a different story.'[6]

❛ Being a parent connects us with the earth. It brings us back to the trees and to biology and to our bodies and to our hearts. I think of what Mother Teresa said, 'If you can't learn to love your own children, and your neighbours, the people who live next door to you, how do you expect the world to change in any way that will bring peace for us? ❜

Jack Kornfield, Parenting as Spiritual Practice

Recently, mythologists have begun investigating fatherhood imagery, and guess what they have found: an alternative paternal archetype who, like the ruler father, can be found in many different cultures. This archetype is an 'earth father', a nurturer whose sphere is the countryside. The god Pan is descended from him, and so is Pluto, King of the Underworld. Earth fathers in the ancient world were often said to live underground, but not because they were regarded as evil. On the contrary, since dead bodies were observed to enrich the soil, the underworld was often seen as life-giving, with new life emerging out of death. Sometimes the earth fathers were shown with erect penises. These, however, did not symbolise dominance. They represented fertility, and at times earth fathers were said to nourish humans. Bacchus, for example, supposedly changed his flesh into corn and his blood into wine every year, to feed mankind.

Earth fathers can also give birth, though in a very different mould from Zeus whose virginal armour-clad daughter Athena leapt from his head like an extension of his thoughts and obligingly set about subjugating rebellious women on his behalf. In Australian aboriginal myth, Karora, buried warmly in the earth, produces bandicoots from his naval and human souls from his armpits, and there are similar tales in Scandinavian and Chinese mythology.[7] Today, such notions are so alien that they can seem aberrant, and with all connection between men and nurture gone, ancient male birth myths are commonly interpreted as envious attempts by men to appropriate an exclusively female province.

It is significant that, in our culture, the ancient association of males with birth and rebirth has been severed. For societies that retain earth fathers in their mythologies tend to accept nurturing behaviour by men towards young children as the norm, while societies which disown earth father imagery perceive such involvement by men with infants as deviant.[8] Fathers in our culture are to be patriarchs. The literal meaning of patriarch is 'father and ruler', and for us the two ideas are so completely identified that it takes a leap of imagination to grasp that there are societies in which father does not mean ruler.[9] Furthermore, because patriarchy is usually seen as a kind of masculine frenzy, a male protection racket exclusively advantageous to the male sex, we seem to have been blinded to the price that men (and, specifically, fathers) have paid for an unquestioned range of benefits.

> ❛ *I go to see my parents*
> *we chew the rag a bit,*
> *I turn the telly on*
> *and sit and look at it …*
>
> *I go to see my son,*
> *I'm like a Santa Claus;*
> *he couldn't like me more;*
> *mad about him, of course.*
>
> *Still years before he learns*
> *to judge, condemn, dismiss.*
> *I stand against the light*
> *and bleed for both of us.* ❜

Evan Jones, 'Generations'

James Levine, Director of the Fatherhood Project at the Families and Work Institute in New York, has described the moment that opened his eyes. It was Hallowe'en 1968 and, as a teacher of pre-schoolers, he was dressed as 'The Great Pumpkin'. The children's parents found it hard to accept his profession: 'What do you *really* do?' they wanted to know. 'That moment a quarter of a century ago,' writes Levine, 'changed my view of the world. It shocked me into realising that gender stereotypes affect men as well as women. Intellectually, of course I knew that such stereotyping was widespread … But this was deeply personal. People didn't expect me to teach or care for young children.'[10]

The uses of enchantment

Men's behaviour as fathers (no less than women's as mothers) has been shaped by a sophisticated mythology. In fact, it can be argued that since the image of the ruler father has been adopted as the nexus of patriarchy, this mythic figure has impacted on domestic fathering even more heavily than myths about motherhood have impacted on mothering. And it's not just the choice of the central figure. The themes attaching to him are equally significant. For myth is PR on a massive scale. It is cultural propaganda which presents a local event or idea as universal and 'natural'.[11] There can be further distortion when the myths are pure symbolism, and many of the epic father–child struggles fall into this category. They can represent struggles between the individual and society, or between social groups, or even between parts of the self.

Fairytale (the artisan's tradition) is somewhat different. Although fairytales sometimes contain a didactic element, they are more about entertainment than instruction, as is shown by the fact that while we regularly invoke myths to support moral principles, we do not use fairytales in this way. Historian Christopher Hill observes that fathers in fairytale are often benevolent figures, whereas in myth they are more likely to be tyrannical, and believes this is because classic myths were used to promote an authoritarian style of fathering behaviour, which could by no means be taken for granted.[12]

6 There are times where if I haven't seen them for a day or two and I find I get in and I have to tell them off: 'Gary stop this and Richard stop that' and I have to give them a smack. Once or twice I've felt like saying to Annie, why don't you deal with it and deal with it at that time? But they play their mother up and she's tired. Sometimes it takes the father to sort it. I feel bad about having to do it, because I want to spend time with them and I don't want to have to smack them. I do it, but with a heavy heart. 9

Ritchie, 34, father of two

If the primary purpose of myth is to shape behaviour, what instructions have our culture's ancient myths been delivering to fathers and their children? The preoccupying themes are obedience and the transfer of property and power, and often the instruction has been more to the child than the father. For example, the son who rebels against his father's rule and kills or castrates him is always punished, even if his father had tried to kill him first (as in the story of Oedipus). The violent father–son imagery from Christianity is also about the child's obedience: 'Thy will be done'. It is interesting to note that violence does not feature in father–son fairytales. Here the transfer of power invariably happens amicably, and obedience is far more gently promoted.[13]

Another recurring theme in Western myth is the willing sacrifice of the beloved child. Sometimes this is a daughter but more often it is a son, as in the story of Abraham and Isaac. Here the instruction is not to children. It is to fathers, who are told to let nothing (not even parental love, which is here recognised to be the supreme love) distract them from the higher purpose of their lives. It is notable that fathers in fairytale are not required to sacrifice their children for a higher purpose, and also that daughters figure more heavily in these stories. Beauty's father loses her unwittingly, Hansel and Gretel's unwillingly.

But whatever the origin or purpose of a myth, it can have an effect over and above its actual storyline, and the main legacy of father–son mythology is the widely held belief that this relationship is destined to be highly competitive and problematic. One of the men interviewed for this book, whose wife was pregnant, was hoping the baby would be a girl because 'there's all that "young stag" stuff between fathers and sons'. Interestingly, this man had not had a troubled or competitive relationship with his own father. And, in the main, daughters express greater disappointment in their relationships with their fathers than do sons. The Australian fatherhood researcher, Graeme Russell, who is himself the father of a son and has been working with fathers and their children since the early 1980s, believes personally (although no research has yet looked into this) that father–son relationships are often very warm and physically intimate, right through adolescence.[14]

Oedipus – schmoedipus?

Father–daughter relationships were, until recently, less heavily burdened by myth. The preoccupying theme has been containment. Daughters have been held in castles or gardens from which they have escaped (like the Twelve Dancing Princesses) or been exiled (like Eve). Again the issues have been obedience and the transfer of property. The dark side of the containment theme is incest, which is much more common in myth than in fairytale, from which it may have been expunged. Much of the current emphasis on sexuality between parent and child (and particularly between fathers and daughters) is due to the story of Oedipus. Although it does not mention daughters, if any myth currently holds the father–child relationship in thrall, it is this.

> 6 Every night she wanted twenty kisses, not sexual kisses at all, but on the lips. I thought, well you know what they say about fathers and daughters. It must be because I'm her father or because I'm a man, and it worried me. I felt awkward. Then one day, I mentioned it to my wife, and she said, 'Oh yes, twenty kisses, she has to have the same from me.' 9
>
> *Bill, 38, father of two*

The 20th century has been called the century of Freud, and the Oedipus complex has been his trademark. Freud seized on the tale (son kills father and marries mother) to back his theory that children desire genital intercourse with the opposite-sex parent, developing the notion to explain away reports by some very distressed young Viennese women of their fathers' strange behaviour. Freud soon found that the ancient myth, which he had invoked to 'prove' the universality of children's desires, had carried him on its shoulders into public consciousness, where it both shocked and reassured his audience. It shocked them because they had thought the family the only safe haven *from* sexuality. It reassured them because they could believe that the children, not the parents, were to blame.

Do children actually want to sleep with the opposite-sex parent, even unconsciously? To suggest otherwise seems to be party-pooping. People today often comment that little girls 'flirt' with their daddies (boys' flirting with mothers isn't mentioned as often), but in fact very many little girls do not flirt with their fathers, or with other adult males. Those who do so may have mothers who relate to men in that way, and may be doing no more than mirroring their behaviour. Often, of course, so-called flirtatiousness is in the eye of the beholder.

Certainly, boys and girls often want to marry the opposite-sex parent, and one five-year-old, when told that fathers gave mothers seeds so that babies could be conceived, remarked to her father: 'I hope you have saved a seed for me'! However, children also regularly say they intend to marry the same-sex parent. To marry and have a child with a parent may seem perfectly logical if you intend to have children of your own one day, as most children do, and if you also have no intention of ever leaving your parents.

Many aspects of Freud's theory are now under review. How 'universal' is the Oedipus myth? Where in other cultures do we find tales of boys (let alone girls) killing one parent in order to have sex with the other? And when the children Freud studied evidenced fears of castration, which he said proved that they had had guilty fantasies about having sex with at least one of their parents, was there a simpler explanation? Had, perhaps, sexually inhibited parents and nurse-maids in late 19th century Vienna failed to explain why boys and girls were different, or threatened to cut off boys' penises when they were found masturbating? Yet despite these reservations, and the now well-known fact that Freud invoked the Oedipus myth to cover up specific adult crimes, the notion of universality has stuck, not only to children but to fathers. The myth invoked to save the reputations of a few men has brought them all into disrepute. As the meaning of child abuse in popular consciousness has moved from battered babies through the full range of physical abuse to centre on sexual abuse, it has sullied the reputations of all fathers.

Graeme Russell also challenges the notion of the father–daughter relationship as sexually charged. While most fathers appreciate their young daughters' beauty and, as they grow towards adulthood may experience sexual responses to some of their friends, a sexual reaction to a daughter is not, in Russell's view, at all usual.[15] Russell's hunch is supported by US research that found very few fathers indeed feeling sexually attracted to their daughters. However, the extent to which the idea hangs heavily on them was shown by the fact that many were aware of, and terrified by, the possibility.[16] Such wariness could be useful if it inhibited incestuous behaviour. Perversely, however, Freud's theory can seem to legitimise it. Because he invoked a myth, and myth suggests that something is 'natural', the 2 per cent of fathers who impose themselves sexually on their daughters can be seen as doing what the other 98 per cent are having actively to *restrain* themselves from doing.[17]

6 They say that it's all about fathers and daughters but, really, touching any child can have a sexual element because you are handling their bodies, and as long as you stay aware of that you should have a pretty good sense of when you are behaving inappropriately. I have never had any trouble with it, and it changes all the time. If I am lifting up my eight-year-old, I don't hesitate to put my hands on her delightfully plump little buttocks, but I wouldn't wash her genitals in the bath. The two-

year-old still has that lovely wobbly baby fat. She is the kind of child you just want to get your fingers into! But recently when I was tickling her and happened to touch the inside of her thighs, her expression changed. You need to recognise what you can no longer do. **'**

Philip, 45, father of three

Godly fathers

Images of fatherhood are not only provided by myth and fairytale, but by our social and economic systems which, for a long while, were essentially Christanity's 'political wing'. During the first millennium AD the Christian Church, as a central plank in its bid for power, had set about establishing control over the matrimonial practices of Europe's pagan tribes. These, regarding sons from any source as useful in battle, had made little distinction between legitimacy and illegitimacy. By the 11th century, however, Christianity had established an institution of marriage firmly tied to legitimate paternity. A married man was assumed to be the father of all children born to his marriage. He was to be responsible for them and to have control over them, even if they were being brought up by their mothers. An unmarried father, by contrast, had no rights because he was to have no responsibilities. Making men responsible for illegitimate children would, the Church thought, encourage women to behave 'immorally'.[18]

Christian marriage soon became the cornerstone of a hierarchical society with God the Father (father of all fathers) at its pinnacle, represented throughout the system via layers of fathers below him. There was the King, who was a father to his people, noblemen and priests, who were fathers to their communities, and household heads, who were not only seen as fathers to their children, but to their servants and apprentices as well. As everyone knows, all this raised fathers' status. But what is less often recognised is that it also sought to limit their behaviour. 'Every family, when directed as it should be, has a sacred character,' announced a famous English preacher, 'in-as-much as the head of it acts the part of both the prophet and the priest of his household, by instructing them in the knowledge, and leading them in the worship of God; and, at the same time, he discharges the duty of a king, by supporting a system of order, subordination and discipline.'[19]

For a long time practical fatherly care was represented by Jesus' adoptive father St Joseph, and the development of his persona tells us a great deal about what was considered right and proper for earthly fathers. In the 15th century there are many illustrations of Joseph's gentle domesticity. In pictures and engravings he is shown drying the Baby Jesus' nappies and feeding him from a bowl of milk. By the 17th century, childcare has ceased to be his province (he is now shown protecting Mary and working to keep her and the child), but in the occasional painting or engraving he still holds the baby, who is softly touching his face. As time passes Joseph's domestic involvement vanishes and, by the 18th century, he is portrayed as a religious contemplative, praying or studying alone.[20] So it came about that fathers, in all their aspects, were relegated to Heaven, elevated or reduced (depending on your point of view) to one-dimensional lawgivers, in the image of whom earthly fathers were to make themselves.

❝ *Fatherly Advice, 1716*
1. My dear son, know thou the God of thy father, and serve him with a perfect heart.
2. Think often of thine own frailty ...
3. Praise and esteem the holy word of God infinitely before the finest of gold ...
4. Take care of thy health ...
5. Beware of passion. Let not anger and wrath infect thine heart ...
6. Beg of God that he would establish thee in the grace of chastity ...
7. Speak the truth alwaysy ...
8. Be just to all men ...compassionate, tender hearted, and mercifuly ...
9. Avoid sloth and idlenessy ...
10. Let divinity be thy main studyy ... My dear child, be of Catholic spirit. **❞**

William Brattle, 1716

The new fatherhood: stage one

As the 18th century progressed, and secularisation and republicanism took hold, fatherhood began to wobble. If there was no God, what gave a father his authority? A solution was offered by the rationalist philosopher Jean-Jacques Rousseau in a moral novel, *Emile*. In this story a foundling, Emile, is adopted by an exemplary father figure, who raises him with passionate dedication. Although

Emile's fictional saviour was a 'new father' (which at that time meant a calm and reasonable man who trusted in children's innate goodness), he was still heavily authoritarian. He was also head of his family, earning this position not as God's deputy, but through his steadfast, masculine rationality. The classic family image after Rousseau shows a seated (submissive) mother, with a standing (dominant) father, raising his child up before him in acknowledgement of paternity.[21]

From this time on, in addition to 'family values', gender was emphasised as the *raison d'être* of fatherhood. What was proposed for the two sexes was not merely role-segregation but role-polarisation. Fathers were to set limits on mothers' dangerous (yet necessary) emotionality and, in order to do so successfully, had to set limits upon their own. Slowly but surely, in a move which paralleled the excluding of women from active involvement in the affairs of the wider world, men's supposed rationality was invoked to disqualify them from intimate involvement with their children.

Interestingly, *Emile* can be seen as a self-consoling fantasy. Its author, Rousseau, had not only been deserted by his own father, but had conceived five children with his working-class house-keeper/mistress. Dedicated to a 'higher purpose' (his writing, through which he hoped to transform the world), Rousseau decided he was unable to support his children. He therefore had them dumped in a foundling hospital from which, theoretically, they could have been adopted. In fact, conditions in these hospitals were such that, as everyone knew, all five babies almost certainly died.

> 6 We have not formed the ancient world, it has formed us …
> We have taken the fairytales of childhood with us into maturity,
> chewed but still lying in the stomach … Often unknowingly,
> unwittingly, we act out the roles we were taught. 9
>   *Andrea Dworkin,* Woman Hating

Paternal propaganda

Perhaps Rousseau's behaviour should not shock as much as it does. For to study the paternal imagery of the last 400 years is to be confronted with an on-going campaign promoting an extremely limited range of fathering behaviours, which did not include involvement or empathy with infants. This is not to infer a conscious conspiracy, but a patchwork of vested interests which, as the study of masculinity has begun to reveal, has consistently required adult males no less than adult females to behave in particular ways.

As early as 1665 the French Clerical Assembly published a treatise on the family in which it urged its community workers (clerics) to pursue fathers, not for child support, but to ensure that they were carrying out their religious duties inside their homes. In Britain similar instructions were delivered by Puritan preachers, and Calvin told fathers that the best and most loving father concealed his tender feelings 'behind a stern exterior'. Corporal punishment was recommended, but in this area mothers were let off the hook ('they very rarely know how to deal with unruly behaviour successfully'). Fathers had no such luck. 'The father strikes his child and himself feels the smart,' wrote the German poet, Ruckert, 'Severity is a merit if you have a gentle heart.'[22]

All over Europe, fathers were shown in heroic or instructive mould. They pardonned errant children, led their families in prayer and presided over frugal meals. Classical reference was summoned, and simile and metaphor pressed into service. A good father was said to be 'a sturdy oak', 'the pillar that supported the house', 'the sun in the family firmament'. As time went on, the link between fatherhood and work was constantly made. A father 'held the reins' and 'navigated the ship', and was 'shepherd of the flock' and 'keeper of the gate'.[23]

> 6 When my little Konrad was four years old I thought it was high time for him to accustom himself to obeying his father unquestioningly … (so, when he refused to give Christel's doll back to her) … I said to him in a severe tone of voice 'Konrad, you must return the doll at once …' 'No!' was his reply. I lashed him one! two! three! Then I whipped him much harder … My heart was sore throughout. At mealtime I couldn't eat. I got up from the table and went to see our pastor and poured my heart out to him … 'You did the right thing, dear Mr Kiefer,' he said. 'When the nettles are still young, they can be pulled out easily; but if they are left for a long time, the roots will grow …' 9
>
> *Konrad Kiefer, 1796*

St Joseph's earlier domesticity was derided, and satire invoked to keep men at a healthy distance from babies and young children. Between the 16th and 19th centuries texts and images depicted a 'world turned upside down', in which the social order was shown inverted and, through irony, reinforced. A key image was that of a man looking after children, and being beaten by them.

Supplementing such techniques of persuasion were frank warnings. It was said that rocking a cradle had a 'weakening effect' on a man, and 17th century French fathers with a penchant for infant-care were offered a picture of a 'poor fool' nursing a baby, while his wife, primping in a mirror, got herself ready for a night out on the town. The moral was clear: only cuckolds cuddle babies.[24]

As significant as what was said or seen was what was not said and not seen. What was missing were images of men with babies. In 1661 a *Life of King Henry IV of France* was published in Paris. Henry was a passionate father and had a brood of children, legitimate and illegitimate, which he brought up all together in the Royal Palace. Included in the *Life* is what amounts to a family photo, an engraving of the King cradling a tiny baby and tickling its tummy.[25]

Just how extraordinary this image was becomes clear if we scan the rest of Western pictorial art. Here we discover that from the late Middle Ages right through to the 19th century, there are only a handful of pictures of men holding babies. A few peasant fathers (in 17th century Dutch art), St Joseph (for whom the nobility of the Christ Child rendered an unusual pose acceptable) and King Henry. While, over many centuries, the maternal bond has been visually represented, only paternal power has been displayed. We have been shown the public face of fatherhood, with intimate fathering ignored, one might even say suppressed.

> 6 I was never quite sure of it [love] with my father, because of the time in history when he was a father and the type of person he was – fathers weren't parents as it were. But then I found that when you give attention and affection and love you get it back, and that fathers are just as important as mothers. One day when Charlotte and I were walking through the station, we saw two tramps and I said they had no homes, and Charlotte said 'They miss their mummies and daddies'. And daddies! Her idea of happiness and security and contentment, it was that simple. That's where it comes from. 9
>
> *Philip, 45, father of three*

A healthy distance?

What has been the reasoning behind the cultural pressure keeping males away from babies and young children? 'No developing society that needs men to leave home and do their thing for society ever allows young men in to hand or touch their newborns,' observed the anthropologist, Margaret Mead, 'for they know somewhere if they did the new fathers would become so "hooked" they would never go out and do their thing properly.'[26] And indeed, when another anthropologist, Carol Ember, studied an African tribe where boys regularly undertook domestic work alongside girls, she found that the more of this work they carried out, the less aggressive they became.[27]

The fear has not been that men, once they became as close to children as women have routinely been, would find the experience unappealing. Rather the fear has been that, once accustomed to it, they would not willingly give it up. Men have been urged to keep at an emotional and physical distance from infants so that they will be cut off from their most tender feelings, so that they will be alienated from themselves. This has helped to condition them to blind obedience, has fitted them to undertake exhausting and degrading physical work, and has prepared them to be an army-in-waiting in times of peace and to kill and be killed in times of war. It is surely no coincidence that only when violence is seen as anti-social, and it is unlikely that young men in large numbers will ever again be called upon to fight for our country, a review of the father's role is deemed possible.

One of the key ways in which distance between fathers and their children has been promoted is through the image and reality of a father as his family's sole provider. This is a relatively recent development. While earlier definitions of the good father could include providing, poor men like St Joseph were seen as good fathers, too.[28] But by the late 19th century, with Rousseau's 'separate spheres' ideology for the two sexes hardened into an economic system, breadwinning was seen not only as fathers' main activity, but their primary function.

> ❢ The thing that makes an economic system like ours work is to maintain control over people and make them do jobs they hate. To do this, you fill their heads with biblical nonsense about fornication of every variety. Make sure they marry young, make sure they have a wife and children very early. Once a man has a wife and two young children, he will do what you tell him to. He will obey you. And that is the aim of the entire masculine role. ❢
>
> *Gore Vidal*

Fatherly breadwinning did not, as is often believed, offer a smooth ride right up to the 1930s, for even in the mid 18th century fathers often found themselves on an economic roller-coaster. One minute, they were in work and respected. The next, they were out of work and despised. As material expectations rose, more and more was expected of them. Soon it was not enough for a father to be a provider, he had to be a *good* provider. 'To be middle class was to consume,' writes fatherhood historian, Robert Griswold, 'and men underwrote the act – constantly battling to keep up with changing definitions of the good life.'[29]

Nowhere is fathers' new pride, and new isolation, seen more vividly than in 19th century pictorial art. In pictures of family meals, fathers had been central figures. Now they were omitted or edged to one side. In a painting entitled 'Many Happy Returns of the Day' and painted in 1856, women and children are clustered around a laden tea-table in an opulent dining-room. The paterfamilias is sitting at the head of the table, but his chair is pushed back and he is gazing out of the painting at the viewer: 'See how I have provided for them,' he seems to say, 'see how it sets me apart.'[30]

The de-skilling of fatherhood

Why did the role of sole provider find such widespread acceptance as a definition of good fathering? Never before had so much been earned by so many, most of whom were male, and this had spin-offs in terms of masculinity. Fatherly breadwinning, when underwritten by women's economic subordination, supplied men with the exclusive status on which masculine identity has traditionally relied. It also served to recompense fathers, as with home and workplace increasingly separated, they lost their grip on family life. For as the 19th century progressed, fatherhood was steadily de-skilled, and mothers and others gradually took over the day-to-day functions which had once bound fathers and children together.

6 Once a father moved out of family life, his work ceased to be something he did for the sake of his family and became work for the sake of work ... He didn't slow down when he'd achieved a level of sufficient comfort ... He worked because he worked; that was what he did because that was what he was. He was no longer paterfamilias, he was homo laboriosus. 9
Frank Pittman, Man Enough

The de-skilling of fatherhood continues. Caregiving is now almost entirely in the hands of women (mothers and family professionals), and the duties of educator and trainer, once shared by parents, are largely split between mothers and teachers. Fathers are no longer assumed to be children's protectors (quite the opposite), and as women take responsible positions in their communities and participate in the wider world, they are no less able than fathers to interpret that world to their children, or provide them with introductions to it. Few sons (or daughters) now enter their fathers' trades (in the second half of the 19th century more than 50 per cent did so) and a 1994 UK survey showed that teenagers not only discuss personal matters more readily with mothers than fathers, but also education and employment.[31] Today, even providing can no longer be seen as the defining function of fatherhood, because it is not an exclusive function. Mothers work too. Between 1985 and 1993, the percentage of working mothers with children under nine went up from 38 per cent to 53 per cent.[32]

Ironically, just when, in the second half of the 19th century, breadwinning duties were exiling fathers from their families in ever-greater numbers, the family was being represented as the generator of psychological adjustment and individual happiness. Fathers, who were worried that the long hours worked outside their homes were destroying their relationships with their children, had to be reassured. As the 19th century turned into the 20th, family experts busied themselves proving that part-time fathering was not only possible but desirable. They declared that a father's detachment from the daily routine enabled him to 'bring a fresh approach and a new perspective that Mother is quite unable to provide'.[33] Psychoanalysts proved particularly obliging. As well as valuing fathers' detachment from mother and child, they suggested that a father's main importance was as a symbol. All the good father had to do, said the great English child psycyhoanalyst D. W. Winnicott, was to 'turn up often enough' for his child to feel he was 'real and alive'.[34]

❢ *Fatherly Advice, 1944*
Play for your side and not for yourself
Keep your eye on the ball
Remember you may become the best bat in the world and still
    not be a sportsman
Do your best to help others
Remember a game is never lost until it is won
Obey your captain without question
Smile in all circumstances ❣
        Herbert Lees, 'Rules of cricket and of life'

The playful father

Although fatherhood had moved out of the political spotlight, it had not entirely lost its political uses. The family was now seen as the cornerstone of democracy, to which the greatest threat was said to come from individuals rebelling against the autocratic behaviour of old-fashioned fathers. Accordingly, the image of the good father underwent a change, and throughout the first half of the 20th century, the image of the father as his children's pal and confidante was relentlessly promoted. Fathers leaping off commuter trains were encouraged to head straight for the playroom. 'In this part of the day Dad should *reign*,' advised *Parents' Magazine* in the 1930s, invoking imagery of yesteryear in a brave attempt to dignify the undignifiable.[35] When not exhausted from rough-and-tumble or half blind from squinting over his offsprings' stamp collections, the New Father was supposed to be involving his children in democratic family-council meetings. 'Democracy,' a leading American child expert told fathers, 'begins at home.'[36]

As an icon for the times, the playful father had it all. The image was softer, more nurturing, more democratic, than any that had been seen before, yet it was essentially conservative. It left intact the gender-division of labour, did not imply father-as-mother and still gave fathers an exclusive role in time that could be spared from the main purpose of their life, which of course was breadwinning. Right up to the 1960s, no listing of ideal fatherly attributes strayed far from the notion of father as king of the kiddies, leading his offspring on recreational expeditions full of masculine purpose. To the science museum, the railway station, the building site, 'Expeditions,' *Child's World* confided cosily in 1965, 'that only daddies can deal with competently.'[37]

By the late 1960s, British social scientists were so certain that fathers played with their children that in a major survey of parenting behaviours, they did not even include a question on the topic, and one mother interviewed even suggested that within families fathers 'should be' the 'light relief'.[38] By the 1980s, researchers believed that playfulness with children came naturally to men, and when it became clear that fathers in some cultures were not at all playful with their children, this roused great interest.[39]

Why has playfulness become as so central to Western definitions of fathering in recent times? The image succeeded because, under the circumstances, it was serviceable. Fathers arriving home after mothers and children had been sequestered together for hours were often required to lighten the atmosphere. They could also gain ready popularity. A 1987 study showed American fathers to be more popular with their young children than Swedish fathers, even though they spent less time with them, and this seemed to be due to their more playful style of behaviour.[40]

> 6 From me they get fun and irreverence. They see me as the light reliever, the person who plays games. I have to balance Barbara who is this great brooding, worrying sort of presence, getting angry, getting sad. They take their problems more to Barbara than to me. I get bored listening to them and always want to give them advice. I do try and focus on it, but it makes me feel sad when they talk about their little lives – they have these feelings and vulnerabilities and anxieties. 9
>
> *Tom, 42, father of two*

Sadly, such popularity often does not last. Older children can find fathers' jokey approach alienating, as several men interviewed for this book remarked. 'Dad was great when we were little,' said one, 'but when we were teenagers he was still making the same stupid faces at the other end of the table.' 'He was a good father for small children, always playing lions on the floor,' said another, 'but he didn't seem to know what to do with us when we got older.' Interestingly, although the playful father is still promoted as the main positive image of fatherhood, even this is no longer seen as a father-only attribute. In a recent television advertisement for Kotex towels, the parent taking a little boy on the dodgems is a mother.[11]

Gradually, the imagery developed to give fathers this special role seems to be marginalising them. In a highly successful *Yellow Pages* commercial, which the advertisers say really has 'hit the spot', a boy efficiently searches the directory for an addition to a trainset for his father's birthday, while the father plays with the set alone in the attic.[42] But, worse still, the king of the kiddies has become a kiddie. A promotion for a gum-gel shows father and baby side by side, looking glumly out of the picture: 'When it comes to mouth pain,' reads the strap-line, 'they're both babies.'[43]

Bad dads

Many of the images we have of fatherhood today are negative. Fathers are seen as absurd, pitiable, marginal, violent, abusive, uncaring and delinquent. 'You can always tell the fathers on TV shows,' wrote a commentator in 1976. 'They're the mindless, ineffectual buffoons.'[44]

Fathers are not only criticised for what they do, but for what they don't do. When fathers first began to work away from their homes in large numbers, their absence was praised, and the classic image of the father lifting his young child into the air was recycled, to show the hard-working father returning home to catch his child in his arms and swing it up in the air. And as Europe plunged in and out of war, soldier fathers (though absent) were often shown as spiritually present. Today, the necessity for heroic absences is all but gone, and with the world of work increasingly distanced from the world of home, the products of daily labour have become harder to envision. As it has become more difficult to give emotional meaning to paternal absence, the image of the absent father has gathered force and negativity, and father-absence associated with the rising tide of out-of-wedlock births has become a symbol of moral degeneration.

The dramatic transformation of the paternal *imago* over the last 100 years cannot be explained solely by fathers' behaviour. Certainly, some fathers behave badly, but some fathers always have and surveys from the 1950s onwards have recorded much individual hostility to mothers, too.[45] Perhaps the mighty fall of fatherhood has resulted from the ruler father's deriving so much of his power from authoritarianism and so much of his influence from blind obedience and the suspension of disbelief. Once the game was up, his de-bunking was, inevitably, a vicious process.

> 6 After your death I met you again as the face of patriarchy, could name at last precisely the principle you embodied. There was an ideology at last which let me dispose of you, identify the suffering you caused, hate you righteously as part of a system, the kingdom of fathers. I saw the power and arrogance of the male as your true watermark; I did not see beneath it the suffering of the Jew, the alien stamp you bore, because you had deliberately arranged that it should be invisible to me. It is only now, under a powerful womanly lens, that I can decipher your suffering and deny no part of my own. 9
>
> *Adrienne Rich*, Your Native Land

If fathers are being punished for the excesses of patriarchy, for being too powerful, they may also be being punished for not being powerful enough. For they have not, as legend decreed, saved us with their thunderbolts or their power over wind or waves. Too often they have been willing to sacrifice us, like the boy Isaac or the five baby skeletons in Rousseau's cupboard, to an all-too-human weakness, or to some higher purpose which they believed it was their duty to pursue.

Fathers v. mothers

Fathers also lose out considerably by comparison with mothers. For more than 150 years now, children have been women's trade. While men have been engaged in production, mothers have been busy with reproduction, and their investment in their offspring has been visible in a way that fathers' often equally committed labour has not been. Many contemporary children perceive themselves as totally dependent on their mothers. 'If you died, mummy, I'd die too!' wept a four-year-old who is raised almost entirely by his mother, since his hard-working father is rarely home before bedtime. When the mother, touched and bewildered, asked why, the child explained, 'I wouldn't be able to reach the stove!'

Such dependence may well result in a need, magnified over many families, to 'keep the mother good', and this may often be at the expense of the image of the father. In her classic study of Jamaican families in the1950s, *My Mother Who Fathered Me*, anthropologist Edith Clarke observed that although mothers regularly beat their children violently (and Ms Clarke witnessed these beatings) fathers' violence would be reported, but mothers' almost never.[46]

The idealisation of motherhood, an idealisation which many commentators have regarded as a deliberate tactic to keep women submerged in childrearing, has gradually worn away at fatherhood.[47] The more idealised mothers have become, the more it has been necessary to 'split off' negative perceptions about them and put them somewhere else. The natural repository has been fatherhood, which has long been perceived as motherhood's polar opposite. Fathers are now paying for the idealisation of motherhood in a manner which was never anticipated.

❝ *Fatherly Advice, 1993*
Big boys don't cry
Always carry a Johnny
Always steer into a skid
It's as easy to marry a rich girl as a poor one
Second place is for losers

Take it easy – but take it
Don't dip your pen in the company ink
Don't get mad, get even
Life's a bitch, and then you marry one
Go and ask your mother **❯**
                        'Papa Don't Preach', GQ Magazine

Latterly, in a new development, fathers are becoming invisible.
Although virgin births are not endemic, we talk of 'one-parent
families' (one-parent *households* would surely be more accurate) and
when 'parents' wishes or opinions or behaviour are reported, often
it is only or mainly mothers who have been studied or consulted. In
'adland' (the world of television advertising) the Janet and John
two-parent family can no longer be taken for granted. In family
scenes in television commercials, even at a wedding or a son's
graduation, there is quite often no father present.[48]

The new fatherhood: stage two

It is customary to deplore the reported slow pace of change in
men's domestic behaviour and the fact that today's nappy-changing
New Father seems only to be appearing in fits and starts, but it
would perhaps be more logical (remembering centuries
dominated by patriarchal imagery) to marvel that he is daring to
show his face at all.

The new father, in fact, is far from being a purely positive figure.
He started life as an inadequate, no less a failure as a father than the
19th century's feckless drunkard. For just as New Woman was
originally accused of being 'sterile' or of 'a neuter gender', so the
sexual orientation of New Man (and the new father) has been
regularly called into question. During the 1950s it was widely asserted
that the children of 'submissive' fathers were likely to develop
schizophrenia or homosexuality, and right through to the 1970s,
househusbands were depicted clad ridiculously in frilly aprons.[49]

Throughout much of the 20th century, fatherhood as a mainstay
of heterosexuality has been a central theme. 'Fathers shouldn't try to
be mothers,' warned an American child-expert, going on to argue,
like advisers in the 17th century, that the daily care of young children
could 'emasculate' men.[50] 'Our culture has employed a fear and
loathing of homosexuality as a weapon,' writes Andrew Samuels, 'to
keep all men as a group tied into the role of provider in the family,
the one who must therefore remain emotionally distant.'[51]

Today public images of true intimacy between fathers and children are still exceedingly rare, and while mothers are regularly shown face to face with their children, this pose is almost never chosen for fathers. The nearest thing to public paternal intimacy is the 'hairless Adonis'. This is the image of the young naked man holding a naked baby against his chest, which is often seen in magazines. But although this suggests softness and strength it can also, unfortunately, imply sexuality.

Men's involvement in childcare is still portrayed negatively or equivocally. Either it is seen as developing from an abnormal situation as in the film (*Jack and Sarah*), or the father is shown as incompetent, failing to put a nappy on correctly (Britannia Insurance TV commercial), or standing helplessly by while his offspring cover themselves in grime (Persil). Incompetent father scenarios are, apparently, developed to flatter mothers, who are the main purchasers of baby-products and who, advertisers believe, like to see fathers fail. However, this is perhaps also a late manifestation of the desire to put distance between men and children. Proving men's unfitness for nursery work serves to revalue their other supposedly more important functions, and the real target may not be the father who can't manage the dirty nappy, but the father who might be thinking of doing so.

> ❝ To this day I still tell my kids that I love them. I don't say any other word and often I give them a little cuddle and say 'I love you Patrick' or 'I love you Sean', something like that, and I have always thought myself that I really do. It is not a negotiable thing. I think it is the way to bring up kids and I can't stand seeing somebody with a young child saying 'Go on give him one' and all that anger 'Do this, do that' and you do get people doing that, as sad as it sounds it does go on. ❞
>
> *Michael, 36, father of two*

New dad ascending?

Nevertheless, there is a sense in which new father images today are subversive, for the context in which they are appearing has changed. It is now regularly suggested that fathers can behave like mothers and still retain their gender identity, and even that the intimate care of young children should be at the heart of men's claim to fatherhood. This change of context impacts on our perception of the new father, and it seems that the Britannia campaign, with its incompetent dad, went down badly with viewers.

At last, among the generally ambivalent new father images, are some that are truly radical. There are a few television commercials and dramas (such as Alan Bleasdale's *Requiem Apache*) in which fathers manage the business of parenting with straightforward competence. *Kramer v. Kramer*, in a stunning reversal of traditional imagery, showed Dustin Hoffman learning to hold his son's body in entirely new ways, eventually cradling him and crooning to him. On the one occasion in that film when the child ran down the path to greet a returning parent and be swung into the air, that parent was the mother.

Yet, although we are presented with contradictory versions of fatherhood, the images remain astonishingly archetypal on the whole. A recent survey of fatherhood images in daily newspapers found that while mothers were shown as ordinary individuals facing a range of choices, fathers were represented either as heroes or monsters, fufilling classic functions as genitors, breadwinners, defenders or saviours.[52] Similarly, when American researcher Shere Hite interviewed people about their parents, she recorded the widespread use of archetypal language in their responses to questions about fathers, but not about mothers.[53] No one quite knows why this happens. It may be that the paternal archetype is being used to plug a gap left by a father who is emotionally or physically absent, or the images may be invoked by writers who have no clear idea of how fathers normally behave. 'Fatherhood has a public face,' wrote one journalist, 'and a privacy that only the individual can discover.'[54]

This private–public 'split' in fatherhood runs deep. Several years ago, an eminent fatherhood researcher was videoing couples interacting with their young children. As expected, the mothers showed the highest levels of interaction, with the fathers staying somewhat aloof. Then the researcher told the couples he was being called away to the phone, and suggested they relax for a moment, but in fact he left the video camera running, without their knowledge. He saw that while the mothers' behaviour remained constant, the fathers' changed, and when they thought they were no longer being observed, they interacted *more* with their children.[55]

⁶ Last night Tim came up and put his arms around me. Now I think a lot of fathers would say to a 17-year-old boy 'What are you doing that for? Go and cuddle your mother!' or be embarrassed by it. Even if they wanted to, they would feel unable to accept the gesture. I just put my arms around him

and we stood there for a few seconds, not a long time, and off he went to buy his cigarettes and I think he just needed that – to put his arms around the guy he identifies with, who might possibly get him through his exams! **)**

Scott, 46, father of two

Fathers' inhibited public behaviour is a problem, both for those who would study them and for fathers themselves. A German nursery leader who set up a 'fathers only' group to minimise the men's self-consciousness discovered that, even then, the vast majority had great difficulties in showing paternal feelings publicly and found it difficult to sing and play freely with their children without embarrassment.[56] This experience has been duplicated in many countries. 'Unlike women, men tend not to talk about their children's caretaking needs in social groups,' explains American fatherhood expert, Kyle Pruett. 'Rather, they "own" their experience privately, as if they have discovered a wonderful secret that can be preserved only by not calling attention to it.'[57]

Rehabilitating fatherhood

Of course we know that in playing 'hide-the-father' men are only obeying cultural rules, but this more or less ensures their invisibility. It means that most of us only get an idea of how fathers behave (fathers other than those we have lived with) when abusive behaviour forces open the 'black box' of the family. It is often said that interest in the sexual abuse of children by fathers is out of all proportion to the amount of abuse there is, but when considered in light of the enormous *absence* of information about other kinds of fathering, this seems inevitable. While abuse is our main window on intimate fathering, our preoccupation with it will persist.[58]

How, then, can the image of the good father be positively reconstructed? When, in 1994, the Disney Corporation launched its blockbuster fairytale, *The Lion King*, a recognised aim of the film was to rehabilitate fatherhood. This did not prove easy. With lions famed for their aloof family behaviour, the film-makers were stuck with a hero who had to be both Top Cat and, in the light of modern expectations, a personable family democrat.

An uneasy compromise was reached. The father lion, though providing no infant-care and periodically terrifying the life out of his cub, was playful and loving and, in a reversal of Christian myth, gave his life for his son's. The little Lion King himself ultimately mounted the throne alongside his lioness, in a spirit of equality. However, when their infant was born, neither father nor mother was seen to hold it. Such are the dilemmas facing all those who would reconstruct fatherhood. If the images chosen are taken from the old armoury, they have the appeal of the familiar and offer fathers an exclusive role. But they also imply hierarchical structures, which are no longer seen as tenable, and emotional distance, which is no longer seen as desirable. We really do not know whether fathers should be dads or patriarchs.

❦ *Prince and Mayte are going to have a baby.*
Congratulations to you both.

We formerly presumed you mad
Though artistically rather rad
The artist 2 B known as Dad ...

For nothing can compare U know
When Pampers, toys and baby-gro
Are strewn around the studio

Then proud with pram in Paisley Park
Oblivious as the fans remark
The artist known as Patriarch ❧
Martin Newell, 'Nothing Prepares U 4'

Why should similarity between the functions of mothers and fathers be considered such a problem and, furthermore, be considered only a problem for fathers? Masculinity fears are probably somewhere around, but it's more than that. Even if mothers' functions become very like fathers' (and it is clear that they are moving perilously close), the fact that mothers become pregnant and give birth still allows them independent identity. Fathers have been given an independent identity through exclusive social functions, and if such functions cannot be found, they run the risk of being termed 'redundant'.

In 1969 Alexander Mitscherlich published a book entitled *Society Without the Father*. This was not, as might be assumed, a volume deploring the daily absence of real fathers from their children's lives. It was, rather, a vision of social organisation bereft of the image of the ruler father so closely associated with the roots of our civilisation.[59] And as Mitscherlich was writing and in the decade that followed, more fathers than ever before were declaring, publicly, that they were seeking intimacy with their children. 'It is not the death of fatherhood which we are witnessing,' wrote the French sociologist, Elizabeth Badinter, responding to a general sense of panic. 'It is the renegotiation of paternal roles.'[60] But although Mitscherlich, too, believed that fatherhood was not drowning but changing, others have not been so sure.

The politics of fatherhood

One group warning of fatherhood's imminent demise, and invoking traditional paternal imagery to save it, is the mythopoetic men's movement headed by poet Robert Bly. Bly is a great supporter of patriarchal structures, without which he insists we will fall prey to a 'sibling society' tearing itself to rivalrous pieces. Leadership is to be provided by adult males who, once they have tapped in to the 'wild man' inside themselves, will be able to pass specialist knowledge on to their sons and keep us all in order.

The foundation stone of Bly's theory is the wild man 'archetype' which he claims to have uncovered in the allegedly ancient ('pre-Greek') folk-tale, *Iron John*.[61] Bly does not think daughters merit serious consideration. They are 'sweet and simple to raise' he declares airily – a view not shared by Andrew Samuels, who is also father of a daughter and who points out that Bly's ambition for girls is limited to their developing into suitable domestic partners for men.[62] Bly's implicit attack on women alienates quite a few fathers of daughters, who might otherwise find this (rare) support for a positive image of maleness attractive.

There are two other problems here. Firstly Bly, like so many before him, is indulging in a spot of myth-making. *Iron John* is not an ancient myth. Not pre-Greek nor even pre-Christian, it is a story of Bly's own creation, loosely modelled on a couple of medieval European tales.[63] Secondly, Bly is not truly interested in fatherhood. His real concern is with *being fathered*, an important issue, but not at all the same thing. This is, similarly, the concern of the British Men's Association for Counselling who in April 1996 announced a national 'talk to your father' day, *not* a national 'talk to your children' day which, one male chat-show host commented sadly 'might have been more appropriate'.

6 I wasn't overly involved in Alessandro's life when he was a child; there was never time to go to school to meet his teachers, for example ... There weren't many things that I told him but

they were important ones. I made it clear that going to school for him was the same as going to the office for me, and that you have to do your best in life … I don't know what's going on from day to day in his life but I expect him not to disappear altogether. **?**

Luciano Beneton

In both the UK and the US, representatives of the New Right also regularly focus on fatherhood, promoting an exclusive role for fathers and running into trouble because they find themselves dealing with a society which no longer has an exclusive role for men. Since the New Right see the father–child bond as secondary to the more intimate and passionate mother–child bond they have only one way of ensuring that fathers remain living with their children. The mothers have to be forced to stay put. This usually means making divorce very difficult and confirming fathers as sole (or main) breadwinners.

The US National Fatherhood Initiative is quite sure that to be 'proper' fathers, fathers must do different things from mothers. Specifically, they must not take on 'the maternal tasks of comforting and nurturing children' but are to 'contain emotions and be decisive'. Rather puzzlingly, the Initiative insists it does not wish to 'turn the clock back to the cold and distant father of the 1950s', a role which (in their view) 'men found unfulfilling and very destructive', although how this would be avoided is not clear.[64]

Traditionally, divorced fathers' groups such as Families Need Fathers have also seemed to take a strong pro-family women-in-their-place attitude. Again, such groups may only have clamoured for a restitution of hierarchical masculinity because that is how the father's role has historically been identified and justified. Fearing that if they are not seen to have something different and special to offer their children, no one will support their bids for increased contact, some divorced men have clung to the notion of a gender-specific role for fathers. And they have done so, however hard it has been to demonstrate and however counter-productive it would be in real terms.

6 It's time to reinforce constitutionalism and reinforce individual and family life. I am in jail. I have done no crime, as the only crime done was to me; that my son was forcibly stolen from me … I have *never* paid child support, as I will not pay to have my son stolen from me … This system that so readily incarcerates fathers and enslaves children to the chains of welfare and the feminist empire, is killing not just this society but civilisation itself … I started a constitutional organisation called the Sovereign Patriot Group ... for clearly, this apartheid against fathers must end. For if we cannot rule and be self-determinate in our own homes, how can we ever rule over government? **9**

Robert Lindsay, Butte County Jail, California

Left with the Right?

At least the New Right has provided a forum in which assent can be given to fathers, even if expressed in old-fashioned terms. What about the political Left? Historically, this constituency has found it hard to say nice things about fathers. The French Revolution was fought by those advocating brotherhood as against fatherhood, and by the 1920s one commentator pointed out that fathers had become widely identified not only with 'monopolist-capitalism' and established religions, but with oppression, aggression and secrecy.[65]

Politically radical and particularly pro-feminist males can have a particularly tough time defending fathers, for they are all too well aware of the damage done in the name of patriarchy, and may fear reinforcing it and undermining women's hard-won autonomy. Andrew Samuels has gone so far as to assure single mothers that by doing the things 'that male fathers do' (namely, engaging in rough-and-tumble play and approving their daughters' sexuality) they need entertain no guilt about depriving their children of a father. They themselves can become 'the good-enough father of whatever sex'![66]

For some people, fatherhood and patriarchal power have been so closely identified that the only terms on which fatherhood has been acceptable is if it mimics motherhood. To qualify as valued parents, fathers must match mothers nappy-for-nappy in intimate care. Other contributions, such as breadwinning, have been ruled inadmissable, even if their dutiful observance has prevented a father notching up the Pampers. Like Andrew Samuels, motherhood writer Sara Ruddock blithely dismisses the one thing that clearly distinguishes fathers from mothers (which is that fathers are men) by nominating her children's biological father, who is apparently a keenly participant parent, to be their 'egalitarian co-*mother*'.[67]

Ruddock, her terminologies thoroughly in a twist, goes on to urge 'mothers of both sexes' to work co-operatively, this despite the fact that even homosexual couples raising children respect sex differences in parenting. Gay male couples do not designate one parent mother and the other father, but tell their offspring they have two daddies or call one of the parents by some other name. Identical strategies around the idea of two mummies are adopted by lesbian co-parents.

❝ Dear Simon,
This week I gave a draft of our contract to Marla, who said she would be our lawyer to create you ... Tim and Scott had little Kati by a surrogate and plan to have another child. With luck, we'll all be going through our pregnancy together ... Are you being a good soul? Are you being patient? As I count on my fingers now, with any luck you'll be here next March!
    Please, God, please; let Simon come to us that day.
    Love, Dad (not to be confused with your Daddy Sam) ❞
                                   Kenneth B. Morgen, Getting Simon

All this may bring a smile to the lips, but it should also bring a chill to the heart. For while liberals have found it impossible to talk positively about fathers, only Robert Bly and the pro-family lobby have provided arenas publicly sympathetic to fathers.[68] Opposite the uneasy figure of the Lion King there is an empty space, and this space can be all too readily filled by misogynists and by frustrated fathers raising their voices in anger against their ex-wives.

Fatherhood and feminism

Since the 1960s, radical left-wing politics and feminism have been fellow-travellers, as have conservatism and the pro-family lobby. These last have not only attacked left-wing politics as providing a charter for immorality, but have swiped sideways at 'man-hating' feminists for supporting single mothers and trying to cut men out of the family. Imagine the confusion, then, when in 1994 an eminent British feminist, Patricia Hewitt, delivered a lecture to social-reform glitterati suggesting that the father–child bond could and should be celebrated at much the same level as the mother–child bond.[69]

The response from leading masculinist, Geoff Dench, was hostile suspicion. In his view, Hewitt and her (female) chums had a hidden agenda. Their real aim was to incapacitate men with childcare so that they could grab all the best jobs.[70] Dench seemed to be locked into the breadwinner/housewife stereotype, and in this he is not alone. When the media is asked to come up with an involved father for a radio or television programme, they invariably choose a househusband, as if the only kind of man who can be close to his children is one who has adopted a traditionally maternal role. Stuck in such polarities, it can be difficult for any of us to grasp a different vision, and to conceive of a society in which neither fathers nor mothers have exclusive roles, and where both are equally valued as breadwinners and intimate parents.

> 6 I make his sandwiches in the morning, before I go to work. I like doing things for him. In the evening I get home as fast as I can. I take him to his bath and I wipe him down and then take him upstairs, read with him, play with him. He talks a lot, you can't stop him bloody yapping! – but I don't mind. Their childhood passes so quickly. Maria feels, and me, we feel that we have had the child for something, and we want to be with him as much as we can. 9
>
> *David, 49, father of three (two families)*

Although a leading US feminist, Louise Silverstein, has written recently in very conciliatory terms about fathers, and even declares that 'fathering is a feminist issue',[71] there is still much hostility among some feminists to the notion of fathers as important to their children or, dare we say it, essential. To suggest such a thing is seen as offensive to single mothers, and as undermining women's autonomy.

This is a correct perception in so far as any improvement in the status of fathers must directly limit mothers' power and influence. However, what is not acknowledged is that the exchange of power between private and public worlds cannot be swapped across bit by bit. And that it is not just mothers' family *responsibilities* that stand in the way of their full social equality, but their enthronement in their children's hearts. The old-style feminist argument seems to be that 'we've invited men in' and they 'haven't been interested',[72] with no recognition given to the fact that there are enormous cultural and structural barriers to men's participation in family life. For men to become close to their children, these will have to be taken as seriously and tackled as consciously as the dismantling of barriers to women's participation in the wider world.

> 6 When I observe a group of people acting in what seem to me irrational ways, the question I pose is not 'What's wrong with them?' but rather 'What are the distorted and distorting features of their situation which make these actions appear rational to them?' Until I have satisfied myself that, if I were in

their shoes, their ... actions would also appear as legitimate options to me, I consider myself not to have succeeded in understanding or explaining anything. **)**

Harry Brod, Men and the Future

Campaigning dads

It is often said that because men in our society do not yet campaign extensively for the right to be participant fathers, it must be concluded that they have no interest in intimate fathering. But, equally, men have not campaigned on their own behalf on health issues, yet no one would conclude from this that they have no interest in staying alive. What these areas have in common is that they can be classified as 'sissy stuff', about which real men have been taught to keep silent.

Men also find it difficult to campaign positively for intimate fatherhood because they have no images to group around. These are locked away in their private lives, and in the public arena they have only female precedents.

(The bottle meant that the father could perfectly satisfactorily feed his own child. Some would be up in the night and take over, but the majority saw it as a treat, perhaps once a day, perhaps twice, and something in which they usually invested trouble and patience. That cameo of so many men hugging the baby to their own sterile nipples and crooning over the full, warm bottle remains in the mind. **)**

Brian Jackson, Fatherhood

Hard as it may be to grasp, it seems that in terms of fathers' or mothers' roles, to talk of exclusivity is no longer helpful, but this is not the only problem. Men are also, very often, confused as to a father's 'proper' functions. If you ask them what fathers are for, they may produce traditional ideas such as providing, protecting and advising. But if you ask them to outline their *own* value to their *own* children, such functions, if mentioned at all, will be towards the bottom of the list. Instead, the fathers prioritise intimacy, tenderness and trust. Despite such confusions, however, the beginnings of a fathers' movement are already there. Some groups are well established; many are in their infancy. A majority, perhaps not surprisingly, have been rights-based, although some are simply activity groups for men and their children. Among divorced fathers' groups, notions of phallocentric supremacy seem to be on the wane and are being replaced by campaigns for shared parenting.

Pulling against these new and radical agendas, however, are and will remain the forces of tradition and fear, which can envision a way forward only in the reconstruction of an imagined past. Today, in a strange alliance, 'progressive' feminists and 'regressive' masculinists can find themselves in unlikely agreement, declaring in an uneasy chorus that, where fatherhood is concerned, men are the problem. In the view, for example, of Sue Slipman, the left-wing-ish feminist ex-head of the UK's National Council for One-Parent Families, men are the 'new rabble' which 'no woman in her right mind would want to take home'.[73] Simultaneously, the American polemicist and spokesman for the New Right, David Blankenhorn, has declared that males are 'not ideally suited to responsible fatherhood'[74] the UK's Geoff Dench, author of *The Frog Prince and the Problem of Men*, asserts that only the hierarchical structures of the traditional family can make men 'tolerably useful.'[75]

That a feminist should indulge in man-bashing comes as no surprise, but why men should join in is less obvious. It will be said that these males are misogynists whose real object in playing at 'bad boys' is to make women responsible for men's behaviour, and so immobilise them, as the Victorians did, on pedestals. This may indeed be part of the story, but it seems probable that there is more to it.

It is a curious trait in human nature to prefer anything, even paralysing guilt, to a sense of powerlessness. Battered wives need not confront their own helplessness if they can believe they are the passive instigators of the violence. The children of divorce need not acknowledge themselves casualties of other people's wars if they can feel they caused their parents' break-up. Religious believers can reclaim some of the power from their God, if they declare themselves sinners. By the same token, men who find themselves alienated from those they hold most dear, their children, may restore a distorted sense of control by declaring that this situation is due to men's own 'nature'.

For it can be more palatable to believe that your alienation was inevitable than to consider that a walk-on part in the central drama of parenting was assigned to you by social forces when you weren't looking. It can be less painful to declare that top billing in 'the family' is needed to recall 'us males' from the 'margins of society' where we 'naturally hang around',[76] than to acknowledge that you acquiesced, unwittingly, in your own estrangement, and that what was sold to you as freedom has turned out to be exile.

'One kiss she gave her mother,' wrote the poet, John Crowe Ransom longingly, as he described his young daughter waking from sleep. 'Only a small one gave she to her daddy – who would have kissed each curl of his shining baby.'[77] Certainly, men becoming fathers were told that Heaven was their proper place. What they were not told was where they would find it.

> ❦ One day when I was skiving off my day-job,
> Sitting writing at my black-ash desk
> Eyes down, intent, you came and stood outside
> The French windows my son likes to look out of
> At age six months. You told me later
> How you'd stayed a moment, unseen, watching me
> At work in this new house, this warm room.
> I imagine, Dad,
> You leaning on your stick, eighty years old,
> Visiting for an instant and then gone. ❧
>
> *Robert Crawford, 'The Look-In'*

Chapter 2
The Private Lives of Fathers: 1790–1990

Historians are fond of declaring – possibly in support of their own jobs – that until we know what we have been, we are unable to see what we may become.

The past doesn't speak of its own accord, however, and on the subject of domestic fathering it is particularly reticent. 'Every year in the first lecture of my family history course,' says Mary Abbott, Principal Lecturer in History at Anglia University, 'I ask my students – who is the missing figure?' Ms Abbott believes the 'missing figure' to be the father of the family, because as she points out 'although there has been much research into women in families, we as yet know very little about the family lives of fathers'.[1]

So powerful has been the image of the patriarchal father – the public face of fatherhood – that relatively few people have realised that his domestic counterpart, his shadow self, has gone missing. And even if it has, whether this is of any significance. But of course it is, because unless we know the truth about domestic fathering behaviours, we almost inevitably apply the public image to the private sphere. For many people, the idea of 'the father' as the classic authoritarian figure is reinforced by the remembered behaviour of their own fathers. For others this isn't the case. But knowing so little about the behaviour of other people's fathers (either now or in the past), even those who have been lovingly fathered tend to assume that the father they knew was all but unique.

> 6 When Sir Thomas More came from Westminster to the Tower-ward again, his daughter, Master William Roper's wife, desirous to see her father, whom she thought she should never see in this world after, and also to have his final blessing, gave attendance about the Tower Wharf, where she knew he should pass by ... Whom as soon as she saw ... hastily ran to him and there openly in the sight of them all embraced him, took him about the neck, and kissed him most lovingly. 9
>
> *Recollected by William Roper, c. 1590*

It has been observed that the era just prior to living memory is by far the hardest part of history for historians or anyone else to grasp. This, it is said, is a kind of 'twilight zone', compelling in its mix of fantasy and remembrance and holding inordinate sway over our imaginations.[2]

Our 'twilight zone' is the first half of the 20th century, an era marked by the hardening of the 'separate spheres' ideology for men and women, by two world wars, and by the rapid increase in travel-to-work times. This means that the history of hands-on fathering in our recent past is very largely a history of absence. As such, it is not typical, but it is widely believed to be so. The remote figure from our 'twilight zone' has become the stuff of which myths are made, his low-level participation in day-to-day fathering endowed with a universal validity and force which, in fact, it does not possess.

That important era, which ushered in the decline of fatherhood, we will consider later. But for the moment we will look further back – to pre-industrial Britain, a time-zone to which the great Cambridge historian Peter Laslett refers, with just a touch of irony, as a 'world we have lost'.

Did fathers care?

When, in the early 1960s, historians first began investigating parent–child relations, they tended to rely for their information on the kinds of public documents considered in the previous chapter: the visual arts, advice literature, religious sermons and so on. Without really considering whether there might be a difference between how fathers were advised or instructed to behave, and how they actually *did* behave, they concluded that all but a few fathers in pre-industrial Britain were emotionally detached and repressively disciplinarian. This theory is still promoted in some recent historical comment on father–child relations.[3] A similar kind of historical mud has been chucked at mothers, though there on the whole it has failed to stick: the maternal bond has been too well publicised.

In pursuit of their vision of the detached disciplinarian so deeply embedded in the Western psyche, the early historians were extremely selective in their use of diaries and other primary sources. When Ralph Josselin, a 17th century vicar, lost his son, he recorded the death in a matter-of-fact way, and this was cited as evidence that 17th century fathers were unmoved by the deaths of their children. In fact, the same father, in the same diary, recorded his deep grief at the death of a daughter, but this was not mentioned by the 'first wave' family historians, because it contradicted their argument.[4]

> **❝** It is not so strange that I love you with my whole heart, for being a father is not a tie which can be ignored. Nature in her wisdom has attached the parent to the child and bound them together with a Herculean knot. **❞**
>
> *Sir Thomas More, 1517*

As time passed, the name 'father' was seriously blackened. It became standard to blame fathers for the use of wet-nurses (a use which, in Britain, has been greatly exaggerated). There was a belief that sexual intercourse curdled breast-milk. Without establishing how pervasive this idea had been, or considering the many other factors that might have discouraged or prevented women from breastfeeding, a wholly unfounded picture was painted of fathers regularly ripping newborns from their wives' breasts, solely in order to satisfy their selfish lusts.

In the late 1970s, one extremely influential historian, dipping into fathers' diaries, recognised – he could hardly have missed it – that many fathers had been intricately and intimately involved in their children's lives. Unimpressed, he sought to show that this was not to their benefit: one such father he described as a 'drink-sodden, idle failure'. Others, whose behaviour proved blameless, he attacked through their children, by reporting in detail on offspring who had failed to cover themselves with glory, and very much dismissing those who had. He did not explore the outcomes for reputedly *un*involved fathers, or their children.[5]

Overall, this early research did nothing to challenge myths about fathering in times gone by, and a number of notions persisted undisputed. For example, it was believed that fathers had never looked after babies, so to describe nappy-changing 20th century fathers as 'New Dads' was substantially correct. Then, it was suggested that fathers had rarely been 'primary caretakers' of children, that when wives had died, men had quickly remarried, or 'reserves of unmarried womanpower had stepped into the breach'.[6] It was also declared that the majority of fathers had ruled by fear, frequently and heartlessly exercising corporal punishment. And, finally, that before the 18th century, few fathers had been tenderly attached to their children.

Then research methods changed, and new information came to light. A group of Cambridge-based demographers began to report on data culled from parish and other records by an army of volunteers nationwide, information which helped to chart the lives of thousands of ordinary people right back to the 16th century.[7] Household historians also turned their attention away from advice given *to* parents and focused on private papers, by analysing diaries, autobiographies and letters in a systematic way.[8] Together these two approaches cast quite a different light on family life in times gone by and, in particular, on the actions and affections of fathers.

> ❛ Now I pray, give me leave to ask you a question, and that is, How you like my little girl … ? I must tell you that she hath been lapt in the skirts of her father's shirt, for she is beloved where she comes, and I love her very well, and so doth she me; and yet sometimes I can whip (smack) her and love her too. You must excuse me for using this language, for when I cannot see my children it does me good to talk of them. ❜
>
> *Thomas Meauty, 1632*

The hearts of fathers

The fathers who have left diaries and letters seem, in the main, to have treasured their children 'above gold and jewels', as Ralph Josselin, the 17th century vicar, put it, valuing them for the joy and grief they caused as well as for the support they might offer in later life as 'comfort … to our grey haires'.[9]

Contrary to popular belief, even aristocratic fathers could be close to their children. Philippe II of France, when away on a sea-voyage during the 16th century, wrote his two teenage daughters 34 loving letters (not intended for publication), which show that he was closely involved in their day-to-day lives. He missed them greatly, worried about their health, their relationship with their younger siblings, and their studies, and sent them gifts and looked forward to their letters.[10]

From every historical period fathers are revealed as being deeply attached to their children, and struggling with many of the same issues which worry fathers today. 'My dear son, You are now at a time of life when every temptation is daily exciting you to join in pleasures and dissipations … that may injure your health and for ever ruin your constitution,' wrote a worried father, Christopher Parker, to his student-son in 1832. 'God grant that you may by your own prudence escape danger … You have ability, you want nothing but exertion, and pray indulge me by its use.'[11] Many fathers resolved to be 'better' parents than their own fathers. A 17th century French nobleman, the Prince de Ligne, whose violent father ' ... didn't like me – I don't know why, for he hardly knew me', resolved to be his own son's 'loving father and loving friend'. He succeeded. And in the 18th century, a John Stedman condemned physical violence in childraising, as a reaction to his own upbringing.[12]

By our standards, infant and child mortality was high, but there is no evidence of fathers not 'investing' emotion in their children in case they died. Nor was family size as large as has generally been believed: in pre-industrial Britain, the average couple would have had about five children, and would have expected to raise almost three quarters of them to the age of 15. The older the children were when they died, the more intensely fathers seemed to grieve, and their grief was just as deep for daughters as it was for sons. The high mortality rate seems to have heightened their anxiety, and when children were ill, fathers, as well as mothers, would watch over them for hours. 'Sat up all night with Nathaniel [aged nine],' wrote an American father, Increase Mather, in 1675 when his little son was sick. A century later, in England, the Canon of St Paul's sat up with his young son for two nights. 'My little boy is, thank God, recovered,' he later wrote.[13]

6 On going into the library the window looks into the little garden in which I have so many times seen her happy. O gracious and merciful God! Pardon me for allowing any earthly object thus to engross my feelings and overpower my whole soul! ... I [have] buried her in my pew, fixing the coffin so that when I kneel it will be between her head and her dear heart ... that when the great author of my existence may please to take me I may join my child ... 9

Arthur Young, 1797
(he never recovered from his 14-year-old daughter's death)

Christianity had an effect on our ancestors' subjective lives which is difficult for us to imagine today, and, when death threatened their children, fathers often struggled painfully with their religious beliefs. 'There has been much health in my family for a long time and God has spared the lives of all my children,' wrote Mather when both his sons were very sick, 'but I have not been thankful and humble as I should have been, and therefore God is righteous in afflicting me. I have nothing to say but to lie down abased before him.'[14]

Although their written style was often formal, fathers in earlier times may have been less inhibited than today's fathers in expressing their emotions physically. Many appear to have cried easily. 'Oh my dearest boy,' wrote the Prince de Ligne to his wounded son, 'may the Lord see you safely home. I am counting the days. When you return, I will kiss your poor, wounded knee. I will fall to my own knees in gratitude and relief before you, before Heaven.'[15] It may well be that some fathers in pre-industrial Britain were more 'in touch' with their feelings than many modern fathers. When their children died only some took the role of comforter with their wives, while others showed the greater distress. 'The grief for this child was so great,' wrote Nehemiah Wallington when, in 1625, he lost his four-year-old daughter, 'that I forgot myself so much that I did offend God in it.' His wife reproved him for his excessive mourning: 'God gave us this child to nurse,' she told him, 'therefore let us give him to Him willingly.' But Wallington was not convinced.[16]

> ❜ Farewell, thou child of my right hand, and joy;
> My sinne was too much hope of thee, lov'd boy,
> Seven yeeres, tho' wert lent to me, and I thee pay,
> Exacted by thy fate, on the just day ...
> Rest in soft peace, and ask'd, say here doth lye
> Ben Jonson, his best piece of poesie. ❜
>
> *Ben Jonson (1572?–1637), 'On My First Sonne'*

Design for living

Although, in diaries and other writings, we are given no more than a tantalising glimpse into the lives of just a few hundred fathers, through analysis of their living and working patterns we can learn about more general trends, and specifically the *potential* for paternal involvement in a wide variety of families.

What is perhaps most striking is the day-to-day availability of fathers. Before industrialisation, domestic organisation was synonymous with economic organisation. Even after feudal times, many households had access to land. Ralph Josselin, the 17th century vicar, also managed a small farm with his family. As early as Tudor times, a majority of all households received at least some part of their income from wages or piecework, but only a minority of parents went far away from their homes to work.

From the late 17th century, retailing was a growing occupation. This too was a family concern. Carpenters, brickmakers, weavers, shoemakers, hempsters, grocers all operated in, or near, their homes, even in London, the only major city of the time. In 1619, in a London bakery, the recorded employees were the baker and his wife, four paid workers, two apprentices, two maidservants – and three or four children of the family. Since the business premises were in the baker's house, it would be fair to assume that the baker's younger children, who would spend little time in formal schooling, would play and work around their parents most of the day.[17]

Even in households well supplied with servants, fathers could find themselves in the thick of things. In 1668, the Earl of Lauderdale, whose wife was ill in bed and whose daughter had just given birth, was in '...troublesome government going to and from one sick to another...' when his grandson took convulsions and the smallpox. 'Sure I slept little,' wrote the Earl 'My babe Charles ... slept ill all night, was most impatient for the breast, and was in a cruel heat ... All this while the mother and grandmother knew nothing, for the physicians positively forbade it ... I sent my excuse to the King ... compelled by my wife's sickness and my daughter's lying-in to stay here.'[18]

In most houses, there was no separation between adult and child space or, often, even between working, sleeping and eating space. And architectural evidence before the late 19th century *doesn't* support the contention that upper-class children were brought up in a nursery wing separated from their parents.[19] 'Playing in the village street and fields ... hanging round the farmyards ... thronging the churches ... crowding round the cottage fires,' writes Laslett, 'the perpetual distraction of childish noise and talk must have affected everyone almost all of the time.'[20]

❝ At night, after we were in bed, Veronica [aged six] spoke out from her little bed and said, 'I do not believe there is a God.' 'Preserve me,' said I, 'my dear what do you mean?' She answered, 'I have *thinket* it many a time, but did not like to speak of it.' Said I: 'God made you.' Said she: 'My Mother bore me.' I looked into Cambray's *Education of a Daughter*, hoping to have found some simple argument for the being of God in that piece of instruction. But it is taken for granted. ❞

James Boswell, 1779

Working time

In a sense, since there was so little separation between life and work in pre-industrial Britain, people worked all the time. But formal working hours could be surprisingly short. In 1750, the length of the working year was 2,500 hours (a 48-hour week), compared with 3,000 hours a century later. Underemployment was a common feature of many workers' lives, and whether (and for how long) a father worked in a day was governed by the vagaries of the weather, and by the availability of natural light. Working hours might be long in summer, and short in winter. Although, in theory, men and women had their 'own' tasks, at harvest time everyone aged six and over worked long hours in the fields. Infants and younger children were taken too, and when field work was slack men as well as women worked around the yard and pitched in domestically: preserving food, cleaning, cooking and looking after children.[21] There are indications that child-rearing was a shared activity and that attachment to the mother, or mother figure, was not the universal pattern.[22]

The notion of the work/family team must not be over-stated. Pauper families were split up, and children as young as seven or eight sent away to work. Poor cottagers took employment where they could and journeymen travelled, as their name implies, far and wide to sell their skills. Other men, for example circuit lawyers, soldiers, fishermen, were away from their children for weeks or months or years, and men building up businesses might, like Matthew Boulton (b. 1728) find 'the longest day not enough'. Boulton was reduced to writing affectionate letters to his children as he travelled around promoting the sales of his engines, while Thomas Huxley (b. 1825) had to struggle so hard to keep his head above water in the early years of his marriage, leaving home early and returning late, that his eldest children hardly saw him: and he referred to himself as 'the lodger'.[23] While this mustn't be forgotten, neither must it be allowed to colour the whole picture. In terms of life-organisation, what is clear is that while working patterns today allow only a tiny minority of fathers the opportunities for substantial involvement in their children's daily lives, the potential for this was open to very many fathers in the pre-industrial world. And even fathers who did travel away – whether educated men or fisherfolk – might also spend extended periods at home.

> ❛ Let me say, my honest little girl, that I had had you often in my mind during my separation from you while on the sea, or the land … and now that I have returned to be with you … meeting you daily at fireside, at table, at study, and in your walks and amusements, in conversation and in silence … I want, most of all things, to be a kindly influence on you, helping you to guide and govern your heart. ❜
>
> *Bronson Alcott (to his daughter Louisa), 1842*

The necessary father

From what we now know of family structure between the 16th and 19th centuries, it would seem that fathers were not only relatively available to their children, but that within many homes they would have been an important resource.

In the 17th century children were present in 70 per cent of English households (compared with 30 per cent today) and most of those households consisted of a husband, a wife, three or four children (mainly pre-pubescent), and perhaps a servant or two. Servants were often almost children themselves, and would generally move on after a year. Grandparents were few: age at marriage was mid to late 20s, by which time at least three-quarters of the young-marrieds would have lost at least one parent, a pattern which continued right through to the early 20th century. Nor, once they reached their teens, did many older children remain at home: they went to school or were apprenticed or entered 'service'.

Although life was communal and young children were supervised by neighbours and siblings, local family networks were not the norm. In 1696 in Lichfield, for example, there were 65 households with 52 different surnames. In the much-studied village of Clayworth, 62 per cent of those resident in 1676 were gone 12 years later, with only one third of that astonishing turnover due to birth and death. The rest resulted from migration.[24] In a majority of homes, therefore, there would have been no live-in cohort of female relatives able to take over when the mother of the family was ill (as she so often was) or 'lying-in' after giving birth, or busy at her loom or the market, or up at the local mill grinding the grain, so fathers must often have been the most available caretakers.

> ❢ Hush thee, my babby,
> Lie still with thy daddy,
> Thy mammy has gone to the mill,
> To grind thee some wheat
> To make thee some meat,
> Oh, my dear babby, lie still. ❢
>
> *Anon. Songs for the Nursery, 1805*

It was female employment as much as family structure which made fathers' participation so important. All but a tiny percentage of women contributed directly to the household economy right through to the late 19th century, and most were recognised as having their own trade. Later, in the mid-19th century, throughout the Midlands and the North of England, a survey of living conditions revealed men all over the textile-towns '...taking care of the house and children, and busily engaged in washing, baking, nursing, and preparing the humble repast for the wife, who is wearing her life away toiling in the factory'.[25]

Men in pre-industrial Britain had regularly, if sporadically, undertaken domestic tasks to release their wives for paid work within or near their homes. During a hard winter in Wales in 1789, for example, a Richard Jones reported that 'My father did the housework in addition to the work on the farm and my mother knitted.'[26] And in England in 1795 an eyewitness account recorded that 'In the long winter evenings the husband cobbles shoes, mends the family clothes and attends the children while the wife spins.'[27]

6 Tho' lazy, the proud Prelate's fed,
This Curate eats no idle Bread ...
His Wife at Washing – 'Tis his Lot,
To pare the Turnips, watch the Pot:
He reads, and hears his Son read out;
And rocks the Cradle with his Foot. 9

'The Welsh Curate', c. 1760

Fathers and babies

Did all but the most exceptional fathers draw the line at baby-care, as has so often been suggested? Certainly, as we have seen, fathers' participation was discouraged by contemporary theoreticians, but that is not the end of the story. In childrearing, perhaps above almost anything else, there is often a huge gap between theory and practice. In the 1960s, for example, a study of Nottingham parents and infants concluded that '...contemporary baby books are a rather poor indication of what actually happens in the home'.[28] It must also be remembered that infant-care was previously very labour intensive. Babies and older infants were held or rocked almost continually. They had to be. The swaddling bands which it was (wrongly) believed would help their limbs to 'grow straight' irritated them, and they cried incessantly; while open fires, stone floors and the tools of domestic manufacture made for a hazardous environment.

In the 17th century, Ralph Josselin noted all kinds of details about his babies' progress, including the dates, times and circumstances of their births. It seems that he was in the house for these and, though not in the room, was very much part of the proceedings. In his diary Josselin also noted the removing of swaddling bands, the cutting of early teeth and the taking of first steps. On one occasion, he mentioned that he and his wife had 'decided to wean' a child, as if it were a joint activity. Two American diarist-fathers even seemed to bear *sole* responsibility for weaning their infants. Joseph Green (1675–1715) noted that he left his wife visiting friends and '...came home to wean John'. A century later, Adolphus Sterne wrote that because his wife was ill he himself sat up '...all night nursing the infant Laura who has to be weaned'.[29]

> ❥ 'Lulluby, oh lullaby!'
> Thus I heard a father cry,
> 'Lullaby, oh, lullaby!
> The brat will never shut an eye;
> Hither come, some power devine!
> Close his lids, or open mine!'...
> 'Lullaby, oh, lullaby!
> Two such nights, and I shall die!
> Lullaby, oh, lullaby!
> He'll be bruised, and so shall I.
> How can I from bedpost keep,
> When I'm walking in my sleep? ❥
>
> *Thomas Hood (1799–1845) 'Serenade'*

There can be no doubt that, from the time records exist, strictures against fathers being involved with babies constrained some fathers' behaviour, in public, but in private. 'She and I being alone,' wrote one 18th century British middle-class father, 'I took her on my knee and dandled her, and she was very fond of me, took me round the neck and kissed me; which engaged my heart very much.'[30] Another 18th century father, whose baby daughter was to stay with her grandparents, resisted this on the grounds that she would be 'spoiled'. 'He affects to be too manly to be fond of an infant,' his wife observed. 'He wants a pretence to lament her absence without descending from his dignity.'[31]

Other fathers, however, didn't seem to care what people thought. The critic and historian, Thomas Carlyle, was a close friend of a brilliant preacher, Edward Irving, until in 1824 the latter became a father. 'Visit him at any time, you find him dry-nursing [feeding] his offspring,' wrote the jealous Carlyle. 'Speak to him, he directs your attention to the form of its nose, the manner of its waking and sleeping, and feeding and digesting.' The besotted young father did not seem in the least self-conscious about his behaviour. He carried on in the same way *out of doors*! 'Oh that you saw the giant with his broad-brimmed hat,' moaned Carlyle, 'carrying the little pepper-box of a creature, folded in his monstrous palms, along the beach; tick-ticking to it, and dandling it.' And when Carlyle gave his opinion – that Christian fathers were not supposed to dote so much on their children – Irving had an easy answer: by attending to his child's needs he said, he was '...exercising generosity and forgetting self'![32]

Working-class fathers, if the journalist William Cobbet is to be believed, did not seem to be as self-conscious about displaying their affections, or being seen doing the equivalent of pushing a buggy. 'There is nothing more amiable, nothing more delightful to behold, than a young man especially taking part in the work of nursing the children,' he enthused in 1830, 'and how often have I admired this in the labouring men in Hampshire!'[33] In fact, Cobbett's rather sentimental observations have been borne out by later research, which shows upper-class and upper-middle-class men less likely than working-class men to display affection for their children in public.

Cobbett made a point of working from home when his children were little, so that they would never be left with servants. Diary evidence from the 17th century on suggests that behind closed doors (if not in public) other fathers were doing their bit. In America in 1828, John Toddy was the parent responsible for giving his six-week-old daughter 'her physic': 'Last Wednesday evening I gave her more than an even teaspoonful of salts. She has needed nothing since. When she does, I think I shall give her an emetic.'[34]

❝ The man who is to gain a living by his labour must be drawn away from home, or at least from the cradleside, in order to perform that labour; but this will not, if he be made of good stuff, prevent him from doing his share of the duty due to his children ... What right has he to the sole possession of a woman's person; what right to a husband's vast authority; what right to the honourable title and the boundless power of father: what right has he to all, or any of these, unless he can found his claim on the faithful performance of all the duties which these titles imply? ❞

William Cobbett, 1830

Lone fathers

If the good news is that 'New Dad' is not 'new' at all, the bad news is that neither is family breakdown. In pre-industrial Britain and throughout the 19th century, one in three marriages ended prematurely, through a combination of death and formal separation. This rate is similar to marriage breakdown in Britain today, and to breakdown rates recorded in 'primitive' societies, such as the Aka Pygmies (see next chapter). And this doesn't take into account informal separation or un registered desertion. Family historians are even now only beginning to uncover the extent of this, and it is already estimated to be about 10 per cent.[35]

But marriage breakdown then differed from marriage breakdown now in important respects, one of which was *gender*. Very often, in pre-industrialised Britain the parent–child unit remaining was headed by a man. Divorce wasn't legalised in England and Wales until 1857, although formal separation occurred before this, and before 1839 married fathers were automatically given custody of any children, except in the most extreme circumstances. As males were more likely to be able to earn an independent living, this might well have been in the children's interests.

The other (and most usual) reason for lone-father families was maternal death: about 8 per cent of mothers died in childbirth. This wasn't, of course, the only reason mothers died. Sometimes, after the death of, or desertion by, a mother one of the children would go to live with relatives; or a widower and his children would go as lodgers into another household, or take in lodgers themselves. And of course older siblings would provide care, and ummarried female relatives sometimes came to live in. Widowers might also remarry or move in with relatives, but widowers with children stayed single surprisingly often. In fact their remarriage was only universally approved if they had no sons. Lord Lyttleton, who was under 40 when his wife died in 1857, looked forward to 30 or 40 years of solitary misery. With 12 children and '...very inadequate means' only a mature childless woman with a fortune would do, and he felt he '...might was well think of the moon'.[36]

6 My little Son, who looked from thoughtful eyes
And moved and spoke in quiet grown-up wise,
Having my law the seventh time disobey'd,
I struck him, and dismiss'd
With hard words and unkiss'd,

- His Mother, who was patient, being dead.
Then, fearing lest his grief should hinder sleep,
I visited his bed,
But found him slumbering deep,
With darkened eyelids, and their lashes yet
From his late sobbing wet.
And I, with moan,
Kissing away his tears, left others of my own; **'**
Coventry Patmore (1823–1896) 'The Toys'

In today's world, only 1.3 per cent of British children under 16 living in a single-parent household, live with their fathers. Between 1599–1811, some 24.1 per cent did so. In fact, it has been estimated that more than one in three lone fathers in pre-industrial Britain existed totally without the 'live-in' support of other adults.[37] Even when a divorced or widowed father remarried, or helpful female relatives joined his household, these did not necesssarily take over where the mother had left off. When, in the middle of the 19th century, Charles Dickens left his wife, he took all his children with him and forbade them to see their mother again (it seems they obeyed). He also employed his young sister-in-law as housekeeper. Dickens, however, remained the focal parent.

Lone fathers, particularly Victorian lone fathers, have taken a battering from biographers who often seem blinded by the stereotype of the distant, authoritarian father. 'Widowed fathers have been maligned,' says art historian Sally Kevill-Davies. 'When you really look into it, you're struck by how loving many of them were, and how conscientious, struggling to raise often very little children in the most difficult circumstances.'[38]

Patrick Brontë (father of Anne, Emily, Charlotte and Patrick Branwell) is a case in point. Well loved by family and parishioners, he was represented as both heartless and violent in Mrs Gaskell's influential biography of Charlotte Brontë. Mrs Gaskell's research methods were faulty: she met Brontë once, and relied largely on the testimony of a disaffected ex-employee. Her relationship with her own father was extremely disappointing, so she may have been inclined to believe the worst. Mrs Gaskell's account was indignantly challenged at the time by, among others, ex-servants. 'There never was a more affectionate father, never a kinder master,' protested one. 'He was not of a violent temper at all; quite the reverse.' Corrections were made in the second edition, but these were left out of the third (and subsequent) editions, and it was not until the 1960's that the errors were sorted out. By that time the damage had been done:

Brontë had been blamed for his daughters' deaths and his son's debauchery. The stereotype had been further confirmed, and another nail had been hammered into the coffin of fatherhood.[39]

6 *On being refused custody of his children by the Lord Chancellor (due to atheism and 'immorality'):*
I curse thee [*the Lord Chancellor*] by a parent's outraged love,
By hopes long cherished and too lately lost,
By gentle feelings thou couldst never prove,
By griefs which thy stern nature never crossed; ...
By all the happy see in children's growth
That undeveloped flower of budding years
Sweetness and sadness interwoven both,
Source of the sweetest hopes and saddest fears ...
O wretched ye if ever any were,
Sadder than orphans, yet not fatherless! 9
Percy Bysshe Shelley, 1817

Domestic despots

The last of the major misconceptions about fathers (in their historical dimension) concerns power and control. The assumption is usually that fathers had it all their own way. When not threatening or beating their children into submission, they were playing the 'property card': disinheriting sons, manipulatively rewriting their wills and forcing daughters into arranged marriages. In point of fact, it was downhill all the way for would-be domestic despots from the 16th century on, as the inheritance-based peasant culture gave way in Britain to the wage-earning urban culture. With three out of four children leaving home by early adolescence, very few remained in the vicinity to be ordered about, and in six West Midland manors, land-transfers within families were down to 67 per cent as early as 1500. By 1750 arranged marriages comprised a tiny percentage of the whole and a bride's dowry – where it continued to exist – was less likely to be a favour from her parents than the product of her own arduous scrimping and saving as an independent wage earner.

Within small communities, and most communities were small, there were powerful social controls. But these weren't all paternal. Mythologist have noted that, in classic fairytales, fathers were very often portrayed as ineffectual and have wondered whether fathers were less dominant in many homes than is generally believed. Laslett also questions traditional assumptions about the balance of power within families, observing that in Stoke-on-Trent in 1701 (a fairly typical district) 29 per cent of mothers were older than fathers. 'The experts on the psychology of childrearing,' he writes, 'will have … to judge how the child is affected by the mother's being closer in years to the bread-winner and family head, quite often older and more experienced than he was.'[40]

There was huge variation between the levels of obedience that individual fathers expected. Some seemed unconcerned about imposing their will; others, in theory at least, expected to have total control. All kinds of strategies were tried. Fathers offered advice, scolded, imposed fines and appealed to their children's better natures, or to the Almighty: 'Nompee a bad boy. God amend him!' moaned one indulgent French father who had completely lost control over his son.[41] English fathers often seemed equally distressed and helpless. A few children were disinherited, their possessions burned, or their fathers tried to commit them to insane asylums, but these were extreme actions, and recognised as such. What was threatened was not always carried through. Ralph Josselin considered disinheriting his younger son a number of times, but never did so.

> 6 After the insults which you have this day coolly and premeditatedly offered to your Father – a Father who has overlooked and forgiven similar insults several times, it is incumbent on that Father …to request *nay more, to command his son to leave him* … It is decided by this Father never again to be exposed to similar insults from a son who eats of his bread and drinks of his cup and … up until now, was his best and only true friend. 9
>
> *John Skinner, 1828*

Josselin's interactions with his children are interesting, because they so completely challenge the stereotype. Although he had a small estate to settle upon them, he exercised astonishingly little control over their life-choices. Unlike 19th century fathers, 17th century fathers did not expect their sons to follow in their footsteps as a matter of course: they encouraged their children to go into different trades to 'spread the risk' and a by-product of this was reduced control.

Josselin's daughters, like his sons, were soon out of his direct sphere of influence. They, too, left home before adolescence. Neither Josselin nor his wife had much to do with their children's choice of partners. Josselin occasionally recommended a suitor to one of his offspring, but he never pressed the point if the idea didn't appeal, which it usually didn't. In the end, only one daughter married locally and all his children found their own partners, mostly in London. The younger son even married without his parents' knowledge or consent, though he later introduced his bride to them quite amicably. The elder son, the only one for whom Josselin did begin to negotiate a 'match', didn't marry at all.

> ❝ Yesterday my poor offending child Judy came for the first time since she was deluded away to be unhappily married against her duty, my will, and her solemn promise ... Though I resolved not to let nature discover its weakness on seeing her, I ... burst into tears ... I could not speak to her for some time. ❞
>
> *Landon Carter, 1772*

Father as educator

All the Josselin children were taught by their father at first. He was the local schoolmaster as well as the vicar, and he taught them to read but not, it seems to write. That came later, when they went away to school. But like many fathers (and mothers) in pre-industrial Britain, Josselin was his children's 'educator' in a much broader sense. Education was not simply book-learning, imposed from above: parents had a role in interpreting what was a relatively small and simple world to their children, and could do so with considerable confidence. 'Father used to say, "I shall not leave you much money, but I will teach you every job, then you can always get work",' wrote a 19th century farmer's son from the Forest of Dean 'He showed us every job in the garden and on the farm.'[42]

An illustrated verse-sheet entitled *My Father*, published in 1811, reveals the breadth of a father's expected role as 'educator'. Although even in this idealised fragment he is not seen holding the child while it is a babe-in-arms, *My Father* is a constant presence in the home. He's there to witness his baby's first steps, with his 'sheltering arms' thrown open, to catch the child as it toddles forward. He persuades the infant, with 'sugar plums and cake', to take his medicine, plays with him, explores the world with him hand-in-hand, and supervises his moral education.[43]

It is interesting to note that whereas today a mother's education level has an important bearing on children's academic achievement (bearing out what everyone knows, which is that it's mainly mothers who help with homework) this was not the case in pre-industrial

Britain. At that time it was the *father's* literacy level which was the great indicator of the child's ability to sign his or her name. Literate mothers very often had illiterate children.[44]

Ralph Josselin, like some fathers from all eras – particularly the 16th and 17th centuries in Britain – did not regard the education of his daughters as unimportant, and was just as proud of their achievements as he was of his sons'. His wife shared his views, but in other families fathers who wanted their daughters educated sometimes had a battle on their hands. There is no reason to believe that Josselin's behaviour towards his children was untypical, and it is clear that throughout his life he remained deeply concerned about them. All important decisions about their lives, he seemed to take with his wife, and he divided his estate among them without controversy, through gifts at apprenticeship, marriage and death.

> ❢ I was anxious that [my daughters'] education should be confined to the common branches of a good English education. But the ladies wished to give them lessons in music and drawing ... I again forbade it but the ladies were very importunate ... and thus the useful branches of [my daughters'] education were much neglected and they returned home very little improved in intellectual culture. ❢
>
> *Abelard Guthrie, 1814–73*

The Josselin family was not matricentral. Ralph Josselin knew far more about his father's kin than his mother's, and in later years, he and his wife would take it in turn to pay visits to their adult children, since one would have to stay at home to mind the farm. It is worth noting that though mothers usually went to help with a birth, it was sometimes fathers who visited married offspring when for other reasons they were unwell.[45]

To whip or not to whip?

The aspect of paternal authority that has attracted the greatest amount of attention is corporal punishment. The general view has been that until recently a majority of fathers (particularly working-class and upper-class fathers) regularly attacked their children physically, and that this behaviour has all but disappeared during the 20th century. Neither of these assumptions, however, can be taken at face value. In fact, there has been a running debate since the 17th century between those who have recommended breaking a child's will, and those whose attitudes have been exceedingly liberal even by modern standards, and physical violence by fathers in times gone by has been seriously over-stated by later generations of historians.

A diary entry by one 17th century father, Samuel Sewell, stating that he 'whipped' his son 'pretty smartly' has been regularly quoted to illustrate strict 17th century paternal discipline. But that is the only time in the whole of Sewell's very detailed diary that he mentions hitting his child (he wasn't ashamed of doing so, and there is no reason to believe he would have censored reference to other beatings). Even this 'whipping' may not have been severe: at that time the verb 'to whip' probably meant 'hit' or 'smack', as parents referred to 'whipping' children with 'my hand'.[46]

> ❢ I was teached blindly to obey, without consulting cither my feelings, or my senses. ... All this may be intended for the best and term'd good cducation, but I shall ever insist, that nothing can be worse than never to consult a child's motives or desires which not only makes them miserable, but ten to one must end in making them bad men. ❢
>
> *John Stedman, 1744–97*

From time to time in today's newspapers we are treated to reports of fathers' brutality towards their children. Such events are newsworthy not because they are the norm but because they are the exception, and so they always have been. *The Times* has been reporting, and condemning, cases of cruelty to children since the 18th century; and 300 years before children were formally protected through legislation, child abuse was recognised and punished, and offending adults were set in the pillory and whipped. Parents from every place, period and class have gravely abused their children. In the 17th century Henry Newcome took in his grandchild because he could not tolerate his son's 'shameful abuse' of the boy. In the 18th century, a young girl's autobiography records her father standing over her at breakfast, whip in hand, which he used as many times as was necessary for her to finish her food.[47] In the 19th century, a George Mockford, remembering the 'great dread' he had had of his father, wrote that 'All I did for him was done under fear of the lash'.[48]

Working-class fathers seem to have been more prone to hit their children than middle-class dads (although in this class, too, outright brutality has been exceptional). There is no evidence that aristocratic or highly religious fathers have been more likely to use physical punishment than other men. American fathers, it is interesting to note, have been particularly liberal. Many commentators have tried to prove that fathering was 'better' or 'worse' in times gone by, but this is suspect. We have to accept that some things are lost to history and that the available evidence is simply too scarce. Evidence from diaries and autobiographies is crucial because it is the only first-person evidence we have, but it has its limitations. And, of course, context is all-important: what may be good fathering in one set of circumstances might be disastrous in another.

> 6 *I would never come, to give a child a blow;* except in case of *obstinacy:* or some gross enormity. To be chased for a while out of *my presence,* I would make to be looked upon as the sorest punishment in the family ... The *slavish* way of *education,* carried on with raving and kicking and scourging ... 'tis abominable. 9
>
> *Cotton Mather, 1705*

Public policy on the physical chastisement of children has been changing throughout this century. Although, bizarrely, while licensed English childminders are still allowed to hit children, corporal punishment is banned in children's homes and state schools; and a substantial body of child-abuse legislation exists. Behaviour does not always mirror policy: in 1994, a survey of London women with a tendency towards depression revealed that one in six had, as children, been hit so hard with an implement that bruises, cuts or worse had resulted.[49] In most homes, however, full-scale beatings are – and always have been – rare, and often given as a 'last resort'. 'I this morning beat Sandie for telling a lie,' wrote James Boswell, in 1780. 'I do not recollect having had any other valuable principle impressed upon me by my father except a strict regard to the truth, which he impressed upon my mind by a hearty beating at an early age.'[50]

Throughout history, some fathers have refused demands to act as family policemen, and in written accounts and interviews mothers have regularly complained that their partners are too 'soft'. Although, as a literary theme, the 'good father' protecting his children from the 'bad mother' is almost unheard of (so idealised has mothering become), in real life fathers have often played the protector role inside families. At the beginning of the 17th century, a Thomas Wale continually mediated between his daughter Polly and her mother. In the 18th century John Stedman 'made high words' with his wife after she had given their son a black eye.[51]

❛ The only suffering I recollect was the restraint imposed upon me on Sundays, especially being forced to go twice to Meeting ... Once I recollect being whipped by my mother for being naughty at Meeting ... [but] my mother had not strength to keep me in order. My father never attempted it. ❜

Henry Robinson, 1775–1867

Industrialisation and fatherhood

There is evidence that during the first half of the19th century, harsh behaviour by some British parents increased (as did industrial disruptions) and it has been suggested that insistence on obedience and conformity may have been a reaction to the rapid pace of social change. If fathers were tougher on their children, the world around them was also tough. It was not cruelty but cruel necessity that drove many parents to force their young children to work long hours: poor relief was denied families of 'troublemaker' parents who refused employment for their children.

In 1831, a few parents gave evidence to a Parliamentary Committee on child labour, and revealed the depth of their horror and despair at the conditions under which their children had to work. 'I have thought I had rather almost seen them starve to death than to be used in that manner,' said one father. And in the later part of the century, a working man, remembering no kind treatment from either of his parents, realised (and very emphatically too) that they had been trying to prepare him '... to live in a world that was harsh and hard to the children of the poorer classes'.[52]

Nevertheless, it seems that in Britain across the second half of the 18th century and the first half of the 19th century, while working patterns and widespread migration from countryside to town weakened family ties and social controls, some families became more closely knit. The system of 'proto-industrialisation' which ushered in full-scale industrialisation, could actually reinforce family ties. This involved an entrepreneur supplying a household with materials (and sometimes equipment), and then buying back from the family the goods they had produced. This system flourished alongside the developing factories, and was widespread for more than 100 years.

An historian of the bourgeoisie in Bradford has declared that in the early Victorian era: 'The role of the father in domestic intimacy and cohesian was almost as great as that of the mother.'[53] As late as 1850, factory-workers still comprised barely 5 per cent of the total population and very few workplaces in England or Wales employed more than 20 people. Most men still worked at home or lived close by their employment. In 1870, just 68 per cent of the children enrolled in school attended classes, and three out of four sons entered the same industries as their fathers. 'My work was at the loom side,' remembered one 19th century weaver's son, 'and when not winding my father taught me reading, writing, and arithmetic.'[54]

❝ The most important of all the effects on the family group of the process of modernisation has undoubtedly been the physical removal from the household of the father and other earners for all of every working day. The perpetual presence of the father ... must have had an enormous effect on the pre-industrial family and household ... [especially] in the West, where the predominance of the nuclear family was most pronounced, with children alone in the company of their parents. ❞
Peter Laslett, Family Life and Illicit Love in Earlier Generations

Accounts of middle-class families before 1850 (accounts of working-class families are few and far between) are full of relaxed and approachable fathers: William Wilberforce showing '...simple unaffected joy in the company of his children', or Dr Arnold, the famous Rugby headmaster, allowing his offspring the run of his study. But after the mid-century the notion of remoteness begins to be applied regularly to fathers, not only by those who recommended this style of behaviour, but by the men's own children. Sometimes these remote fathers were forbiddingly judgemental. More often they were physically absent or emotionally removed.[55] 'Of my father I cannot say much for I never understood him'; 'Even when [my father] was free to stay at home he would be immersed in books'; 'I cannot say much about my father, for. . . I was very little under his care'.[56]

One young Lancashire girl was so in awe of her father, a doctor, that, when worried about her mother, she wrote him a note and left it at his surgery rather than talk to him.[57]

From the sheer numbers of such statements, as well as from what we know about differences in living and working patterns, it seems likely that the structural changes which occured after 1870 did indeed have a powerful impact on father–child relations.

Industrialisation and fatherhood: the 'second stage'

By the turn of the century, while working hours were still long (the eight-hour day only became the norm after the First World War), the journey to work was becoming longer, and only 371,000 persons in the whole of England and Wales were calculated to be working at home.

Home was becoming more matricentral. Women retreated into their homes, older siblings remained at home longer, grandparents lived longer and communities stabilised around certain industries. As a consequence, there developed a readily available back-up supply of female kin to share any childcare, thus strengthening the division of labour between women and men. The more identified home became with women, and paid work with men, the more removed men became from caring for their children, and the more women appeared to support this. In Yorkshire communities such as Haworth, right into the 20th century wives commonly worked in the mills and men regularly (and publicly) undertook domestic work. But in areas such as Northampton, where helping at home meant a man was unemployed, working-class men would not even be seen fetching coal or carrying the dustbin out. It is from this era that women began to use the possessive pronoun in respect of housework (my stove, my kitchen) and children (boys as well as girls) participated in domestic duties which their fathers, away at work all day, could no longer undertake. 'I could legitimately say,' reported the son of a miner, brought up in Durham in the 1890s 'that I brought up several of my younger brothers and sisters.'[58]

The more continuous and unrelenting work became, the more men's leisure time became separated from their homes, and the more they appeared to resent any intrusion into it. By the late 19th century, men in districts such as Northampton spent very little time at home, beyond eating and sleeping, passing the time after work with male friends in pubs and clubs.

By now the numbers of sons entering their fathers' trades was down to one in two, and education-for-all had become a reality. In the protracted shift from a predominantly oral to literary culture, external teachers had taken over, and the intimate connection between work and training in the domestic setting was lost. The divorce of the workplace from the household was widely regarded as a calamity, and the way first generation factory workers behaved in their new environments reveals a lot about the way they had been operating at home. Unlike today's workers, men were not task-oriented. To their employers' annoyance, they wandered about, chatted to workmates, stretched out their mid-day breaks to two hours, took Mondays off when the spirit moved them, and saw it as their right to attend a wide array of holiday festivals.[59]

All this suggests that, as home-based workers, men had been used to interruption – and interruption by, among others, their children – and that they had combined a range of activities during their waking hours. The word 'alienation' began its career as an attempt to describe the separation of the worker from the world of his family, which had also been his world of work. Now began the process through which men's emotional lives, like their working lives, would begin to be separated off from the place they called their home.

> 6 It's the School Board what gives 'em these notions, a-stuffin' boys' heads full of pride,
> And makes 'em look down on their fathers – these School Boards I ne'er could abide.
> When I was his age I was workin', a-wheelin' the barrer for dad,
> And a-fetchin' the stuff from the markets, when horses was not to be had. 9
>
> *Attributed to a London costermonger, 1870*

Paterfamilias in question

Although the lives of fathers and children became increasingly divergent, it would be wrong to conclude that emotional estrangement was an inevitable fate. Generalisations are fraught with difficulties, and never more so than when they concern mythic figures – such as the Victorian *paterfamilias* or his working-class counterpart, the *drunken bully*. That there were drunken bullies is not in doubt: beer consumption was at its height in the 1870s, falling only slowly from a peak of 34 gallons per head per annum. 'Father was a drunkard, a great spendthrift, an awful reprobate,' remembered one late-Victorian son. 'Home was like hell.'[60] However, drunken bullies – then, as now – were the exception, not the rule.

As for *paterfamilias*, a classic example must be Archbishop Edward Benson, Headmaster of Wellington College from 1859. Although Benson was a harsh disciplinarian within the school, he didn't beat his own children. He didn't need to. 'All my recollections are of constant vigilance and self-repression, for fear Papa should be vexed,' wrote one of his sons, after his death. When Benson died his children were able to read his diaries, and so learned for the first time how he had adored them. 'That we should so have feared him,' wrote Fred Benson, 'that we should so have made ourselves unnatural and formal with him, when all the time his love was streaming out towards us, makes a pathos so pitiful that I cannot bear to think of it.'[61]

Yet, a question mark must hang over the *proportion* of fathers who were – even in the late-19th and early-20th centuries – as we have been led to believe, either painfully distant or regularly drunk. In the remembrances of the Benson sons, none of whom married, there is the feeling that their situation was exceptional. Their father was not like other people's fathers and this realisation made their grief the greater.

One cannot but wonder, therefore, whether even the most renouned 19th century stereotype might have concealed a different reality. It is worth noting the virtual absence of the traditional *paterfamilias* from the work of the most popular of all the Victorian novelists, Charles Dickens. Dickens' fictional fathers are (like his own father) mostly clowns or runaways or dead. Similarly, Balzac and Hugo, Eliot and Hardy showed ordinary fathers who were very far from the *paterfamilias* stereotype, while diarists continued to reveal a huge range of fathering behaviours. Nor was 'spare the rod and spoil the child' universally accepted as ideal parenting behaviour.

❬ My father was naturally kind and compassionate … Nearly all his evenings were given either to helping us with our lessons or amusing us in several ways … Long before jigsaw puzzles were available he cut cardboard into geometrical shapes and sizes, and coloured them for us to put together. He drew and cut out cardboard figures to stand up … Sometimes he would read suitable passages from Dickens and reputable authors. ❭
Paper-works manager's son, late 19th century

In *Silas Marner*, George Eliot picked up a popular Victorian theme of the adult male redeemed through the innocence of a child. She created an adoptive father who, though he did not actually change nappies (the baby Eppie thoughtfully arrived after the nappy-changing stage), undertook the entire daily care of his tiny charge and, through this, earned the 'right' to be her father. Since Silas was only a humble weaver, it is unlikely that the average middle-class father considered him a role model, yet the moral and

psychological benefits of intimate fathering were outlined in no
uncertain terms. The once reclusive Silas educated himself in the
ways of life, that he might educate Eppie – and his spirit was healed.
'In the old days there were angels who came and took men by the
hand and led them away from the city of destruction,' wrote Eliot.
'We see no white-winged angels now. But yet men are led away from
threatening destruction: a hand is put into theirs. . . and the hand
may be a little child's.'[62]

'Breakfast soon after eight o'clock – feed Dickie porridge and
bread and butter and jam, milk and water,' wrote a Thomas
Cobden-Sanderson (rather more prosaically) in 1887. 'At 11 o'clock
he goes to bed and sleeps till 12.30. Lunch soon after 1 o'clock. I
feed Dickie with Dickie's help, or perhaps vice versa ... After lunch
go upstairs and all play together for a while.'[63]

Twentieth century fathers

To check out the true nature of father–child interaction early this
century, a social historian called Trevor Lummis interviewed 60
members of an East Anglian fishing community born towards the
end of the 19th century. Some of the men had worked away at sea
for up to 20 weeks at a time but had been home for four months of
the year; others had worked four or five nights a week throughout
the year; yet others – 'inshoremen' and non-fishermen – had
worked conventional hours.[64] Lummis asked questions about
discipline, financial management and leisure activities, and about
men's contribution to domestic work and childcare. Thirty-eight
per cent of the men were described as regularly undertaking
domestic work (those at home for extended periods did the most),
and only two had refused as a matter of principle.

> ❝ He was a good father and a good husband. My children
> never knew what it was to get their own water in the morning
> to wash with. Before they went to school he'd clean their shoes.
> On Friday night ... he'd clean through my kitchen. I had a big
> cooking stove in there ... and he'd make that shine like a bit of
> glass. ❞
>
> *East Anglian fisherman's wife, pre-1914*

In this community (as, it seems, in so many others) corporal
punishment had been rare. It was commonly applied by mothers –
and then most often by mothers who did not have the daily support

of fathers. One quarter of the interviewees remembered their fathers frequently playing with them in the evenings, a similar proportion often had days out alone with them, while one in three regularly went out as a family. Another one in four (all boys) spent part of the school holidays with their fathers at sea. The men were much more home centred in their leisure time than, for example, either the fishermen of Hull in the 1960s or the miners of the 1950s. Only one out of six drank heavily (even these were not necessarily habitual drunkards), a finding borne out earlier by a 1913 study of women and infants in Lambeth: there, too, the researcher had openly expected most of the fathers to be heavy drinkers, but had found, to her surprise, that they weren't.

The degree to which Lummis' study challenges the stereotype of the bullying, drunken working-class father alone makes it interesting, but there is something else: he also noted under-reporting of paternal activity. One informant, who had stated categorically that his father never did anything round the house, later revealed that first thing in the morning his father would feed the horses, light the fire, cook breakfast and make the tea, before waking his wife. Lummis concluded that the actual behaviour of fathers in our recent past is not only largely unknown, but most probably '...misrepresented through poor-quality anecdotal evidence'. He also came to believe that the long hours worked by the men in his study had not been a rejection of fatherhood, but a necessary element in it. 'No matter how strong the paternal instincts of the father,' he wrote, 'young children could only see him for a few hours a week.'

❛ Sundays too my father got up early
and put his clothes on in the blueblack cold,
then with cracked hands that ached
from labour in the weekday weather made
banked fires blaze. No one ever thanked him. . .
When the rooms were warm, he'd call,
and slowly I would rise and dress,
fearing the chronic angers of that house,

Speaking indifferently to him,
who had driven out the cold
and polished my good shoes as well.
What did I know, what did I know
of love's austere and lonely offices? ❜
Robert Hayden (1913–1980) 'Those Winter Sundays'

When daddy came home

It is all too easy to mythologise social transformations such as those brought about by 'industrialisation' or 'modernisation' and to present them as change between ideal models of society past and present. Such theories can be immensely misleading, for they typically assume a consistent change from the, allegedly, personal and family-centered societies of the past, to the anonymous urban world of the present. The dynamics of change are far more complex. During the 20th century, for example, families have been tugged by contradictory forces. Children have been staying longer at home, but fewer have been working alongside their parents. More comfortable homes, telephone communication and the trend towards home-based leisure and car ownership have drawn families together, while education, working patterns and travel have pulled them apart. Family breakdown has both increased, as a result of divorce, and decreased with improvements in medicine and public health.

It seems probable that the wide-scale absence (and loss) of fathers during two world wars contributed to fathers' current secondary status in some families. 'Certainly I believe the absence of my father in my early years coloured my own behaviour when I married and had children,' reported one woman. 'I did not include my husband in the children's upbringing as much as I might have done had I the role model of a "hands-on" father.'[65]

Many men returning from war felt that this part of their life could not be shared, and this seems to have impaired communication in many families. 'My grandfather and father came home from the First and Second World Wars, the elder from the trenches and the younger from the desert, and were changed men, ever afterwards remote from their wives and children,' wrote one British journalist. Equally, there were fathers who managed the absence from, and return to, their children with enormous skill. One such father, a Major Cohen of the Royal Artillery, wrote letters directly to his two-year-old daughter, Suzette, whom he had never seen. 'Thanks to Mummy I now have a complete picture of your first two years of life. You have been an adorable child and apart from when you had some new teeth and when you have your hair washed, you have given no trouble or anxiety to Mummy or me but only continued happiness … My whole life is wrapped around you.'[67]

Major Cohen's return was, predictably, stormy. Suzette screamed all day and night. Her father persevered with loving confidence and the turning point came on a holiday in the Lake District. 'When he ran with me in my buggy singing "Up the hills and over the bumps and all the way home", I realised how wonderful it was to have a real live daddy. He became my life-long friend and mentor,' Suzette later wrote.

> 6 I was born 14.10.42. My father was at war in the army ... a stranger in the distance. When he came home he was still a stranger ... Whether my father didn't know how, or couldn't, or didn't want to, is hard to say. I had no love for him whatsoever. Not once did he show me love or give me any encouragement at all. He was just a stranger in the background. 9
>
> *Alwyne Fisher,* When Daddy Came Home

Modern times

If fathers' behaviour in times gone by has been notable for its variety, the same is true today. 'Fathers,' says English fatherhood authority Dr Charlie Lewis, 'are not an homogenous group. They range from the few men who produce sperm but have no contact with their offspring, through to another small minority who take sole charge of their children.'[68] In trying to establish how fathers behave today, researchers have looked at three main areas: the amount of time spent with their children; the kinds of activities they undertake; and their parenting styles.

How much time do today's fathers spend with their children? Back in 1971, four years after the anthropologist Margaret Mead wrote that American men '...are evolving a new style of fatherhood, in which young fathers share very fully with mothers in the care of babies and little children', sociologists Rebelsky and Hanks decided to find out for themselves just what was going on in their nation's nurseries. Unlike earlier researchers, they did not rely on mothers' reports, nor even on interviews with fathers, but hit on the idea of getting their information out of the mouths of the very babes. With strategically placed microphones, in effect they bugged the homes of newborns in two-parent families, and this is what they found: on average, the infants' fathers were interacting with them vocally (via words and other noises) for 37.7 *seconds* every day. This figure has haunted fatherhood researchers ever since, and when the study was replicated more recently in Britain, the results still held.[69]

Measuring the time fathers and children spend chatting, however, tells only part of the story. The average father of a nine-month-old in a two-parent family is around the house for 25–29 hours per week while his child is awake, and interacts with that child for an average of three quarters of an hour on a weekday.[70] Most of that time, however, the child's mother is present. Half the fathers of children under one have never looked after their babies on their own and, in the study mentioned above, only 5 per cent were found to take charge at least once every other day. Even the men left in charge are usually following instructions: fathers rarely choose clothes or toys, decide diet changes or take their babies to the doctor.

    ❝ I can bring him to order quite quickly, but of course he doesn't have the luxury of saying, 'You're a pig and there's my mum and she's great!' Once when a couple of the kids were talking about their parents in a derogatory way, I heard him defend me to the hilt. He was so incredibly loyal to me, so wonderfully connected to me. And I have to say I don't think it was because I am a wonderful father to him. It's because I'm all he bloody well has. ❞

Bob, 39, father of one

After infancy, some fathers do become more involved, with weekday interaction averaging just under two hours and six and a half hours on Sundays, but this decreases again as children go off to school.[71] While 86 per cent of fathers of children aged two to four claim to play with them almost every day (and only 1 per cent say they 'never play'), by the time the children are at primary school, only 17 per cent play or work on projects with their children most days, while the percentage who 'never play' is up to 5 per cent.[72]

When children are of school age, mothers continue to organise their lives, even if they are working full time. They almost always choose and buy clothes and toys, plan activities, pack lunchboxes and schoolbags, supervise homework and invite friends over to play. Although fathers take charge more often in dual-earner households, in most two-parent families fathers' interaction with their children is substantially mediated through their wives. Even when fathers are in charge, mothers often leave lists for them to follow. 'It wasn't that he didn't love us,' said one of the men interviewed. 'He did love us. But it was always mother who called the shots.' While adolescence is commonly thought of as a time when children's relationships with their parents weaken, mother–child relationships often become closer and more affectionate during this period. Father–child relationships, however, appear more distant, with fathers averaging less than an hour a day during the week interacting with their adolescents, and under two hours on Sundays.[73][74]

Although the 'new father' is often thought to be a middle-class phenomenon, working-class fathers do not spend less time with their children than middle-class fathers. Working-class fathers are more likely to work shifts and operate 'relay' parenting with their wives. At fee-paying schools, the only males regularly seen collecting children are chauffeurs, and when working-class children write about their families, fathers figure more heavily than in stories written by middle-class children.[75] Working-class males are more likely to hold stereotypical views about mothers' and fathers' roles However, a couple's behaviour is dictated more by income than by ideology. The more equally they earn, the more equally they share domestic work – and working-class couples are more likely to earn similar amounts.

Research on the time black British fathers spend with their children isn't available, but in the US Afro-American fathers in two-parent families spend more time with their children than white or Puerto Rican fathers.[76] Employed Afro-American men in two-parent families also spend an average of 25 hours per week on household work (compared with 19.6 hours for white men).[77] Mothers' employment may be an important contributing factor.

Behind the averages, however, we again find the kind of variations in behaviour which were evident in the historical research. A recent survey, which found one in three fathers to be 'minimally involved', also found fathers who were spending 40–50 hours a week interacting with their children – and these men were employed![78] Where one father will be at home for just five hours in the week while his infant is awake, another in the same community – perhaps in the same street – will be present for 47 hours. And where one father will spend an hour a day with his child, another will average six and a half hours.[79]

❛ Q: Why did you decide to record again?
     A: Because this housewife would like to have a career for a bit! On October 9, I'll be 40, and Sean will be five and I can afford to say 'Daddy does something else as well.' He's not accustomed to it – in five years I hardly picked up a guitar. Last Christmas our neighbours showed him *Yellow Submarine* and he came running in, saying, 'Daddy, you were singing...Were you a Beatle?' I said, 'Well – yes, right.' ❜

John Lennon, Newsweek

Do minimally involved fathers realise how slight their contribution so often is? Some do, and feel this is quite right and proper. Others are bothered by it and may actively seek to change it. But many more seem to be simply unaware. The Rebelsky and Hanks dads were as shocked as anyone by the 37.7 *seconds* of baby-talk which their observers recorded: they had thought they were chatting away to their babies for a daily 15–20 *minutes*. One of the fathers interviewed for this book, who described himself as having a 'close and passionate relationship' with his three young children, later revealed that on weekdays he only saw them for a short time in the morning, never saw them in the evenings, and also spent at least half of every Saturday in the office. No one could doubt that this father had intense and passionate *feelings* for his children, but whether he had close and passionate *relationships* with them seemed unlikely, and it was clear that no one had challenged his perceptions. Because average levels of father involvement are so low, any father who does more than a very little can be rated 'highly involved' by himself, his partner – and even by researchers.[80]

The playful father

It will be remembered that our cultural stereotypes have latterly designated mothers nurturers and fathers playmates. How real is this division? Certainly, over a seven-day period, the typical father of a young child spends about nine hours in play, and around two hours in caretaking.[81] Overall, however, mothers do not play any less with their young children than fathers, and they often play for many hours longer. But because they also spend between nine and 18 hours a week caretaking, the *proportion* of time a mother spends with her children is not so heavily weighted towards play.[82] However, the play-styles of mothers and fathers differ in our culture. American, UK and Australian fathers are more jokey with their children and engage more often and more vigorously in 'rough and tumble', although older fathers do relatively little of this and for fathers of all ages rough-and-tumble wanes quite quickly, as children grow older (and heavier). Black fathers in the US seem to play less with their children than white males. Due to black women's high levels of employment, these men may be more involved in the nitty-gritty of everyday care.[83] Fathers are more likely than mothers to be interested in sports and there are class differences here: fathers further up the social scale are more likely to encourage sports which develop individual antagonism, while endurance and team sports are more often supported by working-class dads.

> 6 Ricky and I are closer than anybody. Not in a mushy way. It works well on a child level, I suppose, we are on the same wavelength, but also it works – well, we play golf together, things like that, and Arsenal is very important to us. All those sporty levels. It's a bit unfair, perhaps, being able to give him a lot more time and love and proximity than the others ever had. 9
>
> *Alec, 50, father of three (two families)*

Fathers of young children are slightly less likely than mothers to engage them in more intellectual play (such as puzzles or construction toys) and are more likely to choose activity toys such as balls or vehicles, or watch TV with them. But once toy-choice is taken into account, parents' play-styles prove remarkably similar.

Is nurturing, and physically caring for their babies something that only a few fathers do? No. Studies now regularly report 95 per cent of fathers bathing, feeding and changing their babies some of the time, and 30–50 per cent doing so very often indeed. Researchers used to think that fathers were somehow less warm towards their children than mothers, and were less likely to smother their infants with affection. This may be because they are being watched, however, and in private they may behave very much more affectionately. Fathers who are observed to be 'coolest' with their children also score highest on the 'feeling self-conscious' scale,[84] and it is interesting to note that pre-adolescent children do not see 'playful touch' as being especially characteristic of fathers. They report cuddles and kisses as more typical.[85]

It is also perhaps unwise to make too rigorous a distinction be made between play and caretaking. A moving study of fathers and young children on a public fishing pier has described the sensitive transmission of skills and love: parallel movements, smiles, and the fathers' tender guiding of their children's hands onto the fishing-lines.[86]

Disciplining dad

To what extent are today's fathers their families' disciplinarians? Minimally. They simply aren't at home enough. Mothers not only hit their children more often than fathers, but also give more orders and hand out more threats and punishments (and frequently complain that their partners are not tough enough).[87] Nor are fathers more likely than mothers to encourage their children to persist with a task until it is completed. Mothers do this just as often, and sometimes more often.[88] Fathers are not more negative, firm or restrictive than mothers, nor are they more competitive but, like men generally, are verbally more dominating. They interrupt their children more often, and speak over them, and sometimes when they are talking with their young children, they will use oddly complex language. However, both fathers and mothers get 'bossed around' by their toddlers to very much the same extent – a phenomenon which, once again, would not appear to be new.[89]

> ❢ After breakfast he sat down quietly to write to you [his mother] … [while] I told him the words he did not know how to spell … He commanded me to come close to him each time he wanted to know something … [but] as he was asking something every instant, I said I could not keep going to him … I took up the unfinished letter to send you, but he seized it and tore it … [Later] he came down rather crestfallen and, when I asked him, agreed to write if I could get his copybook from behind the drawers where he had thrown it. This I did. ❥
> *John Russell, 1872*

It is often supposed that working-class fathers are most likely to demand obedience and conformity and to hit their children. But although working-class mothers require fathers to discipline children more often, working-class fathers are *not* more likely to hit their offspring than their middle-class counterparts,[90] nor are they less warm towards them. However, there is a sharp rise in serious threats and violence towards children, by both fathers and mothers, in particularly poor and disadvantaged households.[91]

While middle-class fathers *are* more likely to operate democratically there are big variations: 65 per cent of university-trained professional fathers are family democrats, as against 42 per cent of senior executives and just 24 per cent of junior executives. Twenty five per cent of working-class fathers also operate democratically.[92]

Since working-class families generally live in more hazardous environments, we might expect their parenting to be more authoritarian. This also applies to many black fathers. So far there is no published research into the parenting styles of black British fathers, but black fathers in the US are not seen to behave in a more authoritarian way than white fathers. In fact, a recent US study showed that black daughters living in two-parent families were much closer to their fathers, and spent more time with them, than their counterparts in white families. Black fathers' harsh reputations are partly due to the fact that research into black families has focused almost exclusively on poor, inner-city families. US research has found that race has less impact on the way fathers behave than class: the behaviour and attitudes of middle-class black fathers resemble those of middle-class white fathers, more than those of working-class black fathers.

Religious involvement (particularly fundamentalist religions) also encourages authoritarian fathering. Immigration can be significant too. Immigrant fathers, whatever their race, often feel they must act as guardians of their cultural traditions, and some British Asian families have suffered double-migration – via East Africa to the UK.

Sex-role conditioning

Ensuring boys are boys, and girls are girls, has often been regarded as the Western father's most important contribution to child development. It's certainly possible that, once upon a time, a majority of fathers treated their sons and daughters as if they came from different planets, and in some families they still do. However, the average father today does not do significantly more 'sex-role conditioning' than the average mother. Both parents subtly encourage tiny boys to be naughty and to race around toting firearms, even discouraging many of their attempts at communication, while at the same time encouraging their *daughters* to chatter. When talking with three-year-olds about the past, both fathers and mothers use bigger words with girls and keep them talking longer even when the boys' language development is just as sophisticated.[93] The two areas where fathers are consistently more 'sexist' than mothers is in encouraging sons in more aggressive physical play, and discouraging them from playing with girls' toys. One researcher noted fathers who regularly pushed their infants' buggies, refusing to allow their little sons to push a doll's pram in public. Mothers tend to be less uptight about this, but they don't tolerate it for long, either.

Although most fathers are physically bigger and stronger than most mothers and have deeper, louder voices, and although many play more vigorously with their children and chat away to them less freely and equally than mothers do, this is not sufficient to amount to a distinctive, gender-based parenting-style. More tellingly perhaps, is that differences *between* individual couples are likely to be greater than differences *within* individual couples. As parents, couples tend to develop a communal style: if one is punitive and restrictive, so is the other; if one is relaxed, the other is easy-going, too. And when a father is violent towards his partner, she is quite often violent towards the children.[94]

Of course, some fathers behave very differently from their wives, but in the land of averages – where most people dwell – there can be no doubt that, individually (as couples) and collectively (as gender groups), fathers and mothers behave in surprisingly similar ways. It is also the case that they do so even in spheres where their behaviour has been thought to be particularly gender oriented.

Changing times?

Are today's fathers less – or more – involved than fathers at any time this century? This question is difficult to answer because studies have rarely compared like with like, and the belief that fathers are more involved than their own fathers has been around for several generations. Certainly, most contemporary adults do not remember their fathers as being at all involved in infant care. However, a study of parents in Nottingham in the 1960s showed that even at that time one in five fathers regularly changed their babies' nappies, one in three frequently put them to bed and one in two got up to them, at least occasionally, in the night.[95] This would have been remembered by few of their children, and it may well be that even today's nappy-changing 'new dads' will be remembered as uninvolved by many of their offspring.

> ❲ Like everyone else who lives, [my son] will never recall the circumstances of his first years. It seems to be the wisdom of naure that we cannot remember the time we were most loved and tended, for otherwise we could not be fully adult ... None the less I lament ... his loss of memory. ❳
>
> *Tim Hilton,* In Tandem

Some direct comparisons can be made, however, and these point to greater involvement by today's fathers. In 1970, 40 per cent of UK fathers of very young children came home to a sleeping child during the week and 11 per cent were not there at the weekend either. Today only 25 per cent of employed fathers are not home before 7 p.m. and babies may be staying up later – especially when mothers work, too.[96] A clear increase in levels of fathers' involvement in basic baby-care – putting to bed, feeding and bathing – can be traced from the 1950s through to the 1990s in Europe, Australia and North America, and fathers are also involving themselves in a much wider range of tasks. This is despite the fact that men's employment hours, having dipped in the 1970s, are now back to 1961 levels. Nor is it only the men whose partners are employed who are 'hands on'. In families where mothers stay at home full time, the fathers are also much more involved than previously.[97]

In Australia, researchers have now investigated the period 1987 to 1992 and found that over these five years fathers increased the time spent on childcare tasks, by two hours a week. They have also observed that today's dads are taking care of much younger children. Fathers, it seems, are no longer waiting for their children to leave infancy before becoming active parents.[98]

History as myth

Although myth-busting has been a function of this chapter, there is no desire to replace one myth with another – to banish entirely the authoritarian despot and replace him with a soft-hearted democrat. There are, and always have been, oppressively authoritarian fathers. But the point is that this has been *a* way of behaving (and not the most usual). It has been just one in a wide repertoire of paternal behaviour – behaviour which seems, in many important respects, to have been surprisingly similar to mothers'.

That some fathers from all eras have been intimately involved in their children's upbringing is plain. And that, up to the middle of the 19th century, social structures made that involvement possible to an extent that seems unimaginable today is also clear. It is also obvious that the nature and degree of father–child interaction has shown, and still shows, considerable variation, not only across time and place, but also between individuals and even within families, where a father (like a mother) may be close to one child and distant from another.

This information creates both winners and losers: losers among those who claim a distinctive gender-based role for fathers, or who believe today's 'new fathers' to be groundbreakers – men whose presence heralds a new phase in the history of fatherhood. But the information also creates winners, among those who recognise 'new dad' as the latest manifestation in a long tradition of intimate fathering, or who do not believe that fathers' value to their children can be measured only by demonstrably 'masculine' behaviour.

Yet while infant- and child care has certainly not been exclusively *performed* by women in our culture, it has been perceived as being pretty well exclusively *owned* by women, and with that has come the perception that only women have an unreserved right to passionate attachment to their children. Time and again the men interviewed for this book described the birth of their first child as 'the happiest day of my life', yet often when they said these words or described other moments of intense joy or sorrow connected with their children, their embarrassed voices dropped almost out of the reach of the tape-recorder. Fathers' intimate voices from the past have been no less elusive, no less difficult to catch, but they are, at last, beginning to be heard.

> 6 How I love Lucy, the mother of my boy! … For the 'lad' my feeling has yet to grow a great deal. I prize him and rejoice to have him, and when I take him in my arms begin to feel a father's love and interest, hope and pride, enough to know what the feeling *will* be if not what it *is*. I think what is to be his future, his life. How strange a mystery this all is! This is to me the beginning of a new life. 9
>
> *Rutherford Haynes, 1853*

Chapter 3

The Natural Father: cad or dad?

For over four years, ever since Harry and Anna Clements separated, they have shared care of their daughter, Emily. Harry is an engineer, a real 'man's man' who, before his divorce, didn't even know how to work the washing-machine. Now Emily keeps clothes and toys at her 'dad's place' and when Harry returns his daughter to his ex-wife, Anna observes that, 'Harry behaves like a mother to Emily now, as well as a father. Her clothes are ironed, her hair's well brushed and her teeth are cleaned.'

Recently, some pigeons nested just outside her father's kitchen window. When the eggs were laid, and the birds began their vigil, Emily observed not one but two pigeons sitting on the nest. This behaviour she declared 'very unusual', until her biology teacher set her straight. Despite her own experiences of shared parental care, Emily had assumed that one bird would 'mother' and another would 'father'; and that it would be the female who would sit, and the male who would flit. From a lay point of view, the belief that there are broadly consistent, genetically determined roles for mothers and fathers across many species seems well supported. We wander through the countryside and see fields full of sheep and lambs, cows and calves – every one of them a mother-headed family. And when we read Beatrix Potter to our children, we hear tell of Jemima Puddleduck's search for a safe place to deposit her eggs, or of Mrs Rabbit's lonely attempts to discipline her adolescent son Peter, whose father was last seen in one of Mrs McGregor's pies.

Thanks to a plethora of television naturalists who work tirelessly to bring the goings-on in the natural world to us, our minds have been broadened a little. There can't be many children in the Western world who don't know by now that it's the male sea-horses that give birth, and just about everyone has watched classic television footage of male Emperor penguins shuffling around with apparently well-loved eggs tucked into their ankles. But these we regard as anomalies, and they are not enough to make us question what many believe to be the 'natural law' of mummies and daddies.

❬ One important thing that fathers can do is get the hell out
of the way. I recognise that Lianne is the primary giver, she is
the main man as it were, she is the primary parent, they do go
to her more and I am happy to have it that way. But occasionally
I feel a little bit excluded, and probably some men feel more
excluded than others. I mean, working from home I spend
more time with them than Lianne, so if I feel a little bit
excluded then probably some men feel really excluded, and
they should accept that. ❭

Philip, 39, father of three

Biology as metaphor

Fantasies about flopsy bunnies wouldn't matter at all if that's where
they ended. But they don't. Time and again, and often unconsciously,
we apply our impressions of parenting behaviour among fish, fowl
and mammals to human parenting behaviour. We assume a
spontaneous and universal sexual division of labour in the natural
world, which stimulates a belief that mothering and fathering
behaviours are biologically determined and relatively fixed.

American psychologist Louise Silverstein has pointed out that the
current debate concerning families and the needs of children isn't
really about families or children's needs at all. What is at issue, what
exercises the minds and the passions of traditionalists on the one
hand and liberals on the other, is profound disagreement over the
true nature of the functions and capacities of women and of men.[1]
On one side stands a mother, armed with womb and breasts:
symbols and expressions of her nurturing capabilities. Opposite her
stands a father, wombless and breastless, designated the provider
through deficiency not abundance, his paternal identity formed not
from what he possesses but from what he lacks. It is not only women
for whom biology has been perceived as destiny. Men are caught in
the same trap.

The often unspoken belief is that fathers are biologically
programmed to be relatively uninvolved in nurturing their young,
and this has far-reaching consequences. This belief lies behind the
reluctance of many women to involve their men more deeply in
childrearing, and the reluctance of many men to push themselves
forward, as if such investment might be a waste of time. It can be
seen in policies towards teenage fathers, who have traditionally been
excluded from their children's lives. It is seen every day of the week
in law courts: for example, in the judgement by a Scottish judge in a

custody dispute, who ruled in October 1994 that 'All things being equal, the mother should have the child.'[2] The expectation that building relationships with children does not come naturally to fathers has affected virtually every area of family policy, which has not merely failed to strengthen father–child relationships but has often actively undermined them.[3] Again and again, justification for these (and other) gender arrangements has been biological metaphor lurking, often unacknowledged, somewhere below the surface.

❝ I see myself like a wild cat. I've done my duty by the litter and now I'm buggering off, like wild cats always do. They always bugger off at the end. That's what my father did. He buggered off, into insanity. ❞

Gerrard, 43, father of two

Nature's ways

To a biologist, the word motherhood means just one thing – production of ova – while fatherhood means simply the production of sperm. Parenting behaviours which we may associate with one sex or the other – provisioning, grooming, defending – are not necessarily part of the biologist's equation at all, and are certainly not gender-specific. Indeed, from a cross-species perspective, it is diversity, not homogeneity, that is the order of the day.

Many animals – butterflies, turtles, spiders, species of fish – provide no parental care whatsoever. Others share parenting equally, and this is true of over 90 per cent of bird species. Since many birds (female as well as male) are promiscuous, biologists have been keen to establish whether 'paternity certainty' influences the level of care a male bird offers its young. The answer appears to be that sometimes it does, and sometimes it doesn't. Male swallows with faithful partners feed their chicks with more dedication than male swallows whose partners are promiscuous.[4] But razorbills don't seem to mind either way. They go on feeding their chicks and watching over them at night, whatever their mates have been up to.[5] Among many non-human species (including wolves and Adelie penguins) group care is offered by both sexes. Some animals switch roles and, like the Mexican sword-tail fish, may even switch sex, as the need arises. Kestrels and partridges normally have quite a strict division of labour: she feeds, he hunts. But in both these species, if the female dies the male takes on complete care of the young.

All over the world, males are found in sole charge of eggs. In Australia, a single female lilywalker lays many fertilised eggs in numerous nests, which are then sat on by different males. In some species the male remains the dominant (or sole) parent until the young are grown. Male sticklebacks not only attend the eggs but subsequently oversee the young entirely on their own.

‘ As a kind of advertisement for myself, I broke my ban on his watching television so that we could sit through a natural history film together. The subject was the sea-horse, and he saw with me a hugely pregnant male sea-horse spilling tiny miniatures of itself out of a hole in its belly. It's like alphabet soup of one variety only, beautifully upright (baby sea-horses don't crawl) coming out and straight away drifting into sea-horsehood. How do they know their father?' ’

Michael Hofmann, Patrimony

Paternal care can also be selective: among wild cattle, the herd bull looks after male, but not female, calves. Male anemone fish can become stepfathers, and so can male hornbills, for if one dies while still feeding its young, another male takes over the brood. Virgin male rats, like virgin females, will show parenting behaviour if new-born rats are put into their cages

In only one in 10 mammalian species, however, do males provide any form of direct infant-care *in the wild* although many more will do so in captivity. The key to maternal dominance among mammals rests on one simple, biological fact: that the young are exclusively nourished with their mothers' milk at first. Among mammals, it is our nearest relatives, the non-human primates (monkeys, apes and so on), that have attracted most attention; and it is assumptions about their behaviour which, even in the 1990s, continue to underpin family policy and public opinion.

In all probability, the behaviour of non-human primates has no bearing whatsoever on human primate behaviour. Even if primates are our ancestors, and this is debatable, many evolutionary steps divide us. Yet because these ideas are current, they must be explored. And indeed, if gender-specific parenting patterns across many species of apes and monkeys can be shown, then speculation about rigid, gender-consistent parenting behaviours in human primates must at least be entertained.

‘ She is still a Mother – and I'm not sure what that means. She is the person who gave birth to them, she has the breasts they fed from, she has got these characteristics of mother which are contained within her and not within what she does on a day-today basis. So that, although I may do the ironing, although I may prepare their food, when she comes home from work there are ways – very physical ways – in which they wish to relate to her. They want to touch, be in touch with her. It's reassurance. They want to be sure that she is there and she has come home again safely. **)**

James, 59, father of five (two families)

Primates: first impressions

In the period following the Second World War, an academic discipline which came to be called the New Physical Anthropology set out to define the nature and characteristics of Universal Man and, later, of Universal Woman. Much of this work, which relied heavily on studies of monkeys and apes, was carried out for UNESCO, and was motivated by the desire to combat institutionalised racism.[6]

The key primate researchers of that time were charismatic figures. They were all male, and although they never acknowledged their own bias (even to themselves), it is now established that their perceptions were dramatically affected by their gender, their race, their class, their marital status, and by the historical context in which they operated – as well as by the relatively limited data collected at the time. What did these men see? They saw co-operative, nurturing primate females devoted to their young and dominated by aggressive primate males. These they perceived as the Hugh Hefners of the natural world: outright playboys, mating short-term with as many females as possible and generally remaining aloof from their offspring. The luckiest were seen to live in harem-style troupes, with a host of hopeful females jostling for their favours. Hefner's magazine hit the news-stands in December 1953, and it is perhaps worth noting the coincidence of *Playboy*'s colonising of American male fantasy, and the early primatologists' perceptions of male primate behaviour.

By the early 1970s, a leading researcher, Sherwood Washburn, was asserting that a fair proportion of 'Man's' problems arose from the fact that he was attempting to meet '… the problems of the atomic age with the biology of hunter-gatherers',[7] and a neo-Darwinian evolutionary theory was advanced to explain the supposed 'cad' behaviour of primate males. Given that their biological obligation to the next generation seemed to begin and end with the production of vast numbers of sperm, it was suggested that it made reproductive sense for primate males (and, by analogy, human males) to mate with as many members of the opposite sex as possible, and to pay minimal attention to any offspring resulting.

This pleasure was to be denied primate females who, in the eyes of the early primatologists, were biologically programmed to accept what was forced upon them and devote themselves to raising the products of conception. The researchers declared that the female primate's obvious biological function as incubator-cum-milk-machine, plus her comparatively limited capacity for procreation, made it advisable for her to limit her intake of sperm. She was biologically programmed to spend her time and energy parenting rather than mating. Seemingly oblivious to the fact that many female primates sought mating opportunities with a truly breathtaking panoply of partners and were actually *more* promiscuous than their primate brothers, the researchers declared that the ladies were 'coy'. This 'evidence' from the natural world pointed to a truly primal bond which tied mother and child together, and relegated fathers to the outer jungle.

Cads v. dads

Only one thing it was believed could reconcile the irreconcilable: monogomy. Even at this stage in primate research, it was clear that males in a few species were bucking the 'cad' trend. Male marmosets and siamangs, for example, weren't in the least aloof. They were busy, day and night, caring for and carrying their babies, and behaving well, like 'dads'. Justification for this puzzling behaviour was provided by the paternity certainty theory, mentioned earlier, which held that only a male who was sure he was an infant's father could be persuaded to stay around and to invest energy in parenting rather than in mating. Word spread that these nurturing male monkeys were monogomous, and this caught the imagination of policy-makers: it seemed to endorse the nuclear family model of breadwinner husband and stay-at-home wife which was being so heavily promoted in the post-war period. It seemed reasonable to assume that a wife who stayed at home (away from other males) was likely to stay faithful and that, as in the natural world, a faithful wife and family responsibilities would make a 'dad' out of a human 'cad'.

The redemptive power of monogamy is an idea which remains popular today with neo-conservative family politicians, like American Charles Murray. Murray, whose opinions are widely published and applauded in Britain, views the 'cad' state as natural to human males. These he regards as victims of a testosterone-ridden biology which leads them, unless 'civilised by marriage', to 'regard violence as a sign of strength' and to 'sleep with and impregnate as many girls as possible'.[8]

However, many *unmarried* males do not see violence as a sign of strength, nor seem inclined to sleep with and impregnate as many girls as possible – while some of those who *are* married do. Furthermore, statistics reveal that a substantial proportion of the male prison population is married and that nine out of 10 serial killers are or have been wed. These are incompatible realities ignored by Murray and his followers who rate the civilising potential of marriage way above other factors, the provision of which would prove more costly to the Exchequer: parent education and support, good housing and reduced unemployment. In Murray's eyes, human cads (like their primate brothers) can *only* be enticed into domesticity and turned into dads through monogomous marriage, and through a deep conviction that the children who face them across the breakfast table are from their own gene-pool. And indeed, if – as was held by early primatological theory – only the male apes and monkeys who can be confident of paternity will help to raise the young, then maybe it should be 'back to basics' for humans too. But for Murray and his fellow-travellers there is bad news: they have based their arguments on a vision of the primate world that has since been revised.

❝ Yes, the eldest is my step-daughter. I married her mother when she was about three months old, so I hadn't been there at the birth but I have been there in one way or another all her life. And of all my children, I must admit, between you and me and the wall, she's my favourite. ❞

Pete, 45, father of four

Primates: a different perspective

By the 1980s large numbers of female biologists were crawling around Rajastan and other primate arenas. 'Of course I identify with them!' declared Sarah Blaffer Hrdy, who spent years studying langurs (tree-monkeys). 'I sometimes identify with female baboons more than I do with males of my own species.'[9] This new phase of research was not only influenced by the fact that both men and women were observing the animals, but also by the long-term nature of the studies. Some studies eventually spanned 10–15 years and revealed the impact of changing circumstances on primate behaviour. The findings from this 'second stage' of primate research have now been accepted as mainstream.

The first stereotype to bite the dust was that of the sharing, caring put-upon primate female. Not only did the researchers note female primates' promiscuity, but they observed that very often it was the females who determined a troupe's movements and controlled the food sources. It was suggested that single male groups should no longer be referrred to as harems. They could equally well be said to consist of a self-reliant group of females, making use of a mobile sperm-bank. With this new research came another shift in perspective. Certainly the female monkeys and apes studied seemed to show some kind of 'maternal instinct': a new mother would immediately be surrounded by other females, anxious to seize the baby. But, on closer examination, this female interest or 'maternal instinct' did not prove entirely benevolent. Younger females might go off with the infant and then abandon it; older females might refuse to return it to its mother and through a combination of rough handling and failure to feed, cause its death. Sometimes a female, or group of females, would corner the good feeding grounds so that the infants of excluded mothers died of starvation. And a high-ranking female might harass subordinates into miscarrying, if her presence alone didn't stop them ovulating.[10]

If the female–infant bond in primates had been glorified by the early primate researchers, it was now revealed that the male–infant bond had been denigrated. Certainly, males could be a danger to infants (for example, through infanticide when attempting a troupe take-over) but it was also clear that, in terms of infant-welfare, they contributed far more than had been previously thought. It now appears that among half the species of non-human primates (apes and monkeys) males are regularly found providing direct care to infants.

> ❛ I think I always imagined that babies cried all of the time. You know, for no reason. But he has never cried for no reason, only cried because he was tired, until the teething. I was surprised by that, I was actually surprised by how enjoyable it was, I think, to be honest. I had no expectations of enjoyment, least of all feeling as I do now – that it's all going to be over too soon. ❜
>
> *Oliver, 39, father of one*

How do primate males behave, and what bearing does biological paternity have on the degree of their involvement? 'Best fathering awards' go to species like owl and titi monkeys, tamarins and marmosets. Males assist at births, pre-masticate food for newborns and carry them day and night, only handing them to their mothers for feeding. Can these 'New Dads' be sure they're the fathers? Only sometimes. While owl and titi monkeys do seem to be monogomous, tamarins and marmosets aren't. And as for Barbary apes, who also show intensive male caretaking of infants, they're among the most promiscuous primates around.

'Second best fathering awards' can be given to mountain gorillas and savanna baboons. Here, though mothers do most of the infant nurturing, individual males frequently form special relationships with individual infants. Again, paternity certainty seems to be of little import. Mountain gorillas live in troupes headed by a single male who seems to father most of the offspring; and savanna baboons live in multi-male groups where the female, in the week of peak fertility, usually mates with several males. Yet in both these species, males keep close to chosen infants, cuddle and groom them, and comfort them when they show signs of distress.

'Cad awards' go to species such as orangutans, rhesus monkeys, chimpanzees and langurs, all of whom generally ignore juveniles. Again, biological paternity seems to be of little import. Although rhesus monkeys are utterly promiscuous, langurs can be reasonably sure of their genetic contribution: although females sometimes nip out for a bit of extra troupe sex, one male normally monopolises matings among his troupe for years.

6 We do not dismiss sex-role stereotyping in parenting altogether. Pregnancy and the capacity to breastfeed are important physical and psychological factors. Nevertheless, we feel that men's capacity to nurture should be examined more closely. How much parenting is part of a male's biological heritage? How much can he learn to overcome any inborn discrepancies between himself and his wife? 9

Arthur and Libby Colman, The Father

When cads become dads

If it's not monogamy, or even certainty of paternity, that makes dads out of primate cads, what does? Direct care by males can be essential for infant survival. Among marmosets, the male monkey hardly ever puts the baby down, and this seems to be because a marmoset mother usually gives birth to twins, whose body-weight relative to her own, is high. To produce enough milk to feed them satisfactorily, she must eat constantly, and so her mate provides the rest of the infant-care with, it is suggested, his eye on future mating opportunities. These do exist. Thanks to his efforts, the infants are soon independent, the female is in oestrus, and within six months another set of twins is on the way.

Among many species, the best indicator of a male primate's involvement with a baby is his relationship with its mother. Male and female olive baboons, for example, regularly develop non-sexual friendships, and most of the close relationships between males and infants are in this context. It has been suggested that the male olive baboons, like the marmoset males, only take up with babies to 'get in' with their mothers, and so to mate with them later. But many of the baboon friendships remain just that – friendships – and, since a male baboon only develops a relationship with an infant if the mother allows it, it may be that she is evidencing as much (or more) of an ulterior motive as he is: for she may be the one trying to curry favour with a potential mate.

As an explanation for paternal involvement, 'mating effort' often seems as unlikely as 'paternity certainty'. It is not unusual to find orphan baboons adopted by adult males (indeed, such an adoption seems to be a pre-requisite for their survival). Other, less cuddly primate males adopt, too. Gorilla-watchers in Rwanda noted a troupe's leading male, who had previously ignored an infant, take it over completely after its mother's death. From then on, the two travelled together and the infant even slept in the male's nest. In Rajastan, similar behaviour was observed in a langur. This normally detached creature became personal guardian to an infant abandoned by its mother, grooming it continually, and cuddling it when it was cold. In neither case was the male likely to be the infant's father; and in neither could he hope to mate with its mother.[11] What becomes clear is that the forces leading to intensive caretaking by primate males are complex. Researchers now suggest that when a male ape or monkey takes an interest in a baby (or when a female promotes such a relationship) this can be for any of a number of reasons: it may be for advancement up the pecking order, or as part of mating effort, or through paternity certainty. There is also the possibility that individual males simply become attached to individual infants and care for them without ulterior motive, but socio-biologists (who are a hard-headed lot) reject anthropomorphic sentimentality.

Experiments conducted with captive animals have shown the huge potential for flexibility in primate males' behaviour. In one particularly interesting example, a male and female rhesus monkey were put together in a cage with an unfamiliar infant. Rhesus males, it will be remembered, are archetypal cads. In this case, as expected, the female performed 100 per cent of the nurturing and caretaking tasks, actively inhibiting contact between the male and the baby. When the female was removed from the cage, however, everything changed: the male took over and assumed all the 'mothering' responsibilities.[12]

❝ When Sue and I were discussing having a child I said, I am happy to have this child but I will be its father and not its mother. I know this is a sexist thing to say, but I was very involved in my career. And then when Sue killed herself and Peter became more mine ... then, it felt very different. Now, there's no way I would give him up. I have been determined to be there after school and after nursery. I wouldn't like to change that now. I wouldn't like to disappear and not be the one looking after him. ❞

Bob, 46, father of two (two families)

What modern primatology reveals is that fathering behaviours among non-human primates are not only immensely varied, but are far from fixed. Furthermore, they do not so much vary in response to biological imperatives as to changing circumstances. This is an important finding, and a relatively recent one, and it calls into question any tendency we might have to regard human fathering behaviour as naturally rigid and gender-specific, and human fathers as biologically programmed to be uninvolved with their young, or with the young of other males.

From ape to man

In evolutionary terms, the observation that male monkeys and apes regularly respond to infants which are not known to be theirs, and for a variety of reasons, is significant. It casts doubt on the notion of females as civilising agents, and on the mother–child bond as the original and primary family relationship. It also casts doubt on the idea that human males did not take a lot of interest in babies and children, until their biological contribution to procreation was understood. However, comparisons with primates, beguiling though they are, do not in themselves refute theories of fixed, biologically driven behaviour in humans. It may be that all human fathers behave in essentially similar ways, however society is organised. If they do, this could point to biological mandates.

In search of such happy certainties, early researchers set about measuring physical closeness hour by hour between fathers and children in 80 cultures. None of these was a modern industrial culture, the researchers apparently assuming that a pre-industrial life-style was more 'natural' than life in a suburban cul-de-sac. In this research, fathers were revealed to have stunningly low rates of interaction with infants. Even if a 'regular close relationship' between father and infant was defined as one in which the father was physically nearby for *half* the time a mother was near, only 4 per cent of fathers met the required standard. Fathers of toddlers didn't do much better: just 9 per cent were regularly to hand.[13]

Another attempt at father-watching on an international scale, and another attempt to establish species-characteristic behaviour, was undertaken by American social scientist Wade C. Mackey in the mid-1980s. Believing that researchers had seriously misrepresented fathers by focusing only on their involvement (or lack of it) with very young children, and by not taking proper account of their working patterns, Mackey sent teams of researchers into rural and urban environments in 18 countries at evenings and weekends, to observe adult–child groups in public places.[14] This time technologically complex societies were not ruled out.

As in the earlier research, Mackey's measurements were crude. He did not, for example, ascertain whether the men accompanying the children were their biological fathers, nor did he investigate their at-home behaviour. But what he observed, and brought to our attention, was that the male of the species *homo sapiens sapiens* exhibits a wide range of caretaking behaviours with children. In some countries, Sri Lanka and Israel, adult males are found in about 30 per cent of adult–child groups; in others, such as Spain and Hong Kong, the proportions rise to 60 per cent; the average figure is somewhere around 50 per cent.

Adult males were spotted more often with older male children, rather than female, but in all other respects were seen to behave, as parents, exactly like adult females. They paid lots of attention to younger children of both sexes, and less to older. They touched them, watched them in similar ways and kept as close to them. When adult females were present, males tended to interact with children less, but when they were with them on their own, they interacted more intensely than did females in exclusively women–child groups.

❝ I don't think there are deep, profound differences. I think that what Jill and I managed to achieve was very loving and very equal ... I can never remember picking up one of the kids when they were in a tantrum and them saying 'No, I want mummy, I want mummy' or being picked up by mummy and them saying 'No, I want daddy, No, I want daddy'. And I can remember seeing it in other households and really rather dreading it, thinking that would really hurt me. ❞

Andrew, 49, divorced father of two

In Mackey's observations, however, only one in five children (and almost no babies) were found with adult males *alone* in public, and few males associated in groups with other males and children at the same time. When another adult was added to the man–child group, it was usually a female. But, in any society, there was a kind of minimum level of man–child engagement: the less time men spent with women and children, the more they spent alone with children.

Mackey concluded that there is an enormous split between cultural myth concerning father–child interaction and day-to-day reality. Not only did he perceive human males to be competent with, and sensitive to, children, but given half a chance, they seemed to take opportunities to be with them. Indeed, infants excluded, the men were seen to associate with as many children as the women. However, the fact that they tended to hang back when females were around, caused him to wonder whether the threshold for parenting behaviour was innately lower for women than for men. Or were there other forces at work?

Intimate fathers

The tracking of fathers and children through shopping malls has been the least of it. In pursuit of essential truths about father–child relationships, some modern anthropolgists have virtually moved in with selected communities. Minute by minute, day by day, in jungle or suburb, they have observed fathering behaviours. To the click of stop-watches, they have timed men's interactions with their children, and have recorded and analysed their quality. What they have discovered is that fathering behaviours among humans are even more varied than among primates. One study comparing fathers from a farming community in Kenya with American fathers living in a university town, found both groups physically near their young children for about the same numbers of hours per day. However, while the Americans were designated 'primary caretakers' for around 15 per cent of that time, the Kenyan fathers barely interacted with their offspring.[15] Yet this relatively high level of involvement by American fathers would not, of course, be replicated across all American communities. In some inner-city areas, few fathers would even be resident.

> ‘He [a Trobriand Islander father] will fondle and carry a baby, clean and wash it, and give it the mashed vegetable food. The father performs his duties with genuine natural fondness: he will carry an infant about for hours, looking at it with eyes of such love and pride as are seldom seen in those of a European.’
>
> *Bronislaw Malinowski (1927),* The Father in Primitive Psychology

Even the most dedicated American dad would be hard put to match the paternal enthusiasms of the Trobriand Islanders (observed by Malinowski in 1927)[16] or of a tribe called the Arapesh (observed by anthropologist Margaret Mead in 1935).[17] Although not present at the birth – taboos forbade it – the Arapesh father was intensely involved throughout pregnancy. The Arapesh did not believe a child was created through a single copulation, but through a series of couplings over a prolonged period. During infancy, the Arapesh father continued to play an important role: 'The minute day-by-day care of little children, with its routine, its exasperations, its wails of misery that cannot be correctly interpreted,' wrote Mead, 'these are as congenial to the Arapesh men as they are to the Arapesh women. And in recognition of the father's initial contribution, if one comments upon a middle-aged man as good-looking, the people answer: "Good-looking? Y-e-s? But you should have seen him before he bore all those children."

The behaviour of a tribe called the Manus further inspired Mead to question Western assumptions about biological programming in parenting behaviour. Among the Manus, women had exceptionally low status. Although they nursed their children, both boys and girls were encouraged to identify with their fathers and to spend many of their waking hours with them. When Mead offered baby-dolls to the Manus children, she noted that it was the little boys who played with them.

The Aka Pygmies

The most gripping of the modern studies is one carried out by American anthropologist Barry Hewlett during the 1980s.[18] For more than 15 years, Hewlett has been studying a tribe of hunter-gatherer-traders suitably untouched by Western civilisation, who live in a tropical forest region on the northern border of the African Congo. This tribe, the Aka Pygmies, have proved to be the 'stars' of paternal involvement.

Aka fathers do more infant caregiving than fathers in any other known society. On average, they hold, or are *within arm's reach of*, their infants 47 per cent of the time. They often take the child along when they go drinking palm wine and may hold it close to their bodies for up to two hours during daylight hours. At night if the baby cannot be comforted by nursing, they are often the ones to settle it. Aka fathers clean their babies and wipe their bottoms, and if the mothers aren't around and the infants want to nurse, will offer their own nipples for a soothing, if temporary, suck. Could this provide an answer to the vexed question: 'Why do men have nipples'!

Aka babies seek out their fathers. They crawl or lean towards them and ask to be picked up, and their fathers seem to enjoy looking after them. Aka women preparing the evening meal do not carry babies on their hips as women do in other similar societies. Nor do they pass them over to older siblings, although these are available, because, most often, the fathers hold them. The fathers take charge even when mothers have their hands free and are sitting idle or are chatting, and unlike fathers in Western society, Aka fathers do not say they prefer toddlers or older children.

> ❛ Normally the baby was asleep when I left in the morning and normally sleeping when I got home at night and maybe I would see it for an hour or so. For the first nine months I wasn't really inconvenienced. I don't really like small babies very much. ❜
> *Alan, 34, father of two*

While Western children overwhelmingly see their mothers as the family's nurturers, this is not so among the Aka. In fact, Aka mothers are seen as more punitive probably because food-preparation is their responsibility and they spend a lot of time trying to stop their children from stealing it. Aka mothers weren't seen to supply more nurturing or emotional support than fathers, nor were Aka fathers perceived as more playful than mothers. In contrast researchers were struck by the *absence* of playful interactions between Aka father and child. In the Aka community, the most playful relatives are aunts.

Since it seems unlikely that Aka fathers are biologically programmed to behave differently from other fathers, and do not seem to be culturally conditioned in any ideological sense to be particularly nurturing, Hewlett has been keen to establish why their level of infant-caretaking is so high. It all seems connected to the Aka's main subsistence activity, the net hunt. A year-long co-operative family venture to trap small animals, the Akla net hunt is unique. No other tribe has ever been shown to have a family-based, year-long hunting activity. Even the Aka babies are taken along, for there are few older women left in the camp to care for them. The older women are either out hunting as well or, as Aka fertility is high, are still nursing babies of their own.

The absence of older women willing, or able, to take on responsibility may be one reason why Aka fathers are so involved. Another reason may be the ratio of infant body-weight to adult, which is comparatively high and means mothers alone cannot carry the babies over the long distances involved in the net hunt. But Hewlett believes the key lies in the exceptional way in which Aka men and women's lives are intertwined – both in the camp, and out of it, when hunting. Neither the hunting nor the childcare is seen as an activity dominated by either sex. The hallmark of Aka life is co-operation. Hewlett also suggests that the more infant caretaking the Aka father does, the more attached to his child he becomes, and the more caretaking he wants to do. Like a Western mother, the Aka father responds to the baby's initiatives, his lack of playfulness reflecting the extent of his intimate involvement. For however enjoyable and particularly physical play may be, it is essentially imposed by the parent on the child. Unlike the average Western father, the Aka father doesn't impose. More like a Western mother, he takes his cues from his baby.

> ❛ Future child development studies should also attempt systematic observations throughout the night … Among the Aka, it was not uncommon to wake up in the night and hear a father singing softly to his fussing infant. ❜
>
> *Barry Hewlett*, Intimate Fathers

A wider view

Describing behaviour in 'primitive' societies is always risky. Too often the assumption is made that because individuals live in rustic surroundings, their behaviour is essentially 'natural'. This idea has been particularly potent as far as mothering is concerned. The image of native women carrying their infants continually and breastfeeding them for years is often presented as the bench-mark for natural or real mothering. But in an important article written in 1977, anthropologist Robert LeVine challenged this view. Working among the Gusii in Kenya, where infant mortality was high and toddler accidents, such as falling in the fire, depressingly common, LeVine became aware of the fact that the constant carrying of infants and young children, while not necessarily good for their cognitive or physical development, often preserved their lives.[19] LeVine began to see childrearing practice everywhere as 'cultural adaptation'. In a non-industrial community, where the terrain was dangerous and sanitation poor, where there was no satisfactory alternative to breast-milk and no available contraception, the behaviour of the Gusii made perfect sense. Long-term breastfeeding helped delay the return of ovulation in the mother, and also meant an infant was kept close to the only available safe source of food and liquid. And restricting a young child's mobility, through continual carrying, and responding quickly to its cries, kept it from a host of dangers.

The behaviour of Aka fathers can also be seen very much as cultural adaptation. It is not better, or worse, or more natural than the behaviour of fathers in industrial societies, or in other pre-industrial cultures. The Aka father is responding, no less than British or American fathers, to the *environment* in which he finds himself and, like them, is probably largely unaware of the fact.

❦ The other evening I was actually home in time to read Luke a story and we went to the shelf beside the bed to get a book for him to read and there was a complete range of books that I had never seen before. I suddenly realised that in the last two years, while I've been working so hard, Beth had been out there buying these books and I had absolutely no part. I suppose it's all right and proper but I was a bit miffed that somewhere along the line I must have missed out. ❧

Alan, 34, father of two

Although the amount (and quality) of time fathers spend with their children is specific to each individual family, anthropologists have now been able to define cultural and environmental factors which predispose towards intimate involvement. As already seen among the Aka, high fertility rates and a communal life-style are important. Near equal contribution to diet by males and females also helps, as does an egalitarian ideology, the involvement of women in activities other than childcare, and low levels of warfare locally. Where young families do not move away and grandmothers and other kin are available to help with the children, fathers' involvement is lower. By contrast, fathers in 'new towns' may often be substantially involved, because their input is more necessary.

Paternal caretaking also tends to be higher in communities with relatively little violence against women and children, and where men's daily labour is carried out close to or with their families. For this reason, where large-animal hunting is the main subsistence activity, paternal involvement is often low, even if women do a lot of the hunting. Where men have more than one wife they tend to be less involved in their children's lives, presumably because they have to divide their time between different families. None of these factors on its own seems to make the difference, but taken together they are significant.[20]

What does all this mean for fathers in the West today? Environmentally, they would seem in some respects to be at the low end of the involvement scale. Through divorce and remarriage, or the equivalent, they often have more than one wife (serial monogamy is becoming the norm), and their daily labour is usually carried out at a distance from their children, while in some districts, they live among violence. On the other hand, egalitarian ideology is spreading; women are valued as breadwinners and their contribution in the public sphere is more widely recognised. Many nations have been at peace for some considerable time, and levels of violence in many communities are low. Contrary to popular belief many young families still live close to at least one set of grandparents, but increasingly grandmothers themselves are employed, and are not so freely available to help care for grandchildren.

To sum up, as far as the *potential* for fathering behaviour is concerned, the message from the 'natural world' is that anything is possible. Whether we consider the birds in the air or the beasts in the field, or focus on the behaviour of human or non-human primates, what seems 'natural' is diversity and flexibility, and constant adaptation to circumstance. Nevertheless, although a cross-cultural review of fathering behaviours reveals that individual men (or groups of men) can be as intimately involved in infant-care as any woman, the overwhelming picture is one of considerably less involvement by males than females, particularly during their children's infancy and early years. Is this, people are bound to ask, entirely due to environmental factors, or are there underlying biological imperatives which we would be crazy to ignore?

❝ I don't believe in all this stuff about girls and boys being the same. My boy, he loves building things, but you give the girls Lego and they just push the Lego people round the board. ❞
Martin, father of four, two families

Doing what comes naturally

In the mid-19th century, an important discovery was made: innate philoprogenitiveness, a love of having children, could be easily established. All you had to do was examine a woman's skull, where you would find a certain lump. A large lump meant she liked children, a small one meant she didn't. There was, however, no point looking for these lumps on men's heads – there wouldn't be any!

Hunt-the-biological-origin has always been a popular pastime which has been given an enormous boost recently by advances in genetics. Every year or so brings a fresh claim. For example, gay men have 'different' brains, depression is a purely physical condition, aggression is 'hormonal', and criminality is in the 'genes'. To prove such a thing is the dream of many a scientist, for it represents the pot of gold at the end of the test-tube. And because these theories seem to offer simple and guilt-free solutions, they are very seductive. But once the hype is over, and the scientific world settles down to examine the evidence, the result is always disappointing. For to demonstrate a 'human universal' or 'biological imperative' is desperately difficult. Even establishing that something as simple as the human smile is inborn rather than learned, and that it signifies happiness or pleasure in all human societies, has been hard to demonstrate, although it has finally been proven.

By the 1970s with women's liberation and peace movements on the increase, public opinion concerning parenting behaviours changed. Now it was widely held that the only thing that separated mothers from fathers – give or take their genital structures – was social conditioning. A new crusade began. Family professionals, believing that paternal and maternal behaviours would soon be indistinguishable, started to use the word 'parent' instead of 'mother' or 'father'. And parents all over the Western world denied their young sons guns, and forced Lego on their daughters.

Twenty years on, the pendulum is swinging back again. It is once again fashionable to declare that men and women are different (different but equal, of course). Okay, so the 'philoprogenitive lump' didn't work out, but if the scientists had looked inside the cranium rather than on it, they'd have found what *really* distinguishes women from men, mothers from fathers: the size of the hypothalamus, which governs some of the sex differences in hormonal function. And we don't need the biologists to tell us that boys are different from girls. We can swear on our copy of *Non-Sexist Childrearing* that we brought our sons and daughters up the same, and what happened? The boys fashioned deadly weapons from their sisters' Lego; and the girls were found on bended knee in Woolworths, in front of the Sindy counter. Family professionals, too, have grown concerned in case children become confused about their gender identities. In Sweden – a country which is often called the 'laboratory of Europe' – some nurseries have now abandoned gender-neutral play-space, providing instead 'pink' rooms for girls, and starker environments for boys.

Sex and gender

Pace all this, however, although hundreds and hundreds of experiments, surveys and other types of studies have been undertaken, almost nothing definite in terms of sex differences has shown up – so far. It seems incredible (and who knows what will be discovered in the future?), but as of now, differences between women and men in terms of perception, brain function, and intellectual and nurturing capacity seem to be shatteringly small. And, incidentally, the size of the hypothalamus would seem about as relevant as the size of an Easter egg.[21]

❛ Masculinity is a cultural concept. We like to think of masculinity as natural, and there are slight measurable differences between the statistically average boy and the statistically average girl, but the differences are not enough to base a gender on. ❜

Frank Pittman, Man Enough

It seems that even sex differences that were once assumed proven in these areas may not be so. Let us take just one example. Boys' visual-spatial ability, which covers among other things geometry and map-reading, has been shown to be superior to girls' in a battery of tests. But it now seems that, as girls' upbringing becomes less restricted, even this difference is diminishing, and researchers are showing that in infancy both sexes perform with equal competence. Only later do differences develop. Furthermore, among the Inuit, where girls have traditionally been allowed considerable autonomy and the language is rich in words describing geometrical-spatial relationships, no sex-related differences in spatial abilities have been recorded at any age.[22]

The role of testosterone which is regularly credited with inducing aggressive (non-nurturing) behaviour in males also seems open to question. Men taking high dose testosterone pills in male-contraceptive trials do not become more aggressive. And after football matches, when fans on the winning side show raised testosterone levels, the losing fans (whose testosterone levels do not rise) are the more likely to go on the rampage.

So if no clear biological imperative can be discerned, how do we explain the guns and the Sindy dolls? The latest theory is interaction between environment and biologically based tendencies. The idea is, that although gender behaviour is flexible and can be moulded by lots of things, boys and girls are predisposed to behave differently. Boys, for example, may have a natural predisposition to be more visually-spatially skilled than their sisters, and the Inuit environment, which requires close observation of a subtle landscape, may stimulate atypically subtle development in girls.

When something as simple as different hair colour can elicit different parental response, and when even dressed-alike identical twins often turn out to be quite dissimilar (since each is part of the other's environment), it is no wonder boys and girls often develop different interests. Simply by looking around, they see that life is organised for men and women (and mothers and fathers) in utterly different ways. And this is just passive observation. The famous Baby X Revisited experiment showed how adults treated a baby very differently, depending on whether they believed it to be a boy or a girl, while the Eye of the Beholder study showed that they also interpreted boy–girl behaviour differently, regarding an infant's distress to be fear (if they thought the child a girl) and anger (if they thought it a boy).[23]

❛ All the great mathematicians have been men. I have three children and one of them, a girl, she's very bright mathematically and of course it makes me wonder. I'm a statistician, and I know we will never be able to tell whether women can do the same things as men, or men the same things as women until we have an equal society – and until we've been running it for a thousand years. ❜

Wally, aged 38, father of three

Nor are children passive recipients of sex-role stereotyping. They work away at it themselves, aware from about the age of two to which gender group they belong. One study of pre-schoolers watching television tracked their eye movements, finding the children's gaze lingering longer on characters of the same sex. Were they, it was wondered, actively studying behaviour which they considered to be right for them?

So much for environment. What about physiological factors? It would be strange if biology did *not* nudge women more than men towards involvement in parenting, but if it does, no one has yet shown how. In one very interesting study, tapes of crying babies were played to boys and girls aged eight and 14 years, and their reactions were recorded. Their social responses – whether they smiled or frowned – were different, with the girls on the whole showing greater concern. But when their *concealed* responses – their heart-rates, blood pressure and so on – were measured, there were no differences. Both sexes reacted with the same degree of disquiet.[24] And while adult males very often believe themselves to be relatively incompetent with infants, in fact they aren't. Given the chance to interact independently with their newborns, new fathers are just as deft (or clumsy) as new mothers. They are no less responsive to their infants, no less anxious about leaving them with strangers and, if blindfolded, are as able to recognise their babies by the shape of their little hands. Like women, men automatically pitch their voices higher to speak to babies, and even though men in our culture don't chat away to them as much as women do, they are just as tender and as strongly focused.[25]

In all the studies on parenting potential in the West, only one clear physical response difference has emerged: women's pupils tend to dilate when they look at little babies whether or not they are themselves mothers. Men's pupils don't, *until* they become fathers, and then they do. Again, one hesitates to ascribe this response (or lack of it) to 'biology': the dilation of pupils indicates interest, and interest in babies is, as we know, actively fostered in women in our society and suppressed in men.

6 One of the girls was holding her four-month-old baby boy ...
My friends began to chat up the single girls. I joined in, but
found myself more interested in the baby. The nearest I got to
pick-up lines were, 'Does he sleep through the night? Is he
having trouble teething? ...' All this with an idiotic and beatific
grin right across my face. 9

Nigel Planer, A Good Enough Dad

Honey, I raised the kids!

What happens in parenting behaviour as children grow older? Here
there have seemed to be some clear sex differences. Western fathers
have consistently been shown to be less tolerant, chatty, responsive
and expressive than mothers, and more involved in play than
caretaking. They also prefer outdoor activities and physical play to
'intellectual' play-activities (especially with sons), and are rated by
their children as the less-preferred parent.[26] For a long time it was
assumed that this resulted from some kind of reduced parenting
sensitivity on the part of males, and researchers who might have
wanted to think otherwise and who looked into the behaviour of
non-traditional fathers during the 1970s and early 80s to show that
dads could be just as good as mums, were disappointed.

They found that although non-traditional fathers were spending
almost three times as much time with their children as traditional
fathers (averaging 2.25 hours active childcare per working day)
there was little corresponding change in their style of behaviour.
Non-traditional fathers did not behave towards their children very
differently from traditional fathers. Did this mean (the researchers
wondered) that there is a core aspect to fathering which simply does
not change, however much exposure men have to children? And
then further observations were made. Certainly, the non-traditional
fathers were around the house more than traditional fathers and
spent a lot more time interacting directly with their children, but
they were not more likely to have *responsibility* for them. Even in non-
traditional families with a good deal of shared caregiving, it was still
the mothers who were in charge. But perhaps most interesting was
the discovery that some non-traditional fathers might actually be
spending less time with their children *relative to their wives,* than
traditional fathers. One study showed that where fathers spent a
great deal of time alone with their daughters, the girls' mothers
spent *twice* as much interactive time with them compared to other
girls' mothers.[27]

Another group of fathers began to attract researchers' attention. 'Primary caregiver fathers' (men who are their children's main caretakers) spend a minimum of 25 hours per week in *sole charge* of their young children. They can can be distinguished from both traditional and non-traditional fathers in two ways: they are the parent with responsibility, and much of the time they spend with their children, they spend alone.

Who are these men? Have they taken anti-assertiveness training courses, or spent hours in New Age workshops, searching for their Inner Child? No. Most primary caregiver fathers are neither middle-class, middle-aged, nor are they New Age men, and nor do they have an unusually high ideological commitment to the idea of nurturing fatherhood. They come from all walks of life, and have found themselves in the position of 'primary parent' for a variety of reasons. When compared with their children's mothers, many primary caregiver fathers take a relaxed attitude to housework, tidy clothes and clean faces. But what interests researchers is that, in terms of the way they relate to their children, they are almost indistinguishable from mothers. Although in our culture they often still adopt a more playful style, they also exhibit as much patience, sensitivity, baby talk and public kissing of their young children as women who are primary parents. After a time, many primary caregiver fathers even cease to favour outdoor, over indoor, activities. And though they still initiate rough and tumble, they also go in more readily for other kinds of more intellectual play and stimulation.[28]

> ❛ I help Sam with his homework, talk about what's bothering him, teach him carpentry, fix his bike. He helps me cook, or does the dishes. As my role of important parent develops, it's interesting to observe changes in myself. I'm more genuinely affectionate with the children when they've been injured – before, I'd cuddle them, but in a dispassionate frame of mind – and now when they are happy and excited, I sometimes find that I get excited too. ❜
>
> *Rick, 35, father of two*

Very high levels of involvement and responsibility change men's experience of parenting. In the main, such fathers develop stronger-than-average attachments to their young children. Quite simply, they love them more. As parents, they are more confident and more effective, and while they are not necessarily happier, they are more satisfied. Although father and child may clash more often, these fathers feel closer to their children, are more attentive to their development, and feel they are important to them.[29] The benefits to men of involved fathering may even extend to their physical health. One reason women outlive men is that they pay attention to physical symptoms in themselves and seek medical attention, and it is interesting to note that men who are involved fathers also seem to report physical symptoms as they occur,[30] *and* that they are less subject than other men to physical illness.

Getting to grips with the situation

It is clear that fathers who are their children's main carers cross the divide between mothering and fathering, and from this we can learn something important. Parenting styles are determined not by gender but by situation, and differences arise not through the amount of time fathers spend with their children, but the amount of time they spend *alone* with them and the degree of responsibility they hold for their daily routine. This realisation has alerted researchers to the possibility that many of the so-called gender differences between mothers and fathers may be situational in origin. It has been noticed that fathers are more likely to wipe their toddlers' faces in playgrounds or sports' centres, where they feel they're in charge, than in supermarkets or restaurants, which they may see as female territory.[31]

As for fathers' tendency to be less verbal with their children than mothers, researcher Sheila Rossan points out that human beings learn to talk to each other one-to-one, and that few fathers spend much time one-to-one with their offspring.[32] Charlie Lewis suggests that UK and US fathers' famous playfulness may have less to do with either gender or cultural factors than with the fact that they mostly meet up with their children in recreation time. It's also possible that fathers who are away from their children so much that they really don't know them very well get the most positive response if they tickle their tummies or throw them up in the air. The observation that fathers are more likely to watch television with their children than to build Lego models or read to them, has led some people to conclude that fathers aren't interested in more active involvement. However, by the time many fathers get home, they – and their children – may be so tired that to cuddle up on the sofa and watch television together is the most appropriate thing to do.

❛ Men and women have accepted the aphorism that 'biology is destiny' too literally. The advantages a woman may gain from her specialised reproductive system do not necessarily limit a man's nurturant and relational abilities any more than a man's larger size and musculature limit a female's potential assertiveness. ❜

Arthur and Libby Colman, The Father

Although gender-based differences in parenting capabilities are hard to demonstrate, what has been shown – and shown over and over again with almost painful ease – is how sex-role *conditioning* drives a wedge between men and their parenting instincts. In one fascinating study, children were asked to pose for photographs with a baby. First they were to be themselves, and then act as a parent. When posing as themselves, the children stood further from the infant than when posing as a mummy. And when they posed as a daddy, they stood further away again. 'Social roles,' remarks Charlie Lewis, 'are learned early.'[33] Every parent knows that little boys under the age of three explore the feeding, bathing and nursing of babies with a vigour equal to that of girls. And every primary school teacher knows that, by the time those same boys have reached the age of eight, taboos not just on this but on any kind of girlish behaviour are firmly in place. Boys' nurturing has been re-routed to be lavished on pets and, for a while still, the occasional teddy.

In the playground, while girls will run in and out of the boys' games, boys almost never play with the girls, unless it is to spoil their activity.[34] And while girls today are queuing up to join the Scouts, we do not find many boys on the waiting list for Brownies. Given that, in our culture, childrearing is seen as the ultimate girls' game, we should not be surprised when adult males fail to join in. We should, rather, marvel that so many do, and consider whether this alone may not be evidence of a truly powerful instinctual drive.

It is only a few decades since women were widely believed to be sexually passionless, intellectually weak and emotionally flimsy by nature. Today such ideas would be treated with derision. Bearing this in mind, perhaps it is not unreasonable to suggest that before too long we will discard the beliefs currently so widely held that men are by nature less sensitive than mothers to their children and less deeply attached to them. Or that men should defer to women in parenting matters, on grounds of their biological fitness for the task.

❛ It seems rather stupid now but you don't, or certainly I didn't, expect the strength of the physical bonding. It was very intense. It's only a few weeks ago since we had to abandon him for the day – for the first time in nine months we couldn't 'box and cox' our work. And our friends said 'you just go off and we'll look after Freddie', and I handed him over and it was an ache, a physical ache. ❜

Oliver, 39, father of one

Future shock?

In a British newspaper article in 1995, a well-known agony aunt suggested that for fathers to see their children born was not 'natural'. As evidence, she cited the fact that, 'In most primitive cultures, women giving birth are accompanied not by tribesmen husbands mopping their brows, but tribeswomen, who pride themselves on female care.'[35] It is true that in most 'primitive' cultures, as well as in our own as recently as a decade or two ago, the miracle of reproducing the human species has been regarded principally as a female miracle. It is also true that men created reserved domains for themselves which were made inaccessible to women through some kind of genuinely or falsely sophisticated apprenticeship.[36] Yet in today's world most male domains have opened to the opposite sex. We are hard put to cite a single activity specific to men and totally unknown to women. Sindy now plays football and women have been declared by the medical profession, and after exhaustive tests, to be as well-suited biologically as men to carry out all military roles.

Now women's reserved domain – pregnancy and birth – is being opened up to men, for science is blunting biological imperatives. It used to be said that all any reasonable child could expect was that its father be present at its conception. Mothers, however, could be expected to be present at the birth. This is no longer so. Both men and women can be separated from their seed. While neither egg nor sperm donor, are usually considered to be the parents of babies born from their biological donations, the law is becoming increasingly confused. Recently, an American surrogate who had carried to term an embryo grown from a commissioning-couple's ovum and sperm, was ruled not to be the mother of the baby boy to whom she had given birth (and for whom, in the words of one commentator, 'her breasts had filled with milk'). The donors were confirmed as the child's true parents.[37]

Today definitions of motherhood are no less problematic than definitions of fatherhood and the significance of biological, over social, fatherhood is growing. Thanks to DNA testing, a man need be no less certain than a woman that the child he is raising is his own, and both men and women can raise the products of a laboratory conception. In the USA it is estimated that 5,000 or 6,000 male homosexual couples have already become parents through private adoptions, or by commissioning babies from surrogate mothers.[38] This undermines fatherhood's last stand in terms of exclusivity – the notion of fatherhood as a mainstay of heterosexuality – and it also undermines the widely believed essential nature of motherhood.

> 6 Week twenty – the halfway point in the pregnancy ... Claire had explained why she felt it was OK to have a baby for two gay men. She felt that because there was no woman in the picture she would not be jealous ... We met a number of other gay (male) doctor couples like us; two who both had infants by artificial insemination ... When I saw them holding their babies, I wanted to cry. I didn't dare hold the children for fear of breaking down. More and more couples like us seem to be succeeding in building families. 9
>
> *Kenneth Morgen,* Getting Simon

It seems there is more to come. Within the next few years effective male hormonal contraception will be widely available, contraception which will protect men from women who might 'kidnap' their sperm, ensuring that no man need be a father without his knowledge. While in the realm of what sounds like Schwarznegger-inspired Hollywood fantasy, scientists speak of the 1984 Kinsey Institute symposium where there was discussion of the technology said to be available to allow a man to incubate a baby, and no shortage of male volunteers anxious to be pregnant.[39] That is as may be. For now all we can be sure of is that human beings are mastering reproduction in a way which has hitherto been unimaginable.

Today, as part of routine screening, fathers can see the living image of their child on a television screen within a few weeks of conception This is fundamentally altering their experience of pregnancy, and drawing them into that previously exclusive female miracle long before they do – or don't – enter the labour ward. This is not to suggest that the experiences of pregnancy and birth are the same for women and men. Of course they are different. But what we are slowly beginning to realise is that they are not as different as once was thought and that the very real differences don't have to govern the rest of the parenting experience.

What is clear is that the 'nature' of fathering is not fixed and inevitable, but characterised by flexibility and adaptation. Fathers are not 'cads' or 'dads'. They are both and neither – their behaviour shaped less by biologically determined rules than by socially constructed roles. And as journalist Barbara Ehrenreich has written, ' "Roles", after all, are not fit aspirations for adults, but the repetitive performances of people who have forgotten that it is only other people who write the scripts.'[40]

6 When you actually see this physical child being born it's just an amazing experience, and it changes your life for ever. I remember seeing a tuft of his hair, the first thing I ever saw of him and then quickly he followed out. And afterwards, going back to the ward, I remember pushing him along – he was on one of these trolleys with a little fish tank – and I remember thinking, 'Why, surely all these people will be looking in and marvelling at this baby!' But they were just carrying on with their work, and I was just another father, pushing his child. 9

Alan, 34, father of two

Chapter 4

Becoming a Father: lessons in exclusion

Why, when fathers' potential ability to parent is so similar to mothers' is their performance so startlingly different? It's not just that boys are brought up to feather the nest and girls to sit in it. In a thousand practical ways, which some say amount to a 'cultural conspiracy against fatherhood', Western males in the process of becoming fathers are forced in a direction that ensures they will be as peripheral to their children's lives as females will be central.'[1]

Fertility

Although, over many centuries, men have made dramatic attempts to control women's fertility, via their sexuality, in order to ensure their own blood line (locking them in chastity belts, for example, or cutting off their clitorises) there is also a sense in which, paradoxically, male fertility has been considered relatively unimportant.

 6 For some men it is apparently insufficient that they can have sexual intercourse; their neurotic need for definite proof (*of their virility*) can only be satisfied by having a child. 9
Reider (1948) quoted in Robinson, Teenage Fathers

In the Christian tradition since Roman times, becoming a father has meant becoming a social father more than a biological father. A father has not usually been defined as someone who could *prove* paternity – for who could? – but as someone willing or compelled to *acknowledge* paternity by raising the child, or by being married to its mother. And while females have been defined in terms of their reproductive capacity, it appears that males have been defined in terms of their sexual function. Today this can be clearly seen in the way doctors approach children born intersex, that is to say, neither obviously male nor female. To create a girl, doctors remove any penile tissue, even though this means that the 'girl' so created cannot experience orgasm; and to create a boy, they remove the ovaries but keep the penis provided it is large enough to function – even if the ejaculate will be infertile.[2]

There have been many spin-offs from our perception of men's fertility as 'off the agenda', not least that their contribution to conception is seen as somehow less important. There has been very little research into causes of and treatment for male infertility even though it is no less often the cause of a couple's joint infertility. The male role in miscarriage and birth defects has also been seriously under-investigated. It wasn't until 1995 that Australian researchers traced the cause of a high level of miscarriage among the families of carpenters and decorators to the regular exposure of the babies' *fathers* to oil-based paints and strong glue. For most men, however, the primary impact of society's lack of interest in their reproductive capacity has been on their diminishing control over conception. It is well known that men have responded overwhelmingly to vasectomy services and that they would be very willing to use hormonal contraception, should it be made available. Whenever advertisements for medical trials for male contraceptives appear, hundreds of men put themselves forward, and once the trial is over, 95 per cent ask the doctors to continue providing them with the drugs. Yet although men are actually better suited to hormonal contraception than women (they do not have a monthly cycle to complicate matters) no male contraceptive pill, patch, implant or injection is yet available and the contraceptive options currently available to men are, to quote a leading WHO contraceptive specialist, 'pitiful'.[3]

> 6 The people I talk to … it's not on the agenda … It's my wife who's had the miscarriage physically, so it shouldn't affect me … I feel incompetent, as though I'm responsible for what happened, and that if I'd been more capable, more caring, more something or other, that it wouldn't have happened. At best I think in terms of my genes – if they had been better genes, then my wife wouldn't have had a miscarriage. 9
>
> *Paul,* The Locker Room

Men also end up knowing far less than women about fertility. Family planning services are designed with women in mind, and make no particular attempts to engage and educate men. And while women's use of contraception is regularly surveyed, no national surveys of heterosexual men's contraceptive use, or even of their contraceptive preferences, exist at all.[4] On one level it makes sense to focus on women who are, after all, the ones normally left holding the baby, but while this not only enables women to control their own fertility (which is quite right and proper) it also allows them to control *men's* fertility. Although few women actually use men as mobile sperm-banks, the fact that women can lie about their use of contraception makes 'sperm-napping' and non-consensual pregancy simple. This easy opportunity both wrests power from males and absolves them of responsibility. We are now a far cry from the time, a mere 30 years ago, when whether or not a man was 'selfish' (willing to practise withdrawal or wear a condom) largely determined whether his partner would bear a child. If anyone is now the passive partner in conception, it is the father.

> ❛ *Small vampire, gorger at your mother's teat,*
> *Dubious claim I didn't know I'd staked,*
> *Like boomerangs your cries reverberate*
> *Till roused, half-blind, I bear you to be slaked,*
> *Your step-and-fetch-it pimp ...*
> *Your fingers writhe: inane anemones*
> *A decent ocean ought to starve. Instead*
> *I hold you, I make tries at a caress.*
> *You should not be. I cannot wish you dead.* ❜
>   *X. J. Kennedy,* Last Child (for Daniel)

Painting by numbers

Nowhere is our lack of interest in men's fertility more apparent than in the virtual absence of readily available statistics on men as fathers. Ask how many women become mothers, how many children they have or how old they are when their first is born and the answers are on your fax almost before you've put down the phone. But to draw a demographic portrait of fathers requires patience and dedication. You get one set of figures from here and another from there. Many simply aren't available, and you have to generalise from small samples or look to countries such as Denmark, which have their fatherhood figures lined up and ready to go.

So who are Britain's fathers? In 1993 some 670,000 men became fathers in England and Wales. The youngest was only 13 years old (in 1992 the youngest father was aged 12!), while the oldest clocked in at 75-plus, and there were 53 in this last category.[5] In the light of such eccentricities, it is perhaps a relief to learn that a majority of the fathers – 56 per cent – were aged between 25 and 34 years. Two out of three of these men were married, but three-quarters of the unmarried fathers registered the births of their babies jointly with the mothers, with 55 per cent living at the same address. The remaining 50,637 fathers, some 8 per cent of the total, were fathers unknown. On these infants' birth certificates beside the mother's name, there was a blank. That these unnamed fathers were important figures in their children's lives is clear from another, sadder, set of statistics, which accompany the first: the statistics on stillbirths. In that same year, 3,855 babies were born dead in Britain, or died within the first week of birth. Where fathers were named on the birth certificates, only 5.5 out of every thousand babies died. But among the group with no named fathers, almost eight out of every thousand did not survive.

❛ All the time I'm willing things to him, I'm saying to him, 'Come on Sean – you can do it'. And after all the operations he has been covered with tubes and everything else and you could hardly see him, there's been blood everywhere, but I've always found somewhere to kiss him – on the head, or on the hands or somewhere – saying to him, 'We love you, you'll be all right', and all that, like. But there is no answer to it, but there have been a lot of tears for him, fighting for him. ❜

Michael, 36, father of two

What else do we know about men as fathers? Currently, some 4.3 million British men (that's a quarter of all males aged 20–59) are living with dependent children in two-parent families, with a further 1.2 million in more complex family structures (perhaps including a grandparent). Since black Britons make up only 5.3 per cent of the population of England and Wales the vast majority of Britain's fathers – 93 per cent – are white; 4.4 per cent derive from India, Pakistan and Bangladesh; and only 1.4 per cent from Africa and the Caribbean. Among this last group, approximately 50 per cent are of Jamaican origin.[6]

A few more figures

Men start their families later than women: on average, in Britain, at around the age of 28.[7] American statistics show Afro-American males becoming fathers younger than white males, and it is not unreasonable to anticipate the same pattern in the UK.

There are, however, far fewer teenage fathers than teenage mothers, of whatever race: only one in three fathers of a baby born to a teenage mother is actually a teenager himself.[8] Although men are mostly older than women when they first become parents, they go on having children for longer. It isn't until men are aged 49 that their fertility rates drop as low as those of women in their early 40s.[9] Parenthood is more common among women than men. Most women (more than four out of five) will have had at least one child by the time their childbearing years are over. But Danish statistics reveal that no more than three out of four men eventually become fathers.[10] Neither homosexuality nor (allegedly) plummeting sperm counts seem to be the cause: physiological infertility affects fewer than 8 per cent of men, and recent surveys suggest that fewer than one male in 20 is exclusively homosexual.

> ❛ Sam bought diapers, receiving blankets, a hooded bath towel. Looking at the tiny articles of clothing spread out in front of me brought back that feeling of unreality. Were we really going to have a baby? We're too old. We're gay. We don't even have a room for him yet … But even as I thought the words, I knew the doubts were evaporating. ❜
> *Kenneth Morgen,* Getting Simon

Every year, around 6,000 infertile British men agree to their wives' being inseminated with other men's sperm and around 1,500 become fathers after such inseminations. Despite images of medical students queuing up eagerly with test-tubes and copies of *Mayfair*, men are actually no keener to donate sperm than women are to donate eggs. In fact, in Britain there are currently 2,239 registered sperm donors to 2,289 registered egg donors. No more than 10 children are conceived from any one donor's offerings.[11]

Although men of all social classes are less likely than women to become parents, they tend to have more children once they do: 1.8 each in Denmark, as against women's 1.73. All over the world, it is generally the poorest and least well-educated women who have the largest families. But the opposite may be true of men. In Denmark again, it is better-off and better-educated males who are more likely to become fathers, and to have the largest number of children.[12] And certainly in Britain too, middle-class males are more likely than working-class males to remarry or cohabit after divorce.

Conception

The process of conception is fraught with ambivalence. Just as the most longed-for pregnancy is often accompanied by feelings of fear and dismay, so few conceptions between consenting adults are truly accidental. 'Forgetting' to use contraception on a possibly fertile day, or deciding to stop taking the Pill 'for health reasons' may mask a desire to check out one's fertility or to have a child, even if the resulting pregnancy is ultimately terminated with relief. Repeatedly, throughout pregnancy, a woman confronts ambivalence and exercises active choice; firstly, through becoming pregnant, and secondly, in continuing with a pregnancy once it has been confirmed. By the time a child is actually born, most Western mothers have made a conscious committment, time and time again, to their baby. If they haven't, they've had an abortion. British women have one in five of their pregnancies terminated.

6 My first wife didn't want to have children. I knew that when I married her. Never waivered. Good on her – people like that shouldn't have them. But I often thought about it from the late 20s-type age, I was always prepared if it came along to deal with it, to enjoy it. It was always at the back of my mind, 'if she got pregnant' … I mean, she was pregnant before we got married, we had a termination when we were 17 or18 and I told her then – I would have been prepared to have the child. 9

Elliot, 38, father of one

Men, as research shows, rarely make a conscious decision to become fathers. A minority joyfully, or grimly, 'try' for a baby but Dr Charlie Lewis, who carried out in-depth interviews with 100 new fathers in 1984, discovered that almost half had never discussed the subject seriously with their wives. Contraception was often abandoned by the woman without joint discussion. Even among men who felt they had agreed to have a child, the pressure was usually seen as coming from the woman.[13] Most of Lewis's fathers, like fathers everywhere, had drifted into procreation. Nor, during the pregnancy, were they required or permitted to make choices. Some of Lewis's fathers expressed the view that any decision to abort, or not to abort, was up to their wives, which was lucky, given that this was their only option. In Britain, the right to abort is the mother's alone, whether she is married or not. But even so, the degree to which fathers' views are discounted in abortion is staggering. In Britain, no information about fathers' attitudes to their partners' abortions has been gathered and at no time are doctors or healthcare professionals obliged to interview fathers. To do so would, in fact, be seen as a 'breach of patient confidentiality.'

Given that men's control over paternity is so limited, are many babies born to men who, had they been women, would never have got pregnant, or would have terminated the pregnancy? Like Charlie Lewis, Bristol researcher Brian Jackson interviewed 100 married or cohabiting fathers-to-be in the early 1980s, and found that one in five were extremely hostile to their partner's pregnancy.[14] Jackson called the unwilling fathers in his sample 'refusers', and it is interesting to note that the one in five refusers mirrors the one in five pregnancies that women have terminated.

> 6 Kids are just a nuisance. If I was to marry again, I wouldn't have any. My old lady wanted to have them. Only trouble was, that made me a father. To start with, they killed our sex life. Then they made so much noise. And they're stupid. It's not their fault, but you've got to admit their conversation *is* boring. And they cost money. Add that lot together and what does a father get out of it? Damn all. 9
>
> *Father quoted in Jackson,* Fatherhood

At least these refusers were living with their pregnant partners. Add to these men the 7 per cent who, at the time of their baby's birth are not living with the mother, plus the 8 per cent who are not only living somewhere else, but whose names don't even appear on the birth certificates (most of these fathers, though not all, one can assume to be minimally committed to fatherhood) and it seems that almost one pregnancy in three may involve a man who is, to a quite significant degree, a reluctant parent. This is not to say that some unwilling fathers don't eventually come round. Many do. 'I wonder now what all the fuss was about,' said one of our interviewees, who had been dragged kicking and screaming into fatherhood. However, others do not. A man's disinclination to have a particular child is a strong predictor of his behaviour afterwards, and two years on Jackson found many of his refusers with a neutral or negative attitude to their toddlers, and separation from the mothers on the cards.

Even when pregnancy is welcomed, however, it is plain that an individual who is not obliged to take an active decision to become a parent (as few men are) is positioned right from the beginning as a bystander – the sleeping partner in the venture of parenthood.

Fatherhood and masculinity

This does not mean that men do not desire children. Among Lewis's sample, 76 per cent of the men had assumed they would become parents, 44 per cent knew exactly how many children they wanted, and several had concealed a (strong) wish for children from their wives on the grounds that it would be wrong to put pressure on them: '[she's] got total responsibillity,' said one, 'I'm here to sort of help.'

Men's desire for children is often hidden from themselves. A 'real' man can declare, 'I want a son', but is not often heard to say, 'I'd like a baby'. He must rely upon his partner for the expression of these unmanly words and perhaps, even, of this unmanly thought. Lewis found that the men most eager for children (those who had raised the subject of having them with their partners) had then tended to make light of it. Even men in childless marriages, who may risk the terrors of international adoption, or who mortgage and remortgage their homes to obtain fertility treatment for their wives, can mask their own wishes under concern for their partners, expressing it instead, wordlessly, in steadfast support.

> 6 All those years when she never conceived, I think I probably lost sight of my own feelings. When there are babies there, I am looking out of the corner of my eye at my wife's reactions, not seeing how I am reacting. In fact it was only recently, two summers ago, when we were at a favourite place down in Cornwall sitting on this tiny little beach and I looked around and everyone else is a family and it suddenly hit me and I felt thoroughly miserable and had to go indoors. 9
>
> *Oliver, 39, father of one*

Although our notions of masculinity, of what we expect of men socially, are powerful inhibitors to men's participation in active fathering, this is not to say that fatherhood itself is outside masculinity's remit. On the contrary, begetting, providing and protecting are fundamental to many cultural definitions of masculinity, including our own.[15] But while young women have been pushed towards maternity, young men have been urged to go out and conquer the world, and since people typically choose partners from their peer group, there is a clear mismatch between the timing of men's and women's desires for children. Although by early middle age there has been a 'catch up' response and almost exactly the same numbers of men and women are keen for children, men are consistently less interested than women in becoming parents throughout their twenties and thirties.[16] Since most children are born to people in these age groups, it would seem that many men are having children before they are ready.

But at any age, intimacy with young children is not part of Western culture's masculinity scenario. Real men, as studies of TV images of masculinity repeatedly show, are overwhelmingly found in the world of objects rather than of family and relationships. They occupy high status positions, initiate action, operate from the basis of the rational mind as opposed to the emotions,[17] and are expected always to be in control, not only of their own feelings, but also of the situations they are in.[18]

> ❛ We was going down the lift with him to the operation, and she's crying and you're sort of rubbing her back and saying 'Don't cry – look these people are the best in the world', and you're sort of gutted yourself and you're just talking, it's just coming out. And only one's allowed into the theatre, and he's shouting back, 'Daddy I love you' and all that crack. And then he is sort of saying, 'They're not going to get the knives out are they?' and you're going through all this and you're thinking to yourself, 'I don't know what on earth is going on'. ❜
>
> *Michael, 36, father of two*

The antithesis of male control is Nappyland, where tantrums rage and edicts are constantly ignored, a club which few boys dare join if they value their heterosexuality. For the milky world of mother-and-child represents, in our culture, the very essence of femininity. And deep within our psyches, notions of femininity and male homosexuality are closely intertwined. In practice (and as the Ancient Greeks well knew) some of the most committed homosexuals are, by any definition of the word, ferociously masculine. But still the fear of being branded not 'man enough' continues to make men agents of their own exclusion, and drives a wedge between them and the development of skills necessary to be an active father.

Pregnancy

There can be few times in a man's life when he is less in control than during his partner's pregnancy. Co-author of the process he may be, but what is happening is in someone else's body. When Brian Jackson asked pregnant women if he could interview their husbands, the most common reaction was astonishment. 'Whatever for?' asked one woman, 'I mean – I know he's the father, but where does he fit in?'[19]

Not so long ago, pregnancy was thought to leave fathers-to-be relatively unmoved. Now we know that most expectant fathers experience huge swings of emotion, that men whose babies are unplanned suffer extreme emotional distress and that many fathers are deeply affected by miscarriage ('I sat on the toilet in the hotel and howled,' admitted one man interviewed). Where babies are planned, fathers-to-be feel exalted and delighted, responsible and frightened, and describe the unfolding pregnancy in much the same terms as mothers. They become attached to the foetus and are entranced when they see it on the scanner, hear its heartbeat, or feel it move.

> ❢ We saw scans at 11 weeks, 18 weeks and 32 weeks. And that was great. Each time I went in there I had a look at the screen and saw the developing girl and it was just fantastic. I felt myself bonding with this sort of image on the screen (which was pretty bizarre!) but each time we would come out and talk about how she looked. ❢
>
> *Elliot, 38, father of one*

Pregnancy has been found to be a time of great togetherness for many couples, and expectant fathers may go to great lengths to get close to their unborn children. Among Jackson's interviewees was one who made a stethoscope out of beer glasses in an attempt to hear his baby's heartbeat, and another who would lie at night with his sleeping wife's belly pressed against the small of his back, relishing the sensation of being alone with his child in the dark. Jackson developed four categories for the fathers he met. In addition to the *refusers* (20 per cent), there were the *spectators* (20 per cent) who were fundamentally supportive but professed themselves unaffected ('We've both seen babies on TV, so it'll be all right I should think.') and the *sharers* who were the great majority (50 per cent), who said things like 'No, I've never been to the hospital or these classes. I wait till Liz comes back and then I want all the news.' The final group were the *identifiers* (10 per cent), who tried to experience the whole thing with their wives.

Most expectant fathers pore over the ultrasound scan photos their wives bring home, listen eagerly to details of classes and antenatal appointments, and watch or help their partners with their exercises. But the information they are receiving is second-hand: they are rarely found at parentcraft classes or antenatal appointments, and they read little about pregnancy and less about childbirth.

> 6 If you exclude yourself from that process, or if you are excluded from the process, I think that's terrible. It's a gap in the child's life which is very difficult to fill later on. I went to everything, all the tests and the ultrasound scans, I thought to hell with it – the rest of my life has to be chucked out. I was going to have these nine months, it was going to be my time as well as hers. 9
>
> *Steven, 44, father of one*

Some of this behaviour can be put down to fear of hospitals and doctors, or the 'masculinity thing'. If you attend a parentcraft class, someone (almost certainly a woman) may ask you to change a doll's nappy, in *public*; if you seek out information, it underlines the fact that you don't know what the hell's going on; if a book tells you about your negative feelings, you'll close it pretty quickly if you feel obliged to pretend you don't have any. Researchers have discovered that, during pregnancy, most men think they need to behave like 'sturdy oaks', and are less likely than at many other times, to share their worries with their partners.

Alienating fathers

It's just not possible, however, to blame it all on men's 'resistance' to a female world, or on the fact that they're not the ones who get pregnant. Structural disincentives for male involvement in pregnancy are legion. Whenever parentcraft classes are held at night, midwives report that fathers' places are booked up months in advance in many districts, but such opportunities are rare. Antenatal classes are given by women, are overwhelmingly directed at women and, to accommodate hospital and tutors' schedules, are generally held during the day, with, at the most, one 'father's evening' and one hospital tour scheduled.

Antenatal appointments are also held in the daytime, and there is no awareness among professionals of any need to improve upon a casual invitation to fathers ('You can come if you like'). Lewis discovered that while one man in three took his wife to at least one antenatal appointment, only one out of 100 got beyond the waiting room; and Jackson found not one father being offered a stethoscope and invited to listen to the heartbeat of his unborn child. Ultrasound suites are often in a separate location within hospitals, and it may be that when fathers reach this point more will join in, but there is no data on fathers' attendance. Some centres (or individual operators) may welcome fathers; others most certainly do not, a common complaint being that fathers 'ask a lot of questions', which may prolong the consultation or cause embarrassment to the operator if 'something wrong' is detected.

> ❝ As young parents do, we read many books about babies and child development. They all seemed very nice and sensible. How do you get a bit of grit out of baby's eye? With the tip of mummy's tongue. Of course no one suggests that gross old dad should start licking away at his child's cornea. All parenthood seemed to me to be examined from a feminine point of view. ❞
> *Tim Hilton,* In Tandem

The average expectant father is killed off through lack of interest, his concern tolerated at best (and discouraged at worst) by health professionals completely out of touch with paternal experience. At no time during pregnancy does any medical worker assess the average father's response directly or help him identify sources of support. And in the 1995 edition of the book which many healthcare professionals use as their bible, *A Guide to Effective Care in Pregnancy and Childbirth*, fathers appear just once in the index under 'support during labour'.[20] The dismissing of fathers' experience during pregnancy is bad enough on its own account. But what compounds the crime is that talking with an expectant father can tell a skilled medical worker a lot about what will happen in the family afterwards: whether the man will have trouble bonding with his baby or is at risk of post-natal depression; whether his partner will manage to breastfeed, be very involved with her baby, or become depressed.[21]

Counselling and educating fathers at this stage can pay off in other ways, improving the quality of father–child attachment, mother–child involvement and breastfeeding rates. Jackson felt that, with proper antenatal preparation, many of the fathers he interviewed would have moved a category closer to involvement – refusers to spectators, spectators to sharers and so on.

Our blindness almost to the very existence of fathers during pregnancy is driven by the view that there isn't much they can do, other than be supportive. They should learn how to change nappies so they can *help*, and may attend the birth for the good of their wives. Support, their consolation prize for not being able to have babies themselves, is to be their *raison d'être.*

Concealed in the word support, however, is a command. For a father to be truly supportive, he cannot be autonomous. After all, *mother* knows best. If she thinks she doesn't, she may lose confidence, and if she loses confidence (or so it is said) then she will not be a good mother. Underlying this attitude is the belief that only mothers matter, that the child's wellbeing depends totally on hers, and that being 'right' is a mother's prerogative. In speaking to fathers during the preparation of this book, we were astonished at the number of men who told us they always supported their wives' way of parenting even if they didn't like what they saw. They felt that if they didn't, the baby, from the first hours and weeks of life, 'will play us off against each other'!

> 6 We have seen wise and gentle male paediatricians, capable of the most complex and loving behaviour toward their infant patients, defer to their painfully inexperienced wives ... [And] in the early years of our own family, Arthur, who had had months of experience with babies in emergency wards and clinics, would often watch from a distance as Libby fretted and fumbled with a sick child. 9
> *Arthur and Libby Colman,* The Father

Heaven forbid that fathers should *disagree* with mothers: what kind of support would they be then? Fathers are to be present, but not too evident, learn a little, but not too much, for knowledge confers power and can all too easily lead to dissent. The father's job, it seems, is self-censorship: not just of his own opinions, but of his own potentially independent relationship with his child.

Informing fathers

There is a lot that expectant fathers need to know and some of it is subversive stuff. Are women really 'natural' experts? What is meant by 'quality time' and how little time with children is enough? What is paternity leave for, and how can you get some if you aren't entitled to any? A father needs facts, so that he can make his own choices. What cultural forces are shaping his thinking and determining his preferences? Is he going to be a family man or a company man, and are the two incompatible? If unmarried (one in three fathers), or not living with the mother of his child (one in six), or a serial father (possessed of a previous family), a father will need information about his rights and obligations: parental responsibility, child support, the redrawing of wills.

There is a lot expectant fathers need to do, and much of it is on their own account. In order to be proactive parents and build their own relationship with the developing foetus, they need to attend antenatal appointments and read properly informative books and publications. To be equipped to handle the birth, let alone the baby (let alone a sick or dying baby), they need not just the one parentcraft class, but a dozen.

> ❝ I've got people around me that have sort of never been there before: 'I'm from Family Support Services' – 'I once lost a child myself and I know what it's like' – and I'm thinking, 'Are you talking to me, like?' Then I've got someone else coming over to me and saying: 'There is a Family Support Group upstairs if you need them.' I don't really want to talk to anyone. Because I've always been there on my own. I have never seen this help before, so I'm thinking to myself 'Why are you coming to me now?' ❞
>
> *Michael, 36, father of two*

All this, and more, fathers need to know. But fathers aren't told any of this. To see how excluded men are, all you have to do is to stand in front of the pregnancy section in a major city bookshop. Most of the so-called general publications are clearly directed at women, with illustrations of women outnumbering those of men about 200 to one. When fathers are mentioned, they are treated to patronising enthusiasm: 'Your presence at the birth will make make all the difference!' 'And as for changing nappies, I found I loved that, too!' Popular books specifically aimed at fathers are usually worse. Either over-intellectual or written in a chatty, condescending tone (often by media 'funny men') and frequently illustrated with absurd cartoons, they sport titles such as *The Expectant Father: a guide for the anxious male* and *A Good-Enough Dad, the confusions of an Infant Father*. Advertisers with no faith in their product, these books seek to sell the experience of fatherhood to a readership they assume to be: a) uninterested, and b) terrified (but not admitting it). By contrast, most books for mothers-to-be are serious in tone, even when written by professional comediennes, and allow for the full gamut of emotions.[22]

Ridiculing fathers

Lewis found his interviewees 'confused and alienated' by the publications directed at them. No wonder: without exception, they portray fatherhood as problematic and typically present the expectant father as a greedy child vying with the foetus for his wife's attention, or as a self-obsessed hedonist sweating over how soon she will be available for sex (does that episiotomy-thing really have to heal?). When this version of fatherhood is the one presented, expectant fathers are perhaps best advised to read nothing at all.

> ❪ I had piles of books thrown my way, bookshelves full of the stuff, but I chose to ignore most of it, not because of any particular arrogance or anything but I was just going to have this thing as a very private personal experience. I was going to observe it with an open mind not with anyone's theories as to how I should be feeling, I just wanted to feel it and I did. ❫
>
> *Phil, 38, father of three*

Any man who dares show a close interest in pregnancy itself is batted off by talk of the couvade syndrome, which features heavily in the psychological literature and finds its way with relentless regularity into popular fatherhood books. Couvade syndrome refers to pregnancy-like symptoms which are supposedly experienced by large numbers of fathers-to-be but, in fact, are hardly experienced by any. Lewis found just 6 per cent of his fathers reporting physical symptoms, many of which, such as claustrophobia, did not bear any resemblance to routine pregnancy symptoms.

Most pregnancy researchers, unlike Lewis, are thrilled by the idea of the couvade syndrome. They hunt for symptoms with huge enthusiasm and reject (or fail to consider) alternative explanations; for example, that a father-to-be's weight gain may result from a new life-style ('I stay in with her now, haven't been to the gym in ages,' said one man interviewed) or from a change in his partner's cooking or eating habits, as she celebrates release from years of dieting.

The use of the word *couvade* is similarly misleading. Originally coined by 19th century anthropolgists to describe tribal fatherhood rituals involving such things as food-taboos and the male taking to his bed and 'labouring' beside his partner, true *couvade* rituals have a practical purpose and are consciously undertaken. Since they are only found in societies where marriage ties are weak or property is transferred down the female line, they are now thought to be a means by which men publicly acknowledge paternity.[23] Thus, real *couvade* bears only the most superficial resemblance to so-called *couvade* syndrome which, when it exists at all, consists of isolated and unconscious stress symptoms. However, by being associated with systemic couvade rituals, the significance of these *ad hoc* responses is inflated and distorted, until they are transformed into something archaic, universal and feminising, an implicit warning to men to keep at a safe distance from the business of pregnancy, lest their manhood be threatened.

Pregnancy is a perilous time, physically and emotionally, and anyone involved in it and not experiencing episodes of acute concern can be said to have misunderstood the situation. It would therefore be strange if some expectant fathers did not manifest physical stress symptoms. It is common for human beings who do not have an easy outlet for their feelings (a position in which, as already observed, many 'sturdy oak' expectant fathers find themselves) to develop psychosomatic symptoms. So while stressed-out middle-managers swallowing painkillers for tension headaches or gulping milk against incipient ulcers can pass without comment, or even be glamorised as 'high-achieving Type A personalities', expectant fathers who develop similar symptoms are pathologised and said to be exhibiting envy of that which they can never have: a womb.

> ❢ I sometimes wonder if all male achievement is not based on this simple fact: since men cannot create human life, they build cultures in an attempt to compensate. And then they tear them down again because the achivement is hollow. ❷
>
> *Richard Seel,* The Uncertain Father

Pathologising fathers

The effect (if not the purpose) of pathologising people's behaviour is to limit it. Let us remember, for a moment, so-called penis envy which first attracted attention at the beginning of this century, just when women were beginning to assert themselves. It was several decades before anyone pointed out that, nice as it must be to be able to pee against a wall, what women were actually envying wasn't so much the penis as what went with it: jobs, education, money, power. Suddenly an absurd pathological condition was transformed into a reasonable concept for women to tackle, rather than avoid.

Womb envy was originally documented by psychiatrist Bruno Bettleheim (who observed this symptom among some severely disturbed *children* he was treating!)[24] and is now referred to as if it were a universal feature of the adult male psyche. In fact, depending on their situation, both women and men can be profoundly (or mildly) envious of each other. As children, we all want to be everything, including other species, but the notion of 'womb envy' as the driving force behind masculine behaviour is hugely suspect. A mind-boggling array of behavioural disturbance has been attributed to the 'archaic feelings of distress' men are said to experience due to their inability to bear children. In addition to couvade syndrome, these include spreading male birth myths, waging war, building cathedrals and engaging in extra-marital affairs.[25]

> ❦ I wasn't a nappy-changer, I think I changed nappies about three times, and that's three times too many. Well, say twice too many, everyone ought to do it once. What is it they say? Try everything once, except incest. ❧
>
> *Geraint, 43, father of two*

The 'extra-marital affair', in particular, is widely reported – courtesy the 1948 Kinsey Report – to be a common male response to pregnancy and childbirth. However, recent research does not reveal expectant or new fathers as particularly at risk of extra-marital affairs (Kinsey's data was notoriously skewed for he relied on volunteers). 'The figures overall,' writes Annette Lawson in her 1993 study of adultery, 'give little support to the idea.'[26] It may even be that men are *less* likely to have affairs when their wives are pregnant or newly delivered than they are at other times. Jay Belsky, one of the leading American researchers looking at the transition to parenthood, uncovered just one extra-marital affair in his sample of 250 new fathers.[27] Other top US experts, Carolyn and Philip Cowan, who studied 72 couples in great depth, noted just three affairs (whether all were by men is not recorded).[28]

> ❦ That the baby is a rival, a threat to male security and confidence, hasn't been my experience. Granted, my wife became immediately and deeply involved with our daughter. But so did I ... This sense of joint responsibility gave us a stronger appreciaton of teamwork and co-operation ... . Nothing can equal the sheer sensual pleasure of slipping back into a warm bed beside a warm partner with a warm baby in your arms, getting the little one fed, and sharing the contentment of the two people who are most important to you. ❧
>
> *Terence Heath,* New Fatherhood

Preparing fathers

Psychosomatic stress symptoms in fathers do not seem to occur in men who are closely involved in their partners' pregnancies, that is the men classified by Brian Jackson as sharers or identifiers. Stress symptoms are almost exclusively found among spectators or refusers.[29] Among those interviewed for this book too, this pattern was clear. Our 'spectators' included a particularly anxious expectant father who was keeping a brave face on things, and who had created a demanding, on-going project for himself, which he referred to as 'my baby' and which kept him out of the house. We also met a father of four who was unable to talk much about his children because he hardly knew them, but who spoke enviously of women's ability to conceive and give birth. It seemed plain that he was looking for something to shock him into parenthood as, he felt, must happen to women through the intensely physical process of pregnancy, labour and birth.

Fathers who are well prepared for their children's births by being closely involved during pregnancy are unlikely to experience weird symptoms and soon discover that while the male experience of pregnancy is necessarily different from that of the female, it need be neither second-hand nor second-class. For there exists a sense in which *both* fathers and mothers are outside looking in, and are building a relationship with a fantasy baby, before its birth. Well-prepared fathers are also less likely to exclude themselves, or be excluded, after the birth.[30] A 1985 German study showed that fathers who had attended infant-care courses did more caretaking than unprepared fathers, keeping closer to their babies, and interacting with them more face to face.[31]

Involved fathers are good for babies. In the German study, the babies of the prepared fathers were, at age nine months, happier and more responsive than the children of unprepared fathers, even though these had now gained experience and were behaving very much like the prepared dads. The prepared fathers, through their early competence, had given their babies a head start.

> ❜ Today I caught sight of my boss at work, slipping a photo of his two-year-old from his wallet and cherishing her: that'll be me soon, I think, and I smile warmly to myself … But there are fears … I can't wait to have a baby, but I am scared of turning into a father. Actually, that's not quite exact. What I'm really scared of is turning into *my* father. ❜
>
> *Jocelyn Targett,* Tiny Fears

In the US, Caroline and Philip Cowan have evaluated group counselling for expectant couples. Interestingly, they found that fathers who attend such counselling prior to the birth are often quite a lot *less* traditionally supportive after it. They may do no more babycare than unprepared men, complain more about the work–family balance, and be more critical of their partner's parenting.

Does this mean that fathers are better left unprepared? Apparently not. Strangely, their wives are happy with their input, however critical. Maybe it gets conflict and disappointment out in the open, maybe the fathers have something useful to say, maybe it shows they care. Who knows? What we do know, is that among the couples prepared for the birth, relationship satisfaction and sexual satisfaction were relatively high afterwards. The mothers were less likely to have become sunk in motherhood, while the fathers didn't allow stress in one area of life to affect another. And things continued to improve. After 18 months, the prepared parents were showing more flexibility in work and family arrangements than the unprepareds, and the prepared fathers were more satisfied about everything than the unprepared fathers, including their partners' parenting. But most significant of all was the fact that while one out of every eight of the *un*prepared couples had split up (together with one out of six of a comparison sample of childless couples), there was not one relationship breakdown among the prepared couples. They were *all* still together, as they were two years on, when the Cowans interviewed them again, and when another unprepared couple had parted.[32]

❮ I loved the whole pregnancy, watching my wife's body changing. I felt a real closeness to a woman that I had never felt before because of this thing that was growing inside – it was part of me. I just used to lie here and watch it growing and growing and as it got bigger, the feelings grew stronger. She was an experienced mother and pregnancy caused no dramas, and I said to her, 'What's happening to me? Why am I feeling like this?' ❯

Bill, 38, father of one

But men who are actively prepared for parenthood are a tiny minority; and the average father, by the time his baby is due to be born, is in a seriously disadvantaged position. Firstly, he has become accustomed to obtaining information about his child indirectly, via its mother. Secondly, he is lagging behind in terms of psychological readiness, still thinking of himself more as a partner than a parent. And thirdly, because he knows so little about anything to do with either pregnancy or birth, he is full of fears and completely unprepared if things go wrong. For when he shows up in the delivery room beside his relatively well-informed wife, he is likely to be in a state of ignorance, comparable with that of women half a century back.

Birth

For fathers hoping to be present at their children's births, 1994 was not a good year. In June, a young man who had missed a court appearance to attend the delivery of his first child was arrested: 'It's ridiculous!' said the magistrate. 'Women have been giving birth for millennia without men there.'[33] And football star Christian Dailly, who skipped a training session to be at his baby's birth, was axed from the team.[34] Nevertheless, the vast majority of Western fathers made it to the delivery room on time. More than nine out of 10 fathers are now present.[35]

> ‘How should I address you, little one,
> on the eve of your birth?
> What can I say that might ease your passage
> through the bloody gates of life? …
> I will be waiting for you; the fat, bald, bearded
> one, looking afraid
> and in the way …’
>
> *Stewart Brown, 'Heart to Heart'*

The phenomenon of such high levels of attendance by Western fathers causes consternation among fatherhood researchers because they know what the rest of us don't. In world terms, it is unprecedented. Not even Aka fathers get to be there when their children are born. In Britain up until the mid-18th century males were usually excluded, and as late as the 1960s British fathers were refused admission to hospital births. This does not, however, mean that no sixties' father saw his child being born: 60 per cent of births then took place at home.[36]

What is a father to *do* at his child's birth? That he may wish to be present on his own account alone has never been considered reason enough. Everyone assumes that fathers have to be of *use.* In 1947, in

America, when men were first admitted it was on condition that they act as a labour coach. In Britain in 1975, one in three obstetricians were still excluding fathers, and when they were allowed to participate in 'the mother's experience' it was to be to the degree 'that she desires it, and he is able to, and wants to *help*'.[37] Given this history, it is understandable that fathers' widespread participation today is still so often met with confusion and suspicion. Fathers are either seen as being 'pressured' to be there (and at risk of post-traumatic stress syndrome); or their attendance is regarded as a stealthy extension of male power. 'Maybe fathers being present at the births would work if they were in pain too. They could at least have their legs waxed, or something!' suggests Rita Rudner in her *Guide to Men*.

Rite – or right?

Recently, it has been suggested that what is really going on is a kind of modern *couvade* ritual. As both non-marital childbearing and divorce proliferate, a man's presence at the birth is said to be a formal way of announcing that he is the father. In fact, in 1968 an anthropologist called Mary Douglas predicted that as family structures changed, men would not only be present in increasing numbers at the births of their children, but that society would become increasingly obsessed with fathers' responsibility for their offspring's mental health.[38] This rather attractive theory may indeed have some validity, although Douglas did not reckon on DNA analysis, which now so easily proves paternity, nor on the fact that cohabitation would be seen as so much of an alternative to marriage. But the major reason for men's presence in the delivery room is, very probably, greater sexual openness. Modesty is no longer an issue. And, importantly, women are inviting men in.

❛ I was up by the mother's head holding her hand comforting her, and then I was sneaking looks, and sort of ducking back down there and I'm saying I can see this little head and then back up here (but I was also very emotional, you know) and giving my wife a commentary on what was going on – because she obviously couldn't see – I think that's a terrible thing about childbirth they can't see what's happening, they are sort of excluded – their husband gets a better look at what's going on. ❜

Phil, 38, father of three

We are often told that men are reluctant to attend, but even as early as 1961 a study revealed more men wanting to be there (22 per cent) than had wives keen for their presence (17 per cent) and by the end of the 1970s a clear male culture of attendance had emerged, with veterans advising novices that this experience was not to be missed.[39] However, most men used to *say* that they were attending 'for their wives', and some certainly only agreed to come along under pressure at the last minute. This has changed. Today 100 per cent attendance is the norm in some areas, and it is not unusual even for men who are not living with the mothers of their children to attend their babies' births. A 1994 study of new fathers in Britain showed 93 per cent of fathers both wanting and planning to be there. Interestingly, in presenting the findings of this survey, the authors gave equal weight in their press release to the 'I did feel pressure' and 'I didn't feel pressure' categories, even though the ratios were completely different: 88 per cent 'no pressure' and only 12 per cent 'some pressure'.[40]

Among younger generations, attitudes are even more surprising. Ninety-five per cent of working-class boys interviewed recently in London, none of whom could be said to be under pressure because none was an expectant father, said they think fathers *should* be present, giving as the most usual reason that it is a father's 'right' to see his children born.[41]

Does witnessing the birth traumatise men? Far fewer than is popularly believed. In fact, one of our interviewees, a lorry driver, commented that he'd found having to keep '… up the head end' during a Caesarian section worrying. ' I would have preferred not to have the screen in front of me and to see the whole thing – it's a fear factor and it just increases that type of fear.' However, another man was relieved to have been spared a Caesarian full-frontal!

Attitudes to cutting the cord were similarly diverse. One Australian father was pleased his child's medical condition had made it impossible (in Australia fathers are routinely given the opportunity). While the only English father offered this privilege had accepted, and reported it as the high point of the birth-experience.

❮ We decided to have Ricky at home and initially I didn't like the idea – had all logical reasons why I didn't want to do it, about being safe in hospital. I think it was to do with the mess and having my space invaded, that was the truth of it. But once we embarked upon it, it was a brilliant experience. We had this wonderful midwife. I think she really liked me. She did

something she said she had never done and she has delivered over 1,000 children, but she got me to get hold of his head and pull him out. And then she let me cut the cord! **'**
Ralph, 37, father of three (two families)

In Britain, only 3 per cent of fathers who witness births say they feel sick and only 9 per cent become really upset. Even then, while medical staff repeatedly provide opportunities for fathers to leave, most, as one midwife put it, '... stick to their partners like glue'. The majority feel a mixture of emotions, but recent research shows that two out of three speak of the experience *only* in glowing terms, and that the vast majority (93 per cent) are positive about it, even if they have also been frightened or upset.[42] 'It was one of the most unpleasant experiences of my life,' said one father, 'and I wouldn't have missed it for anything.'[43] In the light of the marked absence of serious negative reactions, one does wonder what all the fuss about men's supposed inability to handle blood in a delivery suite (though not, one notices, on a battle-field) has been about.

The politics of birth

What it has probably been about is excluding men. Assuring people that they won't be able to cope with a situation, or they wouldn't enjoy it is a common ploy if you want to shut them out. Few of us understand the extent to which in our own culture, as in many others, female-controlled childbirth has been a cornerstone of women's identity. Excluded from other, formal, power structures, this domain has been women's alone and jealously guarded.

In Britain, right up to the mid-17th century and, in many parts of the country, long after this, the way childbirth was staged made it a quasi-religious rite. It took place in a sealed room lit only by flickering candles. Managed and attended solely by women, it was presided over by a female midwife also licensed to dispense emergency baptism, should this be necessary. Midwives were often not very skilled because the low birthrate, combined with the limited geographical area they covered, could mean they sometimes attended no more than two or three births a year. [44]

After men, in the form of male midwives and doctors, 'broke in' to this women's world brandishing forceps and other scientific inventions, there developed a long running battle between midwives (as independent practitioners) and hospital teams. In the post-war period this was largely resolved by enrolling midwives onto these teams, around the same time as the first fathers stepped over the thresholds of the maternity wards.

> 6 I wasn't at their births. I don't like blood and guts. I think it is more important to be there for the late night feeds than for the birth of your child. I remember reading Sheila Kitzinger saying that any man who didn't attend the birth was a feeble pea-brain (or something like that) and I thought – to hell with her! I mean, she didn't even make me feel guilty. 9
>
> *Louis, 45, father of three*

Fathers' participation during labour and birth must remain an option rather than a rule, not least because Britain is a multi-cultural society, and not all cultures regard the idea with equanimity. In fact men from ethnic minority cultures often find themselves dragged in, because they're needed as interpreters.

However, anyone who thinks that British fathers are universally welcome on labour wards today should think again. For although women in general welcome their participation, and most mothers questioned today say they can't imagine giving birth without their partners, some birth professionals, including the charismatic and influential childbirth guru Michel Legrand, are less keen. Monsieur Legrand, in fact, is actively hostile. He ascribes all kinds of ills to fathers' presence, including stressful births, poor post-delivery sex and divorce. This view is not shared by the Royal College of Midwives who are more familiar with the research (which, of course, reveals nothing of the kind) and who say they don't think fathers should actually be excluded. What the Royal College suggests is that the father should not be the sole support. Or, to put it in another way, that his presence be diluted perhaps by a third family member, 'preferably a woman', and, if possible, a woman who has given birth. This, the RCM declare blithely, 'will not undermine the father's role in any way'.[45]

> 6 Sarah obviously needed something for the pain, but when I tried to find out what she wanted, the midwife would interrupt. She kept trying to ignore me and said they would have to consider medical intervention but when I asked what she meant she wouldn't say. I felt marginalised and excluded, not by Sarah who obviously still wanted me close, but by the midwife. Luckily, the midwife on the next shift communicated well with us, telling us what stage Sarah was at and exactly what she wanted her, and me, to do. 9
>
> *Mark Livingston,* At the Birth

Do those professionals, who are less than enthustiasic about fathers' birth attendance, have a point? They, after all, are at the sharp end. Day in, night out, they witness births and meet anxious, unhelpful and even disruptive men. No doubt many of these would be considerably *less* anxious, unhelpful or disruptive if they understood what was going on. But when you ask whether preparing fathers really thoroughly for the birth (and training midwives to use their assistance) might not be done alongside, or instead of, bringing in a third labour partner, you realise you have crossed an invisible line. For this proposal is met with derision. M Legrand is dead against it (he claims that educating fathers makes them 'invasive') and Jilly Rosser of the Midwives' Information and Resource Service simply can't see the point: 'Men aren't helpful in the home, why should we imagine they'll be helpful in the labour ward?'[46]

You would think the idea of educating fathers would be uncontentious. After all, research shows that when labour partners know a lot about pain control, women have shorter labours and are less likely to need epidurals.[47] In some Nordic countries thorough antenatal education for fathers is pretty well a prerequisite of attendance at the birth. But in advocating a greater role for, and the education of fathers you realise that, in Britain, this debate has little or nothing to do with good (or bad) birth practice: you are up to your neck in sexual politics.

Midwives, as noted earlier, have long had to fight their corner against a male-dominated medical establishment, and their identification is with women. The word midwife means, literally, 'with woman'. As for M Legrand who, it has been suggested, may enjoy being the only male in the delivery room, his stance is unashamedly fundamentalist: 'In the old days,' he declares, exhibiting a sketchy grasp of history, 'men got to know their children indirectly through their wives. There was no direct bonding.' This assertion is questionable. Certainly in the late 1950s only one in seven fathers whose babies were born at home, witnessed the actual birth. Nevertheless, records over several centuries show fathers as members of the birth team, albeit usually downstairs or in an adjacent room, and typically meeting their newborns within minutes of delivery.

This is beside the point, for M Legrand is after bigger fish. Does he refute the notion of direct bonding between father and child because it threatens the very foundation of the family? Does he think that once a man realises he can have a relationship with his child *without having one with his wife*, that he will take that child by the hand, and head off on some awfully big adventure? Both M Legrand

and the Royal College of Midwives fear the routine, well-informed and undiluted presence of fathers at the births of their children, and they fear it with reason. Such a practice would undoubtedly increase fathers' power and control, while at the same time raising all kinds of awkward questions. When, for example, does a man's relationship with his child begin? Should presence at the birth be his prerogative, even if his child's mother doesn't want him there? And, has he a 'right' to insist that she continue with a pregnancy, once a child has been conceived?

> 6 We walked into the room where our son lay dead. He looked very peaceful, any pain was over. I said ... to my wife, 'Thank you, darling, for giving me such a wonderful son'. 'He was yours, too,' she said. 9
>
> *J. Way, Compassionate Friends Newsletter*

A personal Everest

Most men who have attended their children's births, rate it as among the peak experiences of their lives, if not *the* peak experience. UK management trainers, Maynard Leigh Associates, report that when men in a group workshop are asked to nominate a personal or professional 'turning point', the event most usually mentioned is witnessing the birth of their child.

Researchers interviewing fathers are accustomed to hearing birth-attending fathers describe it as 'the happiest day of my life', and to hearing men, often still moved as they remember, confess awkwardly that 'I cried'. In fact, according to Brian Jackson, who was actually in the delivery room (with his notebook) when 20 of his interviewees became fathers, 18 were in tears. The only reason the other two weren't, was that they were completely stunned. The other thing Jackson noted was the lovely welcome to the world that almost every father gave his child: holding, looking into its eyes, offering a finger to suck, and speaking. First in an ordinary voice which changed quickly to an intimate whisper; then, instinctively, to higher-pitched baby talk. It was as if, observed Jackson, 'They seemed to have the elements of fatherhood in their blood.'

Although there is no coherent policy on fathers, many hospitals now actively encourage their presence but not, usually, for the father's sake. Women express a great fear of being left alone during labour and overworked staff can do with the back-up. The 52 per cent of men who say they felt 'useful' can be certain they were, and the 14 per cent who felt 'useless' may have been wrong.

There can be no doubt that witnessing the birth makes a man feel closer to his child, although it does not guarantee that he will, later, be a good or attentive father. As we shall see, too many other factors are involved in this. But the shared experience not only unites father and child, it also unites mother and father. This, however, may be where the sharing ends, for as one of the first researchers to tackle motherhood noted ominously: 'If pregnancy unites, birth divides'[48]

> ❬ I have heard more than one man describe the surging joy, the love beyond all anticipation, that came with his first sight of his offspring ... Such a memory calls up the word 'miracle' with surprising regularity ... But, in general, miracles need to be helped along. ❭
>
> *Harry Stein,* One of the Guys

After the birth

Efforts may be being made to accommodate fathers in the delivery room, but once they're out of it, everyone immediately loses interest. These, after all, are *maternity* hospitals, and while some claim to allow dads to visit any time, what they actually mean is *any time as long as it's between 9 a.m. and 9 p.m.*

Since only 1 per cent of births takes place at home, a majority of fathers are forcibly separated from their newborns shortly after birth, as soon as mother is seen as needing to rest. Since no one bears fathers in mind, this is not perceived as an opportunity for men to get to know their babies alone. 'It is hard to imagine a more curious way of treating new fathers than the one we presently operate,' writes Richard Seel, author of *The Uncertain Father.* 'If the father was not involved at all, his absence after the birth would be bearable. But to start a process and then suspend it at its climax seems almost gratuitously cruel.'[49]

First-borns remain in hospital for an average of five days, and subsequent infants for an average of three, unless the birth is by Caesarian section (15.3 per cent of all births) after which a 10-day separation is the norm. Middle-class fathers visit their newborns more often than working-class fathers, and the main reason, apart from access to a car, is their ability to go into work late, leave early, or take extended lunch-hours.[50] This is not to say that fathers have nothing to do during the time between visits. Typically, when not at work or looking after other children, they announce the birth, finish off the baby's room and bring relatives to the hospital. This is all useful stuff, but during this time the mothers, already ahead in the parenting stakes through their greater preparedness, are getting to know their babies one-to-one, and are learning how to handle them.

> 6 When I was younger I lived for a while with a woman who had children and I used to say, it's great I've got an instant family – I haven't had to go through nappies and babies and childbirth or anything. Actually, it was complete crap – and I realised later, when I had children of my own, that this had been part of the problem. It's not so much to do with biology in the strict sense, but the birth and the nappies and that whole thing was an absolutely crucial part of developing a proper and sound relationship. 9
>
> *Kenneth, aged 43, father of three*

Increasingly, first-time mothers offered instruction in baby-care beg hospital staff 'not to show me until my husband gets here', but this is not always possible. And when it is, the very fathers who in the privacy of the delivery room couldn't wait to get their hands on their babies, may draw back self-consciously: 'You see,' said one father, 'there's *married* women who's had one or two kids and they watch to see if you're doing it right.'[51] This is a shame, as there is evidence to suggest that fathers who attend their babies' births and are extensively engaged in the hospital setting afterwards, stay closely involved once the baby comes home.[52]

Coming home

What normally happens? In 1959 fewer than one in three men 'helped' his wife in this period. Today, 95 per cent do so, and while mention of paternity leave may cause ribald laughter among some politicians, ordinary fathers not only take it seriously, but take it.

The most recent British study to include a survey of fathers' leave patterns upon the births of their children is quite old, as is Lewis's, from the early 1980s. Even then he found almost all the men taking at least two days off work, and one in three at least eight. Very little of the leave taken was official paternity leave, which is probably the same today. In the US, a recent survey showed that 19 per cent of men surveyed had an official entitlement to (mainly unpaid) paternity leave under the terms of their contracts, but only 1 per cent took it.[53] Instead, as in Britain, GPs sign sick notes, line-managers pass it 'on the nod' or the men take holiday leave. Using holiday sounds sensible, until you realise that it erodes further the little time that a father will have during that first year, to get to know his child.

Middle-class fathers spend more time at home than working-class fathers. They are likely to have more holiday available, and are less likely to have, or accept, help from relatives. A tiny number of men can't see the point. 'How long could I work on the house?' asked one man, but once paternity leave is paid *and* is socially acceptable, fathers of all classes use it. In Sweden in 1990, 86 per cent of new fathers openly took the full 10 days due (even though these are paid at 80 per cent earnings), and research shows that Swedish men do not use the time for personal leisure, but for housework and childcare.[54]

Why do US and UK fathers rely on *informal* leave? When paternity leave is unpaid, most can't afford to take it, or may simply be unaware of their entitlement. US employers often include it in contracts in order to comply with equal opportunities legislation and then keep quiet about it. A survey of US companies offering leave revealed that 41 per cent didn't expect men to take it![55] Many men fear that formally taking time off when their children are born will reflect badly, careerwise, and given current attitudes in the UK and the US, they're probably right. 'New daddies need paternity leave like they need a hole in the head,' declares American industrialist, Malcolm Forbes (for which read 'my companies need paternity leave like a hole in the head'). In fact, since few men have more than two children and only 4 per cent of a workforce (males and females included) are becoming parents at any one time, the costs of paternity leave are negligible.

> ❢ After the first two she had depression really bad, but this time since I've been home she's been great. I think it's directly due to me being at home ... I can't see any reason other than me being here to explain it. ❢
>
> *father quoted in* Fathers, Childbirth and Work

Why, then, is paternity leave such political dynamite? In 1979, a Private Member's Bill on the subject failed on its first reading, having been described as 'grotesque' and 'an incitement to population explosion'. In 1994, the British Government again ridiculed the notion, as it opted out of European Parental Leave legislation, which it kept calling 'paternity leave' to obscure the issue. Paternity leave terrifies because it is symbolic. It focuses attention on the intimate relationship between father and child and holds it as important. It implies that men have a specific and significant role in the upbringing of their children. It is also seen as the thin end of the wedge. For once it is in place and, particularly, once it is paid, what is to stop the lobby for *parental* leave (extended time-off to care for pre-schoolers) and for *family* leave (allocation for family emergencies) becoming successful?

The birth of children is a peak period for male domesticity: 95 per cent undertake housework and care of older children, with 50 per cent taking the bulk of the responsibility. However, few British fathers engage in any physical care of their newborn baby during the time they are at home, and 25 per cent hardly handle them at all. This is in spite of the fact that barely two out of five UK mothers are breastfeeding after the first fortnight, and that most of the fathers exhibit intense interest in their babies.[56] Don't fathers *want* to handle their infants? Some are frankly scared, others believe that mothers have natural abilities which they lack, yet others feel self-conscious about the increasing skills gap between themselves and their partners. But Lewis believes the most important reason is that nobody expects a father to play a major role with his baby, unless something stops the mother from coping. When this happens, it can provide fathers with a real opportunity.

6 My wife had been in hospital for three months before the baby was born, and our two-year-old had missed her so much that on her first night home the two of them went to bed together, and he was in heaven. That left the baby with me. He cried every time I put him down, so I walked up and down with him all that first night and I always felt in those weeks and months, because my wife and the older lad were making up for lost time, I was really needed. I have always been especially close to this child. 9

Scott, 46, father of two

Goodies and daddies

The father's view of himself as an irrelevance is often reinforced by professionals such as health visitors who, even if the father is present, can quite unashamedly direct all comments to the mother, or tend to patronise fathers when they turn up at the clinic in charge of their babies. One father, who had delivered the baby himself on the front-hall floor, found himself actually shut out by the midwife during postnatal visits. Relatives, too, often look askance at men's attempts to get involved. 'Back in Ireland your father would never have done that!' said the mother of one man interviewed said, as she watched him pushing his newborn along in its pram.

Further discouragement can come from within the couple, in the form of a subtle 'family dance' which one fatherhood researcher, who spent many months observing new parents and their babies, privately describes as 'heartbreaking'. This dynamic is clearly evident in diaries kept by new parents Alex and Jason. They were having great difficulty negotiating parenthood and agreed that the real problem was Jason, the baby's father, who in the three months since baby Jessie's birth had not as he said himself 'sufficiently altered my life-style'.[57] The bare outline of events described in the diaries was this. On the first day Jason had agreed to look after Jessie. However, he kept calling on Alex for help. After the third appeal she '… grabbed the baby and stomped off', and Jason shouted after her 'Can't you cope, then?' On the second day, a Saturday night, when Jessie was sick (twice) Jason left Alex to mop up alone, and went straight back to sleep after having 'grudgingly' provided a towel. On the Sunday he spent an hour in the bath and three hours reading (for pleasure), while the exhausted Alex soldiered virtuously on, trying to 'Make Jess my priority, while trying not to forget Jason is important too'.

A closer reading of the diaries, however, reveals huge complexities. Every time Jason had attempted to look after Jessie, Alex had sabotaged it. On the first day, instead of leaving the house or, perhaps, taking a bath, she had hovered around ready to grab the baby back (and had quickly done so). On the second occasion, during a picnic, her diary revealed that she had 'constantly' directed Jason how to hold Jessie, although she knew it 'irritated him immensely'. She had also told him off for not paying the baby enough attention.

On the Sunday, when he again took the child she actually stayed in the room, criticised his approach and picked the baby up as soon as it made a few 'whingeing noises'. It was after this episode that Jason stomped off to spend an hour in the bath and three hours reading. And when he wanted to take the baby into town for a short car-ride she said he wasn't 'responsible enough', although in another breath she complained that she never had a moment to herself.

What is clear is that Alex and Jason were operating from the shared, but unspoken, assumption that a good mother not only copes but copes *alone*, and that a father's place is on the fringe. This required Jason, an otherwise responsible and respectable 32-year-old and not (as might be imagined from Alex's attitude) a teenage tearaway with drink-driving convictions, to behave 'badly'. It also required Alex to keep control of every detail of her baby's life, although paradoxically she then felt put-upon and completely out of control.

But perhaps the most damaging aspect of the situation, a situation for which neither Alex nor Jason was to blame, but for which both were responsible, was the *mutual* contempt in which they held Jason. When Alex refused on grounds of his irresponsibility to let him take the baby into town, Jason, though upset, murmured only that she was being overprotective.

> ❜ She just told me to stay away. Her parents wouldn't let me talk to her, and my mother said it would be best if I just forgot about her. She'd done the same thing to her boyfriend when I was born. After my daughter was born, I went by a couple of times, but they treated me like I was the devil and wouldn't let me in. After a while I quit trying and today I don't even know where she is. ❜
>
> *father quoted in* Teenage Fathers

The mothers' mafia

Scenes like those take place all over the country every day, and research has shown that a mother's behaviour can determine the degree to which a father will be involved in the care of his infant. The partners of 'new dads' are repeatedly shown to be less intrusive and controlling than those of traditional fathers. In fact, a woman's relationship with her own father can be *more* significant than her partner's to his father, in predicting his degree of participation, as can be her attitude to non-traditional roles for men. 'Mothers are gatekeepers, capable of enhancing or dampening father–infant attachment,' wrote one researcher. 'If they promote a triangle, this opens the way for the child's future attachment.'[58] 'I think we get the partners we deserve,' snaps a British TV presenter, whose husband happily '… does half the childcare, because I let him.'

This is not to make women responsible for men's involvement. Some fathers simply aren't interested in greater participation, however hard their partners push; or they plainly think 'women's work' is beneath them. But it's also clear that the dynamics are complex and that mothers often hold very real power. Mothers' work schedules and their own need for time often dictate their partners' participation.[59] And when men successfully combine work and family with high levels of competence in both areas, their partners are frequently the catalyst.[60] Fathers' behaviour and attitudes don't appear to have a similar impact on mothers' performance. It may be that because fathers' roles are less well defined socially, their behaviour is more flexible. Fathers also seem to respond to need. Fathers of pre-term babies often become very involved parents and where mothers are depressed or ill, fathers can take over.[61]

> ❛ I do most of the essential day-to-day things – shopping, dishwashing, cooking, tidying up. I try to keep the household orderly and clean. This is for the sake of smooth running but also so that there is an aura of sanity about the place which I think helps Deborah to recover her self from the murky world of schizophrenia. It also gives the children a mother who has the capacity to be a good mother, some of the time at least. I am terrified of a mad mother separated from her children. ❜
>
> *Tony, 38, father of two*

When mothers are super-competent and keen, fathers often do the least; and when mothers are less competent or less available, fathers regularly do more. Interestingly, in families in which fathers do a lot of the domestic work, mothers don't necessarily use the situation to their advantage. Research shows that in these families the *children* get more leisure.[62] Many women are still brought up to serve, some love to keep busy and a few may be keen to push themselves to the point of exhaustion: workaholics are not only found in city offices. This is not to suggest that fathers are a *tabula rasa* on which mothers' desires can be written. Some fathers become hands-on parents through a keen personal interest, or to compensate for poor relationships with their own fathers (a pattern particularly strong among fathers of sons). Other men seem to mirror the behaviour of their mothers, or their partners, from whom they will often declare they have 'learned to be a parent'. And the happier a couple are together, the more time fathers tend to spend with their children.[63]

Researchers sometimes report that mothers are keener for fathers to be involved than are the fathers themselves, but appearances can be deceptive. Fathers' attitudes can be determined by their skills and self-confidence (or lack of them). James Levine, who has been studying fathers for more than 20 years, is quite clear that when fathers are assumed to be busy or not interested (or even when they themselves *believe* they're busy or not interested) they are often, in truth, feeling uncomfortable or at a loss.[64] Levine's experience is borne out in Australia, where 'men's health' researcher, Richard

Fletcher, has found that fear of seeming 'sissy' hardly figures as a stumbling block to men's involvement with children when compared with fear of looking like an idiot – of being seen as awkward or incompetent in crucial areas. 'It is important to understand this,' says Fletcher, 'because through training, explanation, gradation, familiarisation you can set up situations where the idiot factor is reduced.'[65]

It's not only fathers who can have mixed feelings. Attitude surveys in the US have revealed that 60–80 per cent of mothers did not want fathers to take a greater part in childrearing.[66] Mothers are used to a world without fathers. They have a mafia all of their own, and their children are their passports to it. Through their babies, new mothers socialise with other women, and full-time working mothers can be especially jealous of the time they have available to spend with their children. And while mothers may welcome fathers as babysitters, they may reject them as equal partners in parenthood, resenting the intrusion of males on their mother-role and unhappy about the quality of their partner's parenting. More than half the mothers interviewed in a Nottingham survey in the early 1990s said they would not like to leave their children with the fathers regularly, and 38 per cent thought that to do so *ever* was a very bad idea. 'I don't know how a man would cope' was a typical comment.[67]

> ❦ With my first wife, it was just assumed she was going to stay at home. But with my second wife, I have taken on the housework and looking after the children. That has needed a lot of negotiation and it has not been entirely trouble-free, because she feels baffled sometimes by the fact that she doesn't know exactly what is in the fridge. Occasionally she will do some of the ironing, she says it is to remind herself how to do it. And I sometimes feel guilty – so extraordinarily fortunate – to know what it is to be at the centre of the kitchen. ❧
>
> *Hugo, 59, father of five (two families)*

Professionals' attitudes

Family professionals may be as resistant to fathers' involvement as mothers. In America a survey showed that only 50 per cent of workers in a pre-school programme supported fathers' involvement. Their reasons for rejecting them ranged from personal mistrust of men, through to a desire to protect the feelings of the large numbers of children growing up without fathers present. Professionals often actively avoid engaging with fathers or simply target services at mothers. Few are aware of how differently they approach fathers and mothers, or even that nurseries or family centres usually look 'father-unfriendly', with walls plastered only or mainly with images of mothers and children.

Researchers often distrust what fathers say and view mothers as more likely to 'tell the truth'. In fact, each parent tends to underestimate the other's contribution and mothers often have no idea how deeply their children are attached to their families. A 1988 study comparing parents' perceptions with independently observed behaviour found fathers' self-reports (rather than mothers') showing the most convergence with the observed behaviour.[68]

A term has now been developed to describe researchers' discounting of fathers. Family research, it is said, is 'gynocentric' (i.e. 'womb-centered'). A clear example is seen in the interpretation by researcher Ann Oakley, author of *From Here to Maternity*, of men's reluctance to handle their babies: 'You do it better than me', 'We have different standards', 'You go out and earn the money, then' were judged by Professor Oakley as being '… all the old dodges dragged in'.[69] She did not seem to consider whether these might be expressions of fear or self-doubt instead.

As recently as 1994, a report by the European Commission Network on Childcare, noting that Danish fathers who took extended parental leave tended to have partners with a high labour-market position and earning power, interpreted this in terms of the strengthened 'bargaining position' of these women, presumably used to 'force' their husbands into taking leave.[70] The proposition that these high-earning women's income might have *freed* some of these men from their obligations as breadwinners sufficiently to be *able* to take time off to spend with their children was not considered.

6 Sometimes I pinch myself and I say, how did I get such an extraordinary stroke of luck? Here I am, 59, with these two wonderful children. I get to see a lot of them so it means we have terrible quarrels and also the time and space to get over them. I support them at school and run around organising their social life and I think – this is incredible! Because the alternative was that I would have been working nine till six or eight till seven or eight till eight and missing it all. I couldn't bear the thought of doing that now. It's pathetic, why does anybody do it? 9

Hugo, 59, father of five (two families)

Jaundiced motherhood researchers have often castigated new fathers for promising more than they ultimately deliver. As if, before their babies are born, men *deliberately* set out to mislead their partners about how much they'll contribute later. And since adjustment to motherhood is shown to be much harder when false expectations have been raised, some have suggested that if fathers aren't going to be fully involved, then they should keep their mouths shut. However, what is becoming clear is that, as a general rule, the only deception practised by expectant fathers is self-deception. Prior to parenthood, men no less than women have absolutely no idea of how their lives will be changed. They really do think they can 'have it all', and are often as angry and disappointed as new mothers when expectation does not meet reality.

Few of the once egalitarian males who become secondary parents once babies come along are chauvinists-in-disguise. By the time a second child is born, such men will have been promoted beyond their partners' former level and, with an entire family dependent on their salary, will find themselves forced to accept whatever the workplace throws at them.[71] Fathers are exalted as breadwinners and scorned as intimate parents by a system which relentlessly promotes in-family care by mothers, not because it is the *best* option but because it is thought to be the *cheapest* option.

Practice makes Papa

One of Britain's research luminaries, who was reporting on the fact that significant numbers of fathers were now looking after children on Saturdays while their wives worked, laughed dismissively when asked whether she had found fathers developing their own ways of doing things, or whether they were simply following instructions left by mothers. 'Fathers have funny ideas about bringing up children!' she said.

Fathers *do* have funny ideas about bringing up children. So do mothers. Inexperienced mothers regularly overheat their babies (resulting, sometimes, in their hospitalisation) or overstimulate them so that they cannot sleep. Some mothers half-starve their infants to stop them 'getting fat' or insist on continuing to breastfeed when their babies are failing to thrive. Conversely, they stuff them with unhealthy foods or 'bulk up' the milk against the advice of professionals, and make them podgy.

Most mothers' funny ideas about bringing up children are, however, relatively harmless and are swiftly abandoned or modified through experience, and through a right which mothers exercise every day: the right to learn by their own mistakes. This right, however, is usually denied to fathers, both by mothers and by the men themselves. 'We were amazed,' exclaimed the Cowans when they observed couples in the weeks following their babies' births, 'at how little time fathers allowed themselves for uncertainty, and how quickly mothers stepped in if father or baby looked uneasy'.[72]

Charlie Lewis found some men, recognising their wives' need to feel in control, actually holding back from doing things for the baby when they would have loved to have done more. But very often when the fathers withdrew, it was because they felt incompetent. And, as the Cowans also found, the more fathers withdraw, the more their partners 'pick up the slack' ... and the more incompetent the fathers feel, the more they withdraw ... and so the vicious circle continues. One in three new fathers suffers depressive bouts[73] and at six weeks, 5 per cent are quite seriously depressed, with the most depressed fathers having wives who are 'over-involved' in the babies.[74]

The most usual interpretation of paternal depression is that the father, a 'greedy child', is feeling displaced, but some researchers have begun to challenge this. It seems probable that in many cases a father's dissatisfaction or depression may spring from his being a potentially active parent who has been disabled. For it has been observed that depression in some fathers lifts when they gain skills and confidence, and feel themselves capable of caring for their infants. The Cowans found that men who felt supported by their wives *in finding their own ways of doing things* were not depressed, and soon developed a strong connection to their infants.[75] As this brought its own rewards, it resulted in even more involvement. But this happens only rarely and in most new families – as already described – fathers typically spend almost no time alone with their (awake) babies, while mothers are alone with them for more than 60 hours per week.

For years, researchers have been presenting 'evidence' that men take longer to adjust to parenthood than women. They have offered this evidence uncritically, branding men less emotionally mature than women, or less willing to accept parenthood. But one wonders whether women's adjustment to parenthood would be as swift if they had as little opportunity to practise as their partners; or if the role were continually presented to them as being paradoxical, as it is to men. For while a new father is expected to share in the trials and tribulations of becoming a parent he is, at the same time, instructed to remain an outsider, and this to a far greater extent than is dictated by the physical realities of pregnancy and birth.

❛ It always seemed to be three o'clock in the morning when I left the hospital after the birth of one of my children ... Like a creature of myth you feel capable of anything. But, filled with the knowledge of your life-creating power, you discover that in fact you are impotent ... And so you wander aimlessly through those night streets until you arrive at home, or at some other destination which ought to have meaning. But the real meaning is locked away in a bed in a ward in a buildng where you are not welcome. It isn't that reality is hard to come back to, rather that reality refuses to allow you in. ❜

Richard Seel, The Uncertain Father

Chapter 5
The Working Father: a different world

For the past eight years, Derek Johnson and his wife Jean, both city-born and bred, have lived in a Dorset village in a thatched cottage down a leafy lane. A civil servant, not very senior and not very interested, Derek considers that his job 'pays the mortgage'. He commutes daily to London, leaving home just after 6 a.m. and returning around 8.30 p.m. Currently, Jean is not employed, for 15 months ago the Johnsons became parents. Derek is delighted with his baby daughter, Abigail, whom he sees at weekends.

Derek is a parish councillor, and in their community the Johnsons are at the centre of a select group who make village life go round. When Baby Abigail ('the Bump') was just five months-in-the-womb, Derek conceived *his* grand idea: their tiny village could mount a massive three-day festival. Cash and community spirit would be raised, the church roof and local school would benefit, and the children, including 'the Bump', would have a wonderful time. For 18 months, Derek hardly sat down, and when he did he was on the phone. The build-up to the festival was an enormous strain but, in the end, worth it. The event was a huge success although Abigail, who was teething, didn't seem to make much of it. Afterwards, Derek took time off work to recover, which he did by playing golf.

Michael Duggan is also a father. A transport manager in central London, he has two boys, Patrick (six), and Sean (four) who has had a heart-lung transplant and is constantly in and out of Great Ormond Street Hospital. Michael himself is the youngest of 12 children, and his own father moved out when he was four years old. He didn't move far, though, and most weeks Michael would trail round to see him. When he was 15, he asked his father why he never gave him a birthday present, not a card, nothing. 'Because birthdays only remind you you are older,' said his dad.

Michael, who lives in a council flat just 20 minutes from the office, works longish hours, eight to six and every other Saturday morning. Like Derek Johnson, he regards his job as a means rather than an end. These days, Michael plays no sports nor is he involved in the community. His complete focus, outside of his job, is his boys. Every morning he gives them their breakfast; every evening he re-enters family life with his sleeves rolled up, ready to talk with them and play with them and put them to bed. At weekends, to give his wife who is diabetic a break, he often takes them out on his own, carrying Sean who tires easily. Michael has seen every single Disney film and knows his children, and the local playgrounds, like the back of his hand. And in many long hospital stays, Sean has never spent a moment alone: when his mother is not there, his father is.

Which of these men is the 'better' father? Is it Derek, whose daughter hardly knows him, but who will run free across the fields, live at the heart of a supportive community and attend a well-funded school? Or is it the ever-loving, ever-watchful Michael, who remembers as a child, 'having nothing whatsoever', and for whom fathering is an act of reparation?

Involvement and investment

One of the considerable difficulties is that, while there are plenty of 'rules' laid down for motherhood, fathers rarely know what is expected of them in any concrete way. 'Even in analytic writing,' points out psychoanalyst and author, Andrew Samuels, 'there is little to be found about the direct relationship of father and infant, not even a description of what ordinary, devoted, 'good-enough' fathering might look like.'[1]

> ❝ I think my children have looked to me for all sorts of things that I wasn't aware they were looking for. Of course you know they want you to give them an ice cream or take them to the cinema, but they also want more subtle, emotional things. If I had been more aware, more analytical of my role, perhaps I would have been better able to put myself into their shoes and think – what do they want from me? I would probably have been a better dad. Maybe it doesn't matter, but I will feel all my life that I have failed in some way. ❞
>
> *Walter, 58, father of five*

In fact, although fatherhood researchers tend to be obsessed with the issue of fathers' involvement (endlessly chewing over how much of it there is, how much there ought to be, and whether levels of involvement are changing), day-to-day intimacy is only one means by which fathers contribute to their children's well-being. Fathers (like mothers) assist their children in many ways, only some of which, such as cleaning or feeding, engage with the child directly. Other input, which may be just as crucial, anthropologists call 'parental investment'. This includes activities which benefit the child, but which the parent would do anyway (such as bread-winning) or services which the parent procures specifically for the child, but which are administered by others (such as education). By this standard, the parental performance of the previously mentioned Derek Johnson doesn't look so bad.

Although involvement is, in fact, only one *form* of parental investment it is much the most highly valued, by parents as well as children. When President-Elect Bill Clinton looked ahead to the possibility of success, he remarked of his daughter Chelsea, 'If I win, she loses', meaning that the time he would have available to spend with her (involvement) would be severely curtailed. And though Clinton's win has been very much his daughter's too, for innumerable doors are now open to her, there was general acceptance of this 'loss' scenario.

Since the late 19th century, these two areas of parental activity, investment and involvement, have been largely divided along gender lines. Investment has been for fathers, involvement for mothers, and there has been remarkably little disagreement about how much of the latter there should be. The more the better has been the general rule. Now, however, a rethink is in progress and 'ideal' levels of (maternal) involvement are being rapidly re-negotiated, and downwards. As the current Government's desire to cut the welfare budget grows, even single mothers are being exhorted to think of themselves as workers first and carers second; and since even two-parent families today can rarely live well on a single income, parents in all social classes recognise that they must make trade-offs between what they do *for* their offspring and how much time they spend *with* them.

6 The most important way to provide for your child is to be a father to him. It's a fifty-fifty business I'm talking about. We should share the same joys and suffering. You need to be here, with your kid, twenty-four seven. Otherwise your pickney is going to turn his back on you one day. He will grow up honouring and respecting only his mother, because she's the one who raised him. Kids aren't blind you know. They can say how their life stays without you. Be careful how you stay Johnny, else one day you'll try and say proudly, 'ah my pickney dat', and

the boy will look on you as if you were a stranger. If you spit in the sky it will fall in your eye. **9**

Patrick Augustus, Baby Father

Involvement v. investment

Is involvement of greater value than investment? There are three factors which, measured in childhood, consistently predict people's success in later life. Success is defined through upward social mobility, fulfilment of potential and the capacity to form and maintain rewarding relationships.[2] Two of these 'success factors' are childhood IQ and psychological competence (i.e. being emotionally healthy), and these we will come to in Chapter 6. The third success factor for children, however, is their parents' *own* success. Successful parents of both sexes serve as role models and provide cash, contacts, coping strategies and useful genes. Since this has nothing to do with involvement at all, it should, at the very least, give us pause for thought.

Examined from this perspective, it seems that even parents who devote time and attention to their own careers for purely selfish reasons need not be dismissed out of hand as 'bad' parents, and that however highly we value involvement, we should not be misled into thinking that the only 'good' fathers (or mothers) are those whose sole concern is the minutiae of their children's lives. The issue here is not whether involvement is better than investment, but how the two can best be balanced. That said, it is plain that few fathers get to choose between investment and involvement, as one of our interviewees found. This man hated his job and looked forward to the birth of his first child as a reason for giving it up and becoming a 'househusband'. His plans went awry when his wife, who had intended to return to work, decided she couldn't leave the baby.

Work patterns are the single greatest determinant of fathers' relationships with their children. Throughout this century, lower-paid white-collar workers – the men who have averaged the shortest working week – have been the group most likely to be closely involved with their children. And the Cowans' research found, among their sample of new fathers, that the kind of father a man wanted or hoped or intended to be had only a relatively slight bearing on the kind of father he ended up as. Forty-six per cent of the variance in fathers' involvement was accounted for by working patterns. The involved fathers were employed fewer hours than other men; and their wives worked more hours outside the home than other women.

❛ When Gary was young I was doing a second job after work and during the week all I would see was the top of his head out of the cot. Sometimes at the weekend, Annie would leave him with me while she went shopping and, right up till he was about four, he might cry for an hour. It made me feel bad, but I didn't see there was anything that I could do about it. We had bills coming in and buying stuff for the house. ❜

Ritchie, 34, father of two

Fathers and employment

What are the hard facts about men's working lives? Increasingly, these are crammed into the years between 25 and 50, coinciding with the time when they are raising children. Today unemployment is often blamed, along with divorce, for the so-called death of fatherhood: fatherhood would be doing just fine (or so it's said), if fathers were able to fulful their natural breadwinner role.

If fatherhood is dying in Britain, however, this would seem to be as a result not of fathers' unemployment, but of their over employment. Eighty-two per cent of British fathers with children under 10 in two-parent families are full-time employed, and are working an *average* of 47 hours a week, and this doesn't include time spent commuting.[3] One in three of these fathers now works more than 50 hours per week. In the two years to 1995 in the UK, weekly workloads for one in five managers increased by more than 15 hours,[4] while in the US, between 1969 and 1995, long working hours added an entire month to the average employee's working year. Britons work the longest hours of all Europeans and 50 per cent of British workers say they come home completely exhausted, compared with 36 per cent in the USA and 17 per cent in Holland.[5]

Since most of the UK's long-hours workers are men, we can assume that most of the truly exhausted British workers are male. Many of them are fathers, and particularly fathers of young children. A 1983 study found new fathers working four times as much paid overtime as childless men,[6] and increased working is often presented as the 'natural' male response to becoming a parent (in contrast to the supposedly 'natural' female response of increased caring). In fact, when new fathers increase their workloads, this would seem to have more to do with the need to make up for the mother's loss of earnings than an innate desire to work harder. In Sweden, where 76 per cent of mothers of under-threes are in paid employment, fathers with very young children work the *shortest* hours of all fathers.[7]

Home-based working often augments the time fathers spend with their children. One in ten British fathers now uses home as a working base[8] and fathers are actually slightly more likely to do this than mothers. Only one UK father in 50 works part time, at home or anywhere else. This is, however, an increase on the mid-1980s, when only one father in 100 worked part time.[9] Around half of these male part-timers are not looking for full-time jobs.[10]

> ❜ It suits really well, working at home, and having people around to help, you can do it. The children love it. They love my presence in the house. I know so much more about their lives. More of it falls on me now. When the nanny's off, or has to leave early, or there's a gap before my wife comes home, then I'm in charge. ❜
>
> *Sebastian, 39, father of three*

Fathers and unemployment

Unemployment increases the time men spend on housework and childcare: 59 per cent of unemployed British males share family work more or less equally with their wives, and 26 per cent take on the main responsibility for it.[11] They are not, however, universally applauded for doing so. One eminent (female) researcher has described what she perceives as the 'heartbreaking' situation in which unemployed men take over at home, leaving their displaced wives to roam the streets in despair. Men, it sometimes seems, can do nothing right!

However, although unemployed men generally spend more time with their children, such is the stigma attached to being without paid work for males, that it sometimes has a bad effect on father–child relations, even if the fathers and children actually see more of each other. Researchers monitoring the Great Depression in the US noted that some unemployed fathers turned to drink and became abusive, while others simply became inattentive: 'He loves them kids and plays with them all the time, except when he's out of work,' explained one mother. 'Then he won't play with them, but just says all the time, "Don't bother me, don't bother me" and of course the kids don't understand why he's so different.'[12] English historians, too, have had little good to say about unemployment and fatherhood, but with some exceptions. Short-term unemployed fathers, or those who have left work voluntarily or have been pensioned off through, for instance, disability, can have a very different attitude. Doris Pilling, who looked into the lives of children born in 1958 with a view to discovering why certain individuals 'made good' in later life, found that many of them had had actively involved fathers, including fathers who were not employed.[13]

Today, those working with executives who have been made redundant, regularly encounter men who, after a month or two at home, have reframed their ideas about the kind of work they are looking for. They want to work, but they want work which will allow them more time with their children. Although unemployment rates of fathers with children under 10 are down only 1 per cent since the mid-1980s, job insecurity is making many men reconsider the relationship between their work and their family. Why put all your eggs in one basket if the bottom may fall out at any time? But despite the huge publicity given to househusbands in the media, these individuals are exceedingly rare. Just 17 out of every thousand fathers have reversed roles to become full-time carers while their partners work full time.[14] Because of the benefits system and the regional nature of long-term unemployment, three out of four UK families with unemployed fathers also contain unemployed mothers.[15]

6 Monday to Friday is hard. The children might want you to go out and some of the time you are inclined to stay indoors because you don't want to be seen as being unemployed. I collected them a couple of times after school but I wasn't happy about it. I would wait until they were almost ready to come out and I would be there, but I would try to make myself invisible and just come out and quickly scurry away. 9

Ritchie, 34, father of two

Since divorce sometimes follows unemployment, and since in the UK, the districts with the highest youth unemployment also contain the greatest number of never-married young mums, it seems likely that unemployment rates among fathers living apart from their children may be relatively high. It is interesting to note that no one as yet has the exact figures. A peculiar aspect of fatherhood number-crunching is that men living in households without children are never counted as fathers, even though many undoubtedly are.[16]

Unemployment among black fathers may have different effects from unemployment among white fathers, simply because it is so much more common. Mothers can be less blaming, and the fathers can take it less personally, because racism, rather than personal failing, may be identified as an important cause. That said, it is plain that racism and unemployment have proved a deadly combination for black fatherhood in the US: the growth in mother-headed families has directly parallelled the drop in employment opportunities for black males.

As is well documented, young working-class males are currently badly affected by unemployment and there are indications that these young men, as has been identified with young working-class women, sometimes conceive children in order to have 'something of my own'.[17] However, despite general moral panic, only one child in every thousand is born to a man aged under 25, just as only one child in every thousand is born to a man aged 50 or older.

A few men are opting for unemployment in order to care for their children, particularly young children. While, historically, married men with children have been the group most likely to have jobs, today they are *less* likely to be in work than than their childfree counterparts. This seems to be directly related to their caring responsibilities. In a pattern once observed only among mothers, fathers of children under five are more likely to be unemployed than fathers of older children. As their children grow older, more of these non-employed fathers re-enter the labour market.[18]

> ❛ It used to be a dilemma whether women went back to work after having children but these days it's a dilemma for men too if they should go back to work. Who wants to miss out on their kids growing up? ❜
>
> *Jonathan Ross*, News of the World Magazine

Sloths or slaves?

In 1989 Arlie Hochschild's book *The Second Shift* hit the headlines, with the claim that full-time working wives were struggling to do two shifts, one at work and one at home, while their husbands coasted along on 17 minutes housework and 12 minutes childcare a day. This book, which has been much quoted since, peddled an idea which has received widespread acceptance: that working mothers (slaves) rush around frantically juggling paid work and family care, while working fathers (sloths) mosey guilt-free through the corridors of power by day, and sit comfortably with their feet up at night. This is, quite simply, not the case. What Hochschild didn't say was that she had restricted her definition of 'housework' to cooking, cleaning, washing and childcare, and had cited weekday figures as though they applied to weekends. She had also used data collected in 1965, although more recent data was available.[19]

Today, a father's place is, increasingly, in the home. Because so many mothers are employed and are often choosing work which uses their qualifications, rather than acecpting jobs with hours that suit the family, fathers' working hours are beginning to form part of working-time negotations within families. Fathers are the most usual 'babysitters' when mothers work, and when mothers work part time, fathers may actually do more childcare than when mothers work full time. In Britain, one in two female part-timers works evenings, weekends or nights; and in only one out of six dual-earner households in the US do partners' schedules *not* overlap.

In the US, the amount of 'family work', which includes administration, repairs and shopping, done by married men increased from 20 per cent in 1965 to 34 per cent in 1985. Similar increases have occurred in Britain. By 1985, women were spending six and a half hours a week *less* on routine housework than their mothers had in 1961 due mainly to increased ownership of domestic appliances, while men doubled their time on housework over the same period. The time men spent on childcare also increased over that time – four-fold.[20] The most recent, highly detailed data from Australia, reveals that between 1987 and 1992, childcare as a primary activity increased for both sexes, but the increase was greater for fathers: up a full two hours per week. Furthermore, while the group most likely to be looking after young children (30–34-year-old women) clocked up three and a half hours *less* per week cooking – probably due to microwave ownership – in this same period the time men spent cooking remained stable. This means that men's relative contribution to family meal-making is growing, and since meal-making, as a primary activity, is often combined with childcare, as a secondary activity, this has implications for fathers.[21]

❖ I went back to work when she was three weeks old. I found it very hard to leave those first few weeks. I just wanted to delay going. I used to make another cup of tea. Whenever I can I change her and I bath her every night – change her first thing in the morning and take her out of her mother's hair so that she can get some sleep. I have her on my arm, walking around, whatever I'm doing. ❖

Alex, 36, father of one

Misrepresenting men

Why does the British press, reporting the findings of the annual General Household Survey which is generally thought to give an 'inside view' on the domestic life of Britons, regularly announce that the New Man is a myth? The reason is that this survey, like many others, such as Mintel's *Men 2000* asks couples the following: which of you *mainly* does the washing (or cooking, or cleaning)? Or is it shared *equally*?

Such tasks are not yet being shared equally, but that doesn't mean that they're not being shared out more *equitably*, and this exactly parallels developments in 'shared' income-earning. The reality is, that among families with young children, both parents are 'Running from morning to night', as one man interviewed put it. There is, broadly speaking, parity between fathers' and mothers' contributions, and although mothers do twice as much family work as fathers, they do only half as much breadwinning, whether this is measured in terms of hours or income. In terms of income, full-time employed mothers in two-parent families typically bring in two fifths of the family wage, while part-timers supply one fifth. This contribution is no less essential than fathers' contribution on the home front: women's wages take family income above the poverty line in one in three families.

In terms of hours, part-time employed mothers and fathers work much the same hours, 17 and 19 respectively, but the big difference comes in the percentages so employed: 35 per cent of mothers as against 2 per cent of fathers.[22] Full-time employed UK fathers (82 per cent) average a 47-hour week, while the so-called full-time employed mothers (18 per cent) average just 25 hours. Only one mother in 16 is employed more than 47 hours per week, and among those employed more than 30 hours per week, one in six is home by 3.30 in the afternoon.[23] And while mothers are more likely to be employed locally, commuting times for fathers are usually longer, too.

Mothers work as long hours as fathers, of course, and mothers of young babies somewhat longer, but these additional hours are worked inside their homes, and in the presence of their children. The division of labour within individual families varies considerably, but the rule of thumb is that where partners are equal breadwinners in terms of the amounts earned, core domestic tasks are most likely to be equally shared.[24]

❛ I do most of the cooking. I do special meals for the kids that they like, there's a 'splog' that I make – splog's a sort of mixture of mashed potatoes, baked beans and stuff like that, they love it – so there is the process of feeding them all, then I have to come back to work at six o'clock, see. So because Carole's still working then, the child minder comes at 5.30 so I hand over to her and I leave at 5.45. ❜

Steve, 39, father of five

Changing values

The fact that women, whose contribution to the family budget is so much less than men's, are not called 'breadwinner sloths', while men are castigated for their allegedly small contribution on the domestic front is interesting. It indicates that although so many mothers today are breadwinners, we do not expect them to be and are, perhaps, still resisting the idea. But we *do* expect fathers to care for children. And while there can be no doubt that some women put pressure on their partners to be more involved as parents, a Europe-wide survey in 1995 revealed that men want this too. Neither men nor women think childrearing should be left mainly to women: 86.3 per cent of men and 87.4 per cent of women thought it was better for a father to be ' … very involved in bringing the child up from an early age'.[25]

Because fathers have been regarded as breadwinners for so long, everyone assumes that men invariably find their greatest life-satisfaction through their employment. This is not the case. Forty-three per cent of British males with children under 12 regard their jobs as 'just a means of earning a living' and 31 per cent would not work if they did not have to.[26] In the US, one in five men surveyed in 1994 said that if the household had enough money to live comfortably, they would prefer to be at home looking after their families.[27] Employed mothers express much higher levels of satisfaction with their work, probably because many of those who prefer to stay at home have exercised that option.

Whether men want to spend more time with their children or not depends on what they believe to be possible or acceptable. Just raising the question seems to bring about changes as individuals reconsider their options. Over a five-year period from the mid-1980s, the numbers of male Dupont employees expressing an interest in adjusting work time to accommodate child time more than doubled. 'Several years ago I wasn't getting any requests for parental leave from men,' says one US childcare co-ordinator. 'Now I get one or two a month'.[28] In Britain, paternity leave, which no one used to talk about at all, is now high on the agenda of non-pay issues during annual wage negotiations.[29]

Men are expecting new things from themselves as fathers. Fatherhood researchers are always struck by the fact that the vast majority of men see their own fathers as negative role-models and say they wish to be very different kinds of fathers themselves. They will usually declare that they want to be closer to their children, both emotionally and physically. Children are also expecting different things from their fathers. London's Institute of Family Therapy reports a marked increase in the numbers of teenagers trying to bring about changes in their relationships with fathers they feel they hardly know.

Since few homes today are built around economic production, parents are not so much valued as educators and trainers, as intimate carers. They look for personal fulfilment in the quality of the relationships they achieve with their offspring, who are increasingly perceived as luxury items, precious and costly. And now that children's physical survival can be largely taken for granted, parents focus more on their emotional well-being. 'I sometimes think I can't do anything right,' said one of the men we interviewed. 'If I don't work the hours, I'm not providing for my kids. If I do, there's also trouble. My youngest boy really plays me up on a Sunday night, because he knows he's not going to see me in the week. I don't know whether to get angry with him or not. I miss him, too.'

> 6 Your children love you. They want to play with you. How long do you think that will last? … We have a few short years with our children when they're the ones that want us around. After that, you'll be running after them for a bit of attention. It's so fast, Peter, just a few years and it's over … and you are missing it. 9
> *Wendy to Peter, in* Hook'

The invisible family

'If concern about their role as father is so significant to men,' asks James Levine, Director of the New York Families and Work Institute, 'why haven't we heard more about it?' The answer is that among the many men who are struggling with the issue privately, few raise it publicly. In a recent British survey of long-hours working, more than half the men thought this put their family relationships at risk, but given their time over again only one in four would take a stand against it.[30]

Men's participation in the world of work has been built on one of the great paradoxes of fatherhood. Since the 1950s, married men have been most sought after as employees: the British car industry, for example, specifically targeted them for recruitment, for their stability and motivation were legendary. But, at the same time, the game played in the workplace is that fathers are single men. 'Work–family is not an issue here,' wrote an American manager in the late 1980s, 'because there are no women in this firm.'[31] And in the Metropolitan Police, family invisibility among police dogs has been elevated to a new level, through a practice that some suggest may one day be popular with officers: thanks to a programme of artifical insemination, busy canines are able to sire puppies without leaving the beat!

You can tell a workplace where families are *not* invisible. In the course of research for this book we visited the head porter of a major oil company, a devoted and very active father, and found his Portakabin plastered with photographs of his children. Swedish researchers also found family visibility when they studied an intensive care unit, and observed photographs were regularly changed and passed around. Children called by or phoned, and little ones were brought in by fathers or childminders to kiss mummy goodnight when she was at work.[32] But in the average workplace, whether inhabited by men or women, everything is designed to fit the employee with no family responsibilities. The photographs of partner and children on the desk or in the cab of a lorry are icons, the inspiration for labour, not troublesome flesh-and-blood human beings. While a father is at work, or so the story goes, they make no demands on him, nor even enter his mind.

In fact, fathers develop a range of strategies to balance work and family, while trying to make sure that no one will notice what they're doing. They may, for instance, park in the back lot so they won't be seen leaving early, or say they're going to 'another meeting' without admitting that it's a meeting with their children.[33] One divorced father we interviewed collects his daughter from school every Wednesday and has done so for the past two years. No one at work is aware of this.

Studies of flexi-time programmes and of compressed week working (when people work, for instance, three or four 12-hour shifts, and have the rest of the week off) show clearly that this kind of non-standard working increases fathers' involvement with their children. Fathers, however, usually keep this quiet. 'I've worked out my time flexibly. I do the paperwork at night,' says a UK salesman, who, since he works from home, regularly cares for his four children while his wife runs her own small business. 'I'm well up on my targets but if the firm found out, they'd be livid.'[34]

6 There is no substitute for spending time with your kids. Nothing else will do. Money, other children, activity holidays – nothing will substitute for your time with them. I think they have had my time, insofar as I could possibly give it to them, with a busy career. They have had everything I had to give, apart from what I give to the job. 9

Scott, 46, father of two

Daddy stress

If it was ever true that the 'two worlds' of work and family life were not in conflict for men, it is true no longer. 'It is no longer possible for workers to leave their personal problems at home, as company cultures dictate,' declares the New York Conference Board, 'because someone is rarely home to solve them.'[35] US research has revealed that, in New York City, the proportion of men reporting significant conflict between work and family increased from 12 per cent to 71 per cent between 1977 and 1989. And a 1992 study found the same degree of work–family conflict experienced by 48.5 per cent of female and 48.3 per cent of male employees.[36] Twenty-eight per cent of male workers reported that family matters regularly got in the way of their concentration at work[37] and, in Britain, an Institute of Management survey revealed 71 per cent of managers saying they thought their relationships with their children were *badly* affected by their working lives (since half the respondents were late middle-aged men it's likely that the stress rates of fathers of young families were nearer 100 per cent).[38]

Working fathers attempt to accommodate family responsibilities to a far greater degree than is generally realised. Twenty-six per cent of first choice applicants refuse relocation for family reasons. And a recent Australian study revealed that one in four fathers had taken time off in the previous 12 months to be with sick children (though their employers had usually been told that they themselves were ill). In Britain 50 per cent of fathers in dual-earner households say they share the care of sick children equally with their wives, a proportion that has risen sharply in recent years.[39]

❛ What I tell managers is to think of me as a single mother and if that's too difficult to think of me as a single father, to pretend I'm bringing up children on my own – and then react. I tell them not to assume I've got a woman at home who is looking after my children. ❜

David Rice, father of two, quoted in Balanced Lives

It is not only the kinds of men who, in the 1950s, would have been called 'family men' who scrabble around, trying to make work fit with home and home fit with work. A recent Swedish study showed career men just as concerned with adapting work to family. They were worrying about the work–family balance, obtaining flexible hours, cutting down on overtime and refusing promotions which would further disturb family life.[40] Looking across north-western Europe to other countries, the researcher concluded that men of all social classes in all countries were becoming more child oriented, and pointed to a recent Norwegian study which revealed that some fathers now thought that developing good relationships with their children was *part of* career success: they believed that the skills they learned at home would be useful to them at work.

Segmentation v. synergy

This would be a novel idea to most UK and US fathers. While working mothers often see positive interrelation (synergy) between their professional and family lives, their partners almost always see the two areas as separate and conflicting (segmentation).[41] This probably stems from the fact that women obtain social status from both work and family, while men's social status and is gained almost exclusively from work and income.[42] But, whatever the reasons, women's synergistic approach can help lighten their load. That's not to suggest that working mothers aren't stressed out. They often are, but their worries can be different from those of working fathers. While, at the end of the working day, mothers are rushing to get to the after-school club before their children are chucked out, fathers are trying to demonstrate their commitment to work by appearing to be in no hurry to leave, and repressing the uneasy feeling (or certain knowledge) that their late departure is disappointing their children yet again.

Although the practical day-to-day responsibility for children's care causes mothers stress it may, paradoxically, actually help them reconcile work and family, for it means they prepare themselves psychologically to move from one sphere to the other. Mothers typically start turning their minds towards home before they leave work, while fathers can still be thinking about work for some time after they have arrived home.[43]

6 Unfortunately, I cannot block what happens at work when I go home. If I've had a bad day at the office, I have less patience with the kids. I suppose everyone knows when I've been home for 10 minutes what my day was like at work. 9

father quoted in Managers as Fathers

Exactly how work worries affect father–child relationships has been shown by a study of male US air-traffic controllers. When the men came home after a stressful shift, they were likely to ignore their children or behave coldly towards them. And when work had been particularly upsetting, they tended to outbursts of anger or acted the heavy disciplinarian.[44] What can make this so damaging is that children, while generally astute observers, are poor interpreters. They'll notice their father is angry or tense, but will rarely ascribe to it the correct reason. Men who are most miserable at work are most likely to report that they have bad relationships with their children. This has enormous implications for cost effectiveness in industry. An American study of 300 dual-career couples found the *only* consistent predictor of men's bad physical health to be whether they had worries or concerns about their relationships with their children.[45] There can also be a ripple effect: one sample of US employees revealed that almost 50 per cent felt other people's childcare problems had disrupted their work.[46]

Is all this just an inevitable result of the greater responsibility men carry for breadwinning? It would appear not. As already mentioned, US fathers who had attended in-depth parent-education programmes before their babies were born, and had come to feel very much *responsible* for what was going on at home even if their wives, being on maternity leave, did most of the infant-care seemed better able to leave their distress about work *at* work.[47]

Clashing agendas

Working cultures can affect fathers' behaviour at home in many ways. For instance, men who are required to be conformist employees tend to value conformity in their children, while those who must think independently produce children who are more independent and self-reliant. And in the 'masculine atmosphere' experienced by army families, relationships between fathers and sons are often unusually strong, and between fathers and daughters unusually weak.[48]

In many traditionally male workplaces, workaholism, emotional detachment, and logic and rationality are rewarded, and managers – until now, mostly male – have been trained to expect unquestioning loyalty and obedience, to issue instructions, always to have the answer, and to pretend to have it when they don't.

> 6 You are always supposed to know and if you don't know, you have got to pretend that you do. If your son asks you how a combustion engine works, you have got to cobble something together or you're not a father. You have to lie a bit. 9
>
> *Geraint, 43, father of two*

Too often, it seems, fathers in managerial jobs try to behave like managers at home, forgetting that the circumstances are entirely different. Many of today's adults remember, with anger or resentment, their fathers' inappropriate work-derived behaviour at home. The father of one of our interviewees, an engineer, used to make professional-looking charts of his children's school results, in the belief that once they could see a downward trend they would be motivated to do something about it, although they never were. Sadly, many of today's fathers may be no more sensitive. A recent US study of 300 managers revealed that fathers planning to spend time with their children almost always picked the activities themselves. The thought of asking the child what he or she wanted to do, and acting upon the answer, was completely foreign to them.[49] Every weekend, all over the country, busy fathers looking forward to delightful outings with their children, find that their offspring have other plans.

Although almost all the managers studied expressed the desire to change their behaviour at home, they had no idea what they needed to do differently, and the fact that they didn't have the skills to negotiate family relationships added yet another layer of stress. When the men did attempt changes, they still seemed to conceive them in terms of workplace culture, only this time, the 'new' workplace culture which emphasises team-work, co-operation and empathy.

One man tried regarding his children as 'valuable consultants'. Another thought he'd try role-play with his kids, and got a nasty shock when he saw his daughter's view of him, strutting around and barking out orders. A third tried thinking of the family as a team and 'allowed' his children to have input into where they wanted to go on holiday. A fourth man gave himself the target of complimenting or thanking each of his offspring three times a week. How they responded to this abrupt change in behaviour is not recorded. A fifth man managed to train himself to stop interrupting his children, but since he still found it impossible to express loving feelings, compromised by writing them letters.

All this no doubt has its uses, but we cannot assume that the current vogue for more democratic and thoughtful management styles will provide fathers with *parenting* skills or that it is more than rhetoric. In 1994, a major British white collar union, MSF, reported an increase in management bullying over the previous five years and found one in 10 employers either tolerating or encouraging a bullying management style.[50] There is also something faintly disquieting about the notion of dad as a 'team leader', a new image for fatherhood which is currently enjoying a vogue in the US. For being a team leader is not the same as being a team player. Being a team leader implies that you have much to teach and little to learn. It suggests and confirms invulnerability, and it leaves fathers in the very position which has led to their being, so often, rejected and reviled: in control, and at the top of the pile.

> ❢ As I've lived through my life, I've learned the secrets of happiness … forgive your parents; join the team; find some work and some play to do, get a partner to do it with and keep it equal; and raise children, wherever you find them. ❢
>
> *Frank Pittman*, Man Enough

Men losing out

Over the past few years, men's interest in undertaking family work has been greatly inhibited by the fact that most discussions of work or family issues have been on a feminist agenda. For the past 30 years, women who have wanted a piece of the action have been telling everyone that childrearing is a terrible job. In fact, childrearing *per se* is not terrible, as a part of life it can be truly wonderful, but this is not something women have chosen to broadcast, in case, thought that they were prepared to go on doing it 24 hours a day, for *free*.

Trying to prompt men to do their bit by making them feel guilty has met with only limited success. Experiencing guilt is not the same as taking action, and this strategy has, counter-productively, fostered the belief that the only people who are currently losers in the work–family dilemma are women. In fact, studies show that both men and women rather enjoy childcare; but what they do hate is routine housework. So convincing, however, has been this talk about the awfulness of spending time with your children, that even males who have a strong personal wish to be involved fathers usually present their participation as a justice issue. 'It seems only fair, when she's had them all week, that I should have them all Saturday,' said the head porter mentioned above who, in fact, greatly looked forward to his weekends with 'my boys'.

This emphasis on justice for *women* masks an important truth that, in terms of the work–family dilemma, men are losers too, most obviously in their relationships with their children, for only one man out of four believes his family relationships are *not* damaged by his working life. However, there are undoubtedly significant numbers of men, and some women, too, who stay at work when they don't have to, for example during the after-work hours, even when they know it is damaging their relationships with their children. There are several reasons for such behaviour. Firstly, they may have insufficient skills or confidence to feel they can take part meaningfully at home. Secondly, they may have learned to rely on work for emotional fulfilment. Thirdly, work in institutions can have an antidepressant effect. The routine, the structures, the clear reward systems and the neutral space can all provide detachment from uncomfortable feelings and supply a sense of achievement and self-worth. 'Even quite humdrum activities', says psychoanalyst Sebastian Kraemer, 'can give you the feeling that you are helping some giant wheel to turn.'[51]

> ❛ Work is more important than anything else. I believe in a sense of contribution and public service and this is the most important thing to me. I have a sense of mission, and it is my belief that I am going to fulfil that purpose, and if I didn't fulfil that purpose I would feel I had failed in my life. ❜
>
> *Tom, 42, father of two*

But there is more to it. To men who do little childcare, the process can look difficult. 'I couldn't stay at home!' said one of our interviewees, a 38-year-old merchant banker, who works 12-hour-days as routine, 'I couldn't stand the strain.' This man's wife is not, as one might think from his reaction, living in poverty and raising a football team. The family has two well-behaved daughters, aged five and seven.

Why does this father perceive childraising to be so difficult? Firstly, his wife, who engages her offspring in a relentless round of Suzuki violin lessons and other improving activities regularly tells him it is. She had a good career once, and although she has elected to stay home, has not done so without resentment. Secondly, when he does turn up before bedtime it's at the worst time of day when his daughters seem to be doing their best to kill and be killed, and he gets the impression that the whole day is spent like this. Thirdly, his childrearing skills are limited because he's had no practice, so when he does look after the children of course he finds it hard. Fourthly, when he is supposedly in charge, in reality he isn't. He's trying to follow instructions left by his wife, and the children object to the fact that he doesn't do things 'like mummy'.

All this adds up to a seriously unrewarding experience. His wife complains that when he does do things with the children ' … it's the fun things', and that he never gets down to the nitty gritty. But, of course, it's the nitty gritty which, in the end, provides the real rewards and through which a parent's self-esteem is built. One of our interviewees was thrilled the day we interviewed him: the night before, when his toddler had been wakened by a bad dream he had called out for 'daddy'.

> **❝** To hear another man say that his kids are driving him crazy seems to the gentleman father an act of treason: it's not suppposed to be work, he seems to be saying, it's supposed to be fun, fulfilling, rewarding. But who said fulfilling experiences shouldn't be difficult, that fun would not be leavened with frustration? In a culture where Forrest Gump seems like a role model … I think it is important to remember that rewarding does not mean painless. **❞**
>
> *Sean Elder,* Dabbling Dads

'Men should play a bigger role at home, to free their wives to go out to work,' declared the then-Employment Secretary, Norman Fowler (somewhat surprisingly) in 1989.[52] What he could not say, and would have been laughed out of the House for saying, is that 'women should play a bigger role in the workforce to *free their husbands to spend more time with their families*'.

Although women have to battle corporate sexism to a degree few men can begin to imagine, it is not women but *people* who are penalised in the workplace for trying to 'have it all', if by 'all' you mean a good job and good family relationships. In fact men who do not play by the old rules almost certainly suffer more workplace discrimination than women for their behaviour, which is seen as even more threatening.

When, in an experiment, a dummy memorandum from an 'employee' who was supposedly requesting one month's unpaid leave to care for three young children, was circulated to 1,500 US employers, leave was significantly less likely to be granted, or thought appropriate, by employers who thought the memorandum had come from a man.[53] In the UK, a leading head-hunting agency believes that while employers can now sometimes be quite accommodating to a woman with childcare responsibilities, it would be the 'kiss of death' for a man to say he needed flexibility for childcare.[54]

> 6 Driven people like to be working with other driven people ... For a manager to come forward and say, 'Yeah, I've been driving right along with you guys for a while but I don't want to drive this fast any more, I want to spend some time with my family', that would be like saying 'I don't want to be part of this club anymore'. 9
>
> *father quoted in* Segmentation and Synergy

Despite these fears, men are increasingly negotiating flexible or reduced working hours, and attitudes may be changing in some areas. Among men whose companies offer part-time working, 70 per cent no longer believe that taking this up would jeopardise their career prospects, if they could afford to work part time.[55] A BT management development specialist with a young son was astonished when his 'totally career oriented' boss agreed comfortably to his request to work a three-day week for a while. And a planning analyst for a multinational corporation is able to leave the office at 4.30 p.m. most days to collect his children, as long as he makes up the time in the evenings and at weekends.'[56]

Paying the price?

Does fathers' involvement in the family have a price-tag? Anyone watching the 1979 film, *Kramer v. Kramer*, would have assumed so. For while the Dustin Hoffman character did get to love and be loved and the Meryl Streep character failed as wife, mother and human being, she made money in the process and gained a rewarding career. Hoffman lost his job and had to take a cut in salary.

When we began our interviews with fathers for this book, one surprising finding was how often our most involved fathers also turned out to be successful in career terms and conversely how often our least involved fathers seemed to be struggling. The workaholics in particular, who before and since their children's births had given virtually everything to their work, were often the men facing career disappointments.

❦ I always used to get up by 6 a.m., into the office by 6.50, and the last four or five years, since the children have been born, there's been the prospect of bankruptcy. We bought the house just at the wrong time. I tend to be driven to sorting out the money matters and that has led to a lot of polarisation between Jane and me. When we lived close to the office it was worse. It was easy to drop in at the weekends. And since it was easy for me to get home in the evenings, I could work fairly late. ❧

Graham, 38, father of two

What does this formal research reveal? Although earlier research studies seemed to confirm the commonsense view that the more time men devote to their children, the further down the organisational ladder they remain,[57] recent research has found this see-saw effect less often. A 1990 study of 300 highly successful US industrialists found that not one was a workaholic, and most had managed to retain a surprisingly good balance between work and home.[58] A similar pattern can be found in the career and life-styles of ordinary fathers. While fathers who work part time or drop out of the workforce for extended periods usually pay a huge price in terms of their careers, high levels of family involvement by *full-time working fathers* are not associated with career-failure, any more than low levels of father involvement predict career success. In fact, when 240 Boston men were monitored from childhood to middle age, it became apparent that those who had spent a lot of time, when compared with other employed fathers, helping their younger children with their school work, and their older children with their social skills, had done particularly *well* career-wise themselves.[59]

How can this be? For a start, fathers do not necessarily trade time with their children for work time. While employed mothers trade family and work time directly hour for hour, one study revealed that for every additional hour fathers worked, the time they spent with their children decreased by just 10 minutes.[60] Successful men may be good at time-management. We found that while the highly involved fathers usually made sure they lived close to where they worked, it was typical of the workaholic fathers to locate their families far away from the office, and therefore spend endless hours commuting.

❛ I leave work around 7 p.m. and am home maybe 8.30. The children are still awake. After the journey it's a strange feeling. You've been pushing yourself on the motorway to stop falling asleep and then you're conscious of relaxing, breathing, closing down. I get through the evening on that sort of basis. ❜

Paul, 37, father of three

Successful men may also be talented communicators with good people skills, and may enjoy their work. Men who are the most committed to, and passionate about, their jobs sometimes achieve the most sensitive relationships with their children, even though they may not spend as much time with them as men who are less satisfied in their careers. The intimate relationships involved fathers enjoy with their children may, in turn, feed back into the workplace, promoting the men's effectiveness at work. The mechanism by which this happens isn't fully understood, but it is thought to hinge on discomfort. The unique experience of parenthood, attachment to another human being for whom you would willingly sacrifice everything, yet who periodically makes demands upon you which you are simply not prepared to meet, unsettles the father profoundly. To cope, he develops new ways of thinking and feeling and acting, and these, in turn, improve his capacity to handle commitments outside his family. Some commentators have called this process 'generativity'.[61]

In some cases, there may be practical reasons for the link between career success and good father–child relations. Successful men may be able to write their own rules, as could (and did) Sir John Harvey-Jones, ex-Chairman of ICI. As the devoted father of a disabled daughter, he left work regularly at 5.15 p.m., to go home.[62] Two of our interviewees, one a very senior civil servant, the other a solicitor now heading up one of the biggest practices in London, had adopted similar strategies.

❛ Because I was so successful early on, I could simply say to my staff 'I go home at 5.30', and because I basically delivered, nobody questioned. So I came home in time to bath my children and be with them and feed them and all those things. Then I worked later in the evening. ❜

Scott, 46, father of two

There was one other factor which we found common to all the men who managed to have both successful careers and successful family relationships: not one had a consuming hobby or played much sport or was very involved in the community. These working fathers, like so many working mothers, seemed to focus on just two main areas; their work and their children.

Father-friendly employment

If fathers are to achieve a better balance between home and work, what do they need? Family-friendly employment, clearly. Lots of companies are in favour of this, as long as family friendly means mother friendly. But telephone a corporation with even the most cloyingly virtuous human resource policies and mention fathers, and the atmosphere changes instantly. They mutter things like 'productivity' and 'Board approval', and ask to vet your copy.

Family-friendly policy making for men is not the same as family-friendly policy making for women. Developing father-friendly initiatives requires an entirely new mind-set, and not one that seems to have been adopted by a single British company yet, presumably out of ignorance, but possibly out of blind terror. Contrast this with the Los Angeles Department of Water and Power (DWP), part of whose mission is to ' … make men feel comfortable about being part of their families'! When asked how this could be achieved, the male DWP employees raised fathering courses as a priority, and DWP now provide an eight-week course for expectant fathers, as well as a mentorship programme through which experienced fathers support new dads.[63]

Women have no trouble accepting family-friendly policies as being for their benefit. In fact, it seems probable that many even see paternity leave in this light. When UK fatherhood researcher Margaret O'Brien asked teenage girls why they thought fathers should be present at their children's births, the most common reason they gave was 'to help the mother'.[64] And although male employees use work place nurseries, childcare vouchers and childcare information lines as often as female employees, they may not perceive them as being 'for them'. They may, rather, see them as a benefit for their *wives*. Men believe they would work anyway, whether or not childcare was available, an illusion that is usually only shattered if they become lone parents, and this belief is reinforced when childcare costs are weighed against women's earnings alone. Most families do this, although one of our interviewees (a youth-club manager whose wife was a dancing teacher) commented, unusually, on the high costs of childcare 'for *us*'.

> ❢ When we first started working with large companies, the groups of men and women sounded very different. If the men complained at all about long hours, they complained about their wives' complaints. Now, if the timbre of the voice was disguised, I couldn't tell which was which. The men are saying: 'I don't want to live this way. I want to be with my kids.' ❥
>
> *Ellen Galinsky, Families and Work Institute, New York*

The fact that fathers' childcare responsibilities have for so long been delegated and met privately within their families means that they have been rendered invisible and so have passed out of our consciousness. Indeed, the notion that fathers are not responsible for childcare has become so deeply ingrained that it even informs the thinking of those who should know better. When, in Britain in 1994, evidence on the difficulties of combining work and family was presented to an all-party Committee of British MPs by pressure groups and family experts, it was riveting to observe only mothers and children hauled forward to sing the praises of after-school clubs or day nurseries. Not one man was brought in to state what is so glaringly obvious that we have all forgotten it: that men, no less than women, can only take part in the world of paid employment if someone else is looking after their children.

In fact no issue is more a fathers' issue than childcare. Childcare support is not only a direct benefit to an increasing number of fathers, it is an indirect benefit to *all* fathers. That is because without an infrastructure of affordable quality childcare women cannot compete in the labour market on equal terms with men, and until they do, men's options, no less than women's, remain limited. Firstly, supporting a family normally takes more than one salary, and if a mother is unemployed or restricted to low-paid or part-time work by childcare responsibilities, her partner will usually have to put in long hours to compensate. Secondly, a part-time or low-paid working woman cannot in any sense bridge the gap if her partner becomes unemployed, so unemployment is seen primarily as a male problem. All this militates against good father–child relations, as we have seen. The third way in which childcare is a father's issue is in the context of divorce. At this point the carer–breadwinner stereotype becomes a parody of itself, for even if breadwinning and caring are shared by a couple beforehand, these functions usually become sharply divided afterwards.

After divorce, if a mother works, fathers are no longer in the house to mind the children. And if a father's workplace value is much higher than his partner's (as it very probably is) and if childcare support is so sparse or so expensive that one parent must be kept available to pick the children up from school and cope with the holidays, then it will make sense, in the awful logic of divorce, for that person to be the mother. Now the father will truly find himself rated as a provider, but this may not now be felt as achievement, but as a humiliation. For his pay-packet will be picked-over and apportioned by strangers, while he faces the loss of most of what being a father has meant to him. 'I just took the children for granted. They were always around, crawling on my lap for a cuddle,' said one recently separated father. 'Now when I wake, I think, what is the point of getting up?'

> ❛ I play for his school assembly every morning – they didn't have anyone who could play the piano. I've arranged it with my line manager and I pop in on my way to work. That way I get to see my boy almost every day, not to talk to but sometimes I get a wink. When I go into the school, everyone knows me and I feel like a parent again. ❜
>
> *Paul, father- of one*

It can be no coincidence that in Canberra, Australia, a city with a 50-year tradition of quality affordable childcare, full-time employment rates among mothers (married, cohabiting, separated, divorced) are unusually high, and the children of divorced couples routinely live part time with *both* parents. For when divorcing couples are enabled to be breadwinners on equal terms, then they can be carers on equal terms.

Is parental leave for fathers?

If childcare is a father-friendly workplace benefit, although often not recognised as such, parental leave arrangements are different again, and here we have another paradox. While some of these may appear to be negotiated for fathers, they often turn out to be benefits only for mothers. No one seriously considers career breaks as being of much use to fathers except perhaps to the tiny number of professional men with highly paid partners who take such breaks. But *parental* leave, time off to care for pre-schoolers, has been so-named because it is *supposed* to be taken by fathers, too. However, parental leave is not automatically a father-friendly benefit. In its full-time form and as a benefit to care for infants (which is how it was originally designed), fewer than 3 per cent of fathers take it. Mothers use it all, usually without discussion and frequently for breastfeeding.

The reasons for low take-up by fathers are simple. Unless parental leave is paid at full salary, the family loses because the father is usually higher paid. Employers don't usually hire replacement labour for the short time the men are away, so a backlog develops at work, and in addition the men fear a negative impact on their careers. At home there are so few other stay-at-home dads that fathers often feel out of place, and spend most of the time on their own with their children. Some very exceptional men have the social skills to deal with the mothers' networks. One tattooed Australian who took over from his wife as their baby's primary carer, put L-plates on the buggy!

> ❬ When I was left with Peter the local mums were very friendly, very welcoming. But I'm not their intimate friend – I am a man. I remember some mothers sort of laughing about wanting to talk about nappies. And I was desperate to talk about nappies, because I didn't know anything about them … So I ran the toddler group Peter was in and then I chaired his playgroup – it gave me a reason to talk to all the mums. ❭
>
> *Bob, father-of-two (two families)*

However, when parental leave is designed with *fathers in mind*, take-up increases. In Sweden parental leave can be taken full or part-time and even in short blocks. It can also be taken for older children – that is, beyond the months normally required by mothers for breastfeeding. Take-up by fathers in Sweden is running at 50 per cent, a figure which should rise even higher now that a non-transferable 'daddy month' quota has been introduced to give men a stronger case when they approach employers. Taking parental leave is then seen less as an indulgence and more as a necessity.

Sweden considers its parental leave policy to have been the single most important factor in increasing fathers' participation in family life. Since most Swedish parents work, parental leave is becoming, in effect, a parenting allowance. Some parents take leave consecutively, to care for infants full time so they don't have to go into nurseries too young, and it has been found that fathers who stay at home alone with their children for a minimum of three months develop independent relationships with them and remain highly involved after they return to work. Other parents take the leave mostly part time and use it to subsidise shorter hours working while their children are small. All this is reducing the need for (expensive) nursery places.

Parental leave is now a major issue for family-friendly employment worldwide and every single country in the European Union, other than the UK, now provides for it, by law. The EU system is, potentially, incredibly radical. Although at the moment it allows for parental leave to be unpaid (and since this is the case, one wonders just what the British Government has been making such a fuss about), it specifies three months' *non-transferable* leave per worker, per child. If, in the long run, this doesn't enable fathers to be involved, then nothing will.

A word about mothers

It is often suggested that since mothers clearly 'want' to stay at home with their children (the evidence cited is that they take most of the parental leave), we should forget about fathers and concentrate on providing longer and longer leave for mothers. To do this would be to ignore the fact that mothers, no less than fathers, make their choices within a specific context: mothers are more likely than fathers to be employed below capability and for low wages; the 'innate' superiority of mother-care is still being trumpeted on all sides; decent childcare is hard to find and expensive; and fathers may be committed to long or erratic hours, for which mothers often feel they have to cover. The women most likely to prefer full-time motherhood are low-waged women who do exhausting physical work. And among the rest, those most likely to be bowled over by maternal instinct and to chuck in their jobs, are the women who were most dissatisfied (often secretly) with their employment or prospects before their babies were born.[65]

> ❛ I always believed that it was best if the mother was there for the children, in the morning and when they came in from school, especially if they had problems at school, such as bullying, they had their mother to confide in. I suppose my mother was always there for me and I suppose that is why I think this. My father worked about seven or eight miles from home, which meant that he left early in the morning, we didn't see him in the morning, and he didn't get in until maybe 7 p.m. at night. ❜
>
> *Ritchie, 34, father of two*

Differentiating between the needs of mothers and fathers in family-friendly policy-making, is crucial. If we go 'gender blind' on this one, we may not serve anyone well and will end up with policies vulnerable to hijack by tradition. Here we must walk a tightrope, being careful not to deny mothers' unique requirements, while remaining aware that all mothers, no less than all fathers, will not have the same requirements. Even mothers' physiological needs vary. Some women, having spent the first trimester of pregnancy with their heads in the toilet, cycle robustly to work during the last three months. For others, the process of pregnancy is a gradual slowing down. And afterwards, while some mothers take a long time to recover, others snap-to in a matter of weeks. Breastfeeding, which can play an important part in the desire to return to, or stay away from, work is another variable: of no interest to some women, a duty to others and to yet others the pinnacle of the mothering experience.

In trying to establish what parents want, we must also remain sensitive to the new mythology of motherhood, which dictates that where women once had to suffer to be beautiful, they now have to suffer to be what society considers good mothers. Extended absence from the workplace, combined with maternal distress (largely brought on by having to cope alone) has now become the hallmark of 'real' mothering. This would be outside the remit of this book were it not for the fact that, in our society, lonely painful motherhood has become the gold-standard against which fathering is measured, and by which it must inevitably fail.

Just as men, throughout this century, have derived their status from exclusivity as breadwinners, mothers have derived theirs from exclusivity as intimate parents, a notion which would shock a Pacific Islander, who doesn't even have a word for 'mother' (mothers and aunts share the same name and responsibilities).[66] In so far as exclusivity represents power, one would not expect the notion of maternal exclusivity to be easily surrendered, and it is interesting to note renewed interest in breastfeeding emerging just when fathers were first being admitted onto the labour wards; and 'breast is best' campaigning at its height during revelations about fathers' capacities to be just as good at 'mothering' as mothers.

To see the exclusive mother model violated comes as a surprise, as we found when we interviewed the youth-club worker with the dancing teacher wife, mentioned earlier. This couple live above the youth club, from which the dancing school also operates. Neither took much of a break from employment when their children were born, but adjusted with the almost limitless flexibility available to them, supported by grandparents, buying in huge amounts of childcare, and co-operating completely. They were busy and tired but, it was plain, in an extremely positive way. When interviewed, they were about to become parents for the sixth time.

> ❛ It is very difficult to plan a sex life by saying, 'Right well every Sunday morning at 10 o'clock,' because you know 10 o'clock on Sunday morning there are maybe five kids in your bed, which is very often the case with us. So I suppose a lot of them have happened through lack of care and also from a position of strength, in as much as we feel quite together in our relationship, we feel quite – I think we both feel that we are quite competent parents and therefore that gives you this sort of gay abandon towards contraception. ❜
>
> *Steve, 39, father of- ix*

Our society may wish for any number of reasons to facilitate long-term, full-time leave for new parents, but if we target this mainly at mothers we need to be aware of the consequences. For what we will get is this: the difference between male and female workers exacerbated, true reconciliation between work and family an illusion, and the workplace more and more sharply divided by gender.

Gendering the millennium

Sweden, which for years had mothers more in mind than fathers, has the most gender-divided workforce in the world. This trend is also well advanced in other countries, including our own, and while it is caused by a range of factors, family-friendly policies designed mainly for women and taken up mainly by women exacerbate the situation.

In certain employment areas, typically charities, financial services and healthcare, women and a few men club together in sufficient numbers to force through some workplace tolerance for workers with family responsibilities. These market sectors then become additionally attractive to women, who congregate more and more heavily in them, and the word goes out that our society is embracing work and family. It isn't. Everywhere else remains untouched.

Gender segregation of the workplace is bad for business. Businesses employing only single-minded, 24-hours-on-the-job male workers find themselves choosing from a narrower and narrower labour pool. The brightest and best of corporate thinking has now accepted the desirability of diverse work teams at all levels in all sectors. Even the Australian mining industry, which admitted women against its better judgement, found not only that the men soon preferred the dual-sex workplaces, but that labour relations improved.[67] Diversity also delivers competitive advantage. Pampers disposable nappies were invented by a grandfather who, by chance, spent the weekend looking after his grandchild and thought 'this will never do!' When workers all have similar assumptions, values and work patterns, risks are not taken, customers' needs go unrecognised and corporate thinking is not creative. This might not have mattered 50 years ago, but it matters a lot today.

Gender segregation of the workplace is famously bad for women, keeping them in low-status, low-paid work. But what is less often recognised is that it is bad for men too, and not only because it traps them in the sole- or main-breadwinner mould. Males working in men-only workplaces find it well-nigh impossible to negotiate family-friendly working, or challenge the long-hours culture, or the ageism that insists they've failed if they haven't made it to the top by 40.

> ‘ I feel like a stranger trying to get to know my own family. I was gone a lot while they were growing up, and when I did come home I was preoccupied with career-related problems. Ten years ago I told my wife and children to just wait until I got established and then I could spend some time with them. Now that I want to get involved with them, I am finding they are more comfortable without me. ’
>
> *father quoted in* Managers as Fathers

When areas are female dominated they become seen as no-go areas for 'real' men, who hesitate to seek employment in them, even as traditional work opportunities for men diminish. Despite widespread worries about unemployment among young males, it wasn't possible to find a single school initiative, let alone a local or national policy, directing boys into careers in education or welfare, although girls are still being enthusiastically directed towards careers in science and engineering. When the no-go areas for boys include, as is the case today, family services (primary schools, nurseries, social work) this can have a negative impact on ordinary father–child relationships. Men seeking employment in these areas are seen as making an eccentric choice, and must be strongly motivated to do so. One thing that sometimes proves sufficient motivation is a sexual interest in children, and so sexual abusers become common in childhood services, relative to other males.

Soon it is thought that *only* an abuser will choose this career and, by extension, it begins to appear as if every man with an interest in children, including fathers in their own homes, is an abuser. Nor is this casting of aspersions the only problem. The more childhood is 'feminised', the higher the percentage of women at retail outlets and in GPs surgeries, among health visitors and social workers, in nurseries and primary schools, the more ordinary fathers back away. They avoid going into the nursery or the school, turn their back on the family centre, leave the parent education and family counselling to mothers, and to female trainers and female therapists. Female professionals usually have little inclination and less understanding of how to engage men, and simply note that fathers 'aren't interested' in family matters, while the social workers joke that when the professional turns up at the front door, '... the father leaves by the back'.

The dominance of women in family services, and the corresponding scarcity of men, is among the most powerful of all the forces which exclude fathers from the lives of their children today. For in this we see the outward and visible sign of what begins to be perceived as an essential truth: that in family life, men are an irrelevance at best, and at worst a danger.

❛ In autumn 1990, I was walking up the Holloway Road with my mate, and we were both carrying our babies in slings on our chests. This car went past with these young blokes in it, and they slowed right down, rolled down the windows, and yelled out 'Child-abusers!' Nothing like that happened 16 years ago when I was going round with my first son, doing much the same things. I think attitudes have changed. I think some men are scared to be seen being intimate with their children. ❜

Phil, 43, father of two (two families)

Having it all

In designing workplace policies for fathers we must not only take into account that fathers' needs vary, but that what a majority of fathers need – or will be able to accept – today, may not suit them tomorrow. We cannot assume, for instance, that the gap between male and female wages will not continue to close, or even that men will remain advantaged in the workplace, or that they will not enter traditionally female areas of employment, or even that their identity will not become intimately tied up in family life. In Sweden, after a relatively short time focusing on fathers' requirements in an informed and sensitive way, more than one man out of three now sees as 'ideal' a situation in which parents share breadwinning and childcaring equally. But given the present situation in the UK, where few people think about fathers at all, it seems likely that the best present you could give a British father would be truly flexible working, and that doesn't just mean being able to come in half an hour late or leave half an hour early. Many men are keen for this and 41 per cent are sure that their companies would benefit if they worked flexibly.[68] In the long term, enabling both men and women to balance the needs of work and family will entail a revolution in working time, but this may be the revolution that is coming.

Increasingly, there is talk of 'time banks', of individuals working shorter or longer hours as the needs of their lives and the workplace dictate. It seems absurd that older and younger people should be without work, while those in the middle stages of life and trying to raise children, are so punishingly overworked. The Australian insurance company, MLC Life, has taken this on in a big way and has designed its customer service teams to include both long- and shorter-hours workers. These last include young people still studying, older people scaling down to retirement, and parents of young children. The company finds it is now meeting the needs both of its customers and its employees, and no doubt its share-holders, *far more effectively* than ever before.[69]

> ❛ Only a minority of employees now work a 'normal working day', and the 'normal working week' is becoming a minority activity too … The organisation of working time is becoming more flexible, more varied and more individualised. We can see emerging from the old model of standardised working time a new model of 'post-industrial' working time – a model much closer to female, than to male, patterns of the past. ❜
>
> *Patricia Hewitt,* About Time

Although MLC Life is unusual in taking the needs of *all* its employees, not just mothers, into account, the push for reorganisation and the drive towards flexible working has arisen for sound business reasons: the need to meet consumer demand and maximise return on capital investment. This is happening all over the world, and fathers, as well as mothers, are turning the situation to their advantage. Many of the fathers now appearing at the school gates are not unemployed, but working shifts or flexible hours. Additional encouragement is afforded by a new blue-print provided by working mothers, who are demonstrating that it is not necessary to be a full-time stay-at-home parent to have intricate and satisfactory relationships with your chidren. Militating against this potentially father-friendly climate, however, is Britain's reviled long-hours culture, which insists that truly committed workers, managers in particular, not only be available to meet work demands at a moment's notice but, in order to prove loyalty and dedication, must stay at work even when there isn't much going on.

This ideology currently has a stranglehold, even though much of it seems to be a mark of business inefficiency: 43 per cent of male white-collar employees believe that if their companies were better organised there'd be no need to work long hours on a regular basis. Indeed, long-hours working seems to do surprisingly few men any real good: only 17 per cent believe their last advancement was due to the hours they put in.[70] This does not, of course, mean that *without* working the long hours, they would have been considered fit for promotion.

Accommodating fathers

When MLC Life canvassed its employees, both mothers and fathers felt confident they could manage the work–family 'dilemma' satisfactorily provided they were given enough *flexibility* to do so. Working *shorter* hours wasn't their top priority. Flexibility is already on offer to British men far more readily than is generally appreciated, as those who request flexibility for reasons of career or personal development often discover.[71] It's when men request flexibility *for family reasons* that disapproval is voiced, and at no time does it seem to occur to anyone that for a father, taking responsibility for his children might, in itself, be a route to personal development.

> ❛ You know in films about the danger of World War Three, to get to the button that launches the missile you have to unlock something, unlock a case for it? Having children unlocked the case for me, it released this explosive volcanic rage and it is shocking, and the thing I try most to do something about. I do not suffer fools gladly and children sometimes are fools. That's got better with each one. I am more understanding now, when Ellie wants to get herself dressed and tries to put every bit of herself through the same hole of the shirt. I have learned a bit more about how people learn, and how you therefore have to teach. ❜
>
> *Philip, 39, father of three*

When researchers investigated shift working in a police station (mainly staffed by men) and an intensive care unit (mainly staffed by women), they found some fascinating parallels – and differences. Among the nurses, childcare needs were openly taken into account when rosters were drawn up, as well as when staff negotiated 'swaps'. Working life in the police station was potentially just as flexible and, in fact, many of the men used shift working to take considerable responsibility for their children at home. This, however, was not something they made public, and when shifts were allocated, the basis for the distribution was entirely different: to give the men equal access to the most lucrative shifts, and to accommodate second jobs.[72] Men have a long tradition of accommodating each other at work. Time is made available for the territorial army, charity and local initiatives, trade union work and commitments to professional organisations, and 'moonlighting'. Why shouldn't this flexibility include recognition of men's responsibilities to their children?

Australian researcher Graeme Russell finds that when the issue is approached in the right way, fatherhood can be put on the company agenda with surprising ease. In one organisation where (male) employees had expressed a desire for three days of their sick leave to be designated emergency family leave, the Board, who had seemed at the outset implacably opposed, reviewed the results of a pilot study and cheerfully offered three days family-leave *on top of* sick leave.

The vision thing: what if ...?

This chapter, so far, has been mainly about the here and now, but what of possibilities for the future? What if our entire attitude to parenthood, and to fathers' and women's rights, roles and responsibilities, were to change? How would the world of childhood look if both fathers *and* mothers (with equal control over fertility, and so with parenthood a truly joint venture) entered on the process determined to make the most of an experience they knew would only come their way once, or perhaps twice, in a long lifetime?

What if parenting leave began before birth (for both partners) with time off to accommodate the kind of preparation for parenthood already offered in the US, and documented by the Cowans (outlined in Chapter 4)? What if we were able to harness the growing flexibility both in working time and in working space (including teleworking in which, recently, there has been an explosion) to permit both mothers and fathers to scale their working hours down towards the birth and up from the birth, as necessary and as desired, supported by excellent 'drop in' childcare provision and child health services? And what if, after the birth, it was standard practice for fathers and mothers to be allowed a period of adjustment, together, as a family? Something rather like a 'honeymoon', that was no doubt very necessary before premarital cohabitation became so widespread. Indeed, it is probably fair to say that many men today spend more time on a honeymoon getting to know women they have been living with for years than they spend at home after the birth of their baby!

❛ I feel it's a question of making flexible working for men happen (if that's what someone wants) rather than assuming 'It can't be done in our company'. My expectation was that, and I was wrong. I think perhaps a lot of men might have the belief there's no point in trying because I know the answer will be no. Well, in some cases it might be no, but it might be possible to make something happen, or at least to raise awareness. ❜
management trainer quoted in Balanced Lives

And what if during this 'baby-moon', parent education and training continued, building on networks established before the birth, so that couples were enabled to develop baby-care skills *in tandem* and both felt part of a wider community? Then women would no longer be left to cope alone, day and night, prey to exhaustion and postnatal depression; and men could wake in the small hours to feed their child or change it and hand it to a breastfeeding mother, without despairing about having to go to work in the morning.[73] From where we stand now all this looks inconceivable, and many will even say undesirable. But 30 years ago it was inconceivable (and widely accepted as undesirable) that men attend the births of their children, or that women continue working once they were mothers.

One of the most important lessons to be learned from the Swedish experience is that extensive public education campaigns are necessary before fathers are taken seriously as intimate parents. For it is now understood that much of what fathers can do for their children, and children for their fathers, depends on the value accorded their interaction by the local and wider community. This is just as important as what actually goes on between fathers and children in everyday life. If a culture is saturated with indifferent or clearly negative attitudes to close father–child relationships, then this often results in such a relationship (even one that actually works well on a day-to-day basis) being felt to be of little importance, or problematic.

Time and again when talking with parents, we came up against the notion that fathers are of little importance in themselves. That it didn't really matter if daddy was never home before bedtime, provided mummy was, and that as long as she was clapping and smiling at the swimming gala everything would be OK. It's not that a father's presence wasn't desired. Often it very much was. But the belief seemed to be that it was not necessary, that mothers could deputise well enough for their partners in respect of the children, much as they might when taking the car to be serviced.

Whether or not this is the case will be examined in the next chapter. But what is certain is that the *belief* that fathers are replaceable (and mothers are not) profoundly influences the day-to-day behaviour of working fathers. For, while even mothers who work exceedingly long hours rarely spend less than an hour on a (working) day interacting with their children because they somehow, against all the odds, *make* that time, fathers do not do this. Fathers are far less likely than mothers to rush home from work to snatch half an hour with their kids before bedtime, not because they don't love or value their children but because they don't value *themselves* at home. Because they do not believe their presence and attention there to be of the highest importance, or even, let it be said, *of much importance at all.*

> ❛ I don't believe you can trust men as you can trust women. It affects me as a father and I think the kids know that I am like that. They think Barbara is caring and angry, and I am fun. I think it is my natural self to be caring, but I haven't got myself into the caring position with my children, I think partly because of the huge demands of my work. But I do feel also that it is possible that I have shut myself off emotionally from my children. The kids say that I'm going deaf, but I'm not really deaf. I'm just not in their world. I'm in another world completely from them. ❜
>
> *Tom, 42, father of two*

Chapter 6

Divorce and After: bringing fathers back in

Does the fact that a father may consider himself to be in a different world from his children, and spend very little time in their company, really matter? After all, research has shown that the children of full-time working mothers do no less well in later life than the children of full-time housewives, although in the former circumstance mother and child spend much less time together.[1] The notion of quality time may be derided, but in parent–child relationships quality is indeed more important than quantity.

Yet here's the rub: the two are connected.[2] There seems to be a certain minimum requirement in terms of quantity which, if it is not met, affects quality. This makes intuitive sense. It is hard to relate constructively to someone you don't know very well. Most working mothers seem to meet the necessary level of involvement: not only do they rarely interact closely with their young children for less than an hour a day, but because they remain 'in charge' of their lives, are continually consulting with them and their caretakers, staying in touch with their development and needs. This is not usually the case with working fathers. What is their minimum requirement? Or, to put it another way, how little fathering is fathering enough? 'What we want to know,' said a leading UK journalist, speaking (or so he said) on behalf not only of himself but of ' … every other anxious father in the newsroom, is how much time do you need to spend with your children to stop them, you know … taking drugs and so on?'

❝ I never felt close to my parents. If I look back at my childhood and think what time did I spend with them I can't actually think of very much. I don't want to make the same mistakes with my children. Something that bothers me quite deeply is that I still feel a bit detached from them as I do from most people and I have been very busy with other things since they were born … I hope it's not too late. I suppose I hope pretty strongly that much of the bonding between parent and child takes place in the later years. **,**

Nigel, 44, father of four

The cowardly answer to how much fathering is enough would be, 'how long is a piece of string?' Not only can skilled fathers make a lot out of a little, but child development depends on many things. It depends on health, wealth, education and support; on environment; on the child's personal characteristics and those of its siblings; on the confidence and competence of its caretakers; and on the quality of its parents' relationship. In fact, the single most important indicator of maladjustment in children is their parents' active hostility – to each other.[3]

None of this, however, lets fathers off the hook. The more extensive a father's involvement with his children at ages 11 and 16, the higher their education and career aspirations; and the greater his participation when they are seven and 11, the less likely they are to become delinquent.[4] Even boys whose fathers have criminal records are less likely to get into trouble themselves if their fathers spend a lot of time with them.[5] Bearing these simple facts in mind, it seems probable that many working fathers should think twice before accepting all the overtime offered, even if it does enable them to be better providers. The losses may outweigh the gains.

How does quality mitigate or exacerbate the effects of quantity? Poor father–child relationships (poor can mean either negative or distant) are *clearly* linked to substance abuse by adolescents, and both emotionally distant and bullying fathers feature heavily in the histories of anorexic and bulimic women. Nor do 'close-binding' fathers, who hamper their children's independence through anxious over-involvement do them any good. This, too, is linked with anorexia and bulimia, as well as with other stress-related conditions such as asthma.[6]

Children cannot be relied upon to see their father's focus on matters outside his family as a positive. Some may buy into 'Daddy's working all weekend because he loves you so much', but others experience this as rejection and may rationalise the situation by concluding that what they have to offer their apparently detached parent can't be of much interest.[7] Adolescent delinquents often have fathers who don't pay much attention to their comings and goings, or who react unsupportively or defensively towards them.[8] One of our interviewees, a man whose adult adjustment had been very troubled, recalled how, when he had rushed in to tell his parents he had won a scholarship to the best university in the land, all his father had said was, 'Look at that mud you've trekked across the hall'!

> "I saw this face with glasses behind the locked gate ... It was Scott. It was about a year before he died of an overdose ... Dad did his best. But of course, Dad was always super busy. And when he was making a movie he just wasn't available ... When someone you love and need can only see you now and then for just a few hours, you feel love and hate ... When you really love someone as Scott loved Dad, you hate the fact that he can't be with you."
>
> *Paul Newman's daughter, quoted in,* Fathers and Sons

Alcoholic fathers and fathers who are depressed tend to spawn children with adjustment problems (although, interestingly, the school performance of children of alcoholics does not necessarily seem to suffer). Genetically, we are only just beginning to understand the subtlety of fathers' contributions: 30 per cent of the sons of alcoholic fathers will, themselves, become alcoholic. Such a strong link is not found with daughters' alcoholism, although they show higher than average rates in marrying alcoholics.[9]

The good father

What benefits children enormously is *positive* involvement, and plenty of it, with their fathers. This is not only of terrific value in itself but can act as a buffer to negative circumstances, such as economic hardship or a hostile or difficult mother. Adolescents with depressed mothers do better in life if they have had good relationships with their fathers.[10]

In the previous chapter it was pointed out that parental achievement was an important predictor of positive outcomes for children, and that effective breadwinning was one of the most vital functions of parenthood. That is so, but it does not tell the whole story. Life success very often comes to the 'emotionally intelligent', to individuals whose psychological competence has enabled them to optimise their intellectual gifts. Emotional intelligence can develop over the whole life-span but it is forged in our families of origin, and in particular, in our relationships with our parents, fathers as well as our mothers.[11]

> "If I've been around enough, then things can be left half said. If not, then things need to be fully said. If they are having problems with their homework, say, then I would know

it may be because of what happened yesterday. If I can't do that, then I'm not spending enough time with them.

Roger O'Connell, quoted in Go on, leave. They'll survive without you.

For a long time it was believed that babies formed just one 'primary attachment' (usually with their mothers) on which their emotional health depended. And, certainly, children with only one main caretaker are substantially dependent on that person's well-being. However, we now know that tiny infants develop simultaneous attachments with anyone in regular cooing distance. A father doesn't 'interrupt' a more significant attachment between mother and child, and his function in infant development is not secondary to hers unless circumstance (or his own desire) makes it so. Positive high-level engagement by fathers matters *from birth*. Babies so blessed in the first four weeks of life are performing better than their peers on their first birthdays. Well-fathered six and seven year olds not only achieve better at school – socially and academically – but have higher IQs.[12]

Sensitivity to the child seems to be the key, and it may well be that a minimum level of involvement is not so hard to achieve. A study of Israeli fathers of nine-month-olds showed that employed fathers who had spent 45 minutes a day actively engaged with their children 'understood' them as well as the (non-employed) mothers. This meant that, when playing with their infants, they offered the right toy or response, which in turn stimulated the baby's achievement.[13] Right through adolescence, and in many different ways, the benefits to children of positive and substantial father involvement can be measured: in self-control, self-esteem, life skills and social competence. Adolescents who have good relationships with their fathers take their responsibilities seriously, are more likely to do what their parents ask and are less limited by traditional sex-role expectations. The boys have fewer behaviour problems in school, and the girls are more self-directed, cheerful and happy, and willing to try new things.[14] Among adults, both men and women, the strongest predictor of empathic concern for others is high levels of caretaking by their *fathers* when they were little. Father involvement is also one of the major predictors of whether adults in their twenties will have progressed, educationally and socially, beyond their parents.[15]

However, even the best fathering is not a cure-all. While 80 per cent of women who feel emotionally distanced from husbands or lovers have had bad experiences with their fathers, and 90 per cent of those whose parents split up do not settle easily into satisfying love relationships, 40 per cent of well-fathered daughters also have trouble settling down to domestic bliss.[16]

❛ I don't know if men ever have long and intensive discussions about personal relationships. Well, you do with your wife, but not with other people. My daughter feels that this is a problem. She feels I don't tell her I love her, I do not talk to her about herself, everything. I say I'm here, but then she doesn't talk, she gets embarrassed. ❜

Alec, 50, father of three (two families)

Fathers and families

Fathers are of value to their children in many ways – as carers, companions, providers, protectors, educators and life-models – as well as through their potential to be 'irrationally emotionally involved' with them. That is, to love them madly and remain loyal to them for life. Children and biological parents measure themselves against each other in unique ways, and although substitute fathers can, and often do, fulfil many of a father's functions, a man who has created a child and is then lovingly involved in its upbringing supplies it with a unique touchstone for life.

Fathers also have symbolic importance: they are important because our 'social discourse' rates them important. Most of us long for the good father, as we long for the good mother, and may spend much of our lives looking for him. Children are never fatherless in their imaginations, for if they do not know their fathers, they make them up.

Involved, facilitative and affectionate fathering is good for families not only, as pointed out in Chapter 4, because divorce rates among couples where fathers have been prepared for parenthood can be zero.[17] First-born children who have good relationships with their fathers are more accepting of a new sibling,[18] and in later life brothers and sisters will get on better.[19] Women whose partners are involved fathers are more satisfied with their marriages, and long-term research shows a clear connection between involved fathering and the happiness and stability of the parents' marrige in mid-life.[20] The importance of fathers' involvement for marital stability also seems indicated when we bring together two facts: divorce is less common in families with sons, and fathers are more involved in family life when they have sons.

Fathers are a resource within families, and in many important ways a greatly under-used resource. However, one of the saddest findings of fatherhood research is that even in two-parent households, the vast majority of fathers are not around enough to pass much on to their children *of themselves*. This may well explain the bewilderment of some high-achieving fathers who come home to children they love, but with whom they feel they have curiously little in common.

> ❛ I was earning a lot of money, but I was leaving at seven in the morning and getting home at seven at night and working most weekends. I don't know if it exactly causes a problem – I mean, I worked with 20 or 30 other guys doing a similar sort of job, and they all had children, and I wouldn't say that they had a problem. It was just that – well, this is how it looked to me – it was just that the children were being raised totally by their mothers. ❜
>
> *Phil, 38, father of three*

Researchers trying to compensate fathers for the obviously miniscule impact so many make, directly, on their children, say things like, 'Indirect patterns of influence are pervasive and perhaps more important',[21] meaning that in many families the man himself (his preferences, values, idiosyncracies) is less important than his wife's reaction to him or his pay-cheque or the social networks (family, friends, colleagues) attaching to him. The importance of the latter for children's well-being must not be underestimated. All kinds of benefits are channelled through fathers to their children from his family and friends – holidays, outings and job contacts as well as less conventional offerings. 'Your mother says our baby will be the best-dressed baby on the estate,' a young girl wrote to her imprisoned fiancé: 'I guess she's been on a shop-lifting spree!'

Ironically, what the average long-hours working breadwinner dad may often be funding is a better relationship between *mother* and child, for it is as support to mothers that many of today's fathers – heading out at dawn, returning at dusk and hovering in the background at home – earn many of their rosettes. A study of army families in Britain showed that even if fathers' actual domestic input was pretty slight, when they were at home mothers of five-year-olds showed 'normal' stress levels; but when the men were working away one mother in four scored 'severe stress' and one in five evidenced a level more usually seen to correspond with serious psychiatric problems![22]

Fatherly fathers

One finding of particular interest to researchers has been that in two-parent households children raised mainly by their fathers do better than those raised mainly by their mothers. Does this mean there is something innately superior about men's parenting? No. These children have *two* actively involved parents: their fathers as day-to-day caretakers, and their mothers devoting more time and energy to them after work than do most breadwinner fathers.

Claims are sometimes made that children from lone-father households are less likely to end up with criminal records than children from lone-mother households, and research shows that lone fathers do follow stricter rules and are more consistent in discipline. This leads to the conclusion that fathers have some special way of disciplining their children that eludes mothers.[23] In fact, lone fathers tend to be older, richer and more middle class than lone mothers, factors which seem far more likely to explain lower criminality than parenting style. They also get more help with parenting – from women!

> 6 One of the major problems in many of the inner-city schools in this area is that the single-parent children are being brought up by women who have got very basically no control over these huge hulking nine-year-olds. I am pretty fierce or can be pretty fierce, so he has been brought up fairly strictly, not desperately strictly, I mean he and I, we're both slobs, and we don't follow the manners and etiquettes that my mum would like us to follow, shall we say! 9
>
> *Bob, 47, father of two (two families)*

Firmer discipline doesn't always pay off, for girls in particular. Children tend to be more compliant with parents of the same sex, and some lone-parent households (headed by mothers or fathers) develop an egalitarian style, which can work very well. It would also be a mistake to conclude that lone fathers have no problems with discipline: they are statistically more likely than lone mothers to batter their children.[24]

In fact, fathers in any kind of household who adopt a parenting style which particularly emphasises authority and limit-setting frequently seem to do more harm than good. This is quite different from 'authoritative parenting', the ideal for both mothers and fathers, in which the parent provides consistent values and boundaries, and supports the child with warmth and confidence. Pre-school boys with bossy fathers are not popular with the other children. By school age they have more behaviour problems and are more likely to be maladjusted, unsociable and without initiative. Children whose fathers hit them a lot are particularly likely to go off the rails at adolescence.[25]

What kind of father makes the best sex-role model? Between 1940 and 1970, when this was thought to be fathers' most important function, it was assumed that boys raised without fathers would tend to be homosexual or, at the very least, would exhibit 'low masculinity' i.e. be wimps. Conversely, it was thought that highly masculine fathers would produce highly masculine sons. Neither proved to be the case. To the psychologists' astonishment, highly masculine fathers often turned out much less masculine sons, and the most highly masculine boys strode out of families where fathers were sometimes quite low in masculinity. These fathers, however, were often warm and intimate with their sons, and it was a couple of decades before it dawned on psychologists that sex-role modelling wasn't enough: a boy had to like and respect his father. It was that which would make him choose to behave 'like a man' – however that was defined by the society in which he lived. Today we know that even sons raised by homosexual fathers are no more likely than the rest of the population to be homosexual themselves.[26]

Researchers have been far less interested in women's sexual orientation or sex-role identity, but the same seems to apply. Lesbian women, like gay men, come from very diverse family backgrounds and some have close and loving relationships with their fathers. But homosexual women are more likely than heterosexual women to speak of their fathers with hostility or contempt. A very high incidence of father–daughter incest is reported by lesbian women.[27]

Although the research shows clearly that the presence of a father is no more essential to a child's healthy development than the presence of a mother, and although the psychologists have concluded that it is the 'characteristics of the father as a *parent*' rather than the 'characteristics of the father as a *man*' which appear to be most significant, it is also impossible to demonstrate that the father's masculine characteristics are of no significance.[28] Who can doubt that, at the present time, men in our society tend to approach things differently from women and have different interests? Generalisations are, of course, fraught with difficulty and 'masculine characteristics' do not necessarily provide a primrose path, even for fathers and sons. Although a common love of sport, for example

undoubtedly unites many boys and their fathers (and some girls),
one of the men interviewed for this book, a football fanatic, has a
seven-year-old son whose sporting passion is reserved exclusively for
snooker; while another, a man who in his own words 'wouldn't cross
the road for a football match', is blessed with a son who sleeps in an
Arsenal strip and a daughter who plays in goal with great relish.

However, male–female differences go deeper than this. For
example, men tend to take more risks than women. This leads them
to die younger, but also leads to astonishing achievement. Men
express anger more readily than women in many situations, are less
self-critical and are more likely to step out into the public arena as
if it were created for their benefit, which in many respects it has
been. All in all, one would be hard pushed to deny the value to a
child of having, readily available to it, a representative of half the
world's population, the male sex.

> ❢ We cuddle a lot. We have a cuddle which we call the 'horse's
> neck', which we devised as a way of cuddling properly without
> me having to bend down and hurt my back! So I sit on a seat
> and she climbs on my lap facing me, and then we cuddle from
> there. Also she has a real routine at bedtime when I kiss her
> goodnight. There is a rhythm that she kisses at. She can do that
> for ages, and she won't let me go until she has done the right
> number of kisses. ❣
>
> Ken, 50, father of three (two families)

A special role for fathers?

In a whole range of ways, writers on fatherhood over the past century,
in attempting to justify the father's role, have hung their hats on the
notion of fathering as a distinct, 'gendered' activity. Fathers have
been said to be of value not simply because they are individuals or
even because they are men, but because the things they do when they
are with their children and the way that they do them are 'different'.

However, as we saw in Chapters 2 and 3, fathers' and mothers'
parenting styles do not, overall, differ significantly and within
couples tend to converge. When they do differ, it is the situation,
rather than the parent's gender that seems to determine behaviour,
and because in the average family mothers are around so much
more, and are ruling the roost, a few qualitative differences are
standard. In particular, the average father scores much lower than

the average mother, on the 'sensitivity to children' scale.[29] Emotional and physical distance from their children (and correspondingly reduced sensitivity) has, for many decades, been credited with giving fathers a distinctive and useful parenting style. The contention has been that fathers' sketchier knowledge of their children's capacities means that they inadvertently stimulate them beyond their expected achievement levels, thus providing them with a bridge to the outside world. Furthermore, daily absence enables fathers (so it is said) to be coolly rational, to provide a foil to 'emotionally embroiled' mothers.[30] ,

There can be no doubt that to be able to step outside an emotionally charged situation can sometimes be of value, although it is hard to understand why only fathers should be expected to do this. On the other hand, to leap in and make judgements when you have only half the facts may not be so useful. A research project in London in 1996 found young men perceiving their fathers as expecting either too much or not enough of them in terms of responsibility, while they felt their mothers gauged their capacities more as they did themselves.[31]

> ❛ I leave talking to their mother – you know, about problems and that. I shout, I smack and if I can't catch them when they run away I sometimes throw my foot at them, which I get told off for, all three, but as I said, I have a short fuse, and I find I can deal with other people's kids better than I can my own. ❜
> *Phil, 38, father of three*

As for the 'bridge' hypothesis, among the Israeli fathers mentioned earlier, those who did not manage the 45 minutes per day needed to stimulate their children's development tended to underestimate, not overestimate, their capabilities. They babied them. And when fathers of pre-schoolers use language that is too sophisticated, this does not seem to spur them on to greater achievement, but rather depresses and discourages them.[32] Conversely, when children are raised by two involved parents, both fully sensitive to their capacities, then their development rattles ahead, probably because both parents are stimulating them appropriately.

Distant dads

Clearly, it is not impossible to foster some differences in parenting styles between fathers and mothers. What is required is for one parent (traditionally the father) to be kept apart from his children for much of the time, while the other (traditonally the mother) builds an intimate relationship with them. That is the situation today, with the result that many children experience their relationships with their fathers as deeply unsatisfying. A survey of teenage boys and girls in Britain's East End of London revealed not only that mothers were their most popular confidantes, but that fathers were not even second in line: a majority of the young people were more likely to confide in their friends than in their fathers.[33]

A national survey of British adults aged between 18 and 45, carried out in 1995, found that even among the youngest age groups, one in five felt they had never received praise from their fathers and more than one in three could remember no hugs and kisses from them. Only half as many, one in six, said they had not been hugged and kissed by their mothers. When facing a major difficulty, two out of three would consult their mothers, but just one in seven would go to their fathers. Twice as many reported having been constantly or frequently afraid of their fathers as were afraid of their mothers.[34]

But the notion that distance might not be merely counter-productive, but could actually mean that many fathers have virtually no impact at all on their children's early development, is not one that occurred to anyone until recently. After all, for most of this century, psychoanalytic theory and social learning theory and just about every other kind of theory have been telling fathers that they have a key role in child development simply because of their gender, even if they are hardly ever at home. Ten minutes morning or evening, an hour or two at the weekend, and dad is enabling infant and mother to 'separate' or providing his toddler with that 'bridge' to the outside world or playing his 'crucial role in the Oedipal drama' or 'modelling masculinity' for his son.

> 6 He is going to be my size – so I mean there is no point trying to be violent with him all the time. I consciously try, these days, to go against my own nature and find ways of explaining things to him. I think you can do that, but to do it you have to be – what is the right phrase? – to be 'under yourself'. You haven't got to be coming forward and diving in. You've got to be parental – you have got to be feminine. That's a sexist way of putting it – we have all got femaleness and maleness, as we know – but you have to be bending. You have got to be able to bend as a parent. 9
>
> *Bob, 47, father of two (two families)*

However, recent research on the process of early child development casts doubt on this notion of a unique and essential role for fathers. Not only have 'father absence' studies over five decades shown the vast majority of boys without fathers developing quite normally in terms of their sex-role identity (and performance) but there is no evidence that, without a father's input, mother and infant fail to 'separate'. They seem to manage it perfectly well.

So minimal is the average father's direct influence early on, in fact, that when researchers analysed the development of more than 1,500 US five-year-olds and took into account factors such as poverty and mothers' age, they found no difference in intellectual or emotional development between children whose fathers had been present from birth, children whose fathers had moved out and then come home again, children who had had a stepfather (or more than one) and children who had had no father or father-figure around at all. In every group, similar percentages of children did well and not so well.[35]

This does not mean that individual fathers are not precious to their children, for they are. Nor that ordinary fathers are without pertinence, for the whole of a child's environment is relevant and fathers are part of that: fat fathers tend to have fat toddlers, for instance.[36] Neither does it mean that fathers *per se* aren't important, for as we have seen, highly involved fathers influence their children's early development profoundly, and a father's characteristics can be relevant, for good and ill, throughout the lifespan.

What it does mean, however, is that the standard for fathers, in our culture, is a standard of absence, and that as far as early child development is concerned, fathers *in their gendered role* might as well take a running jump. For in this crucial process the input of the average, loving, breadwinner-daddy is no more salient than that of the totally unavailable father. The average child separates and forms an identity, decides on a sexual orientation, finds feelings and fulfils capabilities *whether its father is there or not.*

The message emanating from this is that there is no free ride for fatherhood, no magical role for fathers just because they are fathers or just because they are men. It is what each man gives on a personal level that makes him a key player in his child's development. And, in the wider world, it is what men as a group will give to children in respect of intimate care and attention that will enable males to play a key role in their development. Otherwise a father's main value is limited to a pay-cheque and to a lesser extent a support system, and although these are valuable functions they in no way satisfy the aspirations of today's fathers, or their children.

❦ There was a job about three or four months ago, it was almost double the salary that I earn here. Carole read the job description, and it was everything I do and could do and have been trained for and she said 'What about going for that, if you want to make a change?' I thought about it and I said, those people who pay those big salaries they want you there 7.30 in the morning and then part of the job was fund-raising (I do a lot of that now) so it would be like all down the office and functions in the evening. I wouldn't have seen nothing of the kids. ❧

Steve, 39, father of five

Fathers apart

Working patterns are not the only means by which distance is fostered between children and fathers. They are divided through other means. Over a 12-month period, adoption orders are granted on the children of 5,000 British males, half of them in favour of step-fathers,[37] and at any one time there are some 60,000 children in state care.[38] Imprisonment separates at least another 42,000 fathers from their children every year.[39] One per cent of these men are lone fathers, and research has shown that in the great majority of cases the imprisoned fathers (despite their criminality) have significant and often positive relationships with the children they leave behind.[40] Even among fathers in maximum security prisons, one out of three is visited by their children, four out of five speak with them on the phone and nine out of ten men are keen to receive training to improve their parenting skills.[41]

The main mechanism by which men are separated from their children, however, is family breakdown – separation and divorce. Estimates today suggest that 41 per cent of marriages will end in divorce. This may be conservative figure in terms of *parental* separation, since cohabiting parents split three times as often as married parents.[42] US research shows that half of all American children experience some of their childhood in a single-parent household. Currently, one in five US males is a non-resident father; that is, he has at least one school-age child living in someone else's home.[43] And, in Britain, more than one and a half million fathers are in the same situation. But although men in our society so often become detached from their offspring, they frequently end up raising children that are not biologically theirs. Men are seven times more likely than women to become live-in step-parents.[44]

Lone fathers are a rare breed in Britain and quite a few of them – one in six – are widowers. Around 140,000 British fathers are currently in solo charge of children, and are outnumbered eight to one by lone mothers.[45] Although lone fathers are not the only divorced or separated men to live with their children, since around four out of every 100 UK children drift between households after their parents have parted,[46] very few British fathers, once they have separated from a partner, ever live with children from that relationship again.

❛ I have 13 days between the times I see them. I have to divert my attention to other things to fill the gap ... other relationships, sport and other minor ways. Whereas when I was there full time, the children imposed limits on what you could and could not do, which wasn't burdensome, it was something you accept as a parent. ❜

father quoted in Being There: fathers after divorce

Baby fathers

In some communities, non-resident fathers are the norm. In North America 50 per cent of Afro-American males have dependent children not living with them; and even black women earning in excess of $75,000 a year are ten times more likely than their white counterparts to have had a child outside marriage.[47] In the UK, 46 per cent of Afro-Caribbean families are headed by mothers alone, compared with 18 per cent of white families.[48] Within some sections of the black community in the US, the UK and the Caribbean there has now developed a separation between the idea of marriage, or cohabitation, and childbearing. Reflecting this, a new street terminology has evolved to describe someone who is the father, or mother, of your child but with whom you do not necessarily live: *baby father* (my baby's father) and *baby mother* (my baby's mother).

Various theories have been put forward to explain this state of affairs, ranging from tribal patterns (supposedly matriarchal) to slavery (fathers routinely and forcibly separated from their children) and these may be relevant. However, racism and poverty seem to be the primary causes. Up until the early 1960s, black US families were mainly two-parent and stable, and at this time black men had what seemed to be a solid, economic niche in factory jobs. As the manufacturing base caved in, the black workers were the first to go[49]. Today, in the US, even black men with college degrees are three times more likely to be unemployed than whites, and in Britain young black males are almost twice as likely as young white males to be unemployed.[50]

Nevertheless, it is plain that cultural traditions are important. In the UK, Bangladeshi families are among the poorest, yet their incidence of non-resident fatherhood is far lower, presumably because in this community brides have typically moved into the households of their husbands' families. This may well change as the Bangladeshi community becomes less self-contained. Afro-Caribbean men may have other reasons to be unavailable to their children. In the US they have the lowest life expectancy of any group: 25 per cent of those aged 24–29 are behind bars, and many others are dead or substance-dependent. However, it is worth noting the growing incidence of inner-city US fathers taking responsibility for children conceived with drug-dependent mothers.

❦ Little brown baby wif spa'klin' eyes,
Come to yo' pappy an' set on his knee.
What you been doin', suh – making' san' pies?
Look at dat bib – you's ez du'ty ez me ...

Come to you' pallet now – go to yo' res';
Wisht you could allus know ease an' clean skies;
Wisht you could stay jes' a chile on my breas' –
Little brown baby wif spa'klin' eyes! ❧
        Laurence Dunbar (1872–1906), 'Little Brown Baby'

In Britain, as in America, the phenomenon of young men fathering children on a number of baby mothers is beginning to appear as a function of poverty and unemployment, rather than race. It does make a grim kind of sense: if you will never be able to support a child effectively, why defer conception? If you cannot maintain even one child, why stop at one? Throughout Britain, the areas with the highest proportion of never-married young mothers, are also those with the highest proportion of young unemployed males, of whatever colour.[51]

It is by no means clear that this derives, as is sometimes suggested, from a 'stud mentality'. Many of the young mothers make active choices to become pregnant: given their circumstances, it can be their only route to any kind of status. And it is now known that many of the young fathers prove keen to play a part in their babies' lives if they are helped to do so.[51]

Disappearing dads?

Does this mean that all families headed by mothers are fatherless? Not at all. Visiting patterns in Afro-American and Afro-Caribbean communities can be complex, and many non-resident fathers visit frequently, undertake childcare and take the children to the homes of their own relatives. Marriage at middle age is common in some Afro-Caribbean communities, and women and men who have had children together may marry at a later date. And commentators have begun to suggest that Afro-Caribbean families should not be regarded as failed nuclear families. Rather their own coherence and effectiveness should be recognised.[52]

Among European communities, visiting may rarely be as flexible, but here, too, there are many misconceptions about diminished contact between father and child. Often quoted is the '40 per cent rule' which has held that 40 per cent of fathers are out of the picture entirely within five years. This figure, derived from a famous 1991 study of lone-mother families,[53] is trotted out regularly, giving the impression that only stringent social controls prevent the average father doing what comes naturally: abandoning his kids. However, as one commentator pointed out somewhat acidly, 'Asking lone parents about the circumstances of their former partners may not produce the most objective picture',[54] and a more representative national study currently being analysed in Oxford, which has interviewed both mothers *and* fathers, is coming up with very different findings – findings which suggest that the image of the disappearing dad needs revising.

> 6 Basically, the only thing I can do is be there for whenever he wants me. For him to take from the relationship what he needs at any given time. Because you are just having this odd glimpse of him, not just physically, but also in his developmental stage. He may be, the next time he comes, a very different person emotionally, with a different set of needs from last time, because you are just taking a picture at any one time, a time lapse, you know. 9
> *father quoted in* Being There: fathers after divorce

The Oxford research reveals that even five to 10 years after the break-up, three out of four fathers are still in contact with their children, and one out of three sees them at least fortnightly.[55]

Similarly, a 1994 Newcastle study has shown more than one father in three in *at least* weekly contact with his children five years after divorce, and fewer than one in four with no contact at all.[56] Furthermore, children grow up and averages hide the fact that some fathers move into contact as others move out: intermittent communication later may not mean desertion. Although average involvement certainly diminishes over time, a father apparently firmly out of the picture in year one may have reappeared by year two, or even by year seven, and studies regularly show higher numbers of fathers involved two or three years after divorce than in the first year.[57]

Interestingly, the Oxford study has not limited itself to studying divorcing couples, but also has included parents who hardly, or never, lived together. While 85 per cent of the fathers who had 'lived in' saw their children during the first year after the break-up only 50 per cent of the 'never/hardly lived with' fathers did so. This group, it is plain, brings down the averages substantially, for only four out of 50 of these fathers saw their children regularly. Perhaps the truth is not so much that, after divorce, perfectly nice fathers totally disappear, as that men who were peripheral at the outset tend to remain so.

Results from countries which have been more proactive than Britain in encouraging post-divorce father–child relationships further challenge the myth of the disappearing dad. In Australia, three years after divorce, two out of three children still see their non-resident parent at least fortnightly (and generally more often).[58] In California, in the fourth year after divorce, more than nine out of 10 children have had *physical* contact with their fathers in the previous twelve months. Of the remaining few per cent, some will have been in touch by telephone or mail.[59] And the Californian children don't just see their fathers, they see a lot of them. Almost one child in three lives with its father or lives part time with both parents; and even among those living with their mothers, two out of three have seen their fathers *at least once* within the previous month.

> ❛ What shall we do with the child
> Who's got your eyes my hair your smile
> Reminding me that we fell in love –
> but just for a little while? ❜
>
> *Kate Reifsnyder, Nick Holmes, Carly Simon,*
> *quoted in* The Custody Revolution

Dividing the child

Are fathers from the Sunshine State more loving than other fathers? No. Divorce policy is the key. Since 1979 warring Californian parents have been forced to attend mediation, and courts have regularly awarded joint custody or have given the children to the parent most likely to facilitate continued contact with the other. Arrangements for children to live part time with both parents have also been encouraged. Above all, a culture of continuing contact has been promoted, and very many parents find co-parenting solutions without resorting to the courts.

Some shared parenting in California is truly shared, an equal 50–50. Very often the division is one third–two thirds, or even slightly less, with parents exhibiting remarkable flexibility. A few operate the 'birds' nest' system, where the children stay in one home, and the parents rotate residence. Some children live with their mothers, but may see their fathers every day, when, for instance, they pick them up and take them to school. The luckiest can bicycle between their homes while others have to take a plane. Some live with each parent alternately, term to term, or week to week. Others do alternate weekends, or live with one parent in the holidays or when work schedules allow.

Although living in two places clearly has its difficulties, and ghastly tales are told of two-year-olds passed back and forwards with never more than 24 hours in either home, children who are 'shared out' do no worse than children living with just one parent. Where there are differences as, for example, in self-esteem, the two-home children do better.[60] This, it is thought, is because they do not feel deserted by either parent. An overwhelming body of research shows that the children who survive their parents' break-up best are those who maintain significant and positive relationships with *both* parents afterwards.[61]

The big danger with truly shared parenting in separate homes after divorce, however, is that it provides hostile parents with great opportunities to continue fighting. High parental conflict, whether before, during or after divorce, is actually more destructive to children than the loss of a parent.[62] Should mothers then simply get to keep the children in situations where parents really can't agree? Sometimes, but not necessarily. Apart from awarding many children to their fathers (recent research suggests that boys may sometimes do better with fathers and girls with mothers),[63] the Californians have invoked a range of strategies to make co-parenting viable.

Flash points for hostile parental behaviours, such as at hand-overs, can be mediated by third parties and a system of 'parallel parenting' can be developed. This involves the parents never meeting and hardly ever speaking and, although far from ideal, has been found to work surprisingly well in many cases. It sometimes leads, in the end, to grudging co-operation. In California, four out of six divorced couples are parenting co-operatively five years after divorce, and one out of six operates parallel parenting, with only one out of six couples involved in damaging and continuous conflict.[64]

❢ Some of the parents I see, as a solicitor, they seem to have lost all sense of themselves as decent parents. I've had them ask me whether I think their child's distress will look good in court! Often, if it were up to me, I'd say neither of them should get the children. I think we need to come clean and say that what these people are involved in, it's child abuse. ❢

Nick, 47, father of three

There are winners and losers in any system, and it is indeed probable that some children of warring parents are more damaged by the high conflict inherent in continued contact with both than they would have been by remaining with one parent only. However, it seems certain that their losses are more than balanced by the gains of the many children whose relationships with both parents become positive and substantial.

The wrong side of the law?

Recently Britain has superseded even California in theoretical support for co-parenting after divorce. The Children Act 1989, which came into force in 1992, contains a presumption of joint legal custody (now called 'parental responsibility' in Britain) for previously married parents, with the aim of ensuring that parenting is considered a 'job for life' for *both* parents.

However, this can be seen as just so many fine words. Firstly, it lets down completely the one in three fathers who are not married to the mothers of their children. These men have to jump through extraordinary hoops to get parental rights, if the mothers veto them, and even if mothers are supportive, the procedure is long-winded and complex.[65] Secondly, joint *legal* custody (as the Californians have found) doesn't actually mean that children see more of their fathers after divorce, or that the men necessarily have much of a say in their upbringing.[66] What really makes the difference is joint *physical* custody or, as it is called in Britain, 'shared residence'.

Although many divorced parents, particularly the ones who never get to court, quietly get on with parenting in this way (so common is it in France, that French courts have taken note and started considering shared parenting as an option in custody disputes) most British judges are firmly against the idea. Although many of the judges will have packed their own children off to boarding school, they tend to think that two homes are bad for other people's children and that under-fives shouldn't spend a single night away from their mothers. If feeling generous towards a particularly nice father, a British judge may grant him the standard every other weekend, plus one after-school visit (but not an overnight) during the week.

It is sometimes suggested that custody disputes should be resolved by giving the child to the parent who has been the primary carer. This, however, is simply a mother-bias in disguise. Even a father keen to be highly involved has, due to the cultural and economic factors already described, usually developed into a secondary carer within weeks of his child's birth, let alone by the time of divorce. However, the legal system cannot be blamed for everything. The Law does no more than reflect public opinion. 'How can you expect a judge to grant something he dare not ask for himself?' remarked one commentator. Like all of us, judges and the court welfare officers (who make recommendations to the judges) are prisoners of their own experience. One (male) court welfare officer told a divorced father that he should be happy with Saturday afternoon access: 'You see your children more than I do', he was told.

❛ After that particularly nasty fight over visitation, I took her to court again. I got the usual crap from the judge: 'That it's just awful that you fight this way and that you should be ashamed.' Judges always look at me when they say that; their eyes are on me. I think what they mean is that 'You are the only one here who has rationality, you should be stopping this. Also, you're male so you're inherently wrong, that's why I'm looking at you. ❜

father quoted in Arendell, After Divorce

Judges can favour fathers whose life-styles resemble their own. In fact, any British father bidding for custody and planning to give up work to take care of his children may be best advised to keep his plan quiet. The judge may not view him as favourably as he would a father who could show he was an effective breadwinner and disciplinarian.[67] What does happen if British fathers go for sole residence (or custody as it used to be called)? Legal pundits piously declare that there is no obvious mother-bias in the courts because fathers win in custody disputes quite regularly. This may be so, but it entirely misses the point. The fathers who get as far as contesting custody usually have strong cases. The rest will have backed off earlier.

Many such fathers self-censor: they may perceive their wives as better at childrearing, or think children need to see their mothers every day, or feel unable to combine daily childcare with the demands of their jobs. More often than is known, they behave altruistically. Perhaps the most loving and devoted father in our entire sample, a man who spent every available minute with his young son, was separating from his wife (a housewife) at the time of our interviews. When the interviewer asked him if he would be going for custody he shook his head. 'It would kill my wife,' he answered simply.

Those fathers who do not back off voluntarily will usually do so after taking legal advice. How this works was graphically illustrated by a role-play experiment conducted for a British TV programme in 1995.[68] An actress, apparently seeking a divorce and hoping for custody of her child, visited four solicitors. She said she had been career-minded and that her partner had taken the greater responsibility as a parent. She also 'confessed' that she had had an extra-marital affair. Simultaneously, an actor posing as a worried dad was visiting four different solicitors. His story was that, although both he and his wife had been employed, he had been the more involved parent, collecting his son every evening from the minder, for example. He also said he had remained sexually faithful, while his wife had had an affair.

All the lawyers advised the woman to go for sole residence, and she was advised that she would get the child. It was also suggested that she play the 'violence card', although she insisted there had been *no* violence. The man, on the other hand, was told he didn't have a chance of keeping his son. These solicitors were not, themselves, anti-father but were simply reflecting what they knew, or believed to be, the reality. They believed that the judge, as Dustin Hoffman's character's lawyer explained to him in *Kramer v. Kramer* would go '... for motherhood, right down the line'.

❛ A year ago I was seen as a responsible, caring father – today I am going to a court of law to try to prove that my being with my children is in their best interests. The only thing that has changed is their mother and I separated. ❜

father at Father Figures Conference, Glasgow, 1994

Unpacking 'absent' fathers

Clearly most fathers, given half a chance, do not disappear. What motivates those who do, or who allow contact with their children to become infrequent? To a significant degree, divorced fathers' absenteeism has been ideologically driven. As recently as 20 years ago, it was considered beneficial for a father to back off (especially if a stepfather was on the scene) and family professionals concentrated all their energies on supporting the new family: the mother and her children. This 'clean break' mentality, though later discredited by psychologists, was given another boost in the 1980s when financial clean break settlements were, briefly, the fashion.

Even today when, thanks to the Child Support Act, continuing financial support is all but mandatory, the belief that fathers may, and perhaps should, gradually let go on a personal level, is still in circulation. The mother of one of our interviewees, who adored her grandchildren, nevertheless commented approvingly that her divorcing son had moved to his new girlfriend's flat some 30 miles away, and so could only see them at the weekend. She felt it was 'preparing them for the break'. She was disapproving when he assured her that his ultimate objective, once the dust had settled, was to move back to live close to his children: 'It will be very upsetting for his wife,' she stated.

Some men seem to have accepted society's view of fathers as inconsequential and replaceable. The fathers *least* likely to bid for custody or remain in very close touch are often the men who think their ex-wives are good mothers. These men, it seems, can feel that they are simply surplus to requirements (as one of our interviewees put it), especially if a mother's new partner seems well disposed towards the children.

However, the first of the main indicators as to whether a father will lose touch is poverty. Everywhere, the fathers most prone to disengage from their children are the poorest and least well educated, with unemployed fathers heading the list. An unemployed (and disabled) father we interviewed who, after a major struggle, had obtained a Housing Association flat in the town where his son lived, was in despair because the boy's mother had now said she was going to live on her parents' farm in another part of the country. This man was without transport, and the nearest village was four miles from the farm.

It seems unlikely that well-off, well-educated fathers hold a monopoly on paternal love. Poorer fathers, lacking suitable transport, accommodation, and cash for outings, may not even have money for fares. The Child Support Act takes none of these factors into account and 'single' men are at the bottom of the public housing list. To meet a growing need, weekend contact centres have been established in some UK cities. Often sited in community premises staffed at the weekend by volunteers, these provide warm, safe places for non-resident parents to spend time with their children. Staff at the centres are often awed by fathers' commitment: 'We've got one dad who's never lived with his daughter,' said a Scottish worker, 'yet he comes 50 miles on the bus on a Saturday. He's not missed a visit in two years.'

Social factors, however, don't tell the whole story. Some of the fathers who go missing or allow contact to become sporadic, lead chaotic lives, or in rejecting their children are repeating their own experience of rejection by one or both parents. Others stay away because they confuse their relationship with the mother with their relationship to the child, and think that to avoid the one they must deny the other. Yet others are trying to put distance between themselves and guilt (or child support payments). Some focus on alternatives – work, a new partner, the pub – to conceal their distress from others and from themselves ('If they don't need me, I don't need them'). They may also fear, or have been told, that they are not fit parents.

> 6 How many times in one day, after all, can I take my daughter to McDonald's or to the park to swing? I just don't know what to do to entertain her. So we end up renting videos and spending hours just sitting in front of the TV screen. I am restless and bored. She is unhappy and bored although she tries, she really does seem to try. She needs to be out playing with her friends, not stuck here with me. 9
>
> *father quoted in Arendell,* After Divorce

Saturday dads

To understand how father–child relationships fall apart after the break-up, we also need to understand what happens beforehand.

Fathers' relationships with their children are more affected than mothers', by the happiness (or otherwise) of the marriage: happily married men are more sensitive and positive towards their children than unhappily married men.[69] 'I've always been a seven-day-a-week worker,' said one of our interviewees. 'If I'm around the house for more than a couple of hours, there's always rows.'

The journey to family breakdown is typically long, drawn out, and miserable. Contrary to popular belief, few parents separate in haste, and as the marriage deteriorates fathers often withdraw. They may stay out of the house or become non-communicative, and their relationships with their children may enter a long decline.[70] By contrast, during this period, mothers may build alliances with the children, and relationships between them may become closer.

'Visitation fathering' is the second of the main indicators in fathers' losing touch. The biggest drop-off rate is observed among fathers who do not have their children to stay regularly overnight with them.[71] 'Right after the separation he came around often, maybe too often,' said one exhausted and enraged mother. 'Then he started complaining that he didn't know what to do with the children during their visits. The kids began to see less and less of him. It's been three months since their last visit.'[72]

Most studies have found that the fathers who report the closest relationships with their children before the break-up are the most likely to stay in regular touch afterwards. One major study, however, found precisely the opposite. Edward Kruk, interviewing fathers in both Canada and Scotland, discovered that some of the men who seemed to pull back from their children had been, by their own report, the *most*, and not the *least*, involved with them beforehand.[73] Although a more recent study using different methodology has not supported these findings,[74] Kruk's work forces us to confront our goodie/baddie fantasies about divorcing couples, and to recognise that, among the many factors leading to fathers' disengagement, indifference may be the very least. Kruk sugggested that fathers who hadn't spent much time with their children before the break-up might be more content to be weekend fathers, and that their children might also have taken relatively easily to the new arrangements. There is even evidence that, in some such cases, father–child relationships actually *improve* after divorce. But where father and child had had a truly rich and intimate relationship, as is the case in many families, such reduced and unnatural contact could prove insupportable.

Visits can be dreaded, not only for emotions raised or skirted around, but for outright loneliness. Divorced fathers may be unwilling to contact other men in the same position (or may know none) or, working long hours, may not have time. Most are ignorant of local children's activities and networks. 'All I remember,' said one divorced father, 'are the endless Saturdays afternoons. Just the boys and me in the park.'

❝ Every time I pulled up to the driveway to let him off, it was like part of me was dying all over again. I could barely keep myself together long enough to give him a hug goodbye; I knew it wasn't good for him to leave seeing me so visibly upset each time. He would open the door, step out of the car, and I would feel as if I would never see him again … I had to break it off totally, just to survive. ❞

father quoted in Arendell, After Divorce

For fathers whose relationships with their children have been constantly mediated by their partners, solo fathering can be a real shock. When the newly separated Prince of Wales employed Tiggy Legge-Burke to help 'organise his time' with his children, few divorce workers were surprised. Ms Legge-Burke's *real* function (they whispered to each other) was very probably to act as an interface, to help the Prince with the day-to-day business of being a father. And, indeed, the newspapers were soon enthusing about the fun the Prince, the young Princes and their 'surrogate mum' had together.

Although a few Saturday dads comment appreciatively that their offspring are always on their best behaviour, others find the weekends a battleground. Most mourn lack of conflict, recognising that it means reduced intimacy and trust. 'In fifteen years they have never shown the slightest annoyance with me,' said one man interviewed, sadly. 'It's always sunny side up for daddy.'

Meet the mothers

Although, interestingly, a stormy marriage or even a very stormy break-up, does not mean a father will vanish (fury can motivate him to insist upon his 'rights'), the hostility of a man's ex-partner to his continuing involvement is the third of the key factors in fathers' losing touch; or, to put it another way, in their being 'seen off'.[75] More women than men may enter the post-divorce period feeling angry and let down. Although two out of three divorces are sought by women, the most consistent predictor of divorce is a *man's* dissatisfaction with the partnership.[76] This means that, although a mother may eventually petition for divorce, a father may well have behaved in a way that, in her view, has obliged her to take action.

To make matters worse (and mothers' tempers shorter), after separation the 'custodial mother', as a newly single parent, is usually seriously overburdened. And if the non-resident father lets the children down, or overtires them during visits, or indulges their every whim, or even if he does nothing 'wrong' but is missed because he is so loved, then the mother may suffer the fallout. She, after all, is *there*. Most non-resident fathers recognise the enormous power that mothers hold and some try to build alliances, but there can be no certainty that this will pay off. Contact, or access as it used to be called, is the mothers' area of power and control. While some mothers go to great lengths to promote fathers' involvement, even foregoing child support for fear of alienating them, between 20 and 40 per cent *admit* they impede contact.[77]

> ❛ I know the court order says we should alternate Christmases. I don't know where my head was when I signed that. I'll never let him have these children on Christmas. That's the one day of the year that's too important for me to allow him to have them. I'll go to court if I have to. I'll go to the Supreme Court if I have to. It's only over my dead body that he'll have these children on Christmas. ❜
>
> *mother quoted in* The Custody Revolution

A few women genuinely fear violence or abuse. Some think their ex-partners are lousy parents. Yet others have met up with someone they believe will make a better father, and some are motivated by spite. An American study found almost half the mothers saying that they had impeded contact between father and child at least once, purely out of revenge. One in five custodial mothers say they see no benefit at all from fathers' continued involvement and announce that they are actively working to sabotage it. Many of the mothers who actively inhibit contact between father and child after separation are observed by researchers to be overprotective, to be constantly anticipating violent catastrophes in respect of their children.[78] Maternal overprotectiveness, as outlined in Chapter 4, is, like divorce, most common in families where the fathers have not been well-prepared for parenthood.[79]

While an overwhelming majority of the children of divorce want more contact with their fathers, a few reject them outright. Some have good reason to do so, but others have not. Mothers can easily undermine the relationship between father and child, through emphasising (or lying about) the father's bad qualities. In the US, the term 'parental alienation syndrome' has been coined to describe situations in which children have been brainwashed into rejecting their non-resident parent (usually their fathers). Research has shown that mothers who accomplish this are often violent towards their children, or may terrify them in other ways. The children can be recognised by the spurious reasons they give for 'hating' their fathers: 'He made me help make the bed'; 'The bike at my mother's house is better'.[80]

Rarely is brainwashing necessary, however. Simple lack of support can be enough. One mother in our sample, whose ex-partner was known for his chaotic diary (and towards whom she was fundamentally hostile) reported her delight that after eight years he had made an emphatic request to become involved with his son. Father and child made an arrangement to meet in three months' time, but she didn't check or confirm the details, and then expressed surprise when the father did not turn up. The child has declared that he will never speak to his father again.

When researchers at Britain's Relate Centre for Family Research undertook a project to discover why so many divorced men lost contact with their children, they ended up five years later with a very different perspective. The wonder was not, they concluded, that so many fathers lost contact but, given the difficulties, that so many had stayed in touch.[81]

> ❛ If someone came and stole my child from my house window, there'd be 500 volunteers combing the area. When a wife steals a child, 'Well, go about your work and if you're really good you'll get every other weekend' … I will not be a visiting uncle … I'm a parent and parents do not 'visit' their children. Until I can be a father in every sense, I simply refuse to have any part of this. ❜
>
> *father quoted in Arendell,* After Divorce

Child support

Fathers' groups in many countries are incandescent about the fact that fathers are regularly sanctioned for not paying child support, while mothers who impede father–child contact usually get away with it. This is no longer the case in France, where violation of contact orders has been made a criminal offence, punishable by a prison sentence of up to one year and fines of up to £12,500.[82] British courts, however, almost never imprison mothers for being 'out' when daddy calls. They say that to do so would only harm the children. Curiously, however, the same courts seem to have few qualms about imprisoning lone mothers who fail to pay their TV licences, and it could be argued that the children of the contact-impeding mothers would be in the better position: at least their fathers could look after them.

If divorced mothers use prevention of contact to punish their ex-partners and exert control over the situation, however, they are well matched by divorced fathers similarly using (and abusing) child support. Men's outrage over the Child Support Act has been due not only to the attack on their pockets, as is often assumed, nor even to the measuring of their importance to their children solely in monetary terms. What has shocked and overwhelmed them is the attack on their authority – the undermining of power in the one area over which, after divorce, they had been able to maintain some control.

Fathers withhold money for all kinds of reasons, or rationalisations. They say it's because: 'The kids don't see the money'; or because 'I'm not paying money to *her*'; or 'I never wanted the divorce'; or 'She won't let me see my children'; or 'She doesn't need the money'; or even because a stepfather who ' … has the pleasure of their company' should pay for it. Men who feel the break-up was their fault are by far the most likely to pay regularly.[83] Nevertheless, at first sight, the figures on non-payment of child support, like those on contact levels, read like a testimony to paternal indifference. Prior to the Child Support Act only two-fifths of divorced mothers (and only one in seven never-married mothers) said they received regular maintenance payments.[84]

However, regular maintenance, although of vital importance, is not the only means by which resources are transferred. Fathers may also pay towards mortgages, school fees, clothes, holidays and outings, and there are often discrepancies between mothers' and fathers' accounts, with mothers as likely to under-report payments as fathers are to over-report them. A substantial minority of mothers say they don't want or need money from their ex-partners, and can even be keen to avoid payments in case he ' … wants something for his money'. There are, indeed, clear links between child support and contact: the men who see their children most pay most.[85]

> ❦ Why should I have to pay for children who I do not live with and who I do not have a part in raising? By paying child support, I simply reinforce my ex for having left the marriage and denied me my children. What kind of logic is that? … So I take my chances that they'll throw me in goal. But I refuse to pay. ❦
>
> *father quoted in Arendell,* After Divorce

'I can't understand all this fuss about child support,' said one father we interviewed. 'Surely the only real issue is – who gets the kids?' In many cases, this *is* the underlying issue. We met a recently-separated father who was both withholding child support and 'squatting' in the marital home in the (mistaken) belief that this would force the mother to hand the children over to him. And there are recorded instances of men pursued by the CSA denying paternity of children for whom, in a court on the other side of town, they are bidding for custody.

Won't pay – can't pay?

As might be expected, the fathers who have never lived with their children are least likely to pay child support. This is partly because so many of them are poor.[86] Richer fathers are the best payers. A UK Government White Paper in 1990 noted that separated fathers were younger than married or cohabiting fathers and more likely to be unemployed or on low wages, and concluded that inability to pay, rather than unwillingness, was often the problem.[87]

Nor does it follow that every man whose family relies on state benefit has deserted his children financially. For a majority of divorced or separated couples there is simply not enough money to fund two households adequately, and state benefit has, in effect, acted as a subsidy, helping to mitigate (however slightly) the terrible financial consequences of divorce.

One British study of lone mothers found that more than a third of those asked by the DSS to pass on the address of their former partner had refused to do so.[88] Some did not know it, of course, but since the same percentage also refused to give the address to the academic researchers, the suspicion has to be that at least some had something to hide. The Child Support Agency has also noted that 17 per cent of mothers who are sent a maintenance application form immediately come off benefit. Since not all the women sent the forms were on benefit in the first place, the actual percentage of benefit-receiving mothers who drop their claims must be even higher, suggesting that at least some are receiving support from the fathers of their children.

> ❝ I'm worried about the cost of him coming down here, £10–15 in petrol each time. I'm pleased they see him, it's very important that they go on seeing him. He says if they catch him … he won't be able to get them what they want and he could possibly not be able to come so much. ❞
>
> *mother quoted in* Losing Support

It seems probable that some hard-line non-paying fathers were non-payers before their divorces. Sex and money are the two most commonly quoted areas of disagreement before divorce. Twenty-five per cent of battered wives never received any money from their partners, and as marriages deteriorate even previously generous men tend to hang on to the family's cash.[89] Their partners, of course, may also be squirrelling money away.

It is, however, perfectly plain that many fathers could pay much more than they do. Every single study has shown that once the immediate post-divorce period is over, the majority of non-resident fathers see their effective income rise, while that of their ex-partners and children plummets. And a pre-child-support British study estimated that, using DSS formulae, three out of five lone non-resident fathers and four out of five remarried men could pay more.[90] However, men also probably feel, on some unconscious level, that they have a 'right' to a higher standard of living than their ex-partners, and that they need this. Certainly, to attract another mate they need to be seen to have a bit of money. Low-paid and unemployed males are the least likely to re-partner after divorce.

Although these days as many women as men are in employment, financial inequality between men and women in our society is still so substantial that when a woman starts to live with a man, her effective income rises by 40 per cent, while his falls by 10 per cent.[91] In a sense, therefore, we have been relying, however inefficiently, on private contracts to 'solve' social injustice. Individual men have been taking responsibility for individual women and raising them out of poverty, something they are, understandably, less than keen to do once cohabitation has ended.

Mothers are much more likely than fathers to spend what money they have on their children. This is probably because they have a much more acute sense of their financial needs, how much they eat, how often their shoes need replacing, what toys and games the other children have. Mothers' self-esteem is also more closely bound up with their children. A well-dressed, well-equipped child reflects well on a mother. A father, by contrast, may obtain status more readily from a golf club subscription, or his ability to stand a round of drinks in the pub. Here we see how fathers' sense of being in a 'different world' from that of their children expresses itself in less of a readiness to spend on them directly both before, and after divorce. But if the father is totally in charge of his child, for example on a 'solo' shopping trip, he will often spend freely, which can infuriate mothers.

❛ I signed over my share in the business when I left – it was a kind of 'clean break' if you like – and afterwards I always paid if my ex-wife asked – school fees, and so on. But then, when my younger girl went to university, she came to live with me. I found I spent more on her and gave her more money in that first year than I normally did in two. And it wasn't just my gratitude at having her here. It was that, day to day, I could see what she needed – and when I saw what she needed I made sure she had it. ❜

Colin, 49, father of four (two families)

It is possible that fathers who spend a lot of time with their children after divorce are less likely to re-partner and to become 'serial fathers'. The Newcastle study identified this trend, and the Californian study showed, unusually, no higher levels of fathers re-partnering than mothers re-partnering. This could have positive implications in terms of child poverty after divorce (fathers would have fewer new dependents) as would the fact that the more men see their children, the more of their resources they tend to devote to them.

Paternal alienation

When the UK Children Act came into force in 1992, many fathers were hopeful. Since children would now have more say after divorce, they assumed that more would choose to live with them. This has not happened. And interestingly, when children are enabled to make such a choice (as in California) around half gradually drift back to living, or spending more time, with their mothers.[92] Relatively few move from mother to father, and when they do the move is often a brief, and highly conflicted, one.[93]

Why do children so often choose their mothers? It is thought that stepmothers may be less tolerant than stepfathers towards the presence of a partner's children, and there is social pressure on everyone to acknowledge mothers as the more 'important' parent. ('Why do you have two homes?' the daughter of one man interviewed was regularly asked, 'Why don't you just live with your mummy?') Mothers may also go to great lengths to attract their children back, either because they miss them, or because they feel they've 'failed' if they've lost a custody fight. But mothers may also go easier on rules and regulations or make home more cosy. They are certainly more likely to be connected into local networks, and one child living 50–50 with both his parents told us he preferred being at his mother's house because 'There are more kids there'. An important factor is almost certainly many mothers' greater sensitivity towards their children, which has often developed over years. Sensitivity implies being able to interpret needs, fears and desires with some accuracy, and since this is the hallmark of a satisfying and positive relationship, it should come as no surprise when children gravitate more readily towards their mothers.

Even when divorce policy does its best to bolster father–child contact, very many divorced fathers still end up on the margins before their children have grown. And as the years develop into decades that marginalisation increases, with the adult children keeping in much closer contact with their mothers.[94] It is not just children who, upon divorce, lose out on what researchers call 'intergenerational transfer of resources' – that is, their fathers' love and money. When the fathers are old, the tables are turned.

> ❜ I have given away my son,
> And all the years of patience and of love
> And inexperience is what I've gained,
> To appear virginal when I am grave,
> And travel lightly, having cut the root …
>
> I gave away my son
> Being young myself, having ambition
> To enter a harder race. I was not wise,
> And harnessed neither burden nor remorse.
> I stumble from success onto reverse,
> And even if I win, you are my loss. ❜
> *'Success' quoted in Pirani,* 'The Absent Father'

The seeds of divorced fathers' alienation lie way back: in the upbringing which taught them to suppress empathy for those weaker than themselves; in the cultural overvaluing of motherhood and devaluing of fatherhood; in the construction of the work-day world, which has defined them as secondary parents. No legal system can be expected to step in, after a couple have parted, to right these wrongs. The fact of the matter is that in our society, both before and after divorce, most children are primarily attached to their mothers.

However, fathers can no longer rely on remaining part of their children's lives through their continuing relationship with their children's mothers. Just as women marrying at 20 or even 30 cannot bank on their husband's support in old age (he may not have a job, or they may no longer be married), so within families contemporary fathers, as one man put it, '… have no job-security'.[95] Like women, but for very different reasons, they are beginning to realise that to hand over responsibility for a whole section of your life to even the most seemingly loving and committed partner is no longer a safe bet.

Closing the door?

The solution, for many commentators, is to encourage everyone to get married and then make divorce exceedingly difficult, if not impossible. Even the British Labour Party has latterly evinced a touching, and as far as one can see – given the divorce rate – totally unjustified faith in marriage by entertaining the suggestion that a 'dowry' (i.e. a bribe) be offered to couples who might otherwise merely cohabit. Under what conditions this would become repayable is not clear.

Certainly some fathers would be kept closer to their children if family breakdown were halted. But what would this entail? Tightening the divorce laws might stop divorce, but there is no evidence that it would inhibit desertion. Mothers take to their heels (or are left) with their children when they become educated and employed, and when secularisation prevails. Apart from enforcing religious beliefs (but how? and which ones?), removing women from the workforce (which would shortly engender economic collapse) and reinstating workhouses (or something similar), it would be necessary to outlaw birth control so that virginity again became highly prized, and, of course, to stop educating girls.

Encouraging parents to explore every possible avenue before parting has to be wise, and the UK's 1996 Family Law Bill at least moves in the right direction. Lone parenthood is not, on the whole, a good idea. Lone parents tend to be poor and unable to provide adequate supervision. If they re-partner (and most will) they may have even less time to offer their children or may bring into the family someone whose presence proves destructive. Conversely, if they don't re-partner they may be charged with not being emotionally healthy! Child abuse rates are much higher in lone-parent households (whether headed by a mother or a father) than they are in two-parent families.[96]

❢ No one will score you any deeper than your own child. I am not a violent man, but I have been violent towards him. In the early days the worst was settling him back to sleep at two or

three in the morning. I can recall throwing him onto my bed –
and he was under a year old, for God's sake! I was *throwing* him
(onto a mattress, I wasn't throwing him onto the floor) but you
think – Jesus what have I done! And I remember smacking him
because he shit his knickers when I was trying to potty train
him, and being desperate about him as he cried. **❜**

Bob, 47, father of two (two families)

While individual lone parents can do a good job if they are
sufficiently supported and emotionally healthy, financially and
emotionally stretched parents (i.e. most lone parents) can fall at
many fences, and there is no indication that any society anywhere
feels willing or able to meet their financial needs, Even Sweden,
which has a history of doing a great deal for lone parents, has a
Child Support Agency in the pipeline.

Fathers are part of the 'two-parent advantage' which shows
children from two-parent families doing better than children in lone-
parent households, and children in lone-mother households doing
better if they have even minimal (but steady) contact with even
vaguely pleasant non-resident fathers and better still if such contact
is substantial. However, it is certainly not true, as some right-wing
fathers' groups in the US assert, that an abusive father is better than
no father at all. Where fathers or mothers are abusive or seriously
erratic, children do best if removed from their sphere of influence.[97]

Nor does the evidence suggest that unhappy marriages should be
held together for the sake of the children. Not only is it perfectly
possible for fathers who do not live with their children to have
substantial relationships with them but parental conflict is highly
destructive and when you are living with your enemy there are
round-the-clock opportunitites for combat. No one has yet shown
that children from lone-parent families do worse than children
from highly conflicted (but intact) marriages, i.e. the kinds of
marriages that the children of many lone-parents might have been
subjected to, if their parents had stayed together.

Are fathers dangerous?

It appears that there are three stages in the public acceptance of any
supposedly new idea, such as the notion that fathers and their
children can have relationships as close and mutually rewarding as
mother–child relationships are perceived to be.[98] During the first
stage of acceptance, when traditional values still rule, father-care

will be seen as essentially 'different' from mother-care, and any cross-over regarded as potentially dangerous. The second stage reflects ambivalence. Now intimate care by fathers is accepted as valuable and perhaps necessary, although mother-care is still considered superior. In the third stage, there is general acceptance of father-care as a good thing, but even at this point reservations will be expressed by conservative forces.

> 6 My father spent his Saturday nights ironing our dresses and pinafores ... he would spend hours straightening, braiding and curling our hair so we could look 'Just as nice as the other little girls', the girls who had mothers ... Years later I found myself singing to my daughter a song my father had sung to us at bedtime when we were very little. I hadn't heard that song for twenty years, and I'd never heard anyone other than my father sing it, but it seemed to be waiting in my throat for my baby. 9
> *Karen Hill Anton,* Remembering a father who mothered

Countries such as Sweden and Denmark have reached the third stage in this process, for there the debate does not focus on the wisdom (or otherwise) of drawing fathers into family life, but on how this might be achieved. Britain, it would seem, is entering the second stage. Concern is mounting about the limited amount of time many fathers spend with their children and their apparent lack of commitment after separation and divorce, but serious reservations are expressed by some who perceive men to be a danger to women and children Parents now know that as far as sexual abuse is concerned, stranger-danger is less common than family abuse, and believe that the most likely perpetrators are biological fathers. Mistrust has not been ameliorated by bleatings from the anti-divorce lobby that husbands are less of a danger to women than cohabitees, and that biological fathers are less likely to abuse children sexually than stepfathers.

How dangerous are biological fathers? Ten children in every hundred constantly, or frequently, witness physical violence between their mother and the man with whom she is living, and this occurs mainly in the same or in the next room.[99] Witnessing repeated violence by one parent towards another is, in itself, abusive and this should be taken into account by professionals seeking to foster relationships between abusive men and their children. However, a substantial percentage of the abusive men are *not* the biological fathers of the children living with them and in a minority of causes, the violent partner is the mother. And although violent husbands are more than four times more likely than other men to be violent fathers, most wifebatterers do not physically abuse the children.[100]

What about violence towards children themselves? Around 7 per cent of children are punched, kicked, bitten, burned, beaten, threatened with a knife or gun, or hit with an object by parents (including by step-parents). However, mothers and fathers appear in the statistics to be pretty evenly matched as perpetrators and, surprisingly, the most serious acts of physical abuse are more often committed by mothers than by fathers.[101] Interestingly, because the statistics again lump fathers and father-figures (stepfathers and mothers' boyfriends) together, this means that biological fathers are *less* likely to abuse their children physically than biological mothers

Women who are abused by their partners are twice as likely as other mothers to abuse their children, but partner-abuse does not explain high levels of physical abuse by mothers: the vast majority of women who abuse their children physically are not abused by their partners.[102] Children are also abused emotionally and through gross neglect, and here mothers are more likely to be implicated than fathers, even when statistical adjustments are made concerning with whom the child is living.[103]

> 6 Of course I get angry with Emma, but I tend to pull her away from Jill much more than Jill will ever pull her away from me, to protect her, because I think any anger that I have is within the normal spectrum. Whereas sometimes Jill's anger would topple her over into this irrational rage, and stuff would pour out of her, vitriol at the child. Jill absolutely adores Emma, and then click, just like that she is the focus of her rage. 9
>
> *Ken, 50, father of three (two families)*

Violence, power – and sex

What about sexual abuse? Although sexual abuse by mothers is almost certainly under-reported, their rates, even if doubled or tripled, would still be miniscule in comparison with fathers'. As mentioned in Chapter 1, around 2 per cent of biological fathers have physical sexual *contact* with their children, mainly their daughters. In around half these cases, the sexual event is remembered as a one-off aberration (though, even so, as grossly disturbing). In one case in four, genital intercourse or cunnilingus is involved. It is also probable that another 2 per cent of fathers, while not actually touching their children, have behaved towards them in some sexualised way.[104] This is a rate of about one in 25 for inappropriate sexuality and is shockingly high. Interestingly, it just about matches the percentage of children seriously physically abused by their fathers, and by their mothers.

In sexual abuse, the statistics do distinguish between fathers and father-figures, and it is clear that any mother (of a daughter) who is thinking of bringing a new adult male into her household should think very seriously. Boys are more often sexually abused outside their families.

One stepfather in six will have sexual contact with his stepdaughter before she is 14 years old. Less grave but still inappropriate sexualised behaviour will certainly increase those numbers.[105] However, it is instructive to examine more closely the term stepfather, which is generally used to cover any male who lives in a household as the mother's partner, however temporarily. Sexual contact between stepdaughters and *true* stepfathers – men who have 'stepped into' the shoes of biological fathers and have raised the girls for most of their lives – appears to be at the lower rate of one in 11.[106] This is still substantially higher than the one in 50 found for sexual contact with biological fathers.

Given that, outside their families, males are constantly more sexually abusive than females (towards other men, as well as towards women), the corresponding gender-imbalance in sexual abuse within families seems to make 'gender sense'.

But what about the far greater *parity* between the sexes in terms of the physical abuse of children? Could it be that physical violence, as a strategy to control others' behaviour, which it is generally recognised to be, is one that women are actually quite likely to employ if, as within the privacy of their own homes, they are dealing with individuals smaller and weaker than themselves?

It is often suggested that if fathers spent as much time with their children as mothers do, their rates of physical abuse would exceed mothers' by miles, and clearly rates would rise substantially. But, on the other hand, there is evidence that some of the current physical abuse by fathers (and father-figures) is carried out for mothers, and even at their behest.[107] It may be that increased time with the children would lead to *reduced* violence in some cases. Some fathers might have less need to demonstrate dominance, their parenting skills might improve, and support be offered to them. Mothers supported by networks of other mothers abuse their children less often than more isolated women.[108]

As for sexual aggression, this is also known very often to be more about power and control than eroticism. Of course, some sexually abusive fathers are simply paedophiles who have created for themselves the perfect victims, but very many, it would appear, are not. Research has shown that men most likely to abuse their children sexually often had low levels of involvement with them during their childhoods.[109] If such fathers were enabled to be closer to their children throughout their lives, there would perhaps be no need for them to bid for control and intimacy via sexuality.

> *He'd come in my bed and cuddle me and eat me; then he'd threaten me not to tell. He loved me very much. He just had a sickness. He was a good man in every other way. He went to church and worked six days a week.*
>
> *Paula quoted in Herman,* Father–Daughter Incest

Bringing fathers back in

Since the vast majority of children are not in grave danger from their fathers and in fact, when all types of serious abuse are considered, appear to be in no lesser danger from their mothers, and since all the evidence suggests that increased involvement by fathers would, in the main, be good for families, how could this be achieved?

It should first be said that choice has to be paramount. There is no point establishing some kind of impossible standard by which every father who isn't perpetually focused on his toddler feels he is a guilty failure. People perform best as parents when they are comfortable with the choices they have made. Families change over time and expectations vary according to class and race and locality.

As things stand, however, choice for fathers is severely limited and before choices can be truly made, new options need to be presented. If a new standard were to be established, it would seem likely that one based on higher levels of involvement than exist at present would be beneficial and, in the main, manageable.

It is, however, important to recognise that change is generally brought about more by environment than by ideology, and that change comes slowly. It is now 100 years since the great fertility decline, which more than halved the size of families, took hold in Britain and forced women to begin to review the function of their lives. Yet only now are far-reaching changes in women's aspirations and behaviour being observed. Many of the economic and social changes that are beginning to force men to re-evaluate their functions are, as yet, in their infancy.

There is also no point in simply dumping fathers on their children and children on their fathers. Skill acquisition has to be part of it, and network support, and these do not develop overnight. Stepfathers, in particular, have unique and pressing needs, and there has not been sufficient space to investigate this here. Although their numbers are increasing rapidly, these men are currently given no guidance and support, and this no doubt partly explains their often poor record.

If change were to happen it would need to happen on many levels. The images of fatherhood with which we are surrounded would have to be challenged and broadened, and the reality of fathers' private lives made more visible. Individual awareness is key, awareness by *both* parents that golden opportunities are lost when children are shushed and told 'don't bother daddy', when mothers struggle on until they drop, or childcare is sought from others, even when fathers are available. And when alternative views on childraising are quashed in the interest of unity and 'support'. Even such apparently insignificant routines as fathers always doing the driving, while mothers entertain grumbling toddlers in the back seat of the car, help to remove fathers from their families, keeping them always at the edge of any real involvement.

> ❛ The relationship Luke has with Beth is very strong and he won't have a word said against her even in jest. He just simply cannot bring himself to criticise her. ❜
>
> *Alan, 34, father of two*

Taking risks

Individual change would have to be accompanied by structural change.[110] Chapter 5 looked at some of the steps that could be taken to help fathers reconcile the needs of work and family, and it is plain that family-friendly policies would need to be reframed with men in mind. Trades unions and professional associations (as well as employers and managers) would have to tackle the issue, and a comprehensive programme of leave arrangements would need to be developed in accordance with European standards. This is particularly pressing in Britain, where short-term and part-time contract work is being widely used to strip employees of all employment benefits and rights.[111]

But it would have all to begin much earlier than that. Men's parenting potential would need to be treated with respect, and sex (and relationship) education developed with boys in mind and delivered to them in single-sex groups. Sophisticated hormonal contraception would have to be made available to men, to give them back control over their own fertility, and ensure that every child were a wanted child – wanted by their fathers as well as their mothers.

Perhaps the time has also come to review the connection between marriage and parenthood. After all, as sex and procreation are no longer shackled together, and as life-long sexual partnerships are increasingly rare and one in every three children is already born outside marriage, it does not seem wise to view the relationship between a parent and a child as contingent upon the relationship between the two parents. For then the dissolution of the one seems to imply the dissolution of the other. Marriage could be seen as a celebration of an adult partnership, no less and no more, and religious marriage services rewritten to exclude mention of procreation. Upon the registration of a birth, however, formal and lifelong commitment to the child could be made by each parent independently.

> 6 Her friend's husband worked in the builder's merchants and one day he said to me 'The baby goes for adoption tomorrow.' And when he told me that I just broke down and cried. And I'll be honest it sort of messed me up for relations. I could never sort of get established again. I always thought about this baby every day and then I saw in the paper about this new Children's Act, and I wrote up and asked – could we find out under the new Act, where our children went to? And they wrote back – 'No'. 9
>
> *Vince, 59, father of one*

The management of the whole process of pregnancy and birth would need to be revamped, with fathers' responses directly assessed early on, antenatal examinations and appointments offered at non-standard hours, and specially designed parent training delivered to fathers, with meetings and assistance for both parents continuing after birth.

Family professionals would have to review their assumptions. It would not be enough simply to whine that 'we work with the parent presented to us'. Environments would need to be made father-friendly with pictures of fathers and children in plenty, and staff reviewing their own, often very different, behaviour towards women and men. Within the community fathers would need to be targeted directly, and their fears, expectations and working patterns taken into account. If the current priority given to repairing relationships between abusive mothers and their children were to be maintained, it would seem only just that a similar approach be adopted in respect of fathers.

The Exchequer would also have to fund an infrastructure of affordable, quality childcare as well as public housing for separated fathers who had shared residence agreements. Only then would both parents be enabled to be both breadwinners and carers. The costs of this would be offset at least in part through a reduction in post-divorce benefit outlay due to fathers' continuing involvement and mothers' greater employment.

6 Later, when I found where her adoption records were, I phoned up. I said, 'I'm a birth father. I understand that I am allowed by law to leave a letter on my daughter's file.' He said, 'Yes you are.' I went to see the chap. I went smartly dressed in my best suit, and he looked me up and down. He took out some bits and pieces from the file. He said, 'You mustn't see these, as they've got names and addresses on.' Then he handed me the rest of the file. I saw, written down, 'Does the father approve the adoption?' Although no one had ever asked me, it had got a 'yes' beside it. I got my pen out and, in front of the chap, I crossed it out and put 'NO'. 9

Vince, 59, father of one

Parents, whether separated or living together, who could not (or did not wish to) 'box and cox' care for their children would have to share it with professionals, which in Britain would mean a major rethink since the common perception is that nursery care is grossly inferior to family-based care. (In fact, *quality* of care is what matters in any setting, and infants and toddlers who have spent substantial amounts of time in well-run day-nurseries often do particularly well, and by school age are outperforming home-reared children on virtually every measure.)[112]

The challenges to women would be considerable. Since employing men substantially in education and welfare is crucial to broadening the definition of fathering, women would find themselves facing job losses in those areas they currently dominate. They would also have to give up their dominance over their children and acknowledge fathers as equal partners in parenting, while finding the *obligation* to be breadwinners imposed on them as it currently is on men. Today, the parent whose name is on the Child Benefit book (normally the mother) does not have to accept employment while her child is under 16, and we came across a case in which a divorced father whose daughter was living with him half the time was obliged by the CSA to support her while she was with her mother too. This was because the mother (though able-bodied and with no more children) elected not to work. Such a position would no longer be tenable.

It is after separation and divorce that women would really feel the squeeze. They would find themselves obliged to name the fathers of their children, sanctioned through fines and prison sentences if they tried to impede contact, prevented from moving too far away and facing across the courtroom men who would once have obediently handed over their offspring, but who now stand up and fight for them with a good chance of winning.

❝ When I came away from his office and stood on the station, I thought 'I shall never see my daughter', and I cried and cried. But I left the letter on her adoption file. Every birthday and Christmas after that I sent a card to the file, and then one August the chap rang me and said, 'She has been back to her file. I can't say what action she will take, and she is out of the country now until the end of October.' I had a birthday coming up in September. I thought, 'Am I going to get a card?' I got more than a card. I got a letter *and* photographs! At night I put them beside the bed. I kept waking and looking at them, saying to myself, 'Is this true? Is this really my daughter, the daughter I have never seen?' ❞

Vince, 59, father of one

If unmarried fathers were to be given the same rights as married men and if shared residence rather than mother residence were to be considered the norm when parents separate (there is no reason why either of these policies should not be adopted), women would have to recognise that if they dice with becoming pregnant, they risk having to accept their sexual partner, however casual, as their parenting-partner for almost two decades. Just as men who leave their condoms in their wallets now risk paying almost two decades of child support.

All this would mean huge changes, changes which might, as many changes do, fall hardest on the weakest and most vulnerable in our communities first. And since change does not come free, men would face losses, too. 'Everybody wants to rule the world', as the song goes, and there can be no doubt that individual men would lose power to individual women, whose effectiveness in the workplace would be boosted by the greater participation of their children's fathers within the domestic sphere. Some fathers, too, would initially lose out to other males, men for whom parenthood was a nil or low priority. But in the end the rules must change, the sheer force of numbers making it acceptable for both men and women to be close to their children while retaining a substantial connection to the workplace. This would release women, who are in many ways still excluded from full participation in the wider world, and would halt the devastating slide into poverty of separated mothers and their children. It would also release men who, while they may rule that wider world, would seem in the main not to be well acquainted with those for whom they would give it: their children.

❛ There has been five years of it now. He has been cut to pieces. He has scars down his body, a big scar down the front, scars on the side, there is wires in here and tubes in his wrists, tubes in his arms, tubes in his groin. After all that has happened in my life, and I've known sadness and thought things were wrong, personally to myself, but I never knew that there was sadness like this, or pain. It is inside your body and inside your mind. **❜**

Michael, 36, father of two

A new image for fatherhood?

Is this new representation of fatherhood no less a social construction than those that have gone before? Of course it is: why should we, all of a sudden, have broken the habit of centuries? But it is important to recognise that both fatherhood and motherhood are socially constructed, and that both are regularly redesigned to accommodate or promote social change. For example, the notion that children do best if raised almost exclusively by their mothers would once have been considered a nonsense, and indeed it took Western European governments more than 200 years of sustained propaganda to convince a disbelieving majority of their citizens that this was the best option.[113] In fact, promoting an exclusive attachment to one caretaker may not be particularly constructive. Almost one in three children raised by stay-at-home mums exhibit, in psychological testing, an 'anxious attachment', which means that they do not feel sufficiently secure to be able freely to explore the outside world.[114]

Nor is it true that a stable and satisfying relationship with a single adult (usually a female) 'attachment figure' is essential to successful child development. There are many ways to bring up children. Among a tribe in Zaire called the Efe, babies are 'multiply attached'.

They spend relatively little time with their biological mothers and are breastfed by many women and cared for by men, women and children, yet they grow up capable and affectionate.[115] And in the US, observers are already reporting the apparently normal development of children raised from infancy by male homosexual couples.[116]

Adult attachment figures may even be of lesser importance than we have thought. Rhesus monkeys raised without peers turn out more abnormally than those raised without a mother or mother-substitute. And six Jewish children raised in a concentration camp for the first three years of their lives by an ever-changing series of adults (none of whom survived) were, at the last count (1983) leading 'effective lives'. The children had formed a tightly knit group, and it is thought that this peer-support facilitated their successful development.[117] The constant availability of a peer group may be one reason for the developmental superiority of many children raised in quality day-nurseries, and there are already indications that children who have strong and positive attachments to both their parents may develop differently from children raised by one primary caregiver. They do not exhibit the 'separation anxiety' thought by Western paediatricians to be inevitable at around age nine months. This not only occurs later, but is much milder and briefer.[118]

> 6 They will come and look for me if they are hurt as much as they will her. Gareth has this thing, he goes from one parent to the other, like she's the flavour of the month and no one else is allowed to touch him. Then he goes on to me. Like today it's me. I took him to nursery this morning, and she's brought him back, took him upstairs, he won't stay with her. He's screaming and going mad. He wants to come to work with me. 9
>
> *Steve, 37, father of six*

However, although the raising of children in nuclear families is clearly not the only or even, necessarily, the best option, it has been the system of apparent choice in our culture for more than a millennium, and when other methods are tried seems stubbornly to re-assert itself. When Israeli families abandoned the *kibbutzim* it was not because these were unsuccessful (on the contrary, the children so raised ended up neither more nor less neurotic than those raised in conventional families) but because a new generation wished to raise their offspring privately. It is clearly in all our interests that relationships between parents and their children be optimised.

Recognition is currently being given worldwide to the importance of biological parents. In 1989, the UN Convention on the Rights of the Child asserted that children should have the right to know the identity of both their parents and to keep contact if separated from them. This should come as no surprise. Parent–child relationships are increasingly significant in a world in which physical survival can depend on organ or tissue donation from relatives, serial monogomy is the norm, families are smaller and more widely scattered, change endemic and collective responsibility is being replaced everywhere by individual responsibility.

In such a world we can no longer rely, if we ever could, on 'the village' to raise the child and the love between parent and child can be one of very few certainties. Even men who have voluntarily deserted their children never forget them, but carry round with them 'ghost children' with whom they dream of one day being reconciled. For some time now we have recognised the salience of (and sought to maintain) links between children and their biological mothers. Why should maintaining links with biological fathers be considered less of a priority?

The UN Convention did not stop at underlining the centrality of parent–child relations. It established the needs of children as *paramount* and decreed that these be set above the needs of parents. Although far from being in force at present, this radical position is undoubtedly the perspective of the future. And it seems probable that we will shortly consider it bizarre and indefensible that we once denied to children the facts of their parentage and birth, let alone that we failed to support, and in many cases actively inhibited, their relationships with their fathers.

6 I've always thought that when they get older, I would like them to look back and say 'at least he was always there and he cared'. I wouldn't want no special favours, I wouldn't want to be Superman or nothing like that. But I would like them to look back and say 'Well I will say one thing about Dad, he did go swimming with me. He did take me to the pictures. He did sit in McDonald's with me, he did come shopping with me and Mum. He did go to the market with us. We did go to the park together' ... I never had none of that. Never had nothing like that. I think to myself that if they look back and see the opposite to me, I'll have achieved what I wanted to achieve. I'll have got there. 9

Michael, 36, father of two

Notes

Preface

1. Burgess A & Ruxton S (1996) Men and their children: Proposals for public policy, London, Institute for Public Policy Research

Chapter 1

1. Jung CG (1949) 'The significance of the father in the destiny of the individual', reprinted in Samuels A (1985) *The Father: contemporary Jungian perspectives*, London, Free Association Books
2. Samuels A (1985) *The Father: contemporary Jungian perspectives*, London, Free Association Books
3. Jung CG (1949) *op cit*
4. Warner M (1990) *Alone of All Her Sex: the myth and cult of the Virgin Mary*, London, Picador
5. Estes C (1992) *Women Who Run with the Wolves: myths and stories of the wild women archetype*, New York, Ballantine Books
6. Haraway D (1988) 'Situated Knowledge: the science question in feminism and the privilege of partial perspective', *Feminist Studies* Vol 14(3):577-599
7. Colman A & Colman L (1988) *The Father: mythology and changing roles*, Illinois, Chiron
8. Hewlett B (1991) *Intimate Fathers: the nature and content of Aka Pygmy paternal infant care*, Ann Arbor, University of Michigan
9. Badinter E (1989) *Man/Woman: the one is the other*, London, Collins Harvill
10. Levine JA et al (1993) *Getting men involved: strategies that work*, New York, Families and Work Institute
11. Warner M (1990) *op cit*
12. Quoted in Boose L (1989) *Daughters and Fathers*, Baltimore, John Hopkins University Press
13. Bettelheim B (1976) *The Uses of Enchantment*, England, Penguin
14. Graeme Russell, personal communication, 1996
15. *ibid*
16. Hite S (1994) *The Hite Report on the Family*, London, Bloomsbury
17. For prevalence of sexual abuse see Russell DEH (1986) *The Secret Trauma: incest in the lives of girls and women*, New York, Basic Books
18. Sarre S (1995) *Bringing Fathers Back In: fathers and social policy in the post-war period*, Welfare State Programme STICERD, London School of Economics and Political Science
19. John Angell James quoted in Gillis JR (1974) *Youth and History: tradition and change in European age relations 1770-present*, London, Academic Press
20. Delumeau J & Roche J (1990) *Histoire des pères et de la paternité*, Paris, Larousse
21. *ibid*
22. Miller A (1987) *For Your Own Good: the roots of violence in child rearing*, London, Virago
23. Delumeau J & Roche J (1990) *op cit*
24. *ibid*
25. *ibid*
26. Quoted by Giveans DL & Robinson MK (1985) 'Roles Throughout the Life Cycle,' in Hanson SM & Bozett FW (eds) *Dimensions of Fatherhood*, Los Angeles, Sage
27. Quoted in Badinter E (1989) *op cit*
28. Delumeau J & Roche J (1990) *op cit*
29. Griswold RL (1993) *Fatherhood in America: a history*, New York, Basic Books
30. Holdsworth S. et al (1992) *Innocence and Experience: images of children in British art from 1600 to the present.* Manchester, City Art Galleries
31. O'Brien M & Jones D (1995) 'Young people's attitudes to fatherhood' in Moss P (ed) *Father Figures: fathers in the families of the 1990s*, London, HMSO
32. Humbert P (1994) 'Monitoring Child Care Services for Young Children', *Working Paper* V/460/94, Brussels
33. Quoted in Griswold RL (1993) *op cit*
34. Quoted in Badinter E (1980) *The Myth of Motherhood: an historical view of the maternal instinct*, London, Souvenir Press
35. Quoted in Griswold RL (1993) *op cit*
36. *ibid*
37. *ibid*
38. Newson J & Newson E (1968) *Four Years Old In An Urban Community*, London, Penguin

39. Hewlett B (1987) *op cit*

40. Sandquist K (1987) *Fathers and Family Work in Two Cultures*, Stockholm, Institute of Education

41. Mark Simpson 'Added appeal for mum', *Guardian*, London, 7 March 1994

42. Emily Bell (1990) 'In search of the "new man"', *Observer*, London, 17 June 1990.

43. Rinstead Campaign, UK, 1995

44. Quoted in Griswold R (1993) *op cit*

45. Newson J & Newson E (1968) *op cit*

46. Clarke E (1957) *My Mother Who Fathered Me*, London, Allen & Unwin

47. See, for example, Glenn EN et al (1994) *Mothering: ideology, experience and agency*, London, Routledge

48. Mark Simpson (1994) *op cit*

49. Griswold RL (1993) *op cit*

50. Quoted in Badinter E (1989) *op cit*

51. Samuels A (1993a) '*The Good-enough Father of Whatever Sex*', *Feminism & Psychology*, Vol 5(4):511-530

52. Lloyd T (1994) *Analysis of Newspaper Coverage of Fathers and Men As Carers*, Discussion Paper, London, Working with Men

53. Hite S (1994) *op cit*

54. Hilton T (1993) 'In Tandem' in French S (ed) *Fatherhood*, London, Virago

55. Dr Charlie Lewis, Lancaster University, personal communication, 1995

56. Nickel H & Kocher EMT 1987 'West Germany and the German-Speaking Countries' in Lamb ME (ed) *The Father's Role: cross cultural perspectives*, Hillsdale NJ, Lawrence Erlbaum

57. Pruett KD (1993) 'The Paternal Presence', *Families in Society: The Journal of Contemporary Human Services*, Jan:46-50

58. Samuels A (1989) *The Plural Psyche: personality, morality and the father*, London, Routledge

59. Mitscherlich A (1969) *Society Without the Father: a contribution to social psychology*, London, Tavistock

60. Badinter E (1989) *op cit*

61. Bly J (1990) *Iron John: a book about men*, Dorset, Addison-Wesley

62. Samuels A (1993b) *The Political Psyche*, London, Routledge

63. Zipes J (1994) *Fairy Tale as Myth: myth as fairy tale*, Kentucky, The University Press

64. Jonathan Freedland 'Diaper Dads fight for lost manhood', *Guardian*, London, 20 June 1994

65. Hopkins P (1927) *Father or Sons?*, London, Kegan Paul

66. Samuels A (1993a) *op cit*

67. Ruddick S (1990) *Maternal Thinking: towards a politics of peace*, London, The Women's Press

68. Ros Coward 'Make the father figure', *Guardian*, London, 11 April 1996

69. Hewitt P (1994) 'Reinventing Families',The Mischcon Lecture, University College, London

70. Dench G (1994) *The Frog Prince and the Problem of Men*, London, Neanderthal Books

71. Silverstein L & Phares V (1996) '*Fathering is a Feminist Issue*', *Psychology of Women Quarterly*, Vol 20(1):3-37

72. Beatrix Campbell '*Do they want dads or rulers?*', *Guardian*, London, 17 April 1994

73. Quoted in Melanie Phillips 'Is the male redundant now?', *Observer*, London, 26 June 1994

74. Blankenhorn D (1995) *Fatherless America: confronting our most urgent social problem*, New York, Basic Books

75. Dench G (1994) *op cit*

76. *ibid*

77. John Crowe Ransom 'Janet Waking', in *The Norton Anthology of Poetry* (1983), New York, WW Norton

Chapter 2

1. Mary Abbott, author of *Family Ties: English families 1540-1920* (1993), London, Routledge, personal communication, 1994

2. Seccombe W (1993) *Weathering the Storm*, London, Verso

3. See, for instance, Sally Kevill-Davies *Yesterday's Children* (1991) and Maris A Vinovskis 'Historical perspectives on the development of the family' in *Parenting Across the Life-span* (1987)

4. Pollock LA (1983) *Forgotten Children: parent-child relations from 1500-1900*, Cambridge, Cambridge University Press

5. Stone L (1977) *The Family, Sex and Marriage: in England 1500-1800*, London, Weidenfeld & Nicholson

6. George & Wilding, 1972, quoted in O'Brien M (1984) *Fathers Without Wives*, unpublished PhD thesis presented to the London School of Economics and Political Science
7. See, for example, the work of the Cambridge Group for the History of Population and Social Structure, 27 Trumpington Street, Cambridge, UK
8. For example, Pollock LA (1987) *A Lasting Relationship: parents and children over 3 centuries*, London, Fourth Estate
9. Macfarlane A (1970) *The Family Life of Ralph Josselin*, Cambridge, Cambridge University Press
10. Delumeau J & Roche J (1990) *Histoire des peres et de la paternite*, Paris, Larousse
11. Pollock L A(1987) *op cit*
12. Pollock LA(1983) *op cit*
13. Pollock LA (1987) *op cit*
14. *ibid*
15. Prince de Ligne (1790) *Fragments de l'histoire de ma vie*, quoted in Delumeau J & Roche J (1990) op cit
16. Pollock LA (1987) *op cit*
17. Laslett P (1983) *The World We Have Lost: further explored*, London, Routledge
18. Pollock L (1983) *op cit*
19. Hardyment C (1982) *Dream Babies: childcare from Locke to Spock*, London, Cape
20. Laslett P (1983) *op cit*
21. Davidson C (1982) *A Woman's Work is Never Done: a history of housework in the British Isles 1650-1950*, London, Chatto and Windus
22. Laslett P (1983) *op cit*
23. Abbott M (1993) *Family Ties: English families 1540-1920*, London, Routledge
24. Laslett P (1977) *Family Life and Illicit Love in Earlier Generations, Cambridge*, Cambridge University Press
25. Davidson C (1982) *op cit*
26. *ibid*
27. Davies D (1795) *The Case of Labourers in Husbandry*, quoted in Laslett P (1983) op cit
28. Newson J & Newson E (1968) *Four Years Old in an Urban Community*, London, Penguin
29. Pollock LA (1983) *op cit*
30. *ibid*
31. Pollock LA (1987) *op cit*
32. Clarke N (1991) 'Strenuous idleness: Thomas Carlyle and the man of letters as hero,' in Roper M & Tosh J *Manful Assertions: masculinities in Britain since 1800*, London, Routledge
33. Cobbett W (1830) *Advice to Young Men and (Incidentally) to Young Women in the Middle and Higher Ranks of Life*, Oxford, Oxford University Press, 1980
34. Pollock LA (1987) *op cit*
35. Abbott M (1993) *op cit*
36. *ibid*
37. O'Brien M (1983) *Fathers without Wives*, unpublished PhD thesis presented to the London School of Economic and Political Science
38. Sally Kevill-Davies, personal communication, 1994
39. Lock J & Dixon WT (1965) *A Man of Sorrow: the life, letters and times of the Rev Patrick Bronte*, London, Nelson
40. Laslett P (1977) *op cit*
41. Pollock LA (1983) *op cit*
42. Burnett J (1982) *Destiny Obscure: autobiographics of childhood from the 1820s to the 1920s*, London, Allen Lane
43. Reprinted in Kevill-Davis S (1993) *Yesterday's Children: the antiques and history of childhood*, London, Antiques Club
44. Laslett P (1983) *op cit*
45. Pollock LA (1983) *op cit*
46. *ibid*
47. *ibid*
48. Burnett J (1982) *op cit*
49. Bifulco A (1994) 'The first steps on the road to depression', *MRC News*, Vol 63:24-27
50. Pollock LA (1983) *op cit*
51. *ibid*
52. Burnett J (1982) *op cit*
53. Koditschek TS (1981) *Class Formation and the Bradford Bourgeoisie*, unpublished PhD dissertation, Princeton University
54. Gillis JR (1974) *Youth and History: tradition and change in European age relations 1770–present*, New York, Academic Press
55. Thompson P (1977) *The Edwardians: the remaking of British society*, London, Routledge
56. Burnett J (1982) *op cit*
57. Thompson P (1977) *op cit*
58. Davidson C (1982) *op cit*

59. Seccombe W (1993) *op cit*
60. Burnett J (1982) *op cit*
61. Tosh J (1991) 'Domesticity and Manliness in the Victorian Middle Class,' in Roper M & Tosh J (eds) *Manful Assertions*, London, Routledge
62. Eliot G (1861) *Silas Marner*, London, Penguin, 1985
63. Pollock LA (1987) *op cit*
64. Lummis T (1982) 'The Historical Dimensions of Fatherhood: a case study 1890-1914' in McKee L & O'Brien M *The Father Figure*, London, Tavistock
65. Turner B & Rennell T (1995) *When Daddy Came Home: how family life changed forever in 1945*, London, Hutchinson
66. Hilton T (1993) 'In Tandem' in French S (ed) *Fatherhood*, London, Virago
67 Turner B & Rennell T (1995) *op cit*
68. Lewis C (1993) 'Mothers' and fathers' roles: similar or different?', in *Fathers in families of tomorrow*, Copenhagen, Danish Ministry of Social Affairs
69. Charlie Lewis, personal communication, 1995
70. Ninio A & Rinott N (1988) 'Fathers' involvement in the care of their infants and their attributions of cognitive competence to infants', *Child Development*, Vol 59:652-603
71. Pleck JH (1996) 'Paternal involvement: levels, sources and consequences' in Lamb ME (ed) *The Role of the Father in Child Development* (third edition), New York, Wiley
72. Marsiglio W (1991) 'Paternal engagement activities with minor children', *Journal of Marriage and Family*, Vol 53(4):973-986
73. Lamb ME (1996) 'Fathers and child development: an introductory overview and guide' in Lamb ME (ed) *The Role of the Father in Child Development* (third edition), New York, Wiley
74. Pleck JH (1996) *op cit*
75. Erickson RJ & Gecas V (1985) 'Social Class and Fatherhood', in Bozett FW & Hanson SMH (eds) *Fatherhood and Families in Cultural Context*, New York, Springer
76. Pleck JH (1996) *op cit*
77. Shelton BA & John D (1993) 'White, black and Hispanic Men's Household Labour' in Hood JC (ed) *Men, Work and Family*, California, Sage
78. Cohen TE (1993) 'What do fathers provide?' in Hood JC *ibid*
79. Easterbrooks MA & Goldberg WA (1984) 'Toddler Development in the Family', *Child Development*, Vol 55
80. Lewis C & O'Brien M (1987) Re-assessing Fatherhood, London, Sage
81. Dickey A (1987) 'Interrelationships within the Triad' in Berman PW & Pedersen FA (eds) *Men's Transitions to Parenthood*, Hillsdale NJ, Lawrence Erlbaum
82. For much of the information in the following section, I am indebted to Dr Charlie Lewis's chapter 'Fathers and pre-schoolers' (1996) in Lamb ME (ed) *The Role of the Father in Child Developmen* (third edition), New York, Wiley
83. Shelton BA & John D (1993) *op cit*
84. Lewis C (1996) 'Fathers and pre-schoolers' in Lamb ME (ed) *The Role of the Father in Child Development* (third edition), New York, Wiley
85. Russell G & Russell A (1987)' Mother-child and father-child relationships in middle childhood', *Child Development* Vol 58:1573-1585
86. For these and other examples see Lewis C (1996) *op cit*
87. Figures supplied by APPROACH (Association for the Protection of All Children Ltd) 77 Holloway Road, London N7 8JZ
88. Russell G & Russell A (1987) *op cit*
89. Lewis C (1996) *op cit*
90. Kellerhals J et al (1990) 'Social stratification and the parent-child relationship' in Bjornberg U (ed) *European Parents in the 1990's*, New Brunswick, Transaction
91. APPROACH *op cit*
92. Kellerhals J et al (1990) *op cit*
93. Lewis C (1996) *op cit*
94. Sternberg K (1996) 'Fathers, the missing figure in research on family violence' in Lamb ME *The Role of the Father in Child Development (3rd edition)*, New York, Wiley
95. Lewis C (1986) *Becoming a Father*, Milton Keynes, Open University Press
96. *ibid*
97. Pleck JH (1996) *op cit*

98. Bittman M (1995) 'Changes at the Heart of Family Households', *Family Matters* No. 10 Autumn, Melbourne, Australian Institute of Family Studies

Chapter 3

1. Silverstein LB (1993) 'Primate Research, Family Politics, and Social Policy: Transforming "cads" into "dads", *Journal of Family Psychology*, Vol 7(3):267-306

2. Reported by Family Mediation, Scotland, November 1994

3. Haraway D (1989) *Primate Visions*, New York, Routledge

4. Moller AP (1988) 'Paternity and paternal care in the swallow', *Animal Behaviour*, Vol 36(4):996-1005

5. Wagner RH (1992) *Confidence of paternity and parental effort in razorbills*, Washington DC, Smithsonian Institute National Zoological Park

6. Haraway D (1989) *op cit*

7. Quoted in Haraway D (1989) *op cit*

8. Murray C (1994) 'The New Victorians ... and the New Rabble', *Sunday Times*, London, 29 May 1994

9. Hrdy S (1981) *The Woman That Never Evolved*, Cambridge Mass, Harvard University Press

10. *ibid*

11. *ibid*

12. Silverstein LB (1993) *op cit*

13. West MM & Konner MJ (1981) 'The Role of the father: an anthropolgical perspective' in Lamb ME (ed) *The Role of the Father in Child Development* (2nd edition), New York, Wiley

14. Mackey WC (1985) *Fathering Behaviours*, New York, Plenum Press

15. Harkness S & Super CM (1992) 'The cultural foundations of fathers' roles' in Hewlett BS (ed) *Father-Child Relations*, New York, Aldine de Gruyter

16. Malinowski B (1927) *The Father in Primitive Psychology*, London, Kegan Paul

17. Mead M (1935) *Sex and Temperament in 3 Primitive Societies*, New York, Morrow

18. Hewlett BS (1991) *Intimate Fathers: the nature and content of Aka Pygmy paternal infant care*, Ann Arbor, University of Michigan Press

19. Levine R (1977) 'Child rearing as cultural adaptation' in Leiderman PH (ed) *The Child Psychology Series: culture and infancy*, New York, Academic Press

20. Hewlett BS (1991) *op cit*

21. Fausto-Sterling A (1992) *Myths of Gender: biological theories about women and men* (second edition), New York, Basic Books

22. *ibid*

23. *ibid*

24. Lamb ME (1981) *The Role of the Father in Child Development* (second edition), New York, Wiley

25. See the work of Parke RD et al cited in Lamb ME (1996) 'The development of father-infant relationships' in Lamb ME (ed) *The Role of the Father in Child Development* (third edition), New York, Wiley

26. Lamb ME (1989) 'Fatherhood and Father-Child Relationships' in Cath SH et al (eds) *Fathers and Their Families*, Hillsdale NJ, Analytic Press

27. Levant RF et al (1990) 'Non-traditional paternal behaviour with school aged daughters', *Australian Journal of Marriage and the Family*, Vol 11(1):28-35

28. Gbrich CF (1986) *Fathers as primary caregivers: a role study*, paper presented to 2nd Australian Family Research Conference

29. Lamb ME (1989) *op cit*

30. Fulop N (1992) 'Gender, parenthood and health', unpublished PhD thesis presented to the Institute of Education, University of London

31. Lewis C (1996) *op cit*

32. Rossan S (1990) *Giving Meaning to Psychological Research on Fathering*, Brunel University

33. Lewis C (1996) *op cit*

34. Eveline J (1994) *Care with Compliance: changing the worlds of men*, ACGP Working Paper No. 25, Canberra, Research School of Social Sciences, Australian National University

35. Virginia Ironside 'Deliver us from the delivery room', *Independent*, London, 2 February 1995

36. Francoise Heritier, quoted in Badinter E (1987) *Man/Woman: the one is the other*, London, Collins

37. Quoted in Rowland R, 'Donor insemination in *in vitro* fertilization: the confusion grows', *Politics and the Life Sciences*, Vol 12(2) August 1993

38. April Martin, personal communication, 1996

39. Dick Teresi 'How to make a man pregnant: a true story', *New York Times*, reprinted in *Sydney Morning Herald*, 19 December 1994

40. Ehrenreich B (1983) *The Hearts of Men: American dreams and the flight from commitment*, Pluto Press, London

Chapter 4

1. Richman J et al (1975) 'Fathers in Labour', *New Society*,Vol 34:143-5

2. Wijngaard M van den (1991) *Reinventing the Sexes*, Delft, Universiteit van Amsterdam

3. S Reid 'Fertility rights' in *Sunday Times*, London, 29 October 1995

4. Swanson JM (1985) '*Roles Throughout the Life Cycle*' in Hanson SM & Bozett FW (eds) *Dimensions of Fatherhood*, Beverley Hills, Sage

5. OPCS Series FM1 No.22 Table 3.4: Paternities

6. Ballard R & Kalra VS (1994) *The Ethnic Dimensions of the 1991 Census: a preliminary report*, Department of Religions, University of Manchester

7. This figure has been obtained by applying the Danish experience, where first-time fathers are currently 2.4 years older than first-time mothers, to the OPCS figure for British women's age at first pregnancy: 26.5 years in 1994

8. Blythe L (1990) '*Who's helping teenage fathers?*', Nursery World Vol 90(3244):20-22

9. Knudsen LB (1993) *Fertility Trends in Denmark in the 1980s*, Copenhagen, Danmarks Statistik

10. *ibid*

11. Human Fertilization and Embryology Authority, Annual Report 1994, London

12. Knudson LB (1993) *op cit*

13. Lewis C (1986) *Becoming a Father*, Milton Keynes, Open University Press

14. Jackson B (1984) *Fatherhood*, London, Allen & Unwin

15. Gilmore DD (1990) *Manhood in the Making: cultural concepts of masculinity*, New York, Yale University Press

16. *Europeans and the Family*, 1993, Eurobarometer, Brussels

17. Fejes FJ (1992) 'Masculinity as fact: a review of empirical mass communication research on masculinity' in Craig S (ed) *Men, Masculinity and the Media, Sage*, London

18. Dugald McCullouch, Belfast, personal communication, 1995

19. Jackson B (1984) *op cit*

20. Enkin et al (1995) *A Guide to Effective Care in Pregnancy and Childbirth*, OUP, Oxford

21. Berman PW & Pedersen FA (1987) *Men's Transitions to Parenthood: long traditional studies of early family experience*, Hillsdale NJ, Lawrence Elrbaum

22. Lederer H (1995) *'Single Minding'*, London, Coronet

23. Seel R (1987) *The Uncertain Father*, Bath, Gateway Books

24. Badinter E (1989) *Man/Woman: the one is the other*, London, Collins Harvill

25. Badinter E (1989) *ibid*

26. Lawson A (1990) *Adultery: an analysis of love and betrayal*, Oxford, OUP

27. Belsky J & Kelly J (1994) *The Transition to Parenthood: how a first child changes a marriage*, London, Vermilion

28. Cowan CP (1988) 'Working with men becoming fathers: the impact of a couples group intervention' in Bronstein P & Cowan CP (eds) *Fatherhood Today*, New York, John Wiley & Sons

29. French study by Dr Renoux, quoted in Badinter E (1989) *op cit*

30. Brazelton TB & Cramer BG (1991) *The Earliest Relationship*, London, Karnac

31. Nickel H & Kocher N (1987) 'West German and the German speaking countries' in Lamb ME (ed) *The Fathers's Role: cross cultural comparisons*, Hillsdale NJ, Lawrence Erlbaum

32. Cowan CP (1988) *op cit*

33. 'Man accused of theft skips court for baby's birth', *Independent*, London' 14 July 1994

34. Clarke J 'Men are offside in the labour ward!', *Daily Record*, Scotland, 22 September 1994

35. National figures are not available, but the Royal College of Midwives reports almost 100 per cent attendance in some areas, as does a Glasgow obstetrician quoted in the *Daily Record*, 22 September 1994

36. Lewis C (1986) *op cit*

37. *ibid*

38. Quoted in Seel R (1987) *op cit*

39. Lewis C (1986) *op cit*

40. Royal College of Midwives *Men at Birth* survey, December 1994, London

41. O'Brien M & Jones D (1995) 'Young people's attitudes to fatherhood' in Moss P (ed) *Father Figures: fathers in the 1990's*, London, HMSO

42. Royal College of Midwives (1994) *op cit*

43. Mark Livingstone (1995) 'At the Birth', *New Generation*, Vol 14(2):6-7

44. Wilson A (1990) 'The Ceremony of Childbirth' in Fildes V (ed) *Women as Mothers in PreIndustrial England*, London, Routledge

45. 'Fathers in the Delivery Room', press release issued by Royal College of Midwives, 1995, London

46. Telephone interviews, carried out 15 November 1995, London

47. Enkin et al (1995) *op cit*

48. Oakley A (1979) *Becoming a Mother*, Oxford, Martin Robinson

49. Seel R (1987) *op cit*

50. Lewis C (1986) *op cit*

51. *ibid*

52. Keller WD et al (1985) 'Effects of extended father-infant contact during the newborn period', *Infant Behaviour and Development*, Vol 8:337-360

53. Pleck JH (1993) 'Are Family-Supportive Employer Policies Relevant to Men?' in Hood JC (ed) *Men, Work and Family*, California, Sage

54. Carlsen S (1993) 'Men's Utlization of Paternity Leave and Parental Leave Schemes' in Danish Equal Status Council *The Equality Dilemma*, Copenhagen, Munksgaard

55. Quoted in Pleck J H (1993) *op cit*

56. Lewis C (1986) *op cit*

57. Evennett K 'What your rows reveal about you', *She*, December 1995, London, National Magazines

58. Brazleton TB & Cramer BG (1991) *op cit*

59. Grossman FR et al (1988) ' Fathers and Children: predicting the quality and quantity of fathering', *Developmental Psychology*, Vol 24:82-91

60. Bowen GL & Orthner DK (1991) 'Effects of Organisational Culture on Fatherhood' in Bozett FW et al (eds) *Fatherhood & Families in Cultural Context*, New York, Springer Publishing

61. For a full discussion of this, see Lamb ME (1996) 'The development of father-infant relationships' in Lamb ME (ed) *The Role of the Father in Child Development* (third edition), New York, Wiley

62. Waite L & Goldscheider FK (1992) 'Work in the Home' in South SJ & Tolnay SE (eds) *The Changing American Family*, Oxford, Westview Press

63. Cummings EM. & O'Reilly AW (1996) 'Fathers in Family Context: effects of marital quality on child adjustment, in Lamb ME (ed) *The Role of the Father in Child Development* (third edition), New York, Wiley

64. Levine JA et al (1993), *Getting Men Involved: strategies that work*, New York, Families and Work Institute

65. Fletcher R (1996) 'From the Co-Minister for Gender Affairs' in Lloyd T & Wood T *What Next for Men?*, London, Working With Men

66. Lamb ME & Oppenheim D (1989) 'Fatherhood and Father-Child Relationships: five years of research' in Cath SH et al (eds) *Fathers and their Families*, New York, Analytic Press

67. Quoted by Adrienne Katz 'Hello Daddy, it's great to see you', *Independent*, London, 29 April 1992

68. Quoted by Feldman LB (1990) 'Fathers and Fathering' in Pastrick RS et al (eds) *Men in Therapy: the challenge of change*, New York, The Guildford Press

69. Oakley A (1979) *Becoming a Mother*, Oxford, Martin Robertson

70. *Leave arrangements for workers with children* (1994) European Commission, Directorate General V, Brussels

71. Silverstein L & Phares V (1996) 'Fathering is a Feminist Issue', *Psychology of Women Quarterly*, Vol 20(1):3-37

72. Cowan CP (1988) *op cit*

73. Jackson B (1984) *op cit*

74. Ballard C (1994) 'Prevalence of post-natal psychiatric morbidity', *British Journal of Psychiatry*, Vol 164:782-788

75. Pederson FA et al (1987) 'Contrasting Affective Responses of Men Becoming Parents' in Pederson PW & Pederson FA (eds) *Men's Transition to Parenthood*, Hillsdale NJ, Lawrence Erlbaum

Chapter 5

1. Andrew Samuels 'On fathering daughters', *Observer*, London, 26 June 1985
2. Snarey J (1993) *How Fathers Father the Next Generation*, Cambridge Mass, Harvard University Press
3. Figures supplied by the European Commission Network on Childcare
4. Quoted in New Ways to Work (1995) *Balanced Lives: changing work patterns for men*, London
5. *ibid*
6. Study Commission on the Family (1983) *Families in the Future: a policy agenda for the 80's*
7. Nasman E (1991) *Parental Leave in Sweden: a workplace issue*, Stockholm Research Reports in Demography No. 73, Stockholm, Stockholm University
8. Central Statistical Office, *Labour Market Trends*, January 1996
9. Sly F 'Mothers in the labour market', *Employment Gazette*, November, 1994 London
10. Central Statistical Office (1996) *op cit*
11. Mintel International Group Ltd (1994) *Men 2000*, London
12. Quoted in Griswold RL (1993) *Fatherhood in America: a history*, New York, Basic Books
13. Pilling D (1990) *Escape from Disadvantage*, London, National Children's Bureau
14. Sly F (1994) *op cit*
15. *ibid*
16. This position is currently being rectified by Louie Burghes at the Family Policy Studies Centre, London
17. Robinson BE (1988) *Teenage Fathers*, Massachusetts, Lexington Books
18. Sly F (1994) *op cit*
19. Pleck JH (1993) 'Are Family-Supportive Policies Relevant to Men?', in Hood JC (ed) *Men Work and Family*, California, Sage
20. Hewitt P (1993) *About Time: the revolution in work and family life*, London, Rivers Oram Press

21. Bittman M (1995) 'Changes at the Heart of Family Households', *Family Matters*, No. 10 Autumn, Melbourne, Australian Institute of Family Studies
22. Figures provided by the European Commission on Childcare Network
23. Hewitt P (1993) *op cit*
24. Clift C & Fielding D (1991) *The Balance of Power*, London, Lowe Howard Spink
25. *Europeans and the Family* (1993) Eurobarometer, Brussels
26. Jowell R et al (1995) *British Social Attitudes: the 12th report*, London, Aldershot Dartmouth Publications
27. Lewin 1995, quoted in Silverstein LB (1996) 'Fathering is a feminist issue', *Psychology of Women Quarterly*, Vol 20:3-370
28. Catalyst (1988)'Workplace policies: new options for fathers" in Bronstein P & Cowan CP (eds) *Fatherhood Today: men's changing roles in the family*, New York, Wiley
29. 'Happy Families' (1995) *IRS Employment Trends*, 593
30. Austin Knight UK Ltd (1995) The Family Friendly Workplace: an investigation into long hours culture and family friendly employment practices, London
31. Andrews A & Bailyn L (1993) 'Segmentation and synergy' in Hood JC (ed) *Men, Work & Family*, California, Sage
32. Holt H (1993) 'The influence of the workplace culture on family life' in Carlsen S & Larsen JE (eds) *The Equality Dilemma*, Denmark, Munsgaard International Publishers
33. Pleck J (1993) *op cit*
34. Libby Purves 'Fathers of the future?', *The Times*, London, 27 October 1989
35. Friedman D (1987) *Family-Supportive Policies: the corporate decision-making process*, New York, The Conference Board
36. Levine JA (1994) 'Daddy-Stress', *Child*, June/July
37. Rodgers CS (1992) 'The flexible workplace: what have we learned?', *Human Resource Journal*, Vol 31(3):183-199
38. 'Ignore Families at Your Peril', press release issued by International Year of the Family, London, 12 April 1994

39. British Social Attitudes Survey, 1992

40. Bjornberg U (1994) 'Family orientation among men: fatherhood and partnership in a process of change' in Brannen J & O'Brien M (eds) *Childhood and parenthood*, London, Institute of Education

41. Andrews A & Bailyn L (1993) *op cit*

42. Pasick R (1990) 'Raised to work' in Meth RL et al (eds) *Men in Therapy: the challenge of change*, New York, The Guildford Press

43. Andrews A & Bailyn L (1993) *op cit*

44. Repetti RL (1989) 'Short-term and long-term processes linking job stressors to father-child interaction', data presented at the Society for Research in Child Development, Kansas City, UCLA

45. Levine JA (1994) *op cit*

46. Pleck JH (1993) *op cit*

47. Cowan CP (1988) 'Working with men becoming fathers: the impact of a couples group intervention' in Bronstein P & Cowan CP (eds) *Fatherhood Today*, New York, Wiley

48. Bosen GL & Orthner DK (1985) 'Effects of organisational culture on fatherhood' in Bozett FW et al (eds) *Fatherhood and Families in Cultural Context*, New York, Springer

49. Delong TJ & Delong CC (1990) 'Managers as fathers: hope on the home front' in Meth RL et al (eds) *Men in Therapy: the challenge of change*, New York, The Guildford Press

50. MSF Survey on Bullying, February 1996, 50 Southwark Street, London SE1

51. Kraemer S (1995) *Fatherhood past and future*, draft paper, London, Tavistock Centre

52. Quoted in Libby Purves 'Fathers of the future?', *The Times*, London, 27 October 1989

53. Quoted in Feldman LB (1990) 'Fathers and Fathering' in Meth RL et al (eds) *Men in Therapy: the challenge of change*, New York, Guildford Press

54. Quoted in Libby Purves (1989) *op cit*

55. Austin Knight UK Ltd (1995) *op cit*

56. New Ways to Work (1995) *op cit*

57. Snarey JR (1993) *How Fathers Care for the Next Generation*, Cambridge Mass, Harvard University Press

58. Quoted in New Ways to Work (1995) *op cit*

59. Snarey JR (1993) *op cit*

60. Pleck JH (1993) *op cit*

61. Snarey JR (1993) *op cit*

62. New Ways to Work (1995) *op cit*

63. Solomon CJ (1992) 'Work/Family ideas', *Personnel Journal*, Vol 71(10):112-117

64. O'Brien M & Jones D (1995) 'Young people's attitudes to fatherhood' in Moss P (ed) *Father Figures: fathers in the 1990's*, London, HMSO

65. Coward R (1992) *Our Treacherous Hearts*, London, Faber & Faber

66. Ochiltree G (1994) *Effects of Child Care on Young Children: forty years of research*, Melbourne, Australian Institute of Family Studies

67. Eveline J (1994) *Care with Compliance: changing the worlds of men*, Canberra, Research School of Social Sciences, Australian National University

68. Austin Knight UK Ltd (1995) *op cit*

69. Clarke D (1994) *Family-friendly employment: the business perspective*, paper delivered at 'Balancing the Partnership' Conference, Canberra, Work and Family Unit, Commonwealth Department of Industrial Relations

70. Austin Knight UK Ltd (1995) *op cit*

71. New Ways to Work (1995) *op cit*

72. Holt H (1993) *op cit*

73. For this radical perspective see Claire Rayner 'Give us a break', *Guardian*, London, 1 April 1996

Chapter 6

1. Kellerhals J & Montandon C (1992) 'Social Stratification and the Parent-Child Relationship' in Bjornberg U (ed) *European Parents in the 1990s*, New Brunswick, Transaction

2. Easterbrooks MA & Goldberg WA (1984) 'Toddler development in the family: impact of father involvement and parenting characteristics', *Child Development*, Vol 53:740-752

3. Ochiltree G (1994) *The Effects of Childcare on Young Children: forty years of research*, Melbourne, Australian Institute of Family Studies

4. Lewis C *et al* (1982) 'Father participation through childhood and its relation to career aspirations of delinquency' in Beail N & McGuire J (eds) *Fathers: psychological perspectives*, London, Junction Books

5. Farrington DP & Hawkin JD 'Predicting participation, early onset and later persistence in officially recorded offending', *Criminal Behavour and Mental Health*, Vol 1:1-33

6. Phares V (1996) 'Psychological adjustment, maladjustment, and father-child relationships' in Lamb ME (ed) *The Role of the Father in Child Development* (third edition), New York, Wiley

7. Thatcher C (1996) *Beyond the Parapet*, London, HarperCollins

8. Phares V (1996) *op cit*

9. *ibid*

10. Pleck JH (1996) 'Paternal involvement: levels, sources, and consequences' in Lamb ME (ed) *The Role of the Father in Child Development* (third edition), New York, Wiley

11. Goleman D (1996) *Emotional Intelligence: why it can matter more than IQ*, London, Bloomsbury

12. Pleck JH (1996) *op cit*

13. Ninio A & Rinott N (1988) 'Fathers' involvement in the care of their infants and their attributions of cognitive competence to infants', *Child Development*, Vol 59:652-663

14. Pleck JH (1996) *op cit*

15. *ibid*

16. Appleton WS (1993) quoted in Biller HB *Fathers and Families*, Westport CT, Auburn House

17. Cowan CP (1988) 'Working with Men Becoming Fathers: the impact of a couples group intervention' in Bronstein P & Cowan CP (eds) *Fatherhood Today*, New York, Wiley

18. Dunn J & Kendrick C (1982) *Siblings: love, envy and understanding*, Cambridge Mass, Harvard University Press

19. Volling BL & Belsky J (1992) 'The contribution of mother-child and father-child relationships to the quality of sibling interaction', *Child Development*, Vol 63(5):1209-1222

20. Snarey JR (1993) *How Fathers Care for the Next Generation*, Cambridge Mass, Harvard University Press

21. Lamb ME (1996) 'Fathers and child development: an introductory overview and guide' in Lamb ME (ed) *The Role of the Father in Child Development* (third edition), New York, Wiley

22. Richman J 'Depression in mothers of pre-school children' (1976) *Journal of World Psychology and Psychiatry*, Vol 17: 75-78

23. Blankenhorn D (1995) *Fatherless America: confronting our most urgent social problem*. New York, Basic Books

24. Sternberg KJ (1996) 'Fathers, the missing parents in research on family violence' in Lamb ME (ed) *The Role of the Father in Child Development*, New York, Wiley

25. Pleck JH (1996) *op cit*

26. Patterson CJ & Chan RW (1996) 'Gay fathers' in Lamb ME (ed) *The Role of the Father in Child Development* (third edition), New York, Wiley

27. Biller HB (1993) *Fathers and Families*, Westport CT, Auburn House

28. Lamb ME (1996) *op cit*

29. Lamb ME (1996) 'The development of father-infant relationships' in Lamb ME (ed) *The Role of the Father in Child Development* (third edition), New York, Wiley

30. Melanie Phillips 'Dads Behaving Badly", *The Observer*, London, 5 June 1996

31. Lloyd T (1995) *'They are so irresponsible! Aren't they!'*, unpublished research carried out in a London boys' school, London, Working with Men

32. For a full discussion of this see Lewis C (1996) 'Fathers and pre-schoolers' in Lamb ME (ed) *The Role of the Father in Child Development* (third edition), New York, Wiley

33. O'Brien M & Jones D (1995) 'Family and kinship in an East London borough: continuity and change', paper presented at BSA Conference: Contested Cities

34. Creighton SJ & Russell N (1995) *Voices from Childhood*, London, NSPCC

35. Crockett LJ et al (1993) 'Fathers' presence and young children's behavioural and cognitive adjustment', *Journal of Family Issues*, Vol 14:355-377

36. Again, for a full discussion of fathers' impact (or lack of it) on their toddlers' development see Lewis C (1996) op cit

37. Lord Chancellor's Department, 1994, London

38. OPCS, 1993, London

39. Home Office Statistics, 1989–94, London

40. Shaw R (1992) 'Imprisoned fathers and the orphans of justice' in Shaw R (ed) *Prisoners' children: what are the issues?*, London, Routledge

41. Phares V (1996) *op cit*

42. Buck N & Ermish J (1995) 'Cohabitation in Britain', *Changing Britain*, No 3, October, London, Policy Studies Centre

43. Stier H & Tienda M (1993) 'Are men marginal to the family?' in Hood JC (ed) *Men, Work and Family*, California, Sage

44. Haskey J (1994) 'Stepfamilies and stepchildren in Great Britain', *Population Trends* 76, London, OPCS

45. *ibid*

46. Mavis Maclean, Centre for Socio-legal Studies, Wolfson College Oxford, personal communication, 1996

47. F Hidya et al 'Endangered Family', *Newsweek*, Winter/Spring 1990

48. Ballard R & Karla VS (1994) *The Ethnic Dimensions of the 1991 Census: a preliminary report*, University of Manchester, Department of Religions

49. Griswold RE (1993) *Fatherhood in America: a history*, New York, Basic Books

50. S Brata 'Are we colour blind yet?', *Sunday Times*, London, 19 June 1994

51. Robinson BE (1988) *Teenage Fathers*, Massachusetts, Lexington Books

52. Dench G (1996) *Changing Family Cultures and the Place of Men*, York, Joseph Rowntree Foundation

53. Bradshaw J & Miller J (1991) *Lone Parents in the UK*, London, HMSO

54. Burgoyne C.& Millar J (1994) 'Enforcing child support obligations: the attitudes of separated fathers', *Policy & Politics* Vol 22(2):95-104

55. Mavis Maclean *op cit*

56. Simpson B M^{C}Carthy P & Walker J (1995) *Being There: fathers after divorce*, Newcastle upon Tyne, Relate Centre for Family Studies

57. Maccoby EE & Mnookin RH (1992) *Dividing the Child: social and legal dilemmas of custody*, Cambridge Mass, Harvard University Press

58. Gibson J (1992) 'Non-Custodial Fathers and Access Patterns', Research Report, Family Court of Australia

59. Maccoby EE & Mnookin RH (1992) *op cit*

60. Warshak RA (1996) *The Custody Revolution*, New York, Poseidon Press

61. Maccoby EE & Mnookin RH (1992) *op cit*

62. Amato PR (1993) 'Contact with Non-cutodial Fathers and Children's Wellbeing', *Family Matters*, No. 36:32-34 (December), Melbourne, Australian Institute of Family Studies

63. Warshak RA (1996) *op cit*

64. Maccoby EE & Mnookin RH (1992) *op cit*

65. Burgess A & Ruxton S (1996) *Men and their Children: proposals for public policy*, London, IPPR

66. Maccoby EE & Mnookin RH (1992) *op cit*

67. Collier R (1995) *Masculinity, Law and the Family*, London, Routledge

68. *A Bad Time to be a Man* (1996), London, BBC2 presentation, directed by Mike Buckingham

69. Belsky J *et al* (1991) 'Patterns of marital change and parent-child interaction', *Journal of Marriage and the Family*, Vol 53:487-498

70. Cummings ME & O'Reilly AW (1996) 'Fathers in Family Contect: effects of marital quality on child adjustment' in Lamb ME (ed) *The Role of the Father in Child Development* (third edition), New York, Wiley

71. Maccoby EE & Mnookin RH (1992) *op cit*

72. Warshak RA (1996) *op cit*

73. Kruk E (1991) 'Discontinuity between pre and post divorce father-child relationships', *Journal of Marriage and Divorce*, Vol 16(3-4):195-227

74. Charlie Lewis, Lancaster University, personnal communication, 1996

75. Maccoby EE & Mnookin RH (1992) *op cit*

76. Gottman JM (1994) *What Predicts Divorce?*, Hillsdale NJ, Lawrence Erlbaum

77. Pearson J & Thoennes N (1988) 'The denial of visitation rights: a preliminary look at its incidence, correlates, antecedents and consequences', *Law and Policy*, Vol 10

78. Gardener RA (1996) *Parental Alienation Syndrome*, New Jersey, Creative Therapeutics

79. Cowan CP (1988) *op cit*

80. Gardner RA. (1996) *op cit*

81. Simpson B et al (1995) *op cit*

82. Adam Sage 'French children opt for father in wake of divorce', *The Times*, London, 25 August 1995

83. Burgoyne C & Millar J (1994) *op cit*

84. Bradshaw J & Miller J (1991) *op cit*

85. Maccoby EE & Mnookin RH (1992) *op cit*

86. Bradshaw J & Millar J (1991) *op cit*

87. DSS, 1990, quoted in Burgoyne C & Millar J (1994) op cit

88. Bradshaw J & Miller J (1991) *op cit*

89. Jan Pahl, University of Kent at Canterbury, personal communication, 1996

90. Bradshaw J & Miller J (1991) *op cit*

91. Buck N et al (1994) *Changing Households*, London, Policy Studies Centre

92. Maccoby EE & Mnookin RH (1992) *op cit*

93. Cheryl Van Der Waal, Centre for the Family in Transition, California, personal communication, 1996

94. Jalmert L (1990) 'Increasing men's involvement as fathers in the care of children: some gains and some obstacles', unpublished paper, Sweden, Department of Education, Stockholm University

95. GM Jones 'No security for 90's fathers', letter to *Independent*, London, 23 April 1996

96. Sternberg KJ (1996) *op cit*

97. Ruxton S (1996) 'Boys Won't Be Boys: tackling the roots of male delinquency' in Lloyd T & Wood T (eds) *What Next for Men?*, London, Working with Men

98. Rodman H quoted in Ochiltree G (1994) *op cit*

99. Creighton SJ & Russell N (1995) op cit & Sternberg KJ (1996) *op cit*

100. Sternberg KJ (1996) *op cit*

101. *ibid*

102. *ibid*

103. Creighton SJ (1992) *Child Abuse Trends in England and Wales, 1988–1990*, London, NSPCC

104. Russell DEH (1986) *The Secret Trauma: incest in the lives of girls and women*, New York, Basic Books; and Creighton SJ & Russell N (1995) op cit

105. Russell DEH (1986) *op cit*

106. I am indebted to Sue Creighton at the NSPCC, London, for further exploring the data in the *Voices from Childhood* report (Creighton S J & Russell N (1995) op cit)

107. Margolin L (1992) 'Child abuse by mothers' boyfriends: why the overrepresentation?', *Child Abuse and Neglect*, Vol 16:541-551

108. Sternberg KJ (1996) *op cit*

109. Parker H & Parker S (1986) 'Father-daughter sexual abuse: an emerging perspective', *American Journal of Orthopsychiatry*, Vol 56(4):531-549

110. For detailed exploration of the implications for policy and practice, see Burgess A & Ruxton S (1996) *op cit*

111. Hutton W (1995) *The State We're In*, London, Cape

112. Ochiltee G (1992) *op cit*

113. Badinter E (1980) *The Myth of Motherhood*, London, Souvenir Press

114. Ochiltree G (1992) *op cit*

115. Tronick E et al (1992) 'The Efe Forager Infant and Toddler's Pattern of Social Relationships Multiple and Simultaneous', *Developmental Psychology*, Vol 28(4):568-577

116. Silverstein L & Phares V (1996) 'Fathering is a feminist issue', *Psychology of Women Quarterly*, Vol 20(1):3-37

117. Harris JR (1995) 'Where is the child's environment? A group socialization theory of development', *Psychological Review*, Vol 102(3):458-489

118. Lamb ME (1996) *op cit*

Further Reading

Badinter E (1980) *The Myth of Motherhood: an historical view of the maternal instinct*, London, Souvenir Press

Blankenhorn D (1995) *Fatherless America: confronting our most urgent social problem*, New York, Basic Books

Burgess A & Ruxton S (1996) *Men and their Children: proposals for public policy*, London, IPPR

Carlsen S & Larsen JE (eds) (1992) *The Equality Dilemma*, Denmark, Munksgaard International

Colman A & Colman L (1988) *The Father: mythology and changing roles*, Wilmette, Illinois, Chiron

Conference of European Ministers Responsible for Family Affairs (1995) *The Status and Role of Fathers: family policy aspects*, Strasbourg, Council of Europe

Delumeau J & Roche J (1990) *Histoire des pères et de la paternité*, Paris, Larousse

European Commission Network on Childcare (1993) *Men as Carers: towards a culture of responsibility, sharing and reciprocity*, Brussels, European Commission Directorate-General V

European Commission Network on Childcare (1994) *Leave Arrangements for Workers with Children*, Brussels, European Commission Directorate-General V

European Commission Network on Childcare (1994) *Men, Media, and Childcare: newspaper coverage of men as carers in seven EU countries*, Brussels, European Commission Directorate-General V

Fausto-Sterling A (1992) *Myths of Gender: biological theories about women and men (second edition)*, New York, Basic Books

French S (ed) *Fatherhood*, London, Virago

Gardener RA (1996) *Parental Alienation Syndrome*, New Jersey, Creative Therapeutics

Griswold RL (1993) *Fatherhood in America: a history*, New York, Basic Books

Hood JC (ed) (1993) *Men, Work and Family*, California, Sage

Lamb ME (ed) (1996) *The Role of the Father in Child Development* (third edition), New York, Wiley

Lewis C 1986 *Becoming a Father*, Milton Keynes, Open University Press

Lloyd T & Wood T (eds) (1996) *What Next for Men?* London, Working With Men

Maccoby EE & Mnookin RH (1992) *Dividing the Child: social and legal dilemmas of custody*, Cambridge Mass, Harvard University Press

Martin A (1993) *The Guide to Lesbian and Gay Parenting*, London, Pandora

Miller A (1987) *For Your Own Good: the roots of violence in child rearing*, London, Virago

Morgen KB (1995) *Getting Simon: two gay doctors' journey to fatherhood*, New York, Bramble Books

New Ways to Work (1995) *Balanced Lives: changing work patterns for men*. London,

Parke RD (1996) *Fatherhood*, Cambridge Moss, Harvard University Press

Parsons R (1995) *The Sixty-Minute Father: an hour to change your child's life*, London, Hodder & Stoughton

Ricci I (1980) *Mum's House, Dad's House: making shared custody work*, New York, Collier Books

Silverstein L & Phares V (1996) 'Fathering is a Feminist Issue', *Psychology of Women Quarterly*, Vol 20(1):3-37

Simpson B *et al* (1995) *Being There: fathers after divorce*, Newcastle upon Tyne, Relate Centre for Family Studies

Warshak RA (1996) *The Custody Revolution*, New York, Poseidon Press

Resource List

How to use this list

❝ The object is to discover your problems, not to solve them. ❞

❝ Never go anywhere and stop. Take from many different people and many different groups. ❞

❝ Mediation is the way forward at separation, but it seems to be derived from the experience of women. So does most parent training. Question premises. Want everything. Don't lose sight of your expectations to be a total father. ❞

❝ Go to your doctor for a complete check-up. If you are going to die tomorrow, you need to know. ❞

Liam, 40, father of two

The resources

Exploring Masculinity

Everyman
4 Selbourne Terrace
Bradford BD9 4NJ
Contact: Ron Pyatt
tel: 01274 499910
Transformational work for men based mainly in the outdoors

Men for Change Network
Achilles Heel
Flat 6, 75 Dartmouth Park Hill
London NW5 1JD
Contact: Steve Banks
tel: 0171 482 5953

The Men's Databank
25 Randolph Crescent
London W9 1DP
Contact: Derek Shiel
tel: 0171 286 1173

Men's Network Group of Ireland
Balcurris Road
Ballymun
Dublin 11, Eire
tel: 00 353 1 8622194

North London Men's Health Centre
154 Stoke Newington Church Street
London N16
tel: 0171 249 2990

Working With Men
320 Commercial Way
London SE15 1QN
tel/fax: 0171 732 9409
Research into men's issues, also providing
guidance for professionals

Men's Rights

(See also some groups in 'Separation and
Divorce' below)

Child/Father Archive and Research
35 Batchelor Street
London N1 OEG
Contact: Eugen Hockenjos
tel: 0171 833 4394

Family Rights Group
18 Ashwin Street
London E8 3DL
tel: 0171 923 2628
Advice and support for parents whose
children are in local authority care

NACSA (Network Against the Child
Support Act)
PO Box 3159
Fishermead
Milton Keynes MK6 2YB
tel: 01908 665646
Co-ordinating body for anti-Child Support
groups

PAIN (Parents Against Injustice)
3 Riverside Business Park
Stansted
Essex CM24 8PL
tel: 01279 656564
Advice and support for parents being
investigated for alleged child abuse or
neglect

The United Kingdom Men's Movement
(also includes DADS – Dads after
Divorce)
PO Box 205
Cheltenham
Gloucestershire GL51 0YL
tel: 01242 691110
Advice and support for men, particularly
those unwillingly-divorced - strongly anti-
feminist

Fathers and Work

European Commission Network on
Child Care
DGV/B/4
200 Rue de la Loc
B-1049
Brussels, Belgium
tel: 010 322 299 2279
Considers, among other things, men's
employment in childcare services

Men's Inquiry Group
Office for Public Management
252B Gray's Inn Road
London WC1X 8JT
Contact: Ian Gee
tel: 0171 837 9600
Examining men in the workplace

New Ways to Work
309 Upper Street
London N1 2TU
tel: 0171 226 4026
Campaigning and advice organisation, now
exploring the male perspective

Parents at Work
35 Beech Street
Barbican
London EC2Y 8AD
tel: 0171 628 3578
Campaigning and advice organisation

Parenting Skills and Network Support

Local organisations

A Dad's Place
c/o School of Education
University of Newcastle
St Thomas St
Newcastle NE1 7RU
Contact: Robin Duckett
tel: 0191 222 6417
Father-child activity group

Barnardo's Lawrence Weston Family
Centre
Home Farm
Kings Weston Lane
Bristol BS11 AJE
Contact: Colin Holt
tel: 0117 982 4578
Fathers' parenting skills group

Fathers' Family Time
1 Shanganagh Grove
Shankill
Co Dublin
Eire
Contact: Peter Farrell
tel: 00 353 1 2820101
Father–child activity group

Penn Green Community Association
Penn Green Lane
Corby
Northamptonshire NN17 1BJ
Contact: Trevor Chandler
tel: 01536 400068
Father–child support/activity groups

*Other local fathers' groups, can be tracked
down through local councils, social services
departments or churches.*

Networks/national organisations

Care for the Family
136 Newport Road
Cardiff CF2 1DJ
tel: 01222 494431
*Church-based parent education and holiday
service; strong father awareness*

Exploring Parenthood
4 Ivory Place
28 Tredgold Street
London W11 4BP
tel: 0171 221 4471
*Innovative campaigning, research and
training organisation with a strong fathers'
perspective*

Family Caring Trust
44 Rathfriland Road
Newry
Co Down BT34 1LD
tel: 01693 64174
Church-based parenting skills training

Family Nurturing Network
Unit 12F, Minns Estate
7 Westway
Botley Road
Oxford OX2 OJD
tel: 01865 722442
Parenting skills training

National Childbirth Trust
Alexandra House
Oldham Terrace
London W3 6NH
tel: 0181 992 8637
*Information and support in pregnancy,
childbirth and early parenthood; maternal
focus but fathers' groups arise locally*

New Learning Centre
211 Sumatra Road
London NW6 1FF
tel: 0171 794 0321
Parenting skills training

Parent Network
44 Caversham Road
London NW5 2DS
tel: 0171 485 8535
Parenting support and skills training; also
local groups specifically run by and for
fathers

PIPPIN (Parents in Partnership –
Parent–Infant Network)
Derwood
Todds Green
Stevenage
Herts SG1 2JE
tel: 01438 748478
Parenting support and skills training for
expectant and new parents – very *strong*
fathers' perspective

Relate North and West Wilts Training
Services
24a Church Street
Trowbridge
Wiltshire BA14 8DY
tel: 01225 765310
Parenting and relationship education via
schools – for teachers, pupils and parents
(other similar Relate pilot projects are
underway)
Stepfamily
3rd Floor, Chapel House
18 Hatton Place
London EC1N 8RU
tel: 0171 209 2460
Campaigning, information and support
service for stepfamilies – growing awareness
of special needs of stepfathers

Trust for the Study of Adolescence
23 New Road
Brighton
East Sussex BN1 1WZ
tel: 01273 693311
Research, training and resource body

Stonewall Parenting Group
16 Clerkenwell Close
London EC1R 0AA
tel: 0171 336 8860
Campaigning and support group for gay
parents

Crisis Management or on-going
Counselling

Institute of Family Therapy
24–32 Stephenson Way
London NW1 2HX
tel: 0171 391 9150
Couple and family counselling, and
mediation

NORCAP (National Organisation for
the Counselling of Adoptees and
Parents)
112 Church Road
Wheatley
Oxfordshire OX33 1LU
tel: 01865 875000
Support and advice for adoptees and
relatives

Parentline
Endway House
The Endway
Hadleigh
Essex SS7 2AN
tel: 01702 559900
24-hour helpline for distressed parents (see
also local directories for local groups)

Parents Anonymous, London
6 Manor Gardens
London N7 6LA
tel: 0171 263 8918
24-hour helpline for distressed parents

Relate Marriage Guidance
National Headquarters
Herbert Gray College
Little Church Street
Rugby CV21 3AP
tel: 01788 573241
Adult couple counselling (but not crisis
work). 130 centres in England, Wales and
Northern Ireland – see also local telephone
directories

The Samaritans
tel: 0345 909090 (National 24-hour
LinkLine) Although not parent–child
focused, grateful men report terrific support

Child and Family Department
The Tavistock Centre
120 Belsize Lane
London NW3 5BA
tel: 0171 435 7111
Help for couples, parents and children

Separation and Divorce

Organisations offering *mediation* **to**
divorcing or separating couples,
primarily to help sort out arrangements
for children

Family Mediation (Scotland)
127 Rose Street
South Lane
Edinburgh EH2 4BB
tel: 0131 220 1610

Irish Family Mediation Service
Block 1, Floor 5
Irish Life Centre
Lower Abbey Street
Dublin 1
tel: 00 353 1 8728277

National Family Mediation (England
and Wales)
9 Tavistock Place
London WC1H 9SN
tel: 0171 383 5993

Northern Ireland Family Mediation
Service
(Northern Ireland Section of National
Family Mediation)
76 Dublin Road
Belfast BT2 7HP
tel: 01232 322914

Organisations providing meeting places
for children and parents in separated
families

Network of Access and Child Contact
Centres (England and Wales)
St Andrew's with Castle Gate Church
Goldsmith Street
Nottingham NG1 5JT
tel: 0115 9484557

Network of Access and Child Contact
Centres (Scotland)
c/o Family Mediation (Scotland)
127 Rose Street
South Lane
Edinburgh EH2 4BB
tel: 0131 220 1610

Campaigning information and support groups for non-resident parents

Association for Shared Parenting
National Office
28 Garraways
Wootton Bassett
Swindon SN4 8LL
tel: 01793 851544

Families Need Fathers
National Office
134 Curtain Road
London EC2A 3AR
tel: 0181 8860970 (information)
        0891 448690 (helpline – unmarried)
        0891 448696 (helpline – married)
        0181 893 5563 (helpline – crisis)

Kidsfirst
c/o 32 Braemar Road
Brentford
Middlesex TW8 0NR
tel: 0181 568 5634

Parental Equality
1 Muirhevna
Dublin Road
Co Louth
Eire
tel: 00 353 42 33163

Parents Forever (Scotland)
tel: 0141 952 8854
    0131 665 9497
    01333 352 034

Shared Parenting Information Group
85 Duncombe Street
Walkley
Sheffield S6 3RH
tel: 0114 234 3445

SOS Papa
BP 49, 78230 Le Pecq
France
tel: 00 33 3976 1999
fax: 00 33 4247 1847
British contact: Fred Ottavy
Flat 18, 41 Craven Hill Gardens
London W2 2EA
tel: 0171 762 4090
The French 'Families Need Fathers' – very sophisticated and established

Permissions

The author and publisher would like to thank those who gave permission for their work to be used.

Chapter 1

Luciano Beneton quoted by G Montagu in 'Relative Values', *Sunday Times Magazine* 12 June 1994; H Brod 'Fraternity, Equality, Liberty', *Men's Lives*, edited by MS Kimmel & MA Messner, Macmillan (1992); R Crawford 'The Look In', *Masculinity*, Cape Poetry (1996); 'Rules of Cricket and of Life' was sent by Herbert Lees, a civil servant, to his son in the immediate postwar period and quoted in C Heward *Making a Man of Him*, Routledge (1988); Evan Jones 'Generations' *Two Centuries of Australian Poetry*, OUP (1988); J Kornfield 'Parenting as Spiritual Practice', *Fathers & Sons & Daughters* edited by C Scull, Tarcher (1992); K B Morgen *Getting Simon*, Bramble Books (1995); Martin Newell 'Nothing Prepares U 4', *Independent* April 1966; F Pittman *Man Enough: fathers, sons, and the search for masculinity*, Putman (1993); Adrienne Rich *Your Native Land, Your Life*, Penguin Books (1986); Gore Vidal quoted by B Ehrenreich in *The Hearts of Men*, Pluto Press (1993). The Robert Lindsay quotation is from a letter published on the Internet, 14 July 1996. 'Papa Don't Preach' is adapted from 'Fathers and Sons', originally published in British *GQ*, October 1993 © The Conde Nast P.L.

Chapter 2

The historical quotations in this chapter are mainly taken from Linda Pollock's *Forgotten Children: parent-child relations from 1500–1900*, Fourth Estate, (1983) and *A Lasting Relationship: parents and children over three centuries*, Cambridge University Press (1987) and also from J Burnett *Destiny Obscure: autobiographies of childhood and family from the 1820's to the 1920's*, Allen Lane (1982) and P Thompson *The Edwardians: the remaking of British society*, Routledge (1977). We also acknowledge T Hilton 'In Tandem', *Fatherhood*, edited by S French, Virago (1993).

Chapter 3

A & L Colman *The Father: mythology and changing roles*, Chiron (1988); M Hofman 'Patrimony', *Fatherhood*, edited by S French, Virago (1993); K B Morgen *Getting Simon*, Bramble Books (1995); N Planer *A Good Enough Dad: the true confusions of an infant father*, Arrow (1993); F Pittman *Man Enough*, Putman (1993).

Chapter 4

C Bell *Fathers, Childbirth and Work*, Equal Opportunities Commission (1983); S Brown 'Heart to Heart', *Fatherhood*, edited by S French, Virago (1993); A & L Colman *The Father: mythology and changing roles*, Chiron (1988); T Hilton 'In Tandem', *Fatherhood*, edited by S French, Virago (1993); The Locker Room, BBC Radio 4, June 1994; Mark Livingston's *At the birth* and Terence Heath's *New fatherhood* were published in *New Generation*, National Childbirth Trust, June 1995; K B Morgen *Getting Simon*, Bramble Books (1995); B E Robinson *Teenage Fathers*, Lexington (1988); R Seel *The Uncertain Father*, Gateway (1987); J Targett 'Tiny Fears', *Fatherhood*, edited by S French, Virago (1993); J Way 'Hello Dad, How are You?', *The Compassionate Friends Newsletter* Summer 1989.

Chapter 5

S A Andrews 'Segmentation and Synergy', *Men, Work and Family*, edited by J C Hood, Sage (1993); Patrick Augustus *Baby Father*, The X Press (1994); T J & CC Delong 'Managers as fathers: hope on the homefront', *Human Resource Management* Vol 31(3):171-181, 1992; Sean Elder 'Dabbling Dads', *New York Times Magazine* 1993; P Hewitt *About Time*, Rivers Oram Press (1993); *Hook* Tristar Pictures (1991); New Ways to Work *Balanced Lives: changing work patterns for men* (1993); F Pittman *Man Enough*, Putman (1993); Jonathan Ross quoted by Lucy Broadbent 'Jonathan's Paradise Wossed', *News of the World* 17 March 1996.

Chapter 6

K H Anton 'Remembering a father who mothered' *Fathers, Sons & Daughters*, edited C Skull, Tarcher (1992); T Arendell 'After divorce: investigations into father absence', *Gender and Society* Vol 6(4) December 1992; K Clarke (*et al*) *Losing Support: children and the child support act*, The Children's Society, The Nuffield Press (1994); JL Herman & L Hirshman *Father-Daughter Incest*, Harvard University Press (1981); A Pirani *The Absent Father: crisis and creativity*, Arkana (1989); B Simpson, P M^CCarthy & J Walker *Being There: fathers after divorce*, Relate Centre for Family Studies, University of Newcastle upon Tyne (1995); Anne Treneman 'Go on, leave. They'll survive without you', *Independent* 21 June 1996; L Yablonsky *Fathers and Sons: the most challenging of all family relationships*, Gardner Press (1990); The Kate Reifsnyder, Nick Holmes, Carly Simon song is quoted in RA Warshak *The Custody Revolution*, Poseidon Press, (1996). The 'Father Figures' Conference was the first UK Conference on fatherhood, and was held by Children in Scotland, November 1994.

Index